TAKEN

ANGELINE FORTIN

Published by

MY PERSONAL
BUBBLE LLC

ISBN-13: 978-1503219366
ISBN-10: 1503219364 .

DEDICATION

For my dear friends, far and near,
who provide support and encouragement
day in and day out.
I couldn't do this without you.

"People assume that time is a strict progression of cause to effect, but *actually* from a non-linear, non-subjective viewpoint — it's more like a big ball of wibbly wobbly... time-y wimey... stuff."
~ Steven Moffat, *Doctor Who*

1

August 15, 2013
In the Scottish Borders

Give'em what they want.

It had been her father's mantra from the moment fame descended upon her. Which was, in fact, about the same time that what she wanted ceased to matter.

"Miss Thomas! Miss Thomas! Over here!"

Scarlett turned and flashed a practiced smile for the photographer. Putting on a pleasant public face when one was burdened by jet lag was an acting skill Scarlett Thomas had yet to fully master, but the crowd seemed pleased enough by her performance.

"Miss Thomas, how does it feel to be back at Dunskirk Castle?" one of the reporters asked as her agent-*cum*-bodyguard, Tyrone Halliday, ushered her through the throng with a firm hand at the small of her back.

Scarlett considered the looming façade of the medieval castle of Dunskirk, which sat nestled in the lazy roll of the

1

Cheviot Hills of the Scottish Borders not far from England's northern border. Light and shadow marked the six turreted corner towers punctuating the many angles of the curtain walls. Two soaring towers stood like sentinels at the center of the castle, flanking the entrance. The jutting spires drew her eyes upward fifty feet – just as they always had – to the decorative stonework of the crenellations, merlons and machicolations. Fancy words she had learned from an architectural historian that merely named the parts and pieces of the castle fascia that covered the original parapets and more functional battlements beneath.

While Aubroch Castle, the fictional setting of the blockbuster *Puppet War* movies, was written as a dark, gloomy place, Scarlett had been pleased when the location scouts chose this fairy tale location for the final setting. Life within those castle walls had felt more like home than Hollywood ever could throughout the more than five years of filming three movies.

Like Dunskirk/Aubroch, Scarlett often felt she was all gloss and glamour on the outside with so much more veiled beneath the surface. Something, she now feared, might never be seen again.

"It's wonderful," she answered honestly before adding her required publicity blurb when Tyrone's fingers pressed into her back. "I'm happy to be back to mark this momentous occasion."

"There's been rumors Anatolio might be considering another sequel," one of the reporters shouted over the crowd, thrusting his mike at her. "Would you be willing to make another *Puppet War* movie?"

The young adult fantasy series by Marco Anatolio with its three installments, *Marionette, Ventriloquist* and finally *Broken*

Strings, had been literary bestsellers topping the charts for years. The movie rights had been bought a month after the first book's release and at fifteen, Scarlett had been cast as the brilliant but nerdy, Finley Adams, launching her into instant stardom. That had been nine years ago and still she would always be Finley Adams to many.

"I am always open to new projects." Scarlett smiled tightly and moved on.

Flashing another smile, echoed by her agent's, they worked their way up the crowd. The castle door seemed to shrink into the distance as if she was working away from it rather than toward it, but Scarlett forged on, ignoring the reporters. Instead she focused on the fans who lined the cordoned-off avenue, signing autographs and taking selfies with them as she progressed.

"Rowdy crowd here today," Tyrone muttered, blocking off the press of the crowd with one massive arm. "Better watch it. That one might not give your hand back."

"Don't be mean," Scarlett murmured under her breath. "They're just excited. I seem to recall a bit of the same from you when you first met my mother."

"We've been over this," he said with a grimace at the reminder. "I did not fall at her feet. I tripped over the edge of the rug."

Scarlett had to grin at that. Her mother, Olivia Harrington, star of screens big and small, seemed to have many frayed carpets surrounding her person at all times. Assuming what Tyrone claimed was true, of course.

Gently tugging her hand free from her overly enthusiastic fan, Scarlett moved slowly onward toward the canopied platform set up just outside the castle's outer stockade. They *were* a rowdy bunch, Scarlett acknowledged, but she didn't mind. These were her people. She understood them, appreciated them. Probably because she had once been just like them. Scarlett smiled inwardly. Once? She still was. A geek. A fangirl. She understood them better than she had ever gotten anyone in Hollywood.

Like Potterheads, Tributes, and Tolkienites, *The Puppet War* fan base, aptly labeled Puppeteers, was one of the biggest fandoms on the planet. Even years after the last movie, *Broken Strings*, and having never made another movie, Scarlett and her costars were still followed and obsessed over. They all made frequent public appearances at conventions like ComicCon and WizardCon and were constantly targeted by the paparazzi.

"I love your dress, Miss Thomas," one of her fans gushed as Scarlett signed an autograph. Scarlett smiled her thanks. The August day was surprisingly warm and she'd donned a floor-length white cotton maxi dress with an Empire waist and tiny spaghetti straps to offset the heat. Tyrone had insisted she add a jacket for the formality of the occasion, so she'd donned a teal cropped denim jacket. To promote her signature Bohemian style, she wore several long, brown leather necklaces and bangles with silver charms and medallions as well as brown leather gladiator sandals. Cross-wise over her shoulder she carried her favorite Stella McCartney Falabella tote.

"And your hair, Miss Thomas," another gushed. "I love it!"

"Do you really?" she asked, running a hand over her newly-shorn pixie cut. "I've heard it reported that I may have lost my identity in cutting it." Scarlett cast an arch look at her agent, who had agreed with the assessment. She had indeed been known for her long, wavy hair. It was part of the reason she'd cut it so dramatically.

"We do!" her fans assured her and Scarlett cast them all a very genuine smile.

"Thank you so much. You're all just wonderful."

They beamed but another reporter pushed his way through then, ruining the most pleasant moment of her day thus far. She recognized him as one of the sleazy London tabloid reporters who'd had nothing better to do for years other than haunting Dunskirk Castle during taping. "Miss Thomas, what about the rumors regarding a secret romance with your *Puppet War* co-star, Grayson Lukas? Are they true?"

Aren't they always? Scarlett thought bitterly as the crowd held their collective breath waiting for a response, though she refrained from voicing the sour comeback knowing they would only ignore the sarcasm and interpret the words as verbal confirmation of the rumors. The worst thing about fame was that assumption that they all knew her. Knew what she wanted and what she thought.

How she longed for the days before all this had come about, when she had lived her own life or even felt as though she had one. When she hadn't been a star but just a girl who wanted the same thing all the girls wanted.

"Mr. Lukas." The reporter shifted direction when Scarlett didn't answer and she cringed realizing that her former co-star was just a few steps behind her. "What do you have to say to the rumors? Are they true?"

"Aren't they always?" Grayson's intonation of her thoughts was far more kindly presented as he slung a casual arm over her shoulder and gave them all a roguish wink.

Scarlett might have been much like Finley Adams in personality and temperament, but Grayson Lukas completely embodied his character, Flynn Jackson. A more cocksure, vain, cavalier idiot had never walked the earth. In her opinion, he personified the living, breathing proof that every high in life came with a downside.

Once, just once, during the filming of the second movie in the trilogy, *Ventriloquist*, Scarlett had made the mistake of going with Grayson to an awards show, sharing the red carpet with him. Tyrone had imagined it to be a brilliant publicity stunt and he had been right. The media, the paparazzi had latched on to the idea of Finley and Flynn. The nerd and the jock who fought their feelings and were then torn apart in the books and movies, finally together in real life. Rumor, tabloids, Photoshopped pictures. The press had created a relationship for them that wasn't any more factual than the fictional one.

Grayson had thought it should be. It helped them both, he insisted. Kept the spotlight on them. A spotlight Scarlett had been trying to step out of for the past four years.

"Gi' us a kiss!" one of the Scottish tabloid reporters shouted.

They think I actually like this fool! Her lips parted of their own accord, as if she might voice the thought but Grayson took advantage of her moment of silence, bending her back over his arm and taking the kiss the crowd wanted before she could protest. The onlookers went wild and Scarlett knew it would be all over social media the next day.

Back on her feet, Scarlett steadied herself and resisted the urge to swipe the back of her hand across her lips while Grayson waved to their fans.

Turning on her heel, she stalked away while Tyrone rushed to keep up with her. "What an idiot," she hissed from the corner of her mouth. "I can't believe anyone would think

I'm in love with that."

"Appearances, Scarlett."

"I'll tell you what you can do with your appearances, Tyrone."

Reaching the platform, Scarlett determinedly pasted her public smile back on and greeted the Director of Commerce and Tourism from Historic Scotland, the historic preservation society that maintained the castle, and the president of the Scottish Borders Council. "Good afternoon, Miss Thomas. Welcome to Dunskirk Castle! Again, of course. We're so glad that you could be with us today to mark this occasion."

The occasion was the full restoration of Dunskirk Castle and its transference from private property to a national historical site and public museum.

"I'm honored to have been asked." Scarlett smiled at the effusive welcome and shook hands with the others who gathered around; castle staff, government officials, and the director of exhibit operations, Darin Coleridge, who was in charge of the afternoon's festivities.

More hesitantly they greeted Tyrone, who was a harmless as a teddy bear but intimidated effortlessly since he was built like an ox, bald-headed and in possession of a neatly trimmed goatee that Scarlett suspected he maintained solely for its menacing addition to his already sinister persona.

Grayson followed her up on stage while Scarlett turned away to greet two of their other *Puppet War* co-stars who were also attending the ceremony. "Hayden, how are you?" she asked as they brushed air kisses and hugged lightly. "Michael." A more sincere hug. Hayden Walsh and Michael Ford had portrayed Nora Bankman and Christian Cameron in the series, the muscle as it were, in the storyline. Scarlett had gotten on with Michael especially well.

The four of them sank down into a row of chairs set behind the podium. Grayson managed a seat right next to her, but Scarlett studiously ignored him and gave her attention to Coleridge as he stepped up to make his opening remarks.

The photographers in the crowd kept their attention on her and Grayson, snapping away and leaving Scarlett with little choice but to force a brittle smile to her lips.

"…and, of course, we have to thank the director and producers of *The Puppet War* for bringing worldwide attention to Dunskirk by choosing it as the setting for their movies but it is the four young people who are with us today to whom we owe our greatest thanks. Their tireless efforts in promoting Dunskirk and raising the funds to open this museum today will never be forgotten. Now, I heard that Miss Thomas only recently gave a commencement address at Vanderbilt University when she graduated there this spring, *magna cum laude* with a degree in English literature. I thought I might take advantage of her recent practice and asked her say a few words today. She graciously accepted…so, please welcome, if you will, Scarlett Thomas."

Applause swept through the crowd as Scarlett stood once more, swinging her cross-body tote forward and fishing inside for her speech. At the podium, she adjusted the microphone height.

"Thank you, Mr. Coleridge. Your request for a few words is far kinder than what my professors required of me during my recent finals and for that I thank you." She nodded to the director and focused on the crowd before her, ignoring the mocking eyes boring into her back. "Many of you gathered here today know this place only as the living representation of

Aubroch Castle, a piece of *The Puppet War* come to life, but Dunskirk Castle has its own story to tell, one far more profound than fiction. I'm very glad to be back here today as we celebrate its place in the history of the Scottish Borderlands."

"I am no historian as my professors can attest." Scarlett paused as light laughter sprinkled through the crowd, ignoring Grayson's scoff behind her. "No, it's true. Deep down I'm just a fangirl like many of you. Before I first came to Dunskirk, the only castle I ever dreamed of visiting was Hogwarts. Now, knowing each nook and cranny of this dear old thing as I do, I know that Dunskirk will stand a far greater test of time than any book could. Than any movie might dare. I hope you will all keep that in mind as you walk through these halls today."

With a few more short sentences, Scarlett finished and smiled as the crowds applauded. Turning, she shook Coleridge's hand once more and accepted his thanks but before she could return to her seat, Grayson sneered. "Always a nerd, Scarlett."

Irritation roiled through her. "Bite me, Grayson."

"Always."

Unable to sit next to him a moment longer, Scarlett slipped discreetly down the steps and headed for the castle entrance as Coleridge introduced the next speaker.

"Scarlett," Tyrone whispered urgently, rushing to her side. "Come on, the fans love it, the two of you."

Shaking off his hand before he could grasp her arm, Scarlett kept walking. "But I don't. You know I don't."

She didn't have to ask why Tyrone was in favor of promoting a match – even a fabricated one – between her and Grayson. She already knew. Tyrone was close friends with Grayson's agent, close enough to take a favor and give one when necessary. Though Grayson Lukas was known around the world for his part in *The Puppet War*, new roles had been slow in coming and Grayson's Hollywood tastes couldn't survive without either an opportune casting or more opportune publicity.

"I don't know why I haven't fired you yet."

"Because your mother hired me."

"Because you slept with her."

Tyrone just grimaced. "Come back out here. Smile and wave. I'll make it up to you."

"How about you go away and hope I don't shoot either you or Grayson with this stupid pistol you make me carry around?" Scarlett patted the small lump weighing down the bottom of her tote. She'd made her agent angry but couldn't find it in herself to care. The changes she planned on making in the days and weeks to come would no doubt be far more upsetting than her refusal to sit next to her former co-star. Though she'd already told him, he would understand the seriousness of her intentions soon. "I'm going inside. Go say whatever you want, but I'm not coming back out until he's gone."

"Scarlett! Damn it, come back here!"

Scarlett kept walking. She'd lived at the whims of others too long to heed his call. To be at her parent's beck and call another moment. This was her time and she meant to seize it.

2

Once inside the castle doors, the noise of the crowd faded into a mausoleum-like oppression. The thick walls had that effect but the dank, darkness she remembered from the years she'd spent filming in the castle was washed away by the museum quality lighting and dehumidifiers that had been brought in. Today the stone walls were awash with soft light, the great hall now a cordoned-off maze of red velvet ropes leading to a modern desk of light birch standing below a large sign bearing prices for admission.

"Miss Thomas!" A man of later years standing behind the desk straightened as she approached. Despite his neat white shirt and dark slacks, he had an unkempt appearance and rather looked like the house-elf, Dobby, from the Harry Potter movies without the elfish ears. This man's were big enough still, and he had layers of wrinkles folded deeply into his skin. He seemed almost as old as the fortress itself but there was merriment in his twinkling blue eyes and vibrancy in his demeanor that would probably carry him a few centuries more, she thought whimsically.

"Good afternoon," she greeted him as she approached the

desk, skirting around the barriers.

"We werenae expecting ye inside yet, but welcome to Dunskirk, lass. Er, welcome back, I should say. Would ye care to take a turn through the exhibits?" he added in a thick brogue, gesturing to the far end of the hall where a sign reading 'Enter Here' was posted. "I imagine ye could use a bit of time fer yerself. Away from all the fuss."

It was like he was reading her mind. Scarlett wanted nothing more than to escape the people waiting for her outside. No, that wasn't exactly right. Really she wanted nothing more than to escape her life in general. The life that wasn't her own. A life overpopulated with unwanted attention and hateful humans.

"I ken what ye mean, I'd wager ye've a hard go of it."

"Huh? What?" Had she said that out loud? Scarlett groaned. It wasn't like her to make a slip like that in public where any random spectator might hear and misinterpret her words, passing them off – out of context, of course – on social media. If word got out that she was planning a life without them, the circus would be unimaginable. "I meant…"

"Dinnae fash yerself, lass. I kent what ye meant and willnae say a word. On my honor."

"Thank you…"

"Donell, lass," he said, tapping his name badge with one thick, bent finger.

"Donell," she nodded, reaching out to shake his hand. He was stronger than he looked, his handshake firm. "Might I head in, do you think? I'd like to take a peek before all the crowds enter."

"Of course, lass. No' a problem a'tall. Yer deserving of a break from all yer troubles, aren't ye?"

Scarlett smiled and pivoted toward the entrance but paused when he cleared his throat. Turning back, she sighed inwardly as the man lifted a pen and paper suggestively in her direction. "I ken I shouldnae ask but... er, I was wondering, could ye...?"

Her smile wasn't Oscar worthy but it was smile enough to please the clerk who beamed as she neared the desk. "It's no problem at all, Mr..." she referred to his nametag again. "Donell. Shall I make it to you?"

"Nay, lassie," he protested with an engaging grin. "To my granddaughter, Katharine, if ye please, lass. She's quite keen on ye, ye see. An autograph would send her o'er the moon."

Scarlett smiled at that, wondering when she had last been over the moon about anything. She was just so tired of it all. Well, not the fans, she rather enjoyed their enthusiasm, but the daily grind of fame. Fame she hadn't done much to deserve.

"I think ye underestimate yerself, lass. Yer a bonny thing to be sure and sweet, too. No' a'tall like the things they write aboot ye," he assured her. Familiar enough with all the things, true and false, that had been written about her, Scarlett didn't bother to ask what Donell might have read about her, but was confused by his initial statement. What did he mean that she underestimated herself? She started to ask but Donell rushed on before she might question him. "To Katharine, if ye dinnae mind."

"Not at all," she assured the odd little man with a smile and took up the pen and paper Donell pushed across the desk. "Katharine with a K?"

"Aye, lassie," he beamed at her, his eyes twinkling as he watched her write a short note on the page to accompany her signature. "K-a-t-h-*a*-r-i-n-e..."

"Ahh, with an 'a'," she said softly and finished it off with a flourish. "How's that?"

Donell scanned it, and if possible, smiled even more broadly. "Lovely, just lovely, Miss Thomas. You're verra kind, lass, to do this. Thank ye so much."

"I'm happy to do it." Scarlett waited patiently as he stood grinning at her. "Might I go through then?"

"Of course, of course." Donell fanned out several brightly printed brochures on the desk and pushed them toward her. "Some information on the different exhibits."

"Thank you." Scarlett thumbed through them, skimming over the bolded titles distractedly. *Sir Walter Scott: Rob Roy and Beyond, The Great War in Dunskirk, Border Textiles, Flodden: 500 Years,* and *Pong to Playstation: The Infinite Lives of Video Games.* Well, that might be interesting.

"Aye, well, will ye be needing a guide then, lassie?"

"No, I think I can make my way around this particular castle without one," she said with a smile that had him nodding.

"Of course ye can!" The man hastened to assure her, sweeping an arm toward the sign that bore an arrow pointing in the proper direction. "Take yer time, lass. Be sure to mind the armory exhibit, lass," he called after her as she turned to leave. "I'm sure ye'll being interested in what it will show ye."

"I'll be sure to check it out. Thank you, Donell," Scarlett smiled over her shoulder. "You've been very kind."

"No' a'tall, lassie. My pleasure. I hope ye find what yer looking for."

✕ ✕ ✕ ✕ ✕

Her sandals scuffed softly against the stone floors as Scarlett walked the long hall within the castle's curtain wall in silence, flipping idly through the pamphlets Donell had provided but mostly just absorbing the calm nothingness of it all. There had been very few moments like that for her in the past decade and a sigh of contentment escaped her.

The hall was dimly lit with faux torches lighting the way. Backlit displays dotted the wall between the torches giving a historic overview of Scottish borders history along with a timeline. There were castles like Hermitage, Kelso and Jedburgh along with Dunskirk.

Scarlett grazed over the words on the wall absently. She hadn't been joking out there when she said she wasn't a historian. Dates and places meant nothing without the emotion that they evoked in the people of the time. That was why she'd majored in English Lit. It was words that touched her and held her attention.

Once she reached the pele tower, the oldest part of the castle, the hallway widened into a brightly lit gallery dotted with displays on Mary, Queen of Scots. Paintings, jewels, and a reproduction of her death mask. An elaborate gown that looked like it was spun from gold.

Following the path lights to the second floor, she found the armory exhibit Donell spoke of. Pacing slowly around the perimeter of the vast tower, Scarlett studied the paintings on the walls as she circled the room. Most were scenes of the Battle of Flodden done in different styles from the simplicity of the medieval era to the thick oils of the impressionists. Watercolors, drawings. Even a Burne-Jones marble relief. All depicting different aspects of the battle. The glory. The gore. So much red.

Like literature, art had more impact on Scarlett than all the history books in the world's libraries. She could almost see the battle. Touch it. Feel it.

One large oil bore a scene of rugged, kilted soldiers attacking a more tidily-garbed army with swords and pikes. Between the art displays were battle axes, long bows and long pikes fifteen feet in length. On pedestals dotting the room, smaller artifacts from the battlefield – like cannonballs, an Englishman's plate armor, and a Scotsman's broach – were set under Plexiglas. A cannon dominated the center of the room.

One round pedestal bore a heavy sword held up by a Plexiglas stand. Unlike the no-nonsense weaponry on the wall, this one was a Scottish claymore with an ornate grip of dark wood with a swirling grain inlaid with metal filigree that looked like gold. On the hilt and the ends of the pommel and cross guard were huge, smooth stones of amber almost as large as chicken eggs. It didn't look like the sword of a soldier to be sure.

Scarlett leaned in to read the tiny brass plaque on the side of the pedestal: *Scottish Claymore, found on the battlefield of Flodden.*

Running her fingers lightly over the engraved inscription, she pondered the implication of those words. Found on the battlefield of Flodden because its bearer had died there, most likely. Found because there was no one left to pick it up. Unexpected grief squeezed Scarlett's chest. Sorrow too great for the mere mention of some long dead Scotsman, but it gathered heavily in her heart, nonetheless.

Scarlett lifted her fingertips to the sword's edge. Though it looked dulled with age, the blade was unexpectedly razor-sharp and sliced the pad of her forefinger. Flinching back, she watched blood well through the narrow cut and her head swam unexpectedly. The darkness that should have normally accompanied such a head rush was overwhelmed by a blinding gleam of light. Blinking, she found the sword's afterimage burned into her lids.

"Why can't you ever just play along, Scarlett?" She turned to find Grayson Lukas assembling through her still spotty vision as if he were held in a Star Trek transporter beam. "It's publicity. Just publicity."

"It's not just publicity," she argued, sucking the sting away from her fingertip. "It's my life as much as yours and I won't play these games anymore with you. There are people out there who think they know what happened between us when nothing did. People… men who have treated me differently than they should have because of things you've said to the press. I don't want that kind of attention."

Grayson Lukas scowled down at her with none of the boyish charm that had been on display for the crowds outside. The sight wasn't surprising. This was the Grayson she knew. "Bullshit! We all want the attention. It's why we do what we do. We all want it."

"I don't. Especially not that kind of attention."

"No, you're the big, high fashion model now, aren't you, Scarlett?" he sneered, grabbing her upper arm and pulling her close. "Too good for the rest of us?"

"No, just too good for you," Scarlett told him and not for the first time as she swatted at his hands. "We're not teenagers anymore to play at relationships, Grayson. I am not your toy, damn it! I never was and I refuse to lie for the sake of your career anymore."

"You refuse?" His grip tightened painfully.

"Yes, I'm done. With all of it." Scarlett pushed him away harder. Taken unaware, Grayson's hold slipped and she stumbled backward. Her nemesis was close behind, latching on to her jacket to pull her back. It dragged down her arm and Scarlett shook it loose, gaining a few feet of freedom.

He yanked hard and she rotated, freeing the other arm but the jacket caught on her tote, keeping her within arm's length. Her many necklaces were swinging back and forth, then cutting into her neck when Grayson latched on to them and tugged. "What do I have to do to get through to you?"

"Well, this isn't helping your cause," she bit out. Bending, she felt the necklaces slip over her head, heard them clatter to the floor. Grabbing up her skirt, she straightened and brought her foot up hard between his legs. With open scorn, she glared down at him as he curled protectively over his groin. She wasn't afraid of him, merely sickened. "Too bad the paparazzi can't see you now, huh?"

"You bloody bitch!" he yelled, his fist snapping out and catching her on the side of the head as he reared up.

Careening sideways with only one of the pedestals to break her fall, the crash of the column to the floor and the clatter of the ancient sword as it met stone echoed through the tower. With Grayson advancing menacingly, Scarlett tried to right herself but bells were tolling sickly in her head. He grabbed for her again but she managed to block him and twist out of reach. The motion made her head spin dizzily and darkness clouded her vision. She stepped back. Her sandal raked against the hem of her maxi dress and her bottom painfully met the stone floor.

Scrambling backward like a crab, she tried to put some distance between them so that she might defend herself as her self-defense instructor had taught her but her sandaled feet slipped on the floor and again caught on her skirt. She would have to wait until he was upon her to do anything now.

Back farther. Her fingers grazed the warm steel blade of

the claymore and curled around it. Bright white light flared once more as she dragged it closer and found the hilt but the sword was too heavy for her to lift.

Somebody, please...

"What are you going to do, Scarlett? Slay me like one of those bloody CGI dragons from the film?"

"I will if you come a step closer. Just leave me alone!"

With a laugh, Grayson knocked the sword away. It clattered across the floor and Scarlett closed her eyes in dismay then...

Silence.

Shouts sounded from outside, breaking the blessed silence, and Scarlett opened first one eye, then the other in surprise. Grayson was gone.

A metallic clang rang out, and then another followed by a hoarse scream. Still dazed from his lucky punch and more than a little confused by his disappearance, Scarlett scrambled to the window and looked outside. The yelling grew louder, sounding as if it was coming from directly below.

The window was sealed shut but Scarlett pressed close to the wavy bullion glass trying to look directly downward but there was nothing to see.

She frowned.

No wait! There was really nothing to see!

No cobbled drive. No canopy. No crowd. That was odd. Perhaps she had gotten turned around and that was the rear of the castle? She had taken quite a blow to her noggin. Brow still furrowed, she backed away from the window and into a solid object. Cold metal against her neck sent a chill wracking through her as a hard arm wound around her waist.

"Who are ye, lass?" A rough voice asked in a brogue so deep she could feel the man's chest rumble against her back. "What are ye doing here?"

Who was he? A security guard? She doubted it. Unfortunately, she'd had a few stalkers in the past who were far more dangerous than Grayson. "What am I doing here? Just who do you think you are?" Scarlett asked a question of her own with false bravado. In many cases, stalkers wanted her fear as if seeing her cringe or recoil gave them some power over her, but Scarlett Thomas wasn't about to cower before this new threat. "Take your hands off of me! Don't you know who I am?"

"Nay, that's what I'm trying to find out so tell me true, lass, who are ye? What are ye doing in my keep?" There was a sharp prick at her neck and Scarlett realized that the metal touching her wasn't a gun barrel but a knife. He might be nearly unintelligible but he meant business.

"Your keep? Are you crazy?" she bit out, wrapping her hand tightly around his thick wrist. Grayson might have gotten the best of her with that one punch but she wasn't about to become a victim twice this day. "Now take your hands off of me or else!"

"Or else what?" he asked, sounding more confused than challenging with that typical response and the blade at her neck tipped downward as his tight hold slackened.

Scarlett took her chance, throwing back her head and catching him unexpectedly in the chin while at the same time she brought her heel down on his instep. With a vile curse, her attacker released her and she seized the opportunity to pivot out of his hold while twisting his wrist down with her. Pain zinged up her arm as the heel of her other hand caught him in the nose but triumph whisked the sting away.

Spinning away, she started to run but he caught her by the wrist and dragged her back. She was ready for him. With a sharp tug toward his thumb, the weakest point of his grasp, she pulled away and jabbed a kick into the side of his knee. Cursing with pain, he reached for her again.

Damn, but he was fast! This time he held her around the neck and pulled her back against him. Sensing that the same tricks wouldn't work twice with him, Scarlett caught his hand in hers, and sidestepping, brought her other fisted hand down hard into his groin. As he doubled over, she used her shoulder and his own momentum to force his arm upward, rotating it behind him. With one hand, she locked his elbow in place and used the other to force his thumb back to meet his forearm. Triumphantly, she planted a knee between his shoulder blades to keep him down.

Before she could get too cocky though, he reared up almost knocking her off of him but Scarlett used all her weight to pin him until she was practically kneeling on him, adding pressure to her hold on his thumb, forcing it down. Any attempt on his part to lower his arm would only increase that pressure, bringing him more pain.

She had him... for the moment.

With another pained expletive, her assailant stilled. His head whipping around, his eyes filled with icy rage before his gaze met hers. His pale silver eyes widened with surprise. Then drifted slowly downward.

Her expression as she stared down at him couldn't have been any less stunned than his. His appearance was so startling Scarlett almost unwittingly released him to step away. The man radiated anger and savagery from a face so sublime he must have either had the love of one overly benevolent

God or the blessing of one rather diabolical devil.

It was a face designed to captivate, to enthrall. There was no doubt in Scarlett's mind that he had used his looks as an effective weapon against women in the past. What man wouldn't when he looked like that?

He was the devil's own with shaggy dark hair framing his carefully hewn features: the square jaw, enviable cheekbones, aquiline nose and smooth broad forehead. He wore a short, scruffy growth of beard that seemed to enhance rather than hide the hard granite planes of his cheeks and that chiseled jaw. Beneath low, thick brows, his eyes were by contrast as pale grey as a shark's underbelly. His expression just as deadly.

Then she realized that it must have been his shock at being conquered more than anything that kept him on his knees and at her mercy because Lord have mercy! He was huge! Given the bulging biceps and traps of his arm, the thickness of his neck and shoulders, Scarlett was willing to bet that under that linen shirt and bulky kilt was a body of pure muscle. Without a doubt, the enormous, scarred hand she held in hers could break her neck easily.

By the look in his eye, he was considering it.

Thinking of the pistol weighing at the bottom of her tote, Scarlett deliberated whether she might manage to retrieve it, release it from the holster and point it at him before he had time to kill her.

Not likely.

A tremor spiraled through her leaving icy terror in its wake but Scarlett wasn't an actor for nothing and managed to keep her expression cool and confident as she glared down at him. "Enough of this now. I want you to leave me alone. Do you understand?"

The man lowered his head, shaking it slowly. His shoulders jerked and she realized in a flash that he was laughing. Laughing at *her*. "You think this is funny? Are you nuts?"

"Nuts?" he repeated curiously in that deep, thick brogue, lifting his head to look at her once more. "I'm going to forgi' ye, lass, for clearly ye've been ill and are mayhap still a wee bit maddened wi' fever."

If he looked mildly baffled by her words, she was utterly perplexed by his. "Ill? Maddened?" She wrinkled her nose at the suggestion. She wasn't the one who looked crazy. *He* was the one wearing the kilt. Not even a nicely pleated kilt but a mangy dirty one... and was that blood? Then what he said sunk in and her calm slipped. "Wait. You're going to forgive me? Did you really just say that? Forgive me for what? You attacked me, remember?"

"And yer people attacked my hold," he shot back with a blood chilling growl.

"My *people*?"

"Aye, Lindsay, yer people."

"Lindsay? My name isn't Lindsay," she scoffed. "As if you didn't know."

"Are ye the Crawford's get then? Why would he bring ye here dressed thusly?"

Scarlett closed her eyes, taking a deep breath. They were getting nowhere fast with this shooting questions back and forth at each other. And his brogue so much thicker than any other she had heard in Scotland, Scarlett could barely understand him to boot.

The brute flexed his arm and Scarlett fought to keep his elbow locked, adding the slightest pressure to his thumb. It pleased her immensely to see him wince. "Listen. Obviously there has been a mistake. I'm not whoever it is you think I am. So how about I let you go and you walk away. That way I can go back to my hotel, have a nice long bath, a whole bottle of wine and just forget this day ever happened. What do you say?"

"Aboot what?"

"Do ye need help, brother?"

Scarlett looked up at the same time as her attacker and groaned. To her dismay, there was not one man coming to his aid, but a half dozen more dressed much as her hostage. In fact, all of them were wearing the same kilt of faded red plaid with thin yellow and black lines. If that wasn't disconcerting enough, unbelievably they were all armed with long claymores.

"Holy shit." Icy dread gripped her heart as she watched drops of what could only be blood dribble off the tip of one of the swords and spread like a web through the stone of the castle floor. "What the hell is going on here? Who are you people?"

The man at the head of the newcomers took a few steps forward, studying her and Scarlett looked him over as well. Even without him claiming her hostage his brother, she could see the facial resemblance though his expression wasn't quite as murderous. Nor was he as bulked up… which wasn't to say that he wasn't muscular. It would be like comparing a quarterback to a linebacker (if one were into sports analogies). The power was still there. This one also had dark auburn hair instead of mahogany. It was longer, past his shoulders, and combed back from his arresting face.

There was also something about him. Perhaps it was the way he held himself, that self-confident gaze or how his lips curved just so, that was immediately engaging. Certainly he wasn't the humble sort but neither did he radiate cockiness in the off-putting manner some of her former co-stars had. Grayson, for example. Still, this one could have been a movie star in a heartbeat, with fangirls worshiping at his feet.

Having never known a ginger who was dangerous, she felt her wariness ebb.

Meeting his eyes boldly, Scarlett watched the corner of his mouth kick up attractively before his gaze shifted down with some interest to the arm bar she maintained on her attacker. "Is she hurting ye, brother?"

"Nay, Rhys. I'm merely resting."

His 'G' slid into a low hiss when Scarlett bent his thumb downward more forcibly. The other man – Rhys, was it? – smiled broadly as he looked down at her with wicked humor dancing in his silvery eyes. "I like her."

Scarlett raised a superior brow and the man's mischievous grin stretched even wider.

"I think I'd like to take ye home wi' me."

"Thank you, no. I'm fine right here," she shot back and was treated to his delighted laughter as well.

"Rhys, would ye just take her?" her attacker growled out, slapping his free palm against the floor impatiently.

"Perhaps ye should just ask her to release ye." She had to have been mistaken, but Scarlett swore she could see approval in this Rhys' eyes. "She cannae be much of a threat to us. Clearly she's run from her sickbed."

Scarlett looked down at her maxi dress wondering how such a message could be 'clear' when they were the ones dressed so oddly. Like rejects from the local renaissance fair or war re-enactors gone wild.

"Sickbed?" she repeated incredulously. "Do I look sick to you?"

"Are ye no'? Ye must hae been maddened by fever if ye thought to defeat the mighty Laird o' Achenmeade in hand-to-hand combat," Rhys jested with another laugh and a few of the other men swallowed chuckles before the huge barbarian on his knees scowled fiercely, immediately silencing them all.

"Yes, heaven forbid a little girl like me should be able to defend herself against a man intent on harming her," Scarlett retorted, bending the mighty Laird's wrist again until he hissed in pain.

"Bloody hell, Rhys," he swore. "Will ye just take her all ready?"

Rhys met her eyes and shrugged. "Wi' my apologies, lady."

Then his hands were on her shoulders and Scarlett was back to square one. She released the Laird guy who rose shaking out his hand and brought her arms up, arcing them over her new opponent's arms and cutting downward to break his hold.

Odds overwhelmingly against her, Scarlett didn't even try to fight this time but turned and ran. Not a step had she gone before a thickly muscled arm snaked about her waist, lifting her off her feet. Giving her no chance to fight back this time, Laird tossed her over his shoulder as if she didn't weigh an ounce and pinned her there with one arm. Though Scarlett struggled for all she was worth, kicking and hitting, he held her tight, smacking her bottom hard for good measure. Scarlett stilled at the stinging pain. Her self-defense teacher had never addressed how to get out of that particular hold.

"Have a care, brother," the more humorous of the pair said. "She's so frail ye might snap her bones."

"I'm more like to snap her neck," the words vibrated through the thick chest pressed against her thighs. "What else am I to do wi' her?"

Rhys shrugged carelessly. His eyes were still sparkling while Scarlett's were shooting sparks. "She maun hae come wi' the reivers to raid yer keep but why? As sickened as she has clearly been and in her small clothes? I suppose we might ask the Lindsay men who she is if any yet live."

"Aye and we may get a fair ransom for her as well."

Scarlett stilled as that one word stood out from their thick, garbled speech. Ransom! It rang through her head like a peal. She was being kidnapped. So much for him not knowing whom she was.

"Tyrone! Tyrone, help me!" she screamed at the top of her lungs, the plea ending in an undignified squawk as the Laird brought down his meaty hand firmly down on her buttocks once more. With only the thin cotton of her maxi skirt and panties to pillow the blow, her bottom warmed grievously. "Stop it, stop it, *stop it*!" she screamed, beating his back with her fists once more. Not that he seemed to notice, the frickin' brick wall!

With her bouncing against his shoulder, his long jarring steps carried them across the tower and down the stairs. As they were passing through the hall within the curtain wall, Scarlett felt her tote slip over her back and up to the base of her neck. Twisting about, she expected it would fall even farther so that she might be able to reach it.

Let's see what these bastards had to say when she was pointing a gun at them.

But, no. Her bag stayed put. Disappointed, she looked around, hoping to catch sight of any of the castle staff or other guests who might come to her aid. Even Donell, though older, might carry her call for help to the others. But there was no one about other than more kilted marauders. No sound beyond the occasional ring of clashing swords.

"Report," her captor barked out as they emerged from the castle and another armed man rushed toward them without sparing her a single glance. None of the men did. It was as if they didn't even notice her hanging over his shoulder.

Or was it just that common a sight?

"The castle is retaken, m'lord," the newcomer said quickly. "Nae more than a dozen inside and out. None killed. Dougal and Malcolm are rounding up the strays."

Dozen? Scarlett stilled once more at their words. That made no sense. There were at least that many staff members working the castle and more than a hundred spectators and guests present for the exhibit as well. Still, there wasn't a familiar face to be seen.

What was going on here? What had happened to everyone? The crowd? The cameras?

Who were these people?

"At least there is that to stop the feuding. Lock the prisoners in the dungeon and assign a guard to them til Lindsay ransoms them back." Laird turned on his heel then paused a few steps away. "Padraig, bring one of them to me first."

Like a good little soldier, the lackey ran off. Little? Ha, he was as big as the rest of them. It was indeed like coming face to face with a football team. Scarlett, who hadn't been labeled petite since she was ten, was unexpectedly cowed by their collective size.

Not that she planned to show it.

When the Laird dragged her back over his shoulder and dropped her at his feet, she met him glare for glare. The bastard only lifted a single brow, amusement reflected in his eyes if not on his lips.

Oh, if only looks could...

The gun!

Scarlett tore open her bag and dug inside the cluttered tote but was once again thwarted when he clamped both of her wrists in one hand. Though she struggled to free herself, his grip was as effective as a pair of handcuffs. A moment later a rough texture abraded her tender wrist and she stilled in surprise.

He was actually tying her up. Binding her hands in front of her, not with handcuffs or even the taught smoothness of a zip-tie but with roughly braided, hemp rope. "Rope? Who uses rope anymore?"

The brute lifted a brow and jerked the knot tighter.

"Hey! Watch it. That hurts."

"Ye nearly broke my bluidy thumb, lass," he whispered as he bent over to bind her ankles. "And my nose."

"Only nearly? Guess I should have tried harder." Scarlett lifted her knee sharply, feeling a strong sense of satisfaction when she caught him on the side of the head.

"Och, ye bluidy hellion!" He rubbed his ear and glared up at her with deadly menace. "I dinnae like to strike a lady but ye best stand still before I cuff ye to be sure!"

Yes, she supposed she should have been glad that he didn't retaliate with violence as Grayson had. Surely a blow from that brawny fist would kill her but somehow she instinctively knew he wasn't going to hit her. Not now, not when he'd had more than a few chances to do so upstairs.

And in truth, his scathing command chaffed almost as much as the rope around her ankles. She'd spent her whole life being told what do. She had only just started to retake control of her life and now this. Well, she wasn't about to stand for it without being as difficult as possible. If kicking and screaming her way through this whole nightmare would annoy him, it would be worth any effort. "Ouch! Not so tight. Geez, what are you? An amateur? You want a good ransom, the merchandise needs to be returned *unharmed*."

"If ye had bothered to dress yerself ere walking the halls, ye might hae had a thick hose betwixt yer flesh and the rope."

"I am dressed," Scarlett snapped irritably.

He looked down at her dress skeptically and again Scarlett wondered at it. Even without her denim jacket on top of it, there was nothing wrong with what she was wearing but he was looking at her like she was making a dozen fashion faux pas. He certainly didn't look like he could have been a fashion editor for anything more *haute couture* than the Highlands edition of *Field and Stream* or *Kilts Weekly*.

"You're a fine one to talk about fashion with you and your men dressed all matchy-matchy like some Highland marching band. I can't wait to see you pull out the bagpipes."

"Cease yer senseless havering, lass."

"Look, last chance, Laird or whatever your name is," Scarlett warned darkly. "Let me go now or I will make sure you get the book thrown at you hard."

"Mayhap yer more ill than I thought," he said, frowning in confusion and scratching at his whiskered jaw as he studied her. "Why would anyone throw something so dear as books at me?"

Surely that absurd, cantankerous man was going to drive her bat-shit crazy! Scarlett gnashed her teeth. "The *authorities*.

Do you understand that word or do I need to spell it out for you? You will be arrested for this, you know."

Her kidnapper only rolled his eyes dismissively. "My cousin is the Earl of Bothwell, lass, mine uncle the Warden of Middle March. My own father, the Lord High Chamberlain. I assure ye, lass, I willnae find myself in shackles o'er something so minor as this."

Since when was kidnapping 'minor'? "You think a little name dropping is going to scare me?" Scarlett asked boldly. "I can name drop, too. I'll go straight to the top even. I know the Queen!"

Well, *met*, more than knew but the insouciance of the man was beginning to terrify her more than the situation. He didn't seem to care that what he was doing was a crime. The worst kinds of psychopaths were the ones who thought themselves above the law or a law onto themselves. Unfortunately, she knew all too well how dangerous the crazies could be.

And her threat didn't seem to give him pause at all, instead his steely gaze narrowed on her. "Which one?"

Which one? Scarlett shook her head incomprehensively. How many queens did he think were on this freakin' island? "The Queen of England, of course."

If possible, his look became even more glacial. "Are you a spy then?"

"What? No!" Scarlett frowned, still shaking her head as if the motion might deny the absurdity of the entire conversation. "Why would you even ask that?"

"No one in Scotland would admit to an association with the Queen given the discord between our countries."

That discombobulating statement was too mind-numbing for Scarlett to even begin to try to decipher. "Put it this way, if I were a spy would I be so dumb as to admit it?"

He lifted a brow and shrugged as if he questioned her ability to even produce a logical thought. Fair enough. Scarlett felt the same of him. It was as if this Laird guy had been hiding under a rock and had no clue what was going on in the world or how it worked. "I would appreciate it if you would please just leave me alone."

"Unguarded?"

"Have someone else guard me then," she insisted, flicking her fingers toward Rhys. "Like that other guy. The nice one."

"Ye think he will be sweet-talked into letting ye go? He willnae."

"No, I just think he won't drive me as crazy as you do."

4

James Hepburn signaled to two of his men to stand guard over his captive, leaving them with stern warnings not to be swayed by her frail appearance.

As he had been.

Tall but thin as a rail, James would never have considered that such a waifish lass might ever have him at her mercy but surprisingly she had. Shaking out his hand once more at the memory of the horrendous pain she had produced with just a turn of his digits, James crossed the castle yard to where his half-brother was supervising the securing of the captured reivers who would become his prisoners that day.

Sod it all. He hated to detain them so. Most of them were just family men looking to secure food and supplies for their families. Crofters with fields to be harvested. Letting them go, however, would be a mistake. A signal to the Lindsays and the Hepburn's other rival clans that his lands and goods were theirs for the taking.

That would be unacceptable. So ransomed they would be

to their laird, assuming that the Lindsay would be willing to pay a fair price for them.

As for the woman, James didn't know what to make of her.

"What vexes ye, Laird?" Rhys asked with a provoking grin as he neared. "The wee lassie giving ye more pain?"

"Dinnae call me that." James curled his lip not only at the name but at being baited to respond as he had been a thousand times before. "She pains me naught but for the throbbing of my skull when speaking wi' her. She is an impossible harridan, refusing to answer my questions fairly. Evading the truth and talking nonsense. Now, she asks for ye to stand guard over her."

"Me?" his brother questioned with a wicked laugh. "Why me?"

"Yer the *nice* one."

Rhys threw back his head, laughing heartily at James' derisive response. "The nice one?"

"Aye, well she dinnae ken ye well, does she?"

"Nay, she dinnae."

James looked back over his shoulder at his captive who was testing the bounds of the ropes at her wrists. His clever men had tied them to a torch sconce on the tower wall, allowing her little room for movement. "What do ye think of her, brother?"

Rhys turned to look as well, his expression filled with speculation. "Clearly she's a lady. Despite her lack of proper speech, clothing... and hair." James lifted a brow and nodded. Aye, there was that. "She's soft as a pampered bairn's bottom. I'd lay wager she's nae before spent a day at labor or in the sun a'tall. She's more clever than most ladies, as well, me thinks."

James nodded again. Aye, there was no doubt about that. Despite the madness of her words, he could fairly see the wheels spinning in the lass's head with each word she spoke. Puzzling her way out of her predicament much as he was considering the mystery she presented.

He knew not who she was or who her people were. She denied the Lindsay name. 'Struth that was about all he had garnered from her odd speech. Nor could he determine her reason or purpose in walking about the castle unsuitably clothed as she was… or why she was at Dunskirk at all. A raid was no place for a woman.

That she hadn't yet been quelled by his stare or fainted at his feet under his admittedly rough treatment of her person troubled him.

And she had put him on his knees as well!

"She nigh tore the thumb from my hand," he admitted, absently pressing his thumb downward as she had. How had she known how to cause such astonishing pain by holding him thusly? He, a seasoned warrior, had no idea how to induce such agony in such a simple fashion.

"Bloodied yer nose as well," his brother said with a grin and James swiped at his nose impatiently. Rhys went on. "She had skill enough to free herself from my hold, too. Where does a well-bred lass learn such a thing? For what purpose?"

"I dinnae ken nor do I ken what she thought to do next. If she had loosened her hold, I would hae killed her wi' my bare hands." Still as they watched their captive from across the yard, James felt a grudging respect for the lass. He'd not admit it aloud but she had bested him handily. "Me thinks she is no' from Scotland a'tall," he said. "I dinnae ken her speech. Her accent is most odd. France? Even Spain, mayhap?"

"Mayhap. Why would ye think that?"

"She says she knows the Queen."

"Margaret?" Rhys raised his brows in surprise. "One of her ladies? And I thought I knew them all."

"Nay, no' Margaret," James corrected with a grimace. "Catherine. The bluidy queen regent of England."

Rhys whistled and looked over his shoulder at their hostage once more with fresh interest. "'Struth, ye think?"

"I cannae say," James admitted, hating to admit his lack of certainty. "Nor do a know what to do wi' her."

"I say we cart her back to Father," Rhys suggested. "If he cannae find out who she is, Mother will surely know."

James sneered at the recommendation. "I am my own laird. This problem is my own."

"Lindsay is our sworn rival. If she is theirs, 'tis a problem for the whole clan," Rhys reasoned. "If she is a Sassenach, 'tis a problem for our king. If she is simply mad…. Is she?"

"Why dinnae ye go find out?" James grumbled. "Yer the bluidy nice one."

× × × × ×

With her hands tied in front of her and bound to the iron sconce, Scarlett couldn't get to her bag which now hanging down her back despite several attempts to swing it forward. She could reach her dress pocket for her phone, however, and was surprised that they hadn't thought to take it from her right away.

Scarlett quickly dialed Tyrone's number and pressed send, holding the phone as furtively to her ear as she could manage. Nothing but silence. Not a ring or even his voicemail. That was odd, since her agent never turned off his phone. He even left it on when he was in bed with a woman, which was how Scarlett had so inopportunely found out about his fling with her mother.

Thinking to redial and try again, Scarlett glanced down at her screen and noticed that there was no service. Not even one bar. Damn! Of all the times to have no coverage.

Noticing that the men set to guard her were watching her strangely, Scarlett slipped the phone back into her pocket. On an afterthought, she powered down the phone as well. If she were to try again later on, she didn't want to have drained her battery down as it would when constantly searching for a signal.

That baffling Laird guy who had attacked her in the castle was yelling out orders to the other men who hurried here and there, bringing out horses and loading them down with a collection of arms and shields like those she had seen in the exhibit. Watching them, realization dawned. Was that it then? Were they just a bunch of thieves?

Where was everyone then, she wondered once more? Surely someone had heard the raucous even from the other side of the castle? Or had they been somehow subdued?

"Are ye well, lady?"

Shading her eyes against the setting sun, Scarlett narrowed her gaze on the brother as he approached. Rhys, the Laird guy had called him. "Yes, thank you, but I'd be so much better if y'all would just let me go."

"I'm afraid I cannae do that," he said with mock sorrow to match her light sarcasm. "Even though I am the nice one. I thank ye for that compliment, by the by."

Scarlett shrugged, drawing his eye to the bindings on her wrists as the rope attaching her to the sconce swayed. "Being

39

told you're the nice one when compared to the devil isn't really much of a compliment is it?"

"Ye hae a ready wit, my lady. I shall look forward to hearing more of what ye hae to say." He chuckled, pulling a handkerchief – who carried a handkerchief anymore? – out of the pocket of the velvet – yes, velvet… in summer – jacket he wore beneath the long plaid draping over his shoulder. Even the cuffs and collar of the shirt he wore beneath it were unusual, heavily embroidered in gold thread. Gently, he tucked the delicately embroidered linen between the ropes and her wrists and gave them a little pat.

"Thank you."

Rhys shrugged.

"You seem like a reasonable guy. Surely you can't be in favor of this idiocy?"

"Can ye provide a reasonable explanation of how ye came to be here?"

"Of course," she said with an impatient sigh. "I was at the dedication ceremony like everyone else and only went inside for the exhibit…"

Rhys shook his head, cutting her off with an upheld palm. "Cease, lass. Laird had the right of it. Ye've a way of making a man's head pound."

A hint of desperation was building from deep within but Scarlett strove to keep it from her voice. She had to talk some sense into him. "Come on. Just let me go. It'll save you a world of hurt in the long run. Anyone can see you're not kidnappers."

"What makes ye say that?" There was a smile playing at his lips.

"You're taking too long for one thing," Scarlett told him. If her hands were free, she might have slapped the grin right off his handsome face. There was nothing at all amusing about this. "Look at y'all. It's like you're hoping to get caught. Plus you haven't done your homework if you think you'll get a good ransom for me. Despite what you might think, there isn't that much."

"I rather doubt that."

"Celebrity doesn't always equal money, honey," she warned, her Southern roots showing as her agitation grew.

"Celebrity?"

Scarlett was torn between rising anxiety and irritation at their tireless questioning. "Listen, Braveheart, I appreciate the whole medieval thing y'all got going here. It's impressive, really, but you're going about this all wrong. Why don't you just let me go and stick with what you obviously know best?" Though they seemed to know what they were doing pretty damn well. Despite her disbelief at their tactics, apparently a raid in broad daylight was working for them. They must be pretty good if no guards or authorities had come upon them yet. "Take your loot and leave, but let me go."

"Ye think we're naught but thieves, lady?"

"Well, aren't you?"

"Reivers, my lady," he said, rolling out the word with his heavy brogue, his gray eyes twinkling merrily. "In the long and glorious tradition. The Lindsay's are our sworn enemies. We've merely come to take back what they thought to steal." He raised his brows suggestively at her. "And what they hae left behind."

Scarlett rolled her eyes. Yea, she got it, despite his blather. They might not have been ransacking the castle looking for her in particular but a good thief took what was available. Despite his courtesy, he really wasn't going to let her go.

Now that was disappointing. A thick lump tightened her

throat but she swallowed it back, inhaling a calming breath. It wouldn't do to panic just yet. "So you're not going to let me go then? You should. There'll be hell to pay if you don't."

Shit! What else could she do? She really did not want to be kidnapped. "I can pay…"

"A Lindsay as ordered, Sir Rhys," one of the other *reivers* called for his attention and shoved a man wearing a kilt of wide orange and green plaid down at Rhys' feet. Rolling on to his back, he sneered and spit on the ground, all bravado and balls. Scarlett was astounded that he could be so brash as he was bleeding heavily from a gash on his shoulder and in obvious pain.

"You did that?" She gasped at Rhys, shuddering at the sight. "Your people did that to him? He needs a doctor. You need to get him to the ER."

Rhys, his guards and even the man on the ground all looked at her strangely – as if she were the problem – before one of the guards hauled the prisoner to his feet.

"This lass," Rhys said, pointing a finger at her as he spoke to the bleeding man. "Do ye ken who she is?"

The Lindsay man frowned in confusion as he looked between her and Rhys.

Scarlett was genuinely puzzled as well and not just by the entire bizarre scenario. It finally struck her that, even though she couldn't recall the last time someone hadn't recognized her out in public, none of them did. Not when she was hanging over that Laird guy's shoulder or standing on her own two feet. Surely one little haircut hadn't changed all that?

"Seriously?" she couldn't help but ask. "Don't I look at all familiar?"

Four sets of male eyes scanned her from head to toe but she saw no inkling of recognition in any of them. The Lindsay prisoner offered a shrug to boot.

Maybe they really didn't know who they were kidnapping.

Yea, right, she thought to herself. Why the hell would they be kidnapping her then?

There was no need to panic yet, Scarlett reminded herself. According to what she heard, no one in the castle had been killed, so soon – hopefully sooner rather than later – Tyrone would discover she was missing and call the police. Or the Bobbies. Or whatever they were called around here. Either way, Scarlett just needed to bide her time, look for escape if possible and otherwise wait them out.

Unfortunately, she couldn't wait much longer.

"Is that good then, lady? No' too tight?" her guard, Cormac, asked kindly. He'd cut the ropes at her ankles but tied her still bound wrists to the pommel of the saddle. A saddle he had lifted her into as easily as her father might have set her atop a pony at the fair when she was a child. If her father had ever done such a thing, that is.

"I'm fine. Thank you." Thanking her captor seemed silly but Scarlett couldn't blame her guard or take out her frustrations on him. This wasn't his fault. He was just following orders and it didn't seem that anyone, Rhys included, was willing to contradict the big guy. "Is there a smaller horse I could ride though? This one is huge and I'm rather neurotically afraid of heights."

Huge was a modest word for the horse. Gargantuan would have been better.

"My apologies, lady, but nay."

The horse stomped his feet impatiently and Scarlett clung to the tall pommel as if being tied to it wouldn't be enough to save her from a fall. Where on earth did they find horses whose backs were taller than a man's head? The ground looked so far away. It was dizzying. Percheron, Cormac said. Nineteen hands. Scarlett didn't know the exact conversion but was sure it roughly equated to really, freaking huge.

A total of a dozen of Laird's men were mounted and ready to go, leaving an equal number behind at Dunskirk. Each of them dressed in kilts and armed to the teeth. The thought of being surrounded by so many strange, dangerous men was disconcerting. Scarlett shuddered. "Where are you taking me?" she asked her guard as he mounted his own horse and gathered up her reins.

Without giving her an answer, Cormac kicked his horse into motion and Scarlett's obediently followed. Her teeth slammed together and her stomach dropped like a stone as the jarring lift of the rough gait nearly sent her listing out of the saddle.

Oh God! The horse was forgotten as the realization that they were actually leaving the castle robbed Scarlett of her breath. Of course, she knew they meant to but now that they were actually moving.... "Where are you taking me?" She yelled this time, and then screeched out the words at the top of her lungs when she was ignored once more.

Laird pulled his horse alongside of her, looking larger and

even more menacing atop a great black beast that incredibly was bigger than her own. Despite herself, Scarlett was momentarily cowed into silence. She didn't know they made horses that big… or men for that matter. "Where are we…?"

"We travel to Crichton to find out who ye are."

"Crichton? What is that?"

"Cease yer prattle, lass, or by God's might, I shall be tempted to gag ye for the journey," he barked and drew on his reins, turning his mount around and leaving her. Scarlett twisted about in the saddle, bedeviled enough to yell at him once more.

"Hey! Come bac–"

Any other words she might have had caught her throat with a gasp of horror.

The castle – or a good portion of the five-sided goliath – was gone.

Just gone!

Scarlett shook her head and blinked hard but the vision remained.

It made no sense. No sense at all.

In fact, her mind blanked entirely as she watched the building recede in the distance, trying to process what she was seeing.

And what she wasn't.

Most of Dunskirk Castle had disappeared.

All that remained was the massive westerly tower where the armory exhibit had been, a portion of the keep and a shorter curtain wall. It was like she was seeing the castle as it had been a century ago, before fairy tale façade had been added.

But where had it gone?

Where had it gone?

Cold sweat prickled at her skin as her heartbeat accelerated, pounding nauseatingly against her ribcage. She dragged in a painfully shallow wheeze and then another as her head swam dizzily. A horse whinnied close by and Scarlett stared dazedly at one of the kilted men as he rode by, his eyes narrowing on her with what might have been concern though he said not a word.

That rough faded kilt, the short leather boots and the sword at his side. Then there was their odd language. The fighting... with swords, no less. It was outlandish but it all might be easy enough to explain away. There could be a renaissance fair nearby. There might be some historical reenactment going on. There could have been something *some logical reason* for them to be out and about as they were.

Hell, they might all have been escapees from a nearby mental facility, for all she cared.

But *they* could be explained.

Scarlett turned back again, wide-eyed.

The castle though...

That one was tougher.

Their caravan reached the end of the drive to the castle where by all rights an ornate gatehouse and towers flanking a stone arch should stand.

Nothing.

The horses hooves ground against the graveled path that marked the way to the village center. Gravel, not the smooth concrete of the highway. Tall grass waved at her from the open field where the local high school should have been.

Unless sheep had taken to grazing on the golf course to the right, it was gone as well. As was the bustling town she had come to know so well over the years. No inns, no library. No fire station. No pubs. Well, pubs plural. One lonely tavern was all that remained.

No rubble. Not even a small pile of stone to save her from insanity.

Unless alien invaders had somehow surreptitiously vaporized half the castle and three-quarters of the village without catching anyone's attention…

Yes, that would have been bad.

This, this was worse.

How?

How?

How?

✕ ✕ ✕ ✕ ✕

"Are ye well, my lady?" Rhys pulled up alongside her horse, drawing Scarlett's wild stare. Around her, all the mounted men around her began to take notice of her panic. Some eyes widening, others narrowing worriedly at the hyperventilating, crazy woman they had taken prisoner.

One even crossed himself.

Personally, Scarlett didn't think prayer was going to help any of them.

Denial warred in her frantic thoughts for an explanation. *Any* explanation, but her mind was quickly becoming little more than a yawning dark void of horror. "I think I'm going to be sick."

Rhys nodded sympathetically. "Hae ye been ill long then?"

"Why do you all keep asking if I'm ill?" Even to her own ears, the question was a piteous moan. "Do I look sick?"

Eyes looked her up and down and Scarlett could see he

was restraining a nod. "Hae ye no' then?" he asked instead. "Yer to thin and wan. Yer hair shorn and walking aboot in yer bedclothes. What else might we think?"

Too thin? Wan? "Bedclothes?" Dumbly, Scarlett looked down at her white maxi dress once again. To whom would it look like nightgown? Or rather, *when* would it have looked like a nightgown? Not too long ago really. Early twentieth century even. Maybe the 1950s?

Casting a glance about at the dozen men around her once more, Scarlett was fairly certain that she wasn't going to be that lucky. "Ah, since I am so obviously out of it, right now. Would you mind telling me the date?"

"Hae ye suffered so long ye cannae ken the time that has passed?"

"Apparently not," Scarlett muttered to herself.

"'Tis the fifteenth day of August, my lady."

Scarlett nodded, biting her lip. True enough. But...

"And the year?"

Her breath caught and held as the question she tried to convince herself didn't need to be asked popped out anyway.

Rhys lifted a brow warily. "'Tis the year of our Lord, fifteen hundred and ..."

The blood roared in her ears, drowning him out. Fifteen hundred? *Fifteen?* Oh God! This was bad, so very bad. Either she'd gone completely around the bend, her captors all had, or her worst fears had been realized.

A warm hand touched hers and Scarlett flinched, casting a terrified look at Rhys before struggling to regain her composure. "My lady? Lass?" His soft brogue was filled with concern. "I pray that dinnae come as a great surprise for ye, my lady."

The bitter burn of bile rose in the back of her throat but

she swallowed it back with a grimace and shook her head woodenly. Insanity would have been preferable to the alternative, but the truth was undeniable. After all, if you eliminate the impossible…

Scarlett gasped for air, dragging in a ragged breath.

Damn. Sherlock-ed by logic.

How? *How* had it happened? Beyond Sci-Fi, no logical explanation was readily available. Even searching within the genre, she would be hard put to unearth a reasonable explanation.

How then? There hadn't been any blue police boxes about. No mysterious, bow-tied 'doctors'. No big balls of 'wibbly, wobbly, time-y, wimey stuff'.

Scarlett's stomach knotted, threatening a revolt despite her better efforts to remain calm.

"Are ye well, my lady?"

She really wished he would stop asking her that.

6

"Yer looking a wee bit better, my lady."

There wasn't a miniscule bit of humor left within her to even summon a mordant smile at that. If 'better' meant that she was no longer curled up in the fetal position over the pommel moaning "wibbly wobbly, wibbly wobbly" to herself over and over any longer, then sure, she supposed she was better.

That her insides no longer quivered with the persistent urge to be outside of her body was also a good sign. Bodily, she was actually rather numb. Mentally, she was almost deafened by a cacophony of jangled questions, rising like a terrible crescendo until her mind was about to burst. It was almost... *orchestrophic*, Scarlett decided. A nonsensical word being only too perfect for a situation like this.

Picked apart, the questions themselves hadn't changed at all. Questions she had no answer to. How? Why? And how again.

Too emotionally exhausted to go another round with

mental anarchy, Scarlett looked to her companion for distraction. "What's your name? Rhys?"

"Sir Rhys Hepburn of Crichton, at yer service," he told her, bowing from the waist in his saddle. "And ye, lady?"

"Scarlett Thomas."

Rhys's brow lifted even higher at that. "Thomas? An Sassenach name."

"An Anglicized name," she corrected wearily, rocking from side to side with the sway of the horse as they plodded along. The orchestra in her head was dulling to an out-of-tune fifth grade band with a hyperactive ten-year-old beating the living daylights out of the bass drum. "But either way, it isn't Lindsay."

Ha! At least she now knew why none of them had recognized her.

"Is it no'?" he retorted with guarded doubt. "Yet ye expected the Lindsay clansmen to recognize ye, did ye no'? I would even say ye were most genuinely confused when he dinnae."

Yes, she had been but not for the reasons he thought. Should she tell them? Try to explain? Scarlett shook off the thought without hesitation.

One did not simply announce that they were a time traveler. Such a revelation was far more likely to bring her death far more quickly than salvation, no doubt. They might not hunt witches with torches and pitchforks here, but she'd seen enough of *The Tudors* series to know that this was a time when heretics were frequently beheaded or burned at the stake.

If she proclaimed herself a time traveler, even with proof to back it up (the contents of her purse would provide that readily enough), there was little doubt she would be labeled a heretic and probably a witch as well.

Personally, she had no desire to be grilled to a crispy well-done. All this was torture enough.

"Where is yer home then? I confess we find yer speech most odd."

"Memphis."

More doubt, but Scarlett was willing to wager there would be a lot of that going around in the days to come. Days? Weeks? Forever? Bile rose in her throat along with a nauseating quiver in her chest. God, she hadn't even thought of that yet. What if...

"Memphis? Is that no' an ancient city of Egypt?"

Distraction, Scarlett reminded herself. Take it. She couldn't let them see her panic. That shouldn't be too hard; she was an actress and a celebrity. One more than the other made her good at masking her emotions. A deep soothing breath and the mask clicked into place. "It's in Tennessee. I grew up there."

"I dinnae ken such a place. Is it in Spain? France?"

Recalling what Laird had said before, Scarlett felt compelled to reassure him, if only for her own safety. "I'm not a spy."

"We'll see aboot that when we get ye back to Crichton."

Another distraction. One she leapt upon. "Yes, Crichton. That other guy mentioned it. What is it?"

"My family home at Crichton Castle," he told her. "Aboot forty miles north of here. We should arrive there tomorrow evening."

"Tomorrow eve...?" It was Scarlett's turn for an upward brow launch. Now that was a diverting thought, albeit an unpleasant one. "But if it's only forty miles... Wait, do you mean *this* is as fast as we're going to go?"

"We make good time, lady."

Scarlett closed her eyes, stifling the urge the shake her head. He had no idea what 'good time' might really equate to. Then again, he managed to look rather comfortable in the saddle. She wasn't.

"What I meant was, am I going to ride like this the whole time?" She spread her fingers open, gesturing to the rope that bound her wrists. The idea of spending the remainder of that day along with a large portion of the next like that was almost as overwhelming as discovering that she'd somehow landed herself in a different century. "Will you untie my hands?" she whispered rather pathetically. So much for her stellar portrayal of calm. "I promise you, I won't run."

Rhys lifted a skeptical brow. She wished he would stop doing that. Watching it go up and down was rather like watching a carousel go by and just as nauseating. "My brother would hae my head if ye were harmed or if ye were to escape."

Scarlett looked at the big Scot who was now heading their procession. They might be brothers but the two men couldn't be more different. Rhys was humorous, lighthearted and just a wee bit cynical while that Laird guy was... well, *so* not. Both men were handsome beyond reckoning but Rhys, with his leaner features, tamed hair and tidy clothing, seemed so much more polished. The other one simply radiated savagery. "What's with him anyway? What's his story?"

"James? He's naught but my bastard brother."

"Bastard? That's rather rude," Scarlett scolded, eyeing him askance. "What does he call you? His asshole brother?"

"Ye think I cast insult upon him?" Rhys asked after working his way through her words. "While he is somewhat of a bastard in character as well, I was merely referring to his birth."

"His birth?"

"He's illegitimate, no' to put too fine a point on it," Rhys explained. "My father's bastard son by the auld King's bastard daughter. Doubly a bastard, ye see?"

"I think you're a pretty big bastard for caring one way or another. It's not his fault, you know."

His light eyes shone with an inquisitive light. "Yer a curious lass."

Scarlett bit back a dry laugh. "More than you know. If his name is James, why do you keep calling him Laird?"

"Well for one thing, it is his title."

"His title?" Scarlett repeated, hating that she was so dumbly parroting every word they said. She'd thought Laird was his actual name. Like the famous surfer, Laird Hamilton.

"James is Laird of Achenmeade," Rhys explained. "The auld King gave him the title before he died."

"A laird is like a lord, right?"

"Ye *are* a curious lass, aren't ye?" he repeated. "Aye, he's the lord even if over nae one more than himself. He has a tower, lands and a title but nae people as yet. What is a laird wi' nae people?"

Scarlett hoped Rhys wasn't expecting an actual answer to that question since she had no idea of the answer. Just one more thing on the list. "What was the second thing? You said 'for one thing, it's his title'. Was there another reason?"

Rhys grinned. "Aye, because it drives my brother mad, lass. And what better reason is there than that among siblings?"

"I really wouldn't know," she told him, eyeing their leader once more.

Though his back was to her, she was taken by his ease and

grace in the saddle. Not to mention by his size. Beneath the length of plaid trailing down his back, his shoulders were massive under the tautly stretched, ecru shirt, V-ing sharply down to his narrow, belted waist. The massive thighs exposed below the hem of his kilt were bigger around than her waist. He was more innately masculine than any man she had ever met and James, proper and regal, just didn't seem to suit him at all.

Laird, on the other hand... rough, Scottish and manly fit him much better. She had never seen anyone like him, not in Hollywood or beyond. Any woman would feel a thrill just looking at him. Any woman would feel the urge to... Scarlett put an end to that line of thought before it took root. Sure, any woman might be tempted... if he weren't such a huge dick, that is.

"Lass, I maun warn ye," he began; almost as if he knew the direction her thoughts had taken.

"Will you please at least untie my hands?" Scarlett cut in, feeling a flush creep up her cheeks. "I promise you, I will not try to escape."

He considered the request for several long moments before pulling a long dagger from his belt and slicing through the ropes that bound her. With a sigh of relief, Scarlett massaged her wrists as the life rushed back into them. Briefly she considered going for the gun in her bag but decided it wouldn't do her much good to hurt these people. She might have enough bullets to take them down but she wasn't skilled enough to do it before one of them stopped her.

Besides, quite frankly, she didn't want to be dead or even alone right now in this unfamiliar time. "Thank you," she said, passing him back his handkerchief.

"Ye might wi'hold yer gratitude, lass," he said, taking it

and slipping the knife away once more. "Cormac will continue to hold yer reins in case ye get any ideas about fleeing."

"Well, then I thank you even more," Scarlett said dryly. "Since, I have no idea how to steer this thing anyway."

"I dinnae ken yer meaning."

"My meaning is that I don't know how to ride a horse," she said, enunciating clearly. "I mean obviously, I'm riding a horse right now and really, how hard can it be? But I've never actually had to get on one before and I wouldn't want to start with one as big and angry looking as these ones are."

The disbelieving look on Rhys' face faded away and he threw back his head, laughter belting out over the soft sounds of travel. "Ye think me a fool, lady? To trick me into giving ye freely the means to yer escape?"

"No, and believe me, if I ever try to use reverse psychology on you, you won't see it coming."

"Yer speech is most strange, lass," he said, shrugging out of his long-sleeved jacket. Leaning over, Rhys tossed it over her shoulders. "As is most everything about ye. Cover yerself, lass."

"I thought we went over this. I am covered." Scarlett stuck her arms into the garment any way, lacing up the front. The sun was shining brightly and she had no desire to add the sting of sunburn to everything else she had to bear that day. "Since you're being so accommodating, I don't suppose I can just get down off this thing and walk for a while? I mean if this is as fast as we're going to go and all?"

"And set ye free to run? I cannae take that chance however much it might please me to please ye."

A soft sigh deflated her brief rise in spirits. However much it might please him, there were many things Rhys wouldn't be able to provide. Like a way home. Some things were more precious than freedom.

"Dinnae look so aggrieved lass. We'll stop for the night 'ere too long has past," he offered in consolation. "It takes time to secure a proper camp."

"Not the only reivers in the night, huh?" she asked caustically and was rewarded by another mischievous grin.

"I do like ye, lass."

"I'm sorry I cannot – "

"Rhys!" A deep voice boomed and both Scarlett and Rhys looked up to find that Laird had left his place at the head of the train and was riding back toward them with a thunderous look on his face. "Why did ye untie her?"

"No one enjoys a journey bound to a saddle," Rhys explained.

"Tis no' a journey meant for her enjoyment. She's a prisoner."

"We dinnae ken what she is yet," Rhys countered. "She might hae been the Lindsay's prisoner for all we know."

Both looked at her as if they expected an answer but Scarlett couldn't answer their questions when she didn't have any answers herself.

"Relax, Laird, I'm not going anywhere," Scarlett said with light nonchalance as if she were already bored by their bickering, hoping to diffuse a battle for the alpha male.

However, Laird's expression hardened even more. "I cannae believe that as easily as my brother who is to often taken in by a bonny lass."

"You think I'm bonny lass?" Scarlett asked dryly as if that was all she had absorbed of his words.

His jaw worked visibly, clenching and unclenching as he fought back his anger. Well good! It just didn't seem fair to

Scarlett that she should be the only one upset by the entire situation.

"Keep an eye on her," Laird barked at Rhys. "Dinnae let her innocence put ye at ease. If she escapes, 'twill be yer arse."

"We'll stop here," Laird announced, lifting a hand as they arrived at the bank of a wide stream. Bonelessly slouched over in exhaustion, Scarlett's roused herself at his welcome words.

"Oh, thank God," she muttered, almost falling off the saddle as it halted. Hour after hour of riding along being rocked, jolted and shaken had seemed interminable while the sun hadn't seemed to get any lower. It was like being in a very slow, very old roller coaster car as it rattled up a steep incline. No, an excruciatingly sluggish roller coaster.

Cormac dismounted and came to help her down but Laird was there first. Though he looked none too happy about it, he held up his hands. She might have preferred her guard or Rhys to help her down, but Scarlett she was too exhausted to care at that point. She fell into his arms gladly.

Jellied knees wobbled and gave way. Her legs and hips screamed in protest as she straightened them for the first time in hours. Thankfully, he was as solid as a rock as she clung to

63

him, taking her weight as if she were a ragdoll. She felt like one. It was humiliating to feel so weak but for that moment, cradled against his chest and with his strong arms wrapped tightly around her, Scarlett felt...

What? Good? Safe?

Ha! She was none of those things. "Uh, thanks," she said, looking up at him only to find him watching her solemnly. For a moment something in his silvery eyes arrested her before her gaze slid away and he lowered her the rest of the way to the ground.

Hobbling away, Scarlett rubbed her backside. "How do you do that all the time? It's exhausting."

"Ye act as if ye've ne'er traveled," Laird said, handing the reins of their horses over to an eager teenage boy who Rhys had pointed out as Laird's squire, Aiden.

"I haven't. I mean, I have but not like that."

Laird snorted out his reaction to that as if it weren't possible. Scarlett again considered telling the truth of her situation but dismissed the urge. More than likely, the truth wouldn't get her anywhere. Especially with him. Besides, she had more pressing issues on her mind. "Uh, where is the... uh... where can I... you know?"

"Wherever ye care to, lass. We arenae choosy."

Laird waved a hand around and Scarlett felt a flush crawl up her cheeks as she noticed a number of kilts lifted within her field of vision. "Might I find just a little more privacy than that?"

"Ha! So ye can escape?"

"So I can *pee*," she said bluntly, not about to assure him again and again that she wasn't going to run. "If you can't provide a room with a door, I at least want a tree with a nice, fat trunk to hide behind."

It might have been humor but more likely irritation that flashed in his eyes before Laird turned and impatiently strode toward a small stand of beech trees farther upstream. Scarlett limped along behind him, continuing past him when he stopped. Determined to leave all eyes behind at least for a few moments.

"No' too far."

Scarlett rolled her eyes heavenward at the warning and signaled him off with a wave of her arm, fighting off the urge to lift a more specific finger. He probably wouldn't understand the meaning anyway and Scarlett wasn't generally one for outward gestures of profanity. One never knew when the paparazzi might be around just in time to capture the moment.

Like the moment Scarlett Thomas was forced to pee in the woods like a bear. Thank God they couldn't see her now.

Digging into her bag, Scarlett searched for her packet of travel tissues and paused when her fingers touched the cool metal barrel of the handgun. Should she use it to get away? Now was her chance with only Laird nearby. But no, the larger problem remained. Where would she go if she freed herself?

Where *could* she go?

"Hurry on now, lass," Laird called. "We've things to do."

"Nag, nag, nag," Scarlett muttered under her breath as she reemerged from the trees and made for the shore of the nearby stream.

"Lass," he barked.

"Go on if you're in such a rush," she snapped back and knelt beside the water to wash her hands before splashing some more on her face and the back of her neck. She felt as grimy as a rodeo bronc rider just thrown from his horse and was about as sore as she imagined one might be. Cupping her hands, she drank the clear sweet water thirstily.

"Lass…" A big hand enclosed around her upper arm and Scarlett's frustration burst into temper.

"Come on!" she yelled at him, standing to face him as she jerked her arm away. "What is the freakin' rush? Can't a girl go to the bathroom and get a drink of water around here in peace? What is so pressing out here in the hills that it just can't wait?"

Laird lifted a brow and looked down. Scarlett followed his gaze to the bloated leather bag he was holding out to her. It looked like… "Oh."

"To quench yer thirst."

"Uh, thank you." A flush warmed her cheeks. "Sorry. I've just had a really bad day so far, you know? I don't normally lose my temper like that."

"Hae a drink then."

"What is it? Water?" Probably not, from what she had read. What did they drink in medieval Scotland? "Ale?"

"*Aqua vitae.* Made by our local friar."

That didn't ring any bells and Scarlett looked at him blankly.

"Whiskey," he clarified, the word rolling off his tongue in a brogue thick with appreciation. "However Rhys is likely to hae wine, if ye prefer it."

"I appreciate the offer but I'm not much of a drinker." Scarlett eyed the canteen dubiously. It was kind of like the swearing. Never knowing who might be watching had made her rather straight-laced.

"Try it," he urged, holding it out again. "I promise ye, 'twill carry yer woes away."

"That's highly unlikely." But Scarlett considered the bag

once more. Being woe-free sounded pretty damn good right then. "Oh, what the hell. If it will numb the madness of be carried through ti… the wilderness, I'll give it a try." Taking the bag, she lifted it to her lips and took a good long drink. Dragging in a deep breath, Scarlett shuddered as the burn of alcohol hit her gut and radiated through her. "Wow. I mean, *wow.*" Through watery eyes, she saw Laird's pale eyes twinkling with humor though his expression was as solemn as ever. He reached for the bag, but Scarlett turned her shoulder to him and lifted it to her lips once more before handing it back. "What a nightmare that stuff is."

"And yet, already yer far more amiable."

Scarlett bit back a snort. "Ha, if that's how that stuff works, you should drink up."

The corner of Laird's mouth kicked up in a boyish grin that softened the severe scowl that he had been wearing since she first met him. His white teeth stood in stark contrast to his tanned skin and that short, scruffy beard. If he had been attractive before, that touch of humor made him devastatingly gorgeous.

Holy Handsomeness Batman! He was just plain hot.

His gaze never left hers as he tipped up the bag. The muscles in his neck strained and shifted as he took a short swallow but Scarlett shook her head. "No, keep drinking. I think it'll take way more than that to make you more 'amiable'."

His eyes glittered with humor but he upended the bag again.

8

Back at camp, Laird left her by the campfire and disappeared into the woods. One of his men, turning meat on a spit over the flames, offered to fix her a plate but Scarlett wasn't hungry. Even if she had been, the hard bread and inconsistently charred yet bloody meat the men were eating would have only turned her stomach.

Instead she cradled the skin of whiskey close as if the warm bag and its contents offered all the comfort and security of her childhood Teddy bear.

Scarlett snorted at the thought and took another long pull from the bag. How appalling. There was nothing quite as pathetic as wallowing in self-pity. She grinned crookedly. Ha! It was a good thing then that she was choosing to indulge in the pleasant buzz of alcohol instead. No doubt she would be horribly hung over the next day but even with as much of a 'nightmare' the whiskey was, her life was fast becoming a bigger one. She had no idea how she had gotten herself into this impossible situation and no better idea how to get herself back out of it.

Inconceivably, she had traveled through time without even a blue police box or a golden Time-Turner to aid her, and to her way of thinking, she hadn't even gone anywhere good. What was there for her in sixteenth century Scotland? Though her studies for her degree had encompassed the works of the time, Old and Middle English literature weren't her favored cup of tea. *Beowulf* had never resonated with her, and while the romance of Chaucer's *Canterbury Tales* and the Pearl Poet's *Sir Gawain and the Green Knight* bore some pleasurable elements, both of those authors were long dead by this particular point in history.

What was there now but a yawning gap in notable literature? Fifteen… Damn, she'd been so overcome by the first half of the year, she hadn't heard the actual year. Either way, the better part of the sixteenth century focused largely on moral and religious works. Or the occasional play. Poets like Spenser and Sidney or playwrights like Marlowe and Shakespeare weren't even a thought yet.

So why here? Why now? Or did it have nothing to do with her personally at all? What if it were all nothing more than a fluke? An accident? A wrong place, wrong time catastrophe?

Stuck in the rolling grass of the Cheviot Hills with a horde of Lowland reivers?

Scarlett studied Laird's men as they gathered around the fire. She had caught a few of their names along the way. Odd names like Padraig, Cormac, Eideard and Murdo. That last one had given her a momentary pause. She thought the coarsely accented word had been 'murder' before she'd realized it was a name, not an intent. Like their names, the men were, to the last, a rough lot. Rough in speech – what she understood of it any way – and even more so in manners.

Rhys with his too-slick polish was the lone hint of sophistication. As for Laird or whatever his name was, beyond offering her a drink, he hadn't yet displayed enough manners good or bad to form an opinion.

In fact, she hadn't been offered much at all, Scarlett realized as she took another sip of the whiskey.

No, she sat on the bare ground without a blanket to protect her from the growing chill of the night. Where was the vaunted chivalry of the time? The gentlemen who catered to a lady's needs and wishes? These men were largely ignoring her, joking rudely with one another. Bragging about the women they'd had. Still, guys just being guys.

Some things never changed, Scarlett hiccupped before tilting up the bag once more. Nevertheless, there was something about all of this that was niggled on the horizon of her alcohol-hazed mind. Something familiar.

Bothwell, Laird had said his cousin's name was. Why did she know that name? Achenmeade, too. It was there, just out of her grasp.

Scarlett shrugged and pushed the thought away as she took another swig of the whiskey. It would come to her eventually.

She could only hope that a way out of this whole nightmare would also present itself.

WWBD, Scarlett thought tipsily. What would Buffy do? Somehow she doubted that the vampire slayer would have been any more successful than she in finding a quick fix to her unusual situation.

His captive sat on the ground, hunched over his skin of whiskey as if it were her lifeline, James noted as he returned to the campsite. A long conversation with Rhys had revealed even more peculiarities about her. She'd asked Rhys many a question, simple things that anyone should know. The date. What a laird was. She insisted that she'd never rode a horse. Even more strangely, she'd seem to care naught that Laird was a bastard born.

She was an oddity to be sure. Still James felt a grudging respect for her. Other than her initial panic when they'd left Dunskirk, the lass hadn't quailed at all against her circumstances. None of the weeping and wailing he might have expected from a lady. Indeed, she looked him in the eye and spoke her mind. And not always kindly.

She was a fighter. In more ways than one. He couldn't help but admire that. But for all her sharp words and waspish ways, there was sadness in her troubled eyes. Of course, she had been kidnapped and taken against her will but James couldn't help but think that there was some greater worry on her mind.

The firelight cast his shadow over her and she looked up, then proceeded to list to the side in reward for her efforts. A short giggle punctuated by a snort escaped her as she set herself to rights. James fought to bite back a reluctant smile.

It seemed she had chosen to drown her anxieties in drink.

"Yer utterly blootered, aren't ye?" James dropped down on the grass beside her and took the whiskey bag from her. Weighing it in his palm, he lifted a questioning brow. 'Struth, she had actually drunk very little.

The lass straightened her posture and pronounced with something akin to pride, "Yes, I am." She then relaxed against his side, her voice softening like butter as the slight accent that had accompanied her speech all day extended into a long drawl. "Ahh, y'all have no idea. I'm a sweet tea kinda girl, honey. I never drink. Never. 'Specially not the hard stuff since I'm such a lightweight."

"A light weight?" Yet again she was talking nonsense and James didn't think the spirits were entirely to blame. There was something strange about the lass beyond her choice of words and her accent, though he'd be hard-pressed put to put a finger on what troubled him so. "Yer making even less sense now."

"Ha! Like you're Mr. Intelligible. Mr. Comprehensiveable… Comprehens… Ah, bless your heart, I can't understand half of what y'all are talking about half the time either." Scarlett frowned at her own words as James did the same. "Half of half. Wow, I am really fucked up, aren't I? I wish I were more sober so I could appreciate it. Haha!"

She snorted when she laughed and this time James couldn't withhold the rare smile that sprang to his lips at the sound. For all her cantankerous words and nonsense, there was something improbably likeable about the chit and he wondered if he should be more wary of her given his uncharacteristic inclination to soften toward a foe. They didn't know who she was, who her people were. The lass had told Rhys that she was from Memphis. Not the ancient Egyptian city but the Memphis of Tennessee. Neither of them had heard tell of such a place.

And too, she claimed to know the bloody Queen of England. For all he knew, she could well be a spy or nothing more than his enemy's kin.

At best she was nothing more than a sickly, frail lass lacking clothing or possession of her own, in need of protection.

His protection.

If from nothing greater than herself.

Shaking off the charitable urge, James lifted the skin of whiskey away and set it to the side. "Lass…"

Bluidy hell, he didn't even know her name.

His captive canted sideways once more, rolling her face into his shoulder as she chuckled drunkenly. Snorting once more, her laughter drifting away with a long sigh punctuated by a hiccup. "May the good Lord help me if the papa – hic – razzi could see me now."

"I hae nae idea what that is."

"I know, I know," she muttered into his shirt, curling her fingers into the woolen plaid across his shoulder. "You don't even know what a camera is or a pic-ture or a movie or a …"

James looked down at her as she melted against him, uncertain what to do. On and on the ramblings continued until they halted in a soft snore and he jostled her back to consciousness by setting her to rights once again. "Come, lass, to bed wi' ye."

"But I don't wanna go to bed," she murmured though she allowed his assistance in rising, stumbling and swaying once so was upright.

"Och, lass, ye do."

Swinging her into his arms as his men began to bed down for the night around the fire, James carried her a short distance away. He set her on her feet at the perimeter of the fire's glow, and throwing off his sword, began to unbuckle his belt.

"Hey, whoa there," she slurred, weakly pressing her open hand against his chest. "I hardly know you."

"What?"

"I might be a little tipsy… okay, more than a little, but I'm not *that* drunk," she said, her voice clearing with every word. "We're not going to sleep together."

"For certs, we are." James dropped his belt and began to quickly unwind his kilt as the lass swayed on her feet.

$$\times \quad \times \quad \times \quad \times \quad \times$$

A cold splash of water couldn't have cleared Scarlett's head more rapidly than the sight of Laird so casually undressing. Holy crap, he was serious! "No, we aren't!"

"Aye, we are!"

Laird grabbed at her wrist as Scarlett tried to scramble away and pulled her back against his rock-hard body. Horror clouded her mind as she struggled against him but Laird was stronger and probably far more lucid than she. Within seconds she was on the ground, pinned beneath him as he straddled her. Her hands immobilized over her head by his vice-like grip. Chest heaving with panic, Scarlett stared up at him.

Never had she imagined something like this would happen. How could she have forgotten that the medieval times, for all their vaunted chivalry, was also a period of the rape/pillage mentality when it came to war? She didn't want to become anyone's plunder! Not even a guy like Laird. "You won't... get any ransom if I'm... I'm harmed. In any way," she warned brokenly as she twisted futilely beneath him.

Laird's grip eased and his eyes widened as comprehension dawned. Then he laughed at her. "Ye think I'm going to ravish ye, lass?"

Confused, Scarlett stilled as she stared up at him. "I... I... Well, not anymore."

Stilling chuckling, Laird released her hands and lifted himself up on to his knees, still straddling her and intimidating, too, even if he wasn't weighing down on her. "Worry no', lass. Nae man wants a bag of bones in his bed on a cold night. We like a woman with some meat on her. Perhaps when ye've recovered from yer illness though, I might reconsider."

Relief swept through her at his assurance followed by mortification as he winked at her. Overriding it all was indignation. The mighty Laird of Achenmeade might not be very likeable and it wasn't as if Scarlett wasn't glad for his apathy in this particular instance, but she wasn't used to being thought undesirable either. Since *The Puppet War* series had concluded and the geeky teen she had been blossomed into the swan the public adored, she had made a near career, between her college classes, of modeling for the covers of fashion magazines. *Elle, Vogue, Cosmo.* One photographer had said she was built for the runway. Victoria's Secret had even asked her to model for their annual fashion show.

No one had ever called her a bag of bones before. It was more than a little insulting.

"I'm not sick," she ground out for the hundredth time that day. Scarlett bent her knees, planting her feet. Lifting her hips, she launched him – perhaps not over her head as she planned – but at least off to the side with a satisfying lurch.

Anger flashed in his eyes as he righted himself, then humor. "Mayhap no' any longer." He patted her hip as if that might console her.

Warily, Scarlett pushed herself to her knees as he stood and continued to pull off his kilt, which unbelted turned out to be nothing more than a long length of wool. A quick glance back at the fire showed his men all doing the same thing, wrapping themselves in their woolen plaids.

Pulling her tote over her head, she set it aside on a patch of grass but Laird kicked it out of the way, spreading the wool on the ground.

"Hey, watch it!" she cried, snatching up the bag and brushing it off. "You can't just kick it around like that. It's Stella McCartney!"

"Ye named yer bluidy bag?"

Scarlett just shook her head, cradling the leather purse like a baby. There was no way to explain designers and fashion to a sixteenth-century Scottish laird but she had fallen in love with the soft brown leather tote with its silver chain link trim the moment she had seen it. A treat to herself for giving up so much for her parents.

Now it and its contents were all she had in the world.

"You wouldn't understand."

Laird only grunted, clearly in agreement and finished spreading the plaid. He dropped down on it, clad only in his long linen shirt and long stockings, and stretched himself out flicking an impatient wrist at her. Hugging the bag tighter, Scarlett made a face, which garnered her nothing more than a roll of his eyes.

That wrist flicked insistently once more.

Shrugging out of Rhys' bulky jacket and putting it aside with her purse, Scarlett gingerly eased down beside Laird since the evening was already turning chilly but left a foot or more between them. With an impatient sigh, he none-too-gently yanked her close and wrapped the plaid tightly about them, ignoring her protests. "We must both bear it, lass, unless ye wish no' only to be bound once more but to find yer death in the cold this night."

Well, there was no chance of that.

Still she wasn't happy with either option.

Lord, she could feel the heat of his bare thighs through her thin dress. There was little standing between them. Laird seemed to read her thoughts, whispering when she began to protest once more, "When we reach Crichton on the morrow, we will find you some more appropriate clothing."

As if the offer of clothing could make it all better.

Spooned against his big body within the cocoon of his plaid, Scarlett lay stiffly for as long as she could. The proximity of his massive body was unnerving, but fatigue and the effects of the whiskey lulled her.

After a historically crappy day, she felt oddly safe cradled against his solid warmth with the steady rhythm of his heart beating against her back. Logically she should have been terrified of what was happening but in that moment her worries faded and she slowly relaxed against him.

It didn't matter that she didn't like him at all.

She could resume hating him in the morning.

9

It wasn't hard to identify the searing brand pressed against her bottom for what it was. Scarlett sighed and sleepily wiggled her bottom, and was rewarded by a hard, manly – and rather pleasurable – nudge. "Mmm."

Warm breaths tickled erotically at the back of her bare neck, sending a shiver down her spin. Scarlett stretched, arching away languorously and into the calloused palm curled about her bare breast. Snuggling back again, she covered the hand with her own and pressed it tightly against her.

A low grumble vibrated through the hard chest pressed against her back, accompanied by a groggy murmur of desire. Soft lips nuzzled her nape, a beard-roughened chin chaffing against her tender flesh. The fingers covering her breast tightened, then kneaded. Another hand clasped her hip, pulling her back against the rampant erection straining against her. "Mmm, that's nice," she purred drowsily, reaching behind her to run her fingers up the well-muscled arm that held her.

The hand withdrew but a moment later it was back, searing against the bared skin of her thigh. Pushing her dress higher until that rough palm cupped her ass and a sizzling length of male erection nudged against her, sliding with delicious friction against her bottom with only the thin barrier of her panties between them. Her flesh blazoned in the wake of his caress as the hand skimmed over her hip and belly, lured by the mounting heat between her thighs.

"Oh!" Scarlett gasped, coming fully awake as pleasure pierced through her. The warm cocoon she'd fallen asleep within had become an inferno! She clasped her thighs around the hand between them. The body behind hers stilled, then stiffened.

Slowly the hands withdrew. An inch, then two gaped between them, letting the damp chill of morning air waft between their enflamed bodies, cooling them but no more quickly than the realization of what they had been doing... and with whom.

Scarlett rolled on to her back as Laird lifted himself on one elbow to look down at her. Their eyes met and locked but silence reigned with nothing more than the tweet of a nearby bird or the rustle of the grass to greet the morning. The magenta sky haloing Laird's head told her just how early it was. Scarlett imagined her face was about the same shade of red. In shame, she told herself.

Who was she kidding? Despite the situation and the fact that James Hepburn was an ill-mannered bully, she had enjoyed every moment of waking up with him. And what a sight to wake up to! The growth of beard darkening his jaw had just a touch of gray sprinkled through it, she realized. It lent a fierce sexiness to the morning-after look. Scarlett was tempted run her fingers along that prickly jaw and into the wayward tousle of the long, shaggy locks that framed his face.

God but he was gorgeous! Beneath his dark, thick brows, his light eyes were like a silvery glimpse into heaven. His lips, not flattened by irritation or anger, were soft and inviting. Sensuous. Without his perpetual frown, he just looked freaking sexy.

Scarlett bit her lower lip and his gaze fell to them, nostrils flaring. Tension seized her as she waited, hoping he would… *not* kiss her, of course.

"My skinny body seems to be keeping you warmer than you thought it might." She meant to tease away the awkward moment but the words emerged husky, sensual.

Well, there it was.

A furrow appeared between his brows as Laird took a deep breath and looked away, lifting himself further before rising to his feet to tower above her. He should have looked absurd standing there in nothing but his long linen shirt and thickly knit stockings, but with the front of his shirt untied and skewed, baring his broad chest, and his bulging thighs on display below the hem, Scarlett was certain any girl in the world wouldn't have a thought beyond wishing they were gone as well.

"I assure ye it wisnae ye I was thinking of, lass."

"Of course not," she shot back, offended again much as she had been the previous night by his gruff, dismissive words. "No more than I was thinking of you."

He shot her a brief inscrutable look before snatching up his plaid from the ground.

A flash of light caught Scarlett's attention as it was pulled away. On the ground lay a long sword, a Claymore sheathed in a stiff leather casing. The beaming rays of the rising sun winked off three gleaming stones punctuating the ends of the pommel and cross guard of the hilt as if to say 'Hey there, girl, don't I know you?'.

Her throat tightened around a soundless gasp and any lingering desire that warmed her body crystallized into icy dread.

Yes, she did know that sword.

"Oh my God! Where did you get that?"

Still in full-on frown mode, Laird only pulled on his boots before picking up his belt and buckling it around his plaid. Turning his back, he began to pleat the plaid into folds beneath it.

"Laird! Where did you get this?"

Scrambling to her feet, Scarlett tried to lift the weapon but it was even heavier than she remembered and the sheathed tip remained on the ground. Laird took it from her with a shrug, slinging the scabbard over his shoulder so that the sword hung down his back. "I always sleep wi' it wi'in arms' length. For my own protection. I dinnae require such protection from a wee lass like ye, if that was yer thought."

Turning, Laird began kicking his men awake, commanding them to arise so they might be off. Scarlett ran after him, stepping over male bodies grumbling with displeasure.

"It wasn't. But where did you get it?" She might not have killed him in his sleep but she was mighty tempted to do so now if he didn't give her an answer. Scarlett caught his arm insistently, forcing him to stop and look at her. "Where did you get it? Did you steal it? From the castle?"

Laird turned on her. A menacing scowl darkened his expression, his eyes flaring with anger. "Ye dare impugn my honor?"

Fighting the urge to roll her eyes at his machismo, Scarlett shook her head. "No, of course not. It's just..."

Uncertainty and apprehension stalled her words. "Damn it, Laird, please tell me where you got it!"

"It was a gift."

"A gift? From who?" Scarlett pressed, feeling almost frantic now to learn where he had gotten it. The first link she'd discovered between his time and hers. Unfortunately, it was like pulling teeth from an angry grizzly to get a word from him that morning. He wouldn't even stand still. She felt like a fool trotting after him. "Laird, please! Can I just look at it?"

He glanced over his shoulder, lifting that dubious brow she had seen so much of the previous day. "Oh please. I'm not going to stab you."

In a whisper of a moment, Laird unsheathed the sword and leveled it at her so quickly, Scarlett jumped back in surprised. Just as quickly, he flipped the blade so that the hilt was extended toward her. Her hand trembled slightly but then so did her shallow breaths as Scarlett skimmed her fingertips across the smooth amber stones at the hilt.

It was just like the one she had seen displayed in the gallery at Dunskirk Castle though it was not at all tarnished but shiny and new. Scarlett recalled the flare of light that had blinded her when she touched it. The shocking heat and the thin slice of her skin. She ran her fingertips along the blade again, hoping for a miracle, but nothing happened.

Her heart sank.

"A gift?"

From who? An ancient, mystical being who had endowed it with magical powers? A wizard? Oh! Maybe it was a portkey! No, that couldn't be it. Portkeys didn't send people through time.

Neither did they exist. Scarlett knew that Ms. Rowling's

wizarding world and all the magic created in it weren't real beyond the hearts of her devoted fans, but it would explain a lot.

"The king," Laird answered gruffly. "The auld king. My grandfather. He granted me his name, this sword, and my title and lands the day I was born."

A king? That was it? Scarlett was disappointed as Laird slid the weapon back it its scabbard and turned away. Disappointed that there wasn't something more informative for her to work with.

Still, somehow that sword had to be the key to her arrival in this place. It could also be the key back home.

Which meant that Laird was the key.

Suddenly being stuck to his side was right where Scarlett was meant to be. She just had to find a way to stay close.

The memory of him pressed hard against her backside heated her blood once again.

Close, yes, but not too close.

"Break yer fast in haste, lads," Laird barked as he strode away. "I would reach Crichton before the sun sets this day."

$$\times \quad \times \quad \times \quad \times \quad \times$$

"Good morn to ye, Scarlett," Rhys greeted her as she returned to the camp from her short trip upstream.

Scarlett grunted with a curl of her lip, which only made him smile more widely. That Rhys was a perverse sadist, she decided crabbily. And a morning person to boot.

After retrieving her bag and walking not more than a few steps from the camp, the effects of the previous day had caught up with her all too quickly. Her bottom and thighs ached after a day on horseback. Her back and shoulder, too, from sleeping on the ground with no padding beneath her. To make it even worse, her head throbbed from her impulsive affair with Laird's skin of whiskey. She definitely wasn't accustomed to roughing it.

Nor was she used to this frazzled, fidgety restlessness she had been left with since waking in Laird's arms that morning. Or rather, waking fully to the touch of his fingers against her still throbbing core. She had been left wanting… whether she actually wanted the bastard or not.

A splash of the cold stream water over her face and head had done much to revive her. It looked and tasted clean enough so she had enough presence of mind to refill a half-empty Highland Springs water bottle she had found in her purse, since she knew hydration would be key to her recovery. A deeper search of her bag had turned up some painkillers but no doubt it would be awhile before she felt a hundred percent again.

Even longer if she had to get up on that gargantuan horse again.

Laird's men were already mounted and waiting nearby but Scarlett just stared balefully up at the horse awaiting her. Her guard from the previous day, Cormac, stood by patiently to help her mount again but the task seemed akin to scaling at mountain that morning. She was so sore, she wasn't even sure she could lift a foot to the stirrup.

Neither did she want to.

They'd traveled only a handful of hours the day before. Today's journey was to be more than twice as long! It was a daunting thought. "All of the burpees in the world couldn't have prepped me for a day on horseback," she muttered under her breath, taking a resigned step forward.

Something warm and soft squished around her sandal and

Scarlett stilled with a grimace as her stomach revolted again. "Oh, that's just great. This all just gets better and better."

"Mount up, lass," Laird snapped impatiently, drawing his own mammoth horse up close by.

"Do you see this? Do you see what I'm standing in?" she snarled, lifting her skirt and foot to show him the mashed horse dung covering the bottom of her sandal before swiping it furiously across a tuft of grass.

"My apologies," he said sarcastically with a sweeping gesture. "Please take your time."

Scarlett shook her head, finding a rock to scrape off the rest of it. "All the time in the world won't make a bit of difference, Laird. I'm not sure I can get up on that horse again anyway. My legs are like jelly."

"Ye can ride wi' me if ye like, Scarlett," Rhys offered, though he was watching her efforts with amusement. "I shall take ye... despite yer current dilemma."

"God bless you," Scarlett sighed sincerely. His mockery would've only managed to piss her off more if she weren't so thankful for the offer.

Rhys patted his thigh with a roguish grin.

"Really?"

With a laugh, Rhys extended his hand and she stepped forward to accept his help but Laird cut her off briskly. "She'll ride wi' me if she cannae ride on her own."

"Believe me, that's not necessary," Scarlett assured him. "You know I won't run. I couldn't run at all this morning, even if I wanted to."

Of course, she knew she needed to stick with him and that sword, but after their wake up call that morning; she didn't want to be wrapped around him for hours to come. Rhys, for all his flirting and naughty smirks, was far safer. His gray eyes – so similar to Laird's yet so different – stirred her not in the least. He had all the beauty but none of the magnetism.

"Hey!" Scarlett screeched as Laird caught her around the waist and lifted her off the ground before she could reach Rhys. For several long agonizing moments, she hung there, feet dangling, hoping he wouldn't let her fall to the ground before he lifted her with obvious ease and dragged her across his lap.

"I'm in nae mood to take that chance."

"Are you crazy?" she berated him. "You could have dropped me."

With a snort, Laird shook his head. "Unlikely. Ye weigh no more than a sack of flour."

Scarlett pinned the still-laughing Rhys with a glare. "Thanks for nothing."

He raised his hands innocently. "Dinnae blame me, lass, 'twas no' I who dared to rouse the dragon wi' the dawn."

"Yes, the mighty dragon is pretty angry at being roused, isn't he?"

Laird cast her a dark look that told her he didn't appreciate her innuendo and Scarlett cast him a falsely sunny smile. Rhys only laughed and rode off.

Irritated at them both, Scarlett shifted across Laird's thighs awkwardly, grabbing handfuls of the horse's mane to steady herself since Laird seems disinclined to hold her there himself.

"Sit still!" he hissed in her ear.

"I'm trying!" Scarlett ground out, moving her rear from side to side in search of a stable position. "It's not like it's that easy, you know, with nothing to hold on to."

Laird sucked in his breath and finally lifted a hand but not to come to her aid. Instead his fingers wrapped around her throat and Scarlett instantly stilled. *Now* he was going to kill her?

"Enough," his voice was deadly, close to her ear, "or I'll drop ye in the bluidy dirt."

"Then do it, for Christ's sake," she shot back, her fleeting fear gone with his feeble threat. "I'd rather ride with Rhys anyway."

She shifted in his lap again and Laird picked her up, depositing her not on the ground but on the horse's rump behind him with a solid thump. It was an even more precarious position than before and he hardly gave her a moment to get settled before he kicked the horse into motion. Scrambling for purchase, Scarlett had no choice but to hold him or fall as her already sore behind slapped against the bony rear end of the horse with every step.

Could this whole catastrophe get any worse?

"You know, Rhys says you're a real bastard," Scarlett ground out against his broad back. "I'm beginning to believe it."

10

A fairytale-like mist clung close to the ground but Scarlett seriously doubted that what was happening equated to a happily ever after for her.

This was more like being lost in the psychedelic, drug-induced haze of Wonderland... though the Red Queen in this interpretation was little more than a cantankerous Scot in red plaid.

Even so, it was a lovely rabbit hole to have disappeared into, she thought as they rode northward.

Her resentment with Laird faded away as the scenic beauty of the land they traversed snared her attention. The borderlands of Scotland were truly picturesque. The Cheviot Hills laid out before them in sweeping dips and waves of greens, ambers and browns without a telephone pole or paved road to spoil the view. Not a single vapor trail to mar the perfectly blue sky. Just wilderness, actually wild in a way she had never experienced.

And it was so quiet, too. Oh, there was the occasional

noise. The bustle of beast and man, the chaffing of leather and metal but still undisturbed somehow without the electronic hum that accompanied everything in the twenty-first century.

Even her breaths seemed loud here when challenged by nothing louder than the whisper of a breeze, the sigh of the wind moving through the tall grass. The song of the birds. Things Scarlett had never known in Hollywood, New York or even back in Memphis where she had grown up.

It was even different from the Scotland she had discovered while filming there. Edenic. Perfect.

To her surprise, she didn't miss the sounds of the city at all. The honks and horns, cars and trains. The planes continuously flying overhead. Even the Caribbean beaches she had vacationed on weren't this peaceful.

Though she certainly preferred a quick plane ride to the hours on horseback awaiting her again today. Though it seemed like an eternity, they'd only ridden about four hours the previous day leaving many more tedious, painstaking hours to fill the day.

× × × × ×

The sun was high overhead before James called for a break. His captive wilted off his mount's bony backside with a low moan, her knees nearly buckling beneath her. He felt stab of remorse for imposing such an uncomfortable position on her but forced it away. She had brought on her problems without any aid from him.

She – Scarlett, Rhys called her – looked different this day when compared to the last, he realized as he set her on her feet. A rash of tiny freckles dotted her nose and cheeks.

Freckles that he hadn't noticed the previous day with the cosmetics she wore. Nor were her cheeks and lips artificially colored, the dark kohl from around her eyes had been washed away. Many women at court painted their faces, though with far different effect.

He usually preferred a natural beauty and this day in regard to his captive, too, he felt the same. She looked younger and more amicable though her brow was still furrowed crossly and her pointed chin set stubbornly as she limped away.

"Dinnae go far."

The lass raised a mocking brow. "Bossy much? Who died and made you God?"

Though James was taken aback by her blasphemy, it was easy to tell from her tone that her quip was not literally meant. A smile tugged at the corner of his mouth. Even as fatigued as she was, the lass retained her sass.

Scarlett found some privacy over the next rise then washed her hands and face in the nearby stream. Laird had only stopped there for the benefit of the horses, treating his livestock better than his prisoner but she was happy enough to reap the benefits. She drank her fill, hoping she wouldn't regret the indulgence in the hours to come.

Thinking to work off some of her stiffness and pain, she started out along the creek bank in long, therapeutic strides. But not for long. Laird dragged her to a halt not a dozen steps later and glared down at her.

"Need I remind ye that ye swore ye wouldnae run away?" He turned back toward the horses and Scarlett felt her feet dragging. "Can't I just walk around?" she asked. "I won't run away. I just need the exercise and maybe to escape for a little while."

"Is that no' the same thing?"

"Absolutely not. Sometimes one needs to get away from their problems and the people causing them. It doesn't mean that they don't plan on going back," she told him. "Haven't you ever felt that way?"

"Mayhap. What do ye run from, lass?"

Everything. She should have known she couldn't actually get away though. Not even centuries away from her normal life.

"Surprisingly, not the things I normally run from," she said instead.

"I dinnae ken yer meaning." Laird released her arm but turned to continue her projected path down the edge of the winding stream.

Scarlett fell in next to him, taking a moment to consider her response. "You might not understand this, but most days I don't usually have even a moment to myself. I have people demanding my attention, my time. People always watching me. Sometimes, I can't even have five minutes alone and most times, I can't take a walk like this without someone following me." An ironic smile slowly curled her lips. "I still can't, it seems."

"I understand that all too well, lass." Laird lifted his eyes to the northern horizon, looking surprisingly contemplative but Scarlett shook her head.

"I seriously doubt it."

"We all hae eyes upon us, lass."

"Never mind. You wouldn't understand."

He let the matter drop without further argument and they walked a ways in silence. Laird pulled out a piece of dried meat and handed it to her. It was no Slim Jim but she was hungry enough not to care.

"Yer given name is Scarlett?"

Scarlett blinked in surprise at the question. It had been years since anyone had asked her that. Asked her name at all. Introductions were a thing of the past. Everywhere she went, people knew her name and because of it, acted as if they knew her as well.

"If I say it is, will you bother to believe me?"

"Mayhap. Tis an unusual name."

"Yes it is," she agreed. "My mother named me after a character from her favorite book, but believe me, it could have been worse."

"I apologize for not asking it of ye earlier."

"Ha, like before you hand your hand between my legs, you mean?" Memories of the morning flashed through her mind and Scarlett fought the blush warming her cheeks. "Don't worry about it. I'm sure you sleep with tons of women without knowing their names.

"I dinnae do much sleeping with them."

Though she couldn't see his face from her position, Scarlett could hear the smile in his words and felt her lips curl in response. "Oh, I'm sure."

"But I do typically gi' fair time for the usual pleasantries."

"Her name, your name and a quick 'how do you do'?"

His shoulders shook in silent laughter and relaxed. Laird's hand enveloped her shoulder with a light squeeze before he drew away.

Silence fell again, not uncomfortably this time. Laird was definitely a man of few words. Yet, what he conveyed with a look, some small gesture or even shrug told her more about him than anything he had yet to say. There was a wealth of information in that single touch. It told her that, prisoner or not, there was some small part of him that liked her.

She only wished there was something he could do to help

her get home but she couldn't tell him the truth. Not yet. He doubted her sanity enough already.

But he thought she was a 'bonny lass'. Did he find her as attractive as she reluctantly found him? Was he as disgruntled by the fact as she was? Really, this was hardly the time – literally – to be getting all bothered by some hot guy who looked magnificent in a kilt.

Scarlett bit back a laugh. Actually, she doubted there was a better *time* when it came to finding such a man.

Too bad he was such an ass.

× × × × ×

"Awake w' ye, lass. We're here."

Scarlett groaned at the roughly spoken command and snuggled deeper into the tight embrace that held her firmly against a solid male chest. After an agonizing morning perched on that blasted horse's backside, she had no desire to stir from the first real comfort she'd had in days. Or was it weeks? Months even?

With a sigh, she slipped her arms around his narrow waist and settled her cheek against his chest. Fatigue washed over her once more, slumber insistently calling for her return.

"Awake!"

"Laird?" She stretched against him, running her palms up his chest and was shaken hard in return.

"Blast it, lass!"

"Did I fall asleep?" Confusion swamped her at finding herself staring at Laird's face above her when last Scarlett remembered she'd been fighting to keep herself from collapsing against his back.

"Some hours past," he confirmed in a low, rumbling burr

that was quite unlike his usual brusque brogue. Blue skies had faded only to be replaced by vivid twilight. "Ye nearly fell from the horse in yer fatigue."

"Some hours?" Scarlett was even more bewildered to find him looking down at her with far more concern than she had yet seen from him. Considering the contentious day they had spent, it was the last expression she had expected to see on his handsome face.

Surely she must be dreaming?

"What? What is it?"

His curious gaze shuttered as that familiar furrow reappeared between his eyes and he gestured ahead. "We approach Crichton."

Not far away, a castle soared skyward above a low rise. It was no Hogwarts with its arches and spires, nor like any of the other castles Scarlett had visited during her years in Scotland. In fact, there was nothing at all whimsical or decorative about the blockish fortress. Though large, Crichton appeared solidly medieval and had clearly been built for defense.

Medieval? Scarlett wondered whether the term was even in use now. Or was it like Chinese food in China? Simply nonexistent?

Scarlett shook away the nonsensical thought and studied the castle as they approached. Against the vibrant greens of the grassy plains and the brilliant orange, red and purple of the twilight sky, the Crichton seemed dreary and foreboding by contrast. Only a thundercloud looming above it could have made for a more daunting sight. Squared towers connected by recessed curtain walls were all flat and unadorned, rising with nary a window to break the façade. Even the parapets were devoid of any frivolity. The setting sun cascaded over the stone blocks of the outer walls, defining each one clearly.

They penetrated the barrier of the stockade wall and passed beneath a spiked portcullis. Beyond was a low, tunnel-like path lit by torches that opened up in to the castle bailey. A shudder of apprehension chased over her flesh as Crichton loomed above her on all four sides, leaving a rash of goose bumps behind.

The ground level on all four sides was comprised of nothing but bricked archways. Dozens of them with nothing but shadows beyond, she had no idea where they led. The walls above the arches, though broken by larger windows than those on the outer walls, were bricked with thick stones. Each block was about two-foot square and carved to temple outward like diamond facets, giving the impression that the wall was armed and sharp.

It was certainly no fairy tale castle like Dunskirk, or at least the Dunskirk of her time and not just the lone tower of this one. A modernized castle on a tourist's tour was nothing like this. And unlike the other castles she had visited and their sedate tours, this one bustled with activity. An unusual amount, Scarlett thought, since it was almost dark. All around were meanly dressed men and women worked over tables or large pots set over a fire. On closer examination she released some of them were doing laundry. How awful! She hated even throwing a load in her washer. Yet there they were, lifting heavy wads of dripping fabric from the pot with a large wooden lever.

Others were butchering a variety of animals. Scarlett grimaced then gasped when one of the men at a table lifted a thick knife, cleaving the head off a chicken with one swift blow.

The cleaver thunked into the worktable, shaking it and sending a resounding shudder through Scarlett's gut. After a day with nothing more than a piece of dried meat to gnaw on, her empty stomach twisted and heaved in rebellion.

It was a renaissance fair come alive before her, but far more real than any festival she had ever seen. Or perhaps given the historical accuracy, she might more accurately say that it was like a movie set of a historical drama employing a set director not given to creative interpretation.

In any case, it was vividly authentic and far more fragrant as well. Not in the best way. As the stench of dung, blood and animal flesh assailed her, Scarlett covered her nose and mouth with one hand as they came to a halt.

"Grieg!" Laird barked out as they neared a group of men practicing with swords. A blond giant broke from the group and trotted over, nodding respectfully.

"Laird. Sir Rhys."

"What is going on here?"

"There's been a messenger from the king," Grieg told them.

Laird and Rhys shared a look and dismounted hurriedly. When Laird turned to help her down, Scarlett couldn't help but ask, "What's wrong?"

"The king's messenger rarely brings a message of joy, lass," he said grimly, setting her on her feet but Scarlett could not force her legs into any sort of stability beneath her. The sun had dawned that day about four a.m. if she remembered accurately for her own time reference and the sun usually set in August at about eight. That meant she had been on that horse for nearly thirteen hours with only one that one brief break. By her estimation, they had traveled less than three miles per hour. Simple math, but Scarlett'd had plenty of time to do it over and over in her head.

Even if the King himself were waiting on them within the castle walls, Scarlett didn't think she could have made it there.

Comprehending her inability to move, Laird scooped her up in his arms, ignoring her sharp yawp of surprise as he strode toward one of the dark archways after Rhys. Scarlett held on to his shoulders as he bore her weight up a steep stone staircase without even the slightest hitch in his breath. The rest of their men hurried in behind them, anxious to hear what news the messenger had brought.

"Maybe there's a new prince or something?" Royal announcements of a new prince or princess were big news even in her time. That couldn't have changed too much.

"A new bairn was born of the Queen just four months past."

"Oh." It might be bad news then. Scarlett knew that infant mortality rates were high in this day and age. Even kings and queens were not immune to such loss. It was a sobering thought.

He dropped her to her feet as they entered a cavernous room above. Scarlett took a deep breath and immediately wished she hadn't. The malodorous smell that assailed her was much worse than the barnyard below, summoning images of sweaty bodies and high school locker rooms with an undertone of stale beer. Overall it gave her the impression of a bar at closing time. The summer day had been a warm one but not hot enough to inspire such a scent on its own.

Scarlett surreptitiously sniffed Laird. Though he smelled slightly sweaty, it was as warm, earthy and masculine a scent as the one that had greeted her upon wakening and not all together unpleasant. But without a breeze to stir the air, the inside of the castle was hotter and more humid than outside.

She could only conclude that its inhabitants were sweltering beneath their layered garb.

Those inhabitants were gathered around a table near a massive fireplace and Rhys headed that way, with his men and Laird falling in behind him. Everyone looked up and a stern looking woman of about sixty years broke away from the group and hurried toward Rhys with her arms outstretched. "Rhys!"

"My Lady Mother." Rhys took her hands, placing a kiss on each one.

This was Rhys' mother? Scarlett wouldn't have been more astonished to find out she was the original role model for *Sleeping Beauty's* Maleficent.

An elaborate heart-shaped bonnet was set upon her graying head, arching upward over her hairline before pointing down to the center of her forehead. She was richly gowned as well with fur trim edging her collar and her flowing sleeves that draped to the floor.

Bless her heart, Scarlett thought, she had to have been burning up under it all. Then woman's perfume wafted from behind her, thick and musky. It was all Scarlett could do not to wrinkle her nose.

"My son, thank God you're returned safely."

"Naturally we are safely arrived," Rhys assured her. "We are far too arrogant to die."

A sharp snort of amusement escaped Scarlett, drawing the woman's attention. Out of the corner of her eye, she saw both Laird and Rhys wince. Apparently, this wasn't kind of attention one wanted to have.

The woman looked Scarlett over before her icy green eyes narrowed on Laird. A spasm crossed Laird's face before he schooled his features into the arrogant calm she was used to.

He bowed slightly. "Lady Ishbel."

Lady Ishbel did not return Laird's polite greeting but merely swept a chilling scowl over him, extending it to Scarlett as well before greeting each of the other men by name and far more pleasantly. Though Scarlett was surprised by the woman's singular rudeness, Laird seemed to take it all in stride as the woman turned back to Rhys with a questioning look.

"What have we here, my son?"

"A captive, my lady mother, taken during the Lindsay raid on Dunskirk," Rhys said simply.

"And you bring her into my home dressed like this? I would have thought you gentleman enough to give her time to dress before taking her." Then her gaze shifted to Laird suspiciously. "Or am I to assume that her clothes were damaged in the ungentlemanly pursuit of other..." She paused, her nose wrinkling as if she caught the scent of something particularly nasty. "Plunder, shall we say?"

Frowning in confusion, Scarlett looked to Laird for help and saw a sneer curl his lip, incongruously showing both irritation and amusement. "She is asking if yer clothes were torn beyond use when I raped ye, lass," he said quietly, his words laced with bitterness.

Eyes wide and warmth creeping up her cheeks, Scarlett leveled a hard stare on the woman. "He did no such thing! I'm fine. Perfectly fine."

"Humph," Lady Ishbel sniffed doubtfully.

"I thought mayhap ye could identify her," Rhys said smoothly, drawing his mother's attention once more. "She denies any connection to the Lindsay but willnae say true who her people are."

"I told you..."

"She is none of that boorish Lindsay's get," the woman said, talking past her as if Scarlett weren't there either. Somehow that was more offensive than anything else that had happened to her so far, even being tied up.

"Nor does she claim to be."

Lady Ishbel didn't look at Laird at all when he spoke which seemed odd to Scarlett. It was as if the woman would tolerate his words and only barely. She would not deign to meet his eye. Obviously Laird was used to such discourtesy and Scarlett felt a sudden, startling stab of sympathy for her captor though it died in a flash when Lady Ishbel turned her frigid gaze on Scarlett.

Scarlett met her stare for stare, refusing to back down. Still, the lady didn't address her directly. "No doubt she is highborn, though she has clearly been ill."

Scarlett rolled her eyes. "I'm not..."

"Aye," Rhys answered, cutting her off again. "Though there was no lady's clothing at Dunskirk, my lady. We can only assume that she was only left wi' her bedclothes, given her illness, and needed nothing else."

"Strange that she would be there at all."

"Aye."

Well, there was no denying that, was there?

"Laird tho..." Rhys paused, reconsidering his explanation. "We thought to seek a ransom for her return."

The woman cast another frigid glance at Laird.

"I am Lady Ishbel Hay of Kinnoull, daughter of the Earl of Errol," the lady said imperiously, speaking directly to Scarlett at last. "What is your name, child? Or will you refuse me that information as you did my son? Speak up now."

"I did not refuse to answer him, he merely chose not to

101

believe," Scarlett said matter-of-factly and the lady's eyes widened. "My name is Scarlett Thomas. Pleased to meet you."

Now she knew where Rhys got that high arching brow though it didn't suit Lady Ishbel nearly as well. "Perhaps I was wrong regarding your birth? You have quite rudely offered me neither a curtsey nor proper address."

"In my defense, I have been kidnapped and held against my will," Scarlett said sweetly, resisting the urge to argue whose rudeness was worse. Obviously she had offended the woman from the start, though Scarlett wasn't entirely certain how she had managed it since she hadn't even been given a chance to speak. True, when she finally had been questioned directly, she might have been a wee bit pert in her response, as her mother would have said. However, Scarlett didn't feel that she was any more discourteous than they had been in ignoring her and talking over her. "But if you think this is impolite, you should have seen me yesterday." She bobbed a short approximation of a curtsey and added. "Ma'am."

The lady's lips pursed and her green eyes narrowed to slits. "If I were you, I would remember my position lest I find myself chained in the dungeons. Do I make myself clear?"

A chill ran down Scarlett's spine. The woman wasn't joking. "Crystal."

"Mother, enough now. We've more serious matters to discuss than the fate of one wee lass." A tall but wiry man with Rhys' auburn hair spoke authoritatively as he stepped away from the table. He grasped Rhys' forearm before turning to Laird and offering the same. "Greetings, brother."

"Patrick." Laird held his gaze then released him with a nod as Lady Ishbel moved between the two men and speared Laird with another of her glacial stares.

"I am gladdened to see ye returned unharmed," Patrick continued, glancing at Scarlett curiously. "All went well at Dunskirk?"

Laird nodded. "What news here?"

"Our laird and master, Sir William Hepburn, returns three days hence," Patrick told him. "He will bear the King company to Crichton."

A murmur rose among Laird's men, though the others in the room were silent and tense, having already heard this news.

"Wow, the King is coming here?"

Laird looked down at Scarlett. "That is no' likely a good thing, lass." He looked to his brother again. "Is there more, Patrick?"

Lady Ishbel scowled at him. "'Tis not your place to ask questions," she hissed. "'Tis a matter for family." She clutched at her son's arm, trying to turn him away.

Scarlett fought the compulsion to rush to Laird's defense but bit her tongue. Laird was a big boy; he could take care of himself. And he did have an ally already. Patrick shook off his mother's grasp and turned to the table, retrieving a large parchment.

"Aye, brother, there is more. Much more." Holding out the parchment to Laird, Patrick nodded his encouragement for him to take it. "It seems we are to war."

11

War.

Silence fell as all the men stared at him. Not in surprise so much as curiosity. Even so, there was a chill to the word that crossed centuries. Peeking around Laird's arm, Scarlett read along as he scanned the document. The writing was spindly and cramped, running from one edge of the page to the other. She made out little – words like muster and progress, and the scrawling signature and wax seal at the bottom – before he lowered the paper and glanced solemnly around the room.

"Let me have it," Lady Ishbel commanded briskly, holding out her hand expectantly.

Rhys spoke up then. "Pax, Mother. I would rather hear such news straight away than have it forestalled by needless argument."

"Aye, Lady Mother," Patrick chimed in. "None of the men hae yet to hear the details either. Let Laird speak."

Relenting with a mulish frown, Lady Ishbel proceeded to

forestall the news herself, in Scarlett's opinion, by commanding others nearby, probably servants, to bring ale for the men. Everyone took seats around the table and waited until drinks were served before the hush was broken by Rhys asking, "What news?"

"As Patrick said, we are to war."

"With whom?" Rhys asked, making Scarlett wonder how many possible choices there might be.

"The King has received notice from King Louis of France and Anne of Brittany that they have been under siege by Henry at Therouanne. Louis asks that we honor the Auld Alliance and aid him in their war against Henry by invading the north of England in their support."

"Wisnae the Auld Alliance voided by the Treaty of Perpetual Peace?" one of Laird's men, Eideard, asked. "James is married to Henry's bluidy sister, after all."

"No' that Henry ever paid James the dowry as promised in the treaty," Patrick said with a snort.

"Aye," Laird agreed with a nod, tapping a finger against the page thoughtfully. "'Struth, Henry disnae seem to care which treaty we honor of late. The auld or the new. King James has written Henry again and again offering peace if England dinnae attack France, requesting again the dowry be paid if the treaty is to be honored. Last Henry replied that he would sooner consider reasserting his right of feudal overlord of Scotland."

Rhys nodded. "Look what benefits the treaty wi' France has brought us. Their envoy, La Motte, brought wine, munitions and his services as a military advisor."

"But in turn we hae given them the loan of the *Great Michael*," Patrick reminded him.

"The *Great Michael*?" Scarlett asked.

"Och, lass, 'tis only the grandest warship in the land," Murdo scoffed. "Do ye no' ken nothing, lass?"

"Leave her be," Cormac leapt to her defense, shoving the other man nearly off the bench.

"Why is she even here?" Lady Ishbel asked. "Call Graeme to take her away."

"She stays," Laird said flatly and Patrick laid a calming hand on his mother's arm before turning to Laird once more.

"The problem lies in the fact that Henry has ne'er shown James the respect he thinks he deserves. The respect the auld King Henry did. Nor the love shown to him by Prince Arthur, who should hae been king. Henry's been naught but insulting."

"Och," Rhys cut in. "The Sassenach killed James' favorite ship captain, Sir Andrew Barton. *That* is why the King craves a reason to hae at him."

Laird nodded. "Whatever the reason, it seems Henry's hubris has finally given him one."

Treaties and alliances. It was confusing. Still, like the names Scarlett had heard before, there was something familiar about all this though she couldn't put her finger on it. King Henry. Which one? There were eight to choose from. James? Five or six of those, and Scarlett had never been very good with dates unless they dealt with literature.

War. Any war in any time was, regardless of the weapons used, a chilling thought but the idea of doing battle with swords like the ones they all bore in hand-to-hand combat seemed particularly barbaric to Scarlett.

What would happen to them all, she wondered, feeling a rush of concern for Laird, Rhys and the dozen men they had traveled with for the past two days. Her captors might be little more than strangers, but she didn't wish any of them dead.

Remembering the blood dripping from their swords at Dunskirk, she imagined the battle would be a gory one.

What if it was their blood?

She didn't want Laird dead... Scarlett shook her head, dismissing the thought before it took hold. It was only because her future was in his hands, she inwardly reasoned. He was her ticket home. If something happened to him, who knew what become of her?

Laird held the document out to Rhys and looked back at Patrick. "King James has ordered that the Highland clans assemble at Brough Muir near Edinburgh bearing arms and twenty days supplies no later than the seventeenth day of the month."

"That's tomorrow," Rhys pointed out, skimming the parchment.

"Aye, the progress has already begun," Patrick said. "King James sent his personal behest that we raise our forces to fight against the rabble the Queen Regent will surely gather from the north men."

Laird traced his thumb thoughtfully over his lower lip. "Wi' most of England's standing army fighting in France wi' Henry, experienced soldiers will be hard to come by. No doubt that fact only bolsters King James' enthusiasm."

Patrick nodded in agreement.

"It says here the King will join us at Crichton two days hence and we are to join his progress to the second muster point at Ellemford Haugh," Rhys pointed out.

Laird looked to Patrick questioningly. "When did ye receive this message?"

"Only this morn," his brother told him. "I've sent out messengers calling all men of able body to arms. Our clansmen will gather at Ellemford."

"I'm preparing the castle to greet him," Lady Ishbel directed this at Rhys. "A feast, of course. Music and dancing."

"'Tis war, Lady Mother," Rhys said with none of his usual humor. "No' revelry."

"He is our King," she retorted. "And with him comes his court. We must make ready."

Patrick only shrugged. Apparently there was no stopping Lady Ishbel. "And we must make ready as well. I'm glad ye've both returned. I am anxious for yer counsel."

"Aye, ye will hae it," Laird said grimly. "And God help us all."

"My son has no need for your counsel," Lady Ishbel hissed as the men pushed away from the table. "Who are you to think you could advise him? This is a matter for family and Patrick will look to his father when Sir William returns."

"I will aid my brother by his request, my lady," Laird said with strained respect. "We cannae wait so long to make preparation."

"He doesn't need you!" she insisted.

"Mayhap but I will make myself available to him, if he does."

$$\times \quad \times \quad \times \quad \times \quad \times$$

"Wow, pardon my French but what a bee-aatch," Scarlett whispered under her breath as the short conference broke up and the men went their separate ways.

Amusement at her audacious words lightened his mood. Many a time James had longed to voice a similar sentiment aloud when Lady Ishbel so often labeled him bastard and other more graphic epithets that were mostly true but still offensive in his presence.

Aye, there had been a time when he might have liked to rebuke his stepmother in the some manner before he had realized that she would never treat him differently and that his efforts to win her approval were in vain. Over the years, it had become easier to avoid her entirely.

"Why would she assume such a thing?" Scarlett asked step as he took her by the elbow and helped her to her feet. "That you raped me? That's awful."

"Is it? Ye thought I might last night."

"While I think you were perfectly capable of plying me with alcohol and cajoling me into having your way, I don't see you using the kind of violent force Ishbel was implying."

"Lady Ishbel has a rather low opinion of me as do most who reside in this hall," James said with a shrug, though he was warmed by the indirect praise. It had been some time since someone defended him. Longer still since someone hadn't cared a fig for his birth or station. The lass truly seemed unbothered by it all. She was, as Rhys said, a most curious lass. James couldn't help but soften toward her. "I would suggest keeping yer distance from her for the time being."

"Good advice."

"And ye should address her as 'my lady' or 'Lady Ishbel'. Trust me, she can make yer life a living hell if you cross her."

"Like being the by-product and constant reminder of her husband's infidelity?"

James arched a startled brow but nodded brusquely. "Just so."

He looked down at her, his eyes coaxed ever more downward as Rhys' doublet gaped open providing him a distracting vista. The loose bodice of her white undergown allowed just enough shadow to hide her charms from his eyes. All thoughts of war and bloodshed fled with the reminder of her breast cupped so neatly in his palm when he had awoken that morning.

Forcing his gaze upward, he noted the fatigue etched around her eyes. She looked miserably tired, even more so than he.

"Come." He turned away toward a spiral staircase tucked into the corner of the hall, thankful that she followed, albeit slowly. With arousal stirring once more beneath the folds of his kilt, James wasn't certain he could bear cradling her warm body in his arms once more.

The day had been a long one. The lass stewed rigidly behind him as they rode while he tamped down the rush of lust the mere sight of her bare ankle had roused in him. Lust when she was standing in shite! He had been appalled and ill-humored with her as a result. Much as she was with him.

He tried to get some answers from her – who she was, why she had been at Dunskirk, who this Tyrone she screamed for was – but other than their brief, amusing conversation, she maintained her stony silence throughout the morning hours.

After a short break at noontime however, she had softened completely. Her soft breasts pressed against his back. Then she had drooped against him in her exhaustion.

It was only by skill and luck that James had caught her before she tipped off the rump of his horse and pulled her across his lap. She had settled against him with a contented sigh, wiggling her bottom to seek comfort in the same stirring manner that had got her tossed onto the horse's rear so abruptly that morning.

With her curled in his arms and her bottom relentlessly rocking against his groin, James had spent a long afternoon with little else to think about other than stifling the arousal that beleaguered him.

Contrarily, rather than awaken her or give her over to Rhys, he'd carried her in his lap the remainder of the day. To his men, he would have said her continued slumber spared them all her harping tongue.

Inwardly, he could hardly admit the reality to himself.

Neither would he have bared the truth of the matter to save his soul that morning, but he had known very well who was in his arms when he had awoken. He'd done naught but dream of her all night. Dreamt of her body beneath his even though he had laughed off the idea the previous night. He knew from having held her all night and day that she was far more a fair handful than the bag of bones he had teased her being.

The discovery had been a surprising one. His burgeoning desire for her, even more so. Somehow the harridan had bewitched him.

Her shoes scuffed along each of the worn stone stair, marking her presence behind him as he climbed the winding path to the guest wing of the castle.

Though he contemplated briefly taking her to his own rooms – where he might keep an eye over his prisoner, of course – James took the Lindsay's potential wrath into consideration should his clanswoman be harmed either in body or reputation before he might ransom her and opened the door to a chamber directly across from his own.

Twilight cast the room in shadows so James entered ahead of her, lighting a candle next to the bed. His eyes lingered on the down-turned coverlet as the candle spilt its glow upon the sheets. If nothing else might be said for Lady Ishbel, she was an excellent hostess. Beds were always ready for a weary guest to lay their head. Too ready for a man plagued by salacious thoughts.

"Where is this war supposed to take place?"

James turned to find that Scarlett had cast away her bag and was shrugging off Rhys' doublet. The thin strap of her gown was caught by the heavy garment and slipped off her shoulder. His eyes followed it as it fell halfway down her arm, the flimsy bodice catching on the peak of her breast. She wore nothing beneath the gown, James knew. Her small, firm breast rounded enticingly, plump against the shadows of her ribs, contrasting against the fine line of her clearly delineated collarbone.

Hunger gnawed at him, driving away his exhaustion. His fingers itched to trace the bone with the pad of his thumb, his palm burned to feel the weight of her breast once more. Swallowing painfully, he waited as she righted the strap before forcing his gaze upward.

"The King's initial plans are to invade through Newcastle," he said. "Do ye plan to pass that information on to yer friend the Queen?"

The lass rolled her eyes at him while stretching tiredly. Her breasts strained against her bodice, drawing his eye once more. "No, just curious. Wondering if I've heard of it."

"Hae ye?"

"Yes, it's a beer. That's about all I know."

The candlelight cast her shorn hair in flames and licked at her slender, bared neck. Off the curve of her ear. It made him realize that for all the bared bosoms he had laid eyes upon in his life, he had rarely seen a woman's naked ear. Fashion in headdress and hairstyles kept them modestly covered in public. There was something profoundly erotic about the curved shell, the tiny diamond dangling from her lobe.

"Why are you looking at me like that?" she asked. "I already told you I'm not a spy."

A smart girl would have turned and run from Laird Hepburn the first chance she got. Everything about him spelled danger, but instinctively Scarlett knew that he wouldn't hurt her. Not only because he hadn't already but simply because it wouldn't be his style to harm a woman. She'd assumed she was safe with him.

Perhaps she wasn't entirely.

Because that wasn't suspicion written in his eyes, Scarlett realized. No, she must be wrong. Certainly that wasn't desire she was seeing?

Scarlett stilled as he reached out, tracing his finger along the shell of her ear and along the soft edge of her lobe. A shiver ran down her spine that certainly wasn't fear. His gaze shifted downward then, answering her unspoken question and Scarlett felt her lips tingle in response.

Wide-eyed now, she stared at him, the crescent of dark lashes against his angular cheeks before his eyes opened to meet hers. His eyes were not the icy steel she was fast becoming accustomed to but churned like a stormy sky. Or like hot, fluid pewter.

Surely he wasn't…?

But he was.

His head dipped, those heavenly lips brushing across hers ever so lightly. Awakening. Tempting. Scarlett knew she should have denied him. Turned away. Bit his lip even but that kiss, as light as it was, skittered through her leaving pure pleasure in its wake. With a gasp of surprise, her lips parted.

Though by no means an invitation, it was encouragement enough. Laird's lips opened over hers, his tongue sweeping lightly and unhurriedly across hers. Whiskers prickled against her chin and she gave into temptation, raking her fingers along his jaw. Blood roared like a crashing wave in her ears and Scarlett's head swam as if she were drowning in truth.

Pressing both hands to his chest, she tore her mouth from his and pushed him away. Chest heaving, Scarlett stared up at him in surprise, gasping for air and full of questions. Just as it had that morning, the force of her desire overwhelmed her. So quickly had she been aroused that just that single stroke between her thighs had nearly been enough to send her over the edge. Unfulfilled lust had left her irritable and ungracious all day. More irritable than her aching muscles and fatigue might have managed on their own.

All through the morning, she had replayed their brief encounter over and over. Each time hating that she had enjoyed those moments with Laird. And now she was feeling much the same again and after just one kiss! It just wasn't right.

For a moment, she thought he might try to kiss her again but then he turned toward the door. He paused at the open portal, looking back. "What did ye mean when ye said it could have been worse?"

"Huh? What?" she asked, irritated to be fighting to regain her equilibrium when he looked so composed.

"Earlier, ye said yer name could hae been worse?"

"Oh, only that I might easily have been named Sparrow, Speck or Moon Inspektor. You think I'm kidding?" she added when Laird raised a doubtful brow. "Celebrities seem to think it's their duty to outdo one another in eccentricity when naming their children."

His eyes met hers thoughtfully for a long moment. Scarlett could see the questions in his eyes but didn't encourage him further, not knowing how much she could, or should say.

At last he nodded. "I will hae clothing sent for ye. Rest well, lass. I will see ye in the morn."

Scarlett nodded and bit her lip. She shouldn't ask. "Laird?"

"Aye?" He paused, glancing over his shoulder but making no attempt to linger in her chamber.

"Why did you kiss me?"

He shrugged. "My apologies, lass. 'Tis nothing more than a bad habit I hae when I hae a woman in her bedchamber. I meant nothing by it."

"Of course not," Scarlett whispered into the silence as he left, closing the door softly as he withdrew. Flopping on the bed, she grabbed a feather pillow and hugged it close to her chest.

She resisted the urge to pound it against the bed post until it snowed down upon the room.

Ugh. It hadn't been that good of a kiss.

12

The taste of her sweet kiss clung to his lips throughout the night, and James passed the hours tossing and turning, hard and aching, knowing Scarlett was right across the hall from him. Wanting nothing more than to cross that hall and take the lass for his own. To feel that lithe body against his once more.

He'd known the moment they were alone in the room that he should get out of there before something untoward happened. The luscious scent of her, sweet yet spicy, had wafted about him the whole of the day and he had been reluctant to leave her. Despite the effect she had on him.

It was baffling to be so put off by a woman's manner and still want her so. Why? James didn't like her. She didn't like him. But there was something about her that provoked him, something that challenged him. It was similar to the taste of a battle stirring, the anticipation of meeting one's opponent face to face on the field of battle. But it wasn't a sword of iron he wished to be armed with. Such unseemly thoughts had distracted him through matins and even lingered upon his return to the great hall.

Bah. Responsibility and duty awaited him. A true battle where life and limb would be at stake. He didn't have time for such nonsense when he should be focused on the matter at hand. Even if war were not looming, he would do best to avoid her, treat her like the genteel captive she was until he could ascertain her identity and discover her true purpose for being at Dunskirk.

"Good morn, Laird," Rhys called sunnily, joining James at the table in the great hall where James and Patrick had spent the morning pouring over the King's declaration. Men and messengers had come and gone as the hours passed. There was much to consider and more to do before they left Crichton.

"Don't call me that," James muttered by rote and glanced down at his brother's rumpled kilt and linen, unchanged since their journey. "Yer in annoying good cheer this morn. I dinnae see ye at matins this morn nor were ye aboot when I broke my fast. Where did ye rest yer head last night that it kept ye from yer porridge and ale?"

Rhys laughed, slapping James on the shoulder as he slouched down in one of the two massive chairs at the head of the table. "In a far more restful place than ye apparently. How is our captive this morning?"

James scowled at the implication. "I wouldnae ken as I hae yet to see her since last night. Nor does she confide in me. She doesnae even like me, in truth."

"I wouldnae take it personally. No one likes ye, Laird."

That had James scowling even more for his brother's words were not entirely untrue. He knew well enough that there were few in residence at Crichton who cared for his presence. If not for his father's favor, he would not even be welcome there as Lady Ishbel openly scorned him when he was present as she had for the score and seven years of his life. Her unwavering malice was the reason he spent so little time at Crichton, even though his own tower was only partially habitable.

Of late, he'd done little more than travel the countryside or stay at Court until Rhys had brought word of the Lindsay's raid on Dunskirk. Such forays weren't unusual between feuding clans on the border but James had welcomed the distraction from his tedium. Even if the result was an even larger – if not more sightly – one.

"What are we to do wi' the lass now, Laird?"

James frowned. "What do ye mean?"

"Mother dinnae ken who she is. I wouldnae thought it possible," Rhys said. "I would hae sworn she kent every marriageable female in the whole bluidy country. We dinnae ken who she is a'tall, and 'truth, wi' a battle brewing in the days ahead, I dinnae believe ransoming her now to be an option."

The same concern had niggled at the back of his mind all morning.

What was he to do with Scarlett now? When now so much more was on the line? Send her back to her people? He didn't even know who they were.

"What are ye suggesting? That we set her free?"

Rhys shook his head. "Nay, we dinnae yet ken if she spies for England. Recall her claim of friendship to the queen. Wi' this change of events, any suspicion maun be taken seriously."

"If she is a spy, she's done a piss poor job of it," James said, recalling Scarlett's words at Dunskirk. "Do ye think her so senseless that she would admit her association wi' the Queen if she were? Ye said yerself, she is a clever one."

"So ye dinnae think her a spy?"

"Nay, she asked me last night where we meant to invade England," James told him. "As clever as she is, I believe she would be better a better spy than to ask straight out if she were planning to betray us."

Rhys laughed heartily at that. "True enough. She made nae effort to fit in, to talk or act as a lowlander. Also, what intelligence did she hope to find at Dunskirk or from us? There are far superior opportunities for a spy."

"It makes little sense."

"Little aboot her does."

James couldn't disagree with that.

"Unless she kent the King would be coming here," Rhys said, thinking aloud. "Perhaps she has been sent to assassinate him."

A moment of silence, then Rhys laughed while a smile found its way to James' lips. "Nay, she is no murderer."

"But she is hiding something. I cannae deny it. She willnae speak true but there is something..." James paused, shaking his head but the answer did not immediately come to him. "She is frightened. No' of us. I dinnae ken exactly but it is there."

"What do ye propose to do wi' her then?"

James shrugged. "Soon the truth will out as it always does. We will keep her close at hand to deter her from trading in secrets if that is her intent."

"Close at hand, eh? How close exactly?"

"As close as a prisoner maun be kept. Now cease yer badgering," he snapped. "She cannae be our priority now, Rhys. The battle ahead maun hold our attention."

It was as much a reminder for himself as it was for his brother.

War.

Despite the long history of border clashes and clan feuds, a true war with England had not been fought in his lifetime. Aye, he would fight. How could he not? Still, he wondered if the petty squabbling of two overindulged men would be worth the sacrifices that would surely be made.

"Patrick had a private message delivered last night from Linlithgow," Rhys continued, referring to the King's palace west of Edinburgh. Their father, Sir William Hepburn, was recently made Lord High Chamberlain to King James IV. As such, Sir William was more often at the side of the King than at that of his wife. James had often wondered if his father had sought the position in earnest, hoping for such a result or if it had been entirely incidental. He had his own opinions on the subject, no matter what reasoning his father might give. "Father wrote that our cousin was called before the King."

"Bothwell?" James asked, lifting a curious brow. Their first cousin, Adam Hepburn, was second Earl of Bothwell by title but just a lad younger than them both having only one and a score of years on him. Even with his youth, Adam had taken to living life quietly, having already married and born a son to inherit his title one day. He wasn't one to go to Court often or willingly. "For what reason?"

"Bothwell is being named Lord High Admiral of Scotland," Rhys announced, lifting his brows with a nod when James stared at him incredulously.

"Lord High Admiral? Does James think to have a lad lead his men into war?"

"I cannae say. Bothwell is a lad, for certs, but he has earned his spurs as much as any of us." Rhys pursed his lips.

"Father expressed his displeasure that it was his nephew rather than one of his sons who received the honor."

James snorted. "Which of us did he think ranked high enough in the King's regard to earn such a dubious title? Patrick has little interest in war and ye…"

Rhys chuckled. "I am far more interested in other, more pleasurable pursuits. But ye, Laird, ye hae a tie to the throne."

"A rather dubious one. Nay, it wouldnae hae been I the King favored. Yer a more likely choice. Ye've a nose for courtly intrigue," James added, spurring his brother into laughter once more.

"If that is a kind way of telling me I am clever and cunning, I thank ye."

James conceded with a hint of a smile.

"Ah," Rhys said, his gaze shifting beyond James. "Our bonny captive approaches."

It wasn't that he cared to see her in as much as it was to keep an eye on her, of course. James inwardly mocked himself over his edgy impatience. Still, his breathing thinned at the sound of footfall, and turning, he saw her there at last, stepping hesitantly off the bottom step. Her fine eyes were wide as she scanned the hall, her gaze touching and lingering on every object and tapestry as if she had never set foot inside a keep before…

What the hell was she wearing?

Everything hurt. Everything.

Two days ago, Scarlett would have insisted that she was in good shape. She worked out regularly, watched her diet obsessively. But those long hours on horseback had done her in. Well, at least now she knew what to do to get a good core workout.

Descending the stairs on shaky knees took such a herculean effort she was almost tempted to return to her room but Scarlett continued on. Her bed awaited her in her chamber. A bed filled with nightmares more intricately woven than the silk embroidery that decorated every edge of her linens. There was isolation there as well, encouraging gloomy thoughts and anxieties over her time travel predicament. Even the rain that was slapping at her windows couldn't distract her from her utterly moribund dwellings. She would be glad when they left this place.

Below, on the other hand, there was Laird. Captor and conundrum. It would be difficult to face him. Managing to do it without blushing would be even harder, but her unexpected attraction to him was a far more palatable worry than the other.

How had it even happened? Disliking him one moment, in his arms the next. She couldn't possibly have wanted her captor to kiss her. This wasn't the early stages of Stockholm syndrome and stoic warriors without a sense of humor just weren't her type. Moreover, there was no way she liked it more than he had!

Perhaps that was the worst part, knowing he had only kissed her sorry bag of bones because she was there.

Thoughts of seeing him made her even more conscious of the fact that she wasn't wearing any underwear, but only a dress and chemise-type shirt had been left for her. Her lacy panties were now drying on the windowsill after a quick washing, but she was left feeling exposed, vulnerable. Naughty.

None of those things sat comfortably upon her.

Scarlett ran her hand over the stone blocks of the wall as she descended, pushing away the thought in favor of the awe the fortress inspired. Everything about this place was formidable. Even in the morning hours, her room was as forbidding and oppressive as it had seemed the night before even without the nerve-racking picture Laird had presented, hulking beside an equally imposing bed.

Dark wood paneled walls and coffered ceilings, maudlin artwork, and heavy furniture and fabrics. Staying there was almost depressing, most likely subconsciously spurring her morose thoughts. Her own home had soaring ceilings and a curved stairwell as well, but it was well-lit, bright and airy. Here, it managed to make her conversely claustrophobic.

It wasn't just the castle itself. Dunskirk, though much smaller, never made her feel so confined. Perhaps it was just the underlying fact that she was a prisoner of Crichton as well as time itself, but the castle had a very primitive vibe.

Of course, so did Laird, she thought, her thoughts drawn irresistibly back to him. She sensed his presence before she even saw him across the hall. He came to attention and watched her approach with hooded eyes. His height dwarfed her, and like the castle, was overwhelming. Unlike the castle, she didn't feel at all repressed by him.

On the contrary, she felt a strong urge to yield to him in the best possible interpretation of the word. For a modern feminist, it was a rather startling thought but in her defense, Scarlett didn't think that many modern feminists had had the opportunity to come face to face with a rugged, kilted Scottish warrior before.

It changed one's perspective on the matter.

"What's the matter?" she asked, finally noticing Laird's

frown as he studied her from head to toe. "Don't I look okay?"

His gorgeous lips parted then closed. "Ye look… fine."

"You hesitated. Why did you hesitate?"

"I dinnae…"

"Yes, you did. Is it that bad?"

The hurt was there in her eyes, just as it had been the other night when he had falsely called her a bag a bones, saying that no man could desire her. He did. In spades. "Ye look fine, lass. Truly."

"You, sir, are a terrible liar."

Scarlett sniffed and looked down at the dress that had been left on the foot of the bed once more. Initially she had thought Laird had chosen it for her but given the look on his face, she knew that wasn't the case. It wasn't the worse thing she had ever worn. The fabric was a little rough and scratchy against her sensitive skin but the bluish color was not horrible even if it hung on her slender frame like a sack and didn't even reach her ankles.

Did it even matter? There was no one waiting around with a camera to take her picture and splash it all over People magazine's worst-dressed celebrities list. In fact, there wasn't anyone around here to care much about what she wore or even said. It should have been liberating.

However, she did care. Like it or not – bag of bones or not – she wanted Laird to think she looked pretty.

"I think ye look lovely, Scarlett," Rhys said.

"Thank you, Rhys," she said, turning her back on Laird. "You, by contrast, are a very good liar."

Rhys bowed outrageously and, Scarlett supposed, rather gallantly. As always there was mischief written in every line of his handsome face. "I am at yer service. Do me the honor of breaking bread wi' me so that I might flatter ye more."

Now there was a diverting thought. The food, not the flattery. Having had nothing more than a piece of dried meat to gnaw on in the past couple of days, she felt like she could eat a horse. "I would love to."

Rhys offered her his arm and escorted her through the great hall, leaving Laird to follow along with only his great frown as company.

Like the hall, the stone walls of the dining room not dominated by huge fireplaces were covered with large woven tapestries. Though the ones in the great hall bore scenes of battle and castles that lent themselves toward maintaining the overall severity of the castle, the tapestries in the dining area were softer landscapes and boldly patterned coats-of-arms. Large plates of gold and silver replaced the swords, axes and shields displayed in the hall.

On one side of the room, narrow windows were sparsely placed while on the opposite side larger windows were open to the outdoors letting light fill the room. Through them, Scarlett could see another stone wall not far beyond and assumed that this was an interior wall facing the bailey.

Something like straw was strewn across the floor, crunching beneath her sandals. Rushes, Scarlett thought they were called, thinking back on to her freshman history classes. Other than that, there wasn't much about Crichton Castle that jogged any memory of those meager teachings on medieval history.

Long wooden tables were set in a U-shape with the short end closest to the fireplace. Rhys lead her there, and finally giving Scarlett a dose of chivalry, pulled out a heavily carved wooden chair for her. "Can I pour ye something to drink, lady? Ale, wine? Whiskey?" His eyes twinkled and Scarlett cast him a sour look before giving in to a smile.

"Are those my only choices?" she asked, half serious. She would have given her left arm for skim, double shot latte with no whip. "Definitely wine then."

With a laugh, Rhys plucked a pitcher from the table, drawing her attention to the bounty displayed there. There were platters of sausages, pies, fish and meat, their rich aroma overriding everything else. Her stomach stirred once again in approval. "You eat all this for breakfast?"

"We break our fast wi' porridge and bread wi' the dawn," Laird informed her, displaying none of Rhys' humor. "Ye only just made it down in time for dinner."

"Dinner? But it's only 10:30." She had checked the time before coming down.

Both men looked at her curiously but neither one said a word. They were probably as tired as she was of asking for an explanation.

"Well, I won't complain," she said, changing the subject. "I'm starving! But then I'm always starving, so I'm not surprised."

Her words clearly startled them both, since Rhys and Laird

shared a questioning look. This time curiosity must have outweighed the burden of requesting clarification because Rhys asked, "Hae we misjudged yer circumstances, lady? Was it no' illness after all that whittled ye away to a wisp?"

"I did mention, several times in fact," she pointed out, "that I hadn't been sick. I'm this thin because I work hard to be."

"I dinnae understand," Laird said with a frown. "Why would ye want to be so…?" He gestured up and down her length and Scarlett felt another sting of rejection pinch her. His dismissal was unlike anything she had ever experienced. Ugh, what did she care what that ass thought? One odd kiss couldn't change the facts. To him she was nothing but a prisoner. To her, he was an escape route. Nothing more. She should try to remember that, but damn, it smarted to know that a man she found so irresistible thought her no more attractive than department store mannequin.

"I think what my brother is trying to say it that any laird, like the Lindsay, for example, would take it as a sign of his wealth and affluence to see that all those under his care reflected his ability to keep them hearty and hale," Rhys explained. "Certainly his lords and ladies, if no' others in his clan, would be… er… *robust* enough to demonstrate his wealth. Ye ken?"

Scarlett blinked once, then twice before it dawned on her. Looking about the room, Scarlett noticed the few women who were carrying more platters and pitchers to the hall. To a one, they were all plump with ample bosoms and a broad backside. So Rhys was saying…?

That was how they displayed their wealth? Hanging their money up on the wall for everyone to see? Putting more jewels on a golden goblet than was tasteful? Having a little extra padding on their women? So, if you were too thin, everyone would assume you either didn't have the money to keep food on the table or you were too sick for a long while to eat? Well, that was interesting.

And it would certainly explain why men of their station were used to women who were more than a handful. Even if she was burned as a result. "I didn't realize why y'all were finding me so unattractive. I think I understand better now."

"'Struth, I think yer a bonny lass no matter what yer size," Laird said gruffly, surprising her. And himself, if the look on his face was any indication.

"Uh, thanks."

Jaw clenched, he turned away abruptly, leaving them at the head of the table to take a seat on one of the benches farther down the U. Scarlett watched him go, her heart beating just a touch faster than his swift strides.

He was still an ass, of course.

Maybe not a full-on asshole.

Still, an ass nonetheless.

"What's gotten in to him, do ye suppose?" Rhys recalled her attention as he dropped down in a chair next to her, his eyes twinkling with suggestive humor.

"You mean that isn't normal?" Scarlett countered. "I haven't seen him as any other than the bully he is," she added, lying blithely.

"Bully?" he repeated, taken aback. "He... uh, he hisnae mistreated ye, has he, lass? Despite his aura of savagery, Laird isnae normally one to do harm. He held ye throughout our entire journey yesterday like a bairn in his arms even after

I offered to take ye. If I had thought he might…"

"Relax, Rhys," she said, patting his arm. Laird had held her all day? Who was this man who could distrust so completely yet show such caring for her? "I'm fine. I'm not scared of him. I just don't trust him. Or you, for that matter. No offense."

"None taken." The concern fled his eyes to be replaced by his usual good humor. "To be fair, we dinnae trust ye either. Be ye Lindsay or spy."

"Or neither," she pointed out.

"So the fact that we will be invading England through Berwick-On-Tweed rather than Newcastle would be of nae interest to ye?"

"I only asked because I was curious," she told him. Searching her small inventory of historical facts, the name struck no chords however. "But no, it doesn't tell me anything I didn't already not know. I'd ask you to put aside your suspicions but I guess it would be hypocritical of me to get mad about you not trusting me. I don't think I've ever been able to trust anyone in my entire life, wondering if they have a hidden agenda."

"Is yer life so filled with intrigue?" he asked curiously, nodding absently to the flirtatious maid who was placing a wooden trencher on the table between them. With a pout, she turned away without ever gaining his notice. "Sounds like a life at court."

"I wouldn't know much about that but I'll take your word for it."

"Yer a curious lass, Scarlett Thomas. I maun say that I admire yer fortitude. Ye've been captured and made a prisoner, taken half way across Scotland and still ye retain yer sass."

Her lips twisted wryly. "What did you expect me to do? Curl up in the corner and cry like a baby?"

"Most ladies would."

"Yes, but I am not most ladies."

"Nay, yer no'. I'm eager to learn more about what gives ye such brass," Rhys said, biting back a grin as Scarlett's stomach growled loudly. "But why no' eat something first to help ye regain yer health?"

Why didn't she? Scarlett looked at the abundance of food spread and waiting on the table before them. In this time and in this place, she didn't need to worry any more about what she was eating than she did about what she wore. No one here would care if she gained a pound. From their comments and critical looks, they probably wouldn't mind if she gained ten.

She could do something crazy because there was no one here to see her do it.

She could stuff herself without conjecture over her eating habits or kiss a man without rampant speculation regarding her love life.

Scarlett cast a look down the table to find Laird watching her solemnly and felt yet another uncharacteristic blush warming her cheeks. It was a good thing she didn't react so openly in her time. The press would have had a field day!

But there was no press here. No paparazzi.

The sixteenth century was suddenly looking pretty darn good so why not make the most of it? Besides, for the first time eating organic would probably present no problems.

Then Rhys provided a temptation too great to deny. Taking a small loaf of bread from one of the platters, he split it in half and laid the two pieces on the plate they were apparently going to share. She hadn't realized that when he said 'break bread' he literally meant it. The crust was thick and crumbly, Scarlett doubted that there would be any way to bite through it without breaking a tooth but the inside was grainy and fragrant.

Oh, so inviting.

Bread. Even if there had been utensils provided to start digging into the other dishes on the table, Scarlett didn't think she could have denied its yeasty call. It beckoned to her. Tentatively, she dug out a piece of the soft inner loaf with her fingers.

"Is there something amiss, lass?" Rhys asked, his curiosity roused by her hesitance as she did little more than stare at the morsel. "I'll admit it doesnae look like much but it is tasty and filling, I promise ye."

"Oh, it's not that."

$$\times \quad \times \quad \times \quad \times \quad \times$$

Down the table, James, too, watched as Scarlett lifted a hunk of the bread to her nose, inhaling deeply. Eyes closed, her face softened and her lips parted sensually as if she were as aroused by the scent as he was by the sight of her.

What roused her so? James glanced down at the chunk of bread in his hand, resisting the urge to sniff it as she did. It was naught but grain as always.

"What is it?" Rhys asked, voicing the question he was fighting himself not to.

"Carbs."

"What?" Rhys asked, seemingly unaffected by her worshipful tone.

To James on the other hand, the near lust in that word conveyed itself straight down to his groin.

"I haven't eaten carbs in years," she sighed. Against his will, he hardened even more when she closed her eyes and licked her lips in anticipation. "I mean, it's a little overly textured but it's *carbs*."

"Tis no' carbs, lass," Rhys said perplexedly. "Tis just bread."

"Exactly."

She opened her eyes to look reverently upon the morsel she held once more time before sliding it between her lips. Her fine amber eyes burned with the same fire he had seen within them last night. James was like to bound across that table and ravish her if she dared look at the bread like that again.

Her eyes fluttered closed again as she slowly chewed. "Mmm."

That purr of appreciation, much as he had heard when but half-awake the previous morning, incited James even more and he bit back a responding groan. By God, but she roused him as he had never thought possible. Hardly a word, nary a touch and he was throbbing with desire.

It wasn't like him to be so easily provoked. He felt like a beast.

A shuffling around the table told him he wasn't the only one enraptured by her performance. James pinned the spectators one by one with a fierce scowl and a steely gaze until they looked away. Another tiny morsel made its way to her luscious lips in much the same manner and he lifted his tankard to his lips, determined to squelch the desire flaming inside him.

Bluidy vixen.

Over the rim, James found Rhys watching him. His brother's gaze was lit by knowing humor. Slamming the tankard down on the table, James fell into his own meal determined to ignore them all.

The few men who had gathered at the table had long since finished their meal and departed but still James found himself lingering over his ale and sausage, while Scarlett continued to pick her way through that single heel of bread savoring each bite as if it were her last. 'Twas no wonder she remained so gaunt.

He told himself he stayed to assure himself that she consumed a proper meal but James knew it was only to eavesdrop on the conversation at the head table. He'd asked many of the same questions the day before as Rhys put to her now, yet the lass had nary a kind word to say to him. He thought it only because she was his captive but she enjoyed Rhys' company well enough, answering his inquires effusively. He'd learned more about in an hour of eavesdropping than he had in a day's worth of close proximity.

Weren't they both her captors?

But nay, Rhys was the bluidy nice one, he recalled sourly.

"I maun ask aboot something that has been bothering me," Rhys was saying. "How did ye learn to fight as ye did? I ken ye took Laird utterly by surprise but still ye subdued him, a man twice yer size."

"A girl has to be able to protect herself," Scarlett shrugged, popping another piece of bread into her mouth.

"Will ye show me how ye did it?"

"So that you'd be able to counter my moves? No." Her husky chuckle spread like flames across James' skin.

"Ye hae nothing to fear from us, my lady."

Scarlett glanced down the table at James, her whiskey gaze speculative, but even that somehow stirred him. "That remains to be seen."

"Well then, where did ye learn it?" Rhys persisted.

"Self-defense classes," she told him, turning away from James' penetrating stare. "Surprisingly being a celebrity isn't all fame and fortune."

"Celebrity? Ye've used this word before. I cannae think it means to ye what it means to myself. In what way do ye mean for I doubt ye were named by celebration?"

"Celebrity," she repeated distractedly, clearly more enamored with her carbs than his brother's conversation. "You know, famous people? Does that make sense?"

"And ye were born of this celebrity?"

"Yes, both my parents are actors."

"Actors?"

James stiffened in surprise, barely biting back his shocked repetition of Rhys' protest. However, they both looked her up and down again as if searching for something they hadn't seen before. Rhys lifted his gaze to James' acknowledging that he knew James had been listening all along. He raised a questioning brow but James only shrugged. "Ye mean thespians? I had assumed ye a lady born."

They both had.

"I told you that you mistook me for someone else." She hesitated uncertainly.

Rhys looked at James again for direction but he only shook his head, lacking for an immediate response. "How did ye come to be at Dunskirk then, lass? Ye say ye are nae Lindsay nor spy, so why were ye there?"

"The simple answer is that I don't know."

"How can ye no' ken such a thing?" Rhys pressed. "If ye were no' ill, delirious… What other explanation is there?"

Scarlett only shook her head. Her lack of information was as maddening to James today as her silence had been the previous day, and given the manner in which she gnawed nervously at her lip, James got the impression she was giving an unusual amount of consideration to her answers. More consideration than was necessary when honesty might have served her best. "None that would make any more sense to you than it does to me."

"And yer claim that ye ken the Queen of England?"

"I lied," she said quickly. "I was just trying to get away."

"And go where?" he persisted. "Where do ye want to go? 'Tis my inclination, wi' the battle looming ahead, to send ye back to yer people and forgo a ransom. Tell me true from whence ye came and I will see ye safely home."

James started at the unexpected offer and Scarlett looked just as surprised. "You're letting me go?"

"Ye wanted away before. Do ye nae longer?" Rhys asked. Aye, he was a sly one. "Ye made no attempts to escape before. Not one since our arrival here. I'm getting the sense that yer right where ye want to be. Why is that?"

Scarlett's eyes were drawn down the table to Laird. Despite Rhys' distracting conversation, she had been all too aware of his brooding presence throughout the entire meal. Aware that he was watching her every move. Listening to her every word.

What would become of her if they sent her away? Alone and hungry in the middle of sixteenth century Scotland? Her stomach growled in protest, reminding her that she still hadn't filled it. Or perhaps protesting such a future as well.

It was becoming quite clear as her stay in the sixteenth century continued, that she needed these people to feed her, cloth her and keep her sane.

Part of that sanity was maintained by the belief that she would be going home soon. If she had any hope of making her way back to her own time – thus sparing her from insanity - Scarlett needed to be where Laird was. Somehow, his sword was the key to it all. He was the key and she needed to stay close.

While she had already determined there was a 'too close', by contrast, there was also a 'too far away'.

"Nay, Rhys," Laird protested before she could. "Before the lass leaves us, I will hae a satisfactory explanation for her presence at Dunskirk. If she cannae provide it ere our departure to Ellemford, she will join us on our progress and we will find her clansmen or return to Dunskirk when this is over."

Scarlett closed her eyes, exhaling a long sigh of relief.

"Is this acceptable to ye, lass?" Rhys asked, his eyes once again twinkling as if he were somehow pleased by Laird's command. "'Twill be a long journey, fraught wi' danger… and horses."

She grimaced but nodded. "I think I can survive it."

Why was she beginning to think that she was now right where *he* wanted *her* to be?

"Now that that is settled we can make merry once more." Rhys slouched back in his chair, propping his heels up on the table and crossing his feet at the ankles. "Come, Scarlett, tell me more aboot yerself. I confess, I find ye far more diverting than talk of bloodshed. Yer mother? A female on the stage? Tis unheard of at any theater I've attended. Even at court, all the players are men."

Scarlett bit her lip, thinking quickly. "Where I'm from, many women act. It's nothing unusual."

"And your parents? Are their names as outlandish as yours?"

It was a not so subtle interrogation but friendlier than the rapid fire questions Laird had battered her with the previous day. Scarlett rolled her shoulders, forcing the tension away. She had gotten what she wanted, a place by Laird's side and that sword. Would it hurt now to provide some truth to ease their suspicions? "Not really. My father's name is Wesley Thomas and my mother is Olivia Harrington." Rhys waved her on encouragingly. "Of course those are just their stage names. My mother was once simply Thelma Lou Ellis from Memphis, Tennessee and my father was actually born Vasili Trofim Korchinskaiia."

"Ye're Russian?"

Scarlett picked her way through the bread once more with a shrug. "What's wrong with being Russian?" Other than Lenin, Stalin, Communism, Khrushchev, the Berlin Wall, Bay of Pigs and the Cold War and McCarthyism, the American government had never had reason to hate them. Scarlett grimaced. She supposed being Russian in 1950s United States was a lot like being Englishman in Scotland just now.

Suspicion and distrust were everywhere. Wars, Cold and old, seemed to have that in common as well. She'd probably have about as much luck gaining the trust of these men as Stalin would JFK.

"Why would they change their names and deny their people?" Rhys was asking.

"Actors do it all the time to be more marketable, but as for my father, there was another reason entirely," she explained as she continued her meal, thankfully moving on from the bread to the tatties and smoked salmon his brother nudged toward her. "His father had been an actor too but back in the fifties and sixties. Back then, even a hint of Russia clinging to you could get you black-listed so he used a stage name but never legally changed it. My father did that when he was in his twenties. Vasili Trofim in English is Wesley Thomas, you see."

"I dinnae ken this 'black-listed'."

"Umm," she paused, considering. "Blackballed? Boycotted? Ostracized?"

James shook his head in confusion as he listened to Scarlett prattle on. The woman did love to talk once she started. First she was Egyptian, now she was Russian? Och, it must be another lie, he thought, studying her again from head to toe. The Russians were a hardy stock, incapable, he would have thought, of producing a child so delicate of form and face as Scarlett. She was otherworldly, as though she might disappear into an evening mist.

It made a man long to grasp her, like capturing the gossamer wings of a butterfly before it was gone forever. She had a fragility that was innocently alluring. He felt compelled to protect her. Even when he thought her his enemy.

But at the same time…

James shifted uncomfortably on the bench, willing away the tautness that again pained his groin. For all her charms, he could not let his defenses waver.

She was still his prisoner. Still hiding much. Too much about her didn't add up. He'd never known a moment sixty years past when being from Russia might get a man ostracized for being so. It made no sense, but then little of what she said did. She was indeed a mystery, one that was becoming more intriguing with each moment. How was it possible that she could not recall how she had arrived at Dunskirk? It wasn't, and truth be known, there was really no chance her mother acted on the stage. Despite her tales, it simply wasn't done.

Quite likely that everything she was saying was a lie.

"And are ye a thespian as well then?"

"I was," she said shortly.

James could feel the tension return to her posture, her withdrawal as she dropped the fish and pushed the trencher toward Rhys. Clearly, it was not a subject she cared for, it was easy to tell. Another falsehood?

"I would imagine players in the theater make for fine liars."

"You might think so but we're really terrible at keeping…"

Scarlett let the rest her words slip away as a young girl came skipping into the room. She was a pretty, plump girl with apple cheeks and blond hair peeking from beneath her headdress. Bright smiles wreathed her face when she spotted Laird at the table.

"Laird! Patrick told me you were home."

The girl threw herself in his arms as he rose from the table, hugging him tightly and kissing his cheek.

"Hullo, Plumpy," he said softly, returning the embrace affectionately.

Too affectionately. Scarlett felt an unfamiliar curl of tension stir sickly in her gut. "I thought you said nobody liked you here?" she murmured under her breath and saw Laird's lips twitch in response.

The girl stepped back and smiled warmly at Scarlett. She recognized the sort. This girl never met a stranger. "Hello."

"Aleizia, this is Mistress Scarlett Thomas," Rhys introduced her.

"Just Scarlett, please," Scarlett corrected, holding out a hand as she rose from her chair.

The girl looked at her hand curiously before setting her fingers delicately on the edge of Scarlett's and bobbing a curtsey. "It's a pleasure to meet you, Mis... er, Scarlett. I am Aleizia Hepburn of Crichton."

In itself, the introduction was unhelpful in providing Scarlett with anything more than a name. Who was she? A sister? A sister-in-law? Something more to Laird? There was true affection there. In that tender hug. She was awfully young, maybe fifteen or sixteen, but what did Scarlett know? They used to marry relatively young in the middle ages. "Nice to meet you, Aleizia. What a beautiful name you have. Very unusual."

"Thank you," she answered with a broad grin. "I can't wait to hear about what brought you to Crichton."

"No' now, Plumpy," Laird said with a groan.

"That's all right. I don't mind." Scarlett insisted as she didn't object to any open, honest company that kept her from the solitude of her chamber and certainly wouldn't have minded asking a multitude of questions of a person with few filters. "After the testosterone of the past couple of days, I wouldn't mind a some feminine company."

Aleizia blinked perplexedly before smiling once more. "That sounds lovely. We can talk of fashion and the court." She stepped back and looked Scarlett over thoughtfully. "Where did you ever find such a gown? It is a simply horrid! With the King arriving soon…"

"Plumpy!"

"I knew it!" Scarlett slanted an accusing glance upon Laird then glanced over Aleizia's gown. Simply cut but lovely in a way the one she wore could never dream of. Yes, she definitely needed a wardrobe intervention.

And an escape from Laird's probing gaze.

"Why don't ye take Scarlett to yer rooms and help her find something a bit more flattering, Aleizia?" Rhys suggested. "Any lass should be fully armed when meeting the King. Who knows, she might catch his eye."

"Rhys," Laird barked out. "I cannae think that Scarlett would hae much interest in becoming the King's next mistress."

"Absolutely not," Scarlett agreed, but a more palatable option niggled at her brain.

"Come with me," the girl said cheerfully, grasping Scarlett's hands with an exuberant squeeze as she tugged her away from the table. "'Twill be such a pleasant way to while away a rainy day."

James watched them go then turned to his brother with a

dark scowl. "What mischief are ye aboot, Rhys?"

Rhys waggled his booted feet from side to side as he popped a bite of salmon into his mouth with a cheeky grin. "I dinnae ken yer meaning, brother. Did I say something wrong?"

"She isnae yer concern. Stay out of it."

"Stay out of what?" Rhys said innocently, though his eyes were dancing.

With a grunt, James turned on his heel and stalked away. Sod it all! He couldn't have Rhys thinking that he was softening toward the lass. Or attracted to her. What hell could such a trickster make of James' life?

"Aleizia, I'm sure I have no need for so many fancy gowns. Surely just one or two simple ones will do," Scarlett protested as Aleizia piled more and more gowns on the bed. Clothes that weren't even her own.

Having decided that she was too petite and plump for Scarlett to fit into her own gowns, Aleizia had taken it upon herself to raid the wardrobe of young Aileen Hepburn instead. With auburn hair and grey eyes clearly marking her as another Hepburn sibling, Aileen was taller and slimmer than Aleizia, though not so tall as Scarlett. Her clothes would be a closer fit, but the girl, either overwhelmed by Aleizia or Scarlett or both, stayed perched on the edge of the bed watching the growing pile with wide eyes.

Scarlett held a gown of vivid blue velvet up in front of her then tossed it away immediately. No, she would definitely take nothing from Aileen if her first thought on the matter was whether Laird would find her bonnier in blue velvet or green silk. Besides she was feeling rather guilty about ransacking Aileen's closest. "You don't mind if I borrow a couple of gowns, do you?"

"She doesn't mind," Aleizia assured her before Aileen could respond. So far, she'd emptied more than half the wardrobe with her maid's help. "Most of these were made for her trousseau but she's outgrown them already. And you'll need more than a few gowns if you're to travel with the progress. They'll have to be taken down for you, of course, but Piegi here has a fine hand with a needle."

"Trousseau?" The word reminded Scarlett of her earlier curiosity. "How old are you, Aileen?"

"Almost thirteen," she answered, watching Aleizia as she turned to a trunk and lifted the lid. Lofty white linen was added atop the colorful pile.

Scarlett shook her head. No, the reason the gowns didn't fit now because Aileen was still a young girl who wasn't yet finished growing. Just twelve! Scarlett couldn't imagine marrying so young, though history attested it happened all the time. "And you're engaged to Rhys then?" she asked, unable to contain her curiosity. Or Laird?

"Of course not." Aileen lifted her head in surprise, then a shy giggle escaped her. "He's my brother."

"Oh. Then Aleizia is…"

"Patrick's wife," the younger girl answered. "You probably didn't know that, did you? They've been married for three years."

Three years? "How old are you, Aleizia?"

"Sixteen. Why?"

Scarlett shook her head and Aleizia looked up from the trunk. "Are you interested in our brother, Scarlett? In Rhys? He isn't married yet. Neither is Laird."

"I wasn't —"

Aleizia lowered her voice confidentially. "Laird hates being called that. Did you know that? He just hates it but Rhys and Patrick – have you met him yet? – they've always called him that. Just to bother him, I suppose. Because Laird is the oldest and would have been Sir William's heir if he wasn't a... er, well, if he weren't..."

"If he were legitimately born," Scarlett finished for her.

"Yes." The girl's shoulders dropped and she smiled in relief. "I wasn't sure if you knew."

"Does it matter?"

"To many it does. Too many really."

"Not to me," Aileen said softly. "I love Laird... James, whatever name he is called by. He was always an excellent brother to Patrick and Rhys and Adam and Alexander and Arthur –"

"How many brothers and sisters are there?"

"Ten, including Laird, Ayla and Owen."

Scarlett knew why Laird was singled out but...? "Ayla and Owen?"

"Sir William's other bas... recognized illegitimate children," Aleizia corrected. "They do not have Laird's same mother, however. Ayla's mother is the countess of Leeth while Owen's is no more than a milkmaid."

"Recognized?" Scarlett prompted.

Aleizia shrugged. "I imagine there are others."

It was said so indifferently; Scarlett didn't know how to take it but decided that this Sir William must be something of a man-whore. Spreading a little love around where ever he went. That Aleizia could be so casual about it told Scarlett that having a few children outside of his marriage wasn't too unusual for a man in this time. Or was it because of Sir William's position? As a – what did Rhys call him? – Lord

High Chamberlain to the King, perhaps William Hepburn was something of a celebrity himself, and with all the ladies throwing themselves at him, found himself presented with the results from time to time. Like some groupie saying they'd had Adam Levine's love child.

No wonder Lady Ishbel was so discourteous. Not many women would take kindly to their husband bringing the evidence of his infidelity home with him. Still, she shouldn't have taken out her resentment on Laird, as if it were all his fault.

"You didn't say what brought you to Crichton, Scarlett."

"Oh, nothing really. Laird and Rhys are just helping me find my way home." It was the most honest answer, after all.

"Where do you live?" Aleizia asked.

"Here, you should try these on." Aileen held out a pair of shoes.

"Oh, how pretty," Scarlett said in honest admiration, thankful for a reprieve from the difficult question. On a short heel, the shoes were red silk accented at the toes and the top of the curled tongue with what she thought were either real garnets or rubies. Either way, there were more jewels on those shoes than any pair of feet deserved.

Retail therapy had a place in any time, she decided as the shoes spoke to her, brightening her mood. And they looked to be about the right size. "Wow, they're amazing. But I couldn't. They're obviously very expensive."

Aileen shrugged. "My feet have grown and they pinch now." She lowered her voice to a whisper. "I'd rather you have them than Aleizia. She has too many already."

"They *are* beautiful," Scarlett said, tempted despite herself. They were as magnetic as a modern pair of Jimmy Choo's. Her toes curled in anticipation. "They sort of remind of

Dorothy's Ruby Slippers."

"Who's Dorothy?"

"Oh, no one really," Scarlett said as she slipped them on. "She just a character from a story."

"A story!" The girl pounced on the word with the breathless exclamation, a broad smile brightening her solemn face. "I just *love* stories! Can you tell it to me? There is a traveling troubadour who comes around from time to time but Father's regular bard is dreadfully dull without a lick of spirit in his tales."

Scarlett couldn't help but smile in return.

"Please? Do tell us!" Aleizia dropped onto the bed in a pool of skirts and looked up at Scarlett expectantly. Even her maid looked hopeful. No doubt, they were lacking for entertainment without the constant hum of TV and social media around. Scarlett found it all rather peaceful but couldn't find it in herself to deny these two sweet girls.

"All right," Scarlett relented, wondering where to begin. "Well, once upon a time, there was a girl from Kansas named Dorothy Gale…"

✕ ✕ ✕ ✕ ✕

"Then the wicked, green-faced witch leaned close to Dorothy, pointing a spindly finger at her and said, 'I'll get you, my pretty'," Scarlett cackled in her best imitation of Margaret Hamilton. "'And your little dog, too!'"

"Oh, my!"

"That's just what Dorothy said," Scarlett nodded, repeating the words in a perfect, softly breathless imitation of Judy Garland. "Then the Wicked Witch of the West circled around, waving her broomstick at all the cowering

Munchkins with an evil laugh before disappearing in a cloud of red smoke." Scarlett cackled dramatically again for effect while the maid crossed herself. She was beginning to enjoy herself.

"What happened then?" Aileen asked excitedly.

"Glinda, the Good Witch of the North told Dorothy that if she wanted to go back to Kansas she must go to the Emerald City to seek the help of the awesome and powerful Wizard of Oz. Only he would be able to help her," she continued. "Not knowing the way, Dorothy asked how she was to get there."

"How?" Aleizia asked as if she just couldn't help herself.

"'Just follow the yellow brick road', Glinda said, before she transformed into a lovely pink bubble and floated away as the Munchkins waved goodbye. 'Follow the yellow brick road?' Dorothy repeated as she noticed the spiraling path that began in the middle of Munchkinland. Dorothy put the toe of her ruby slipper on the first stone." Scarlett lifted the hem on her skirt and placed her foot tentatively on the imaginary road before her. "'Follow the yellow brick road,' she said. 'Follow the yellow brick road. Follow the yellow brick road, follow the yellow brick road.'" Her voice grew more confident as she repeated the phrase over and over and paced the imaginary road. Then she began to sing. "'Follow, follow, follow, follow, follow the yellow brick road. Follow the yellow brick, follow the yellow brick, follow the yellow brick road. Da-da, da-da, da! We're off to see the wizard. The wonderful wizard of Oz!'"

Aleizia and Aileen clapped their hands with delight as Scarlett began to skip across the room as she sang with a breathless laugh. "'We hear he is a wiz of a wiz, if ever a wiz there was. If ever, ever a…'"

Circling at the end of the room, Scarlett turned and spied Laird lingering at the door. His arms were folded over his broad chest as he shouldered the door frame lazily. He looked huge in the narrow opening, overwhelming.

Heart pounding, Scarlett stumbled to a halt, dropping her skirt.

God, he was gorgeous! Would the sight of him never stop stealing her breath?

His light eyes raked down the length of her before lifting, holding hers. She'd never seen a man with eyes like Laird's. So pale in contrast to his dark hair, beard and brows, as if they were lit from within. Lit with interest. With desire?

For all his dismissive words earlier, those eyes told another tale entirely.

Her sudden halt had every pair of eyes in the room also turning to the door and James became aware that it wasn't just Aileen, Aleizia and her maid but several of the castle maids and pages crowded into the room as well. He'd been so focused on Scarlett's lively performance, and the sight of her slender calves, that he hadn't even noticed. Now, each and every one of them sported a scowl for James's interruption of what he knew to be the liveliest entertainment Crichton had seen for some while.

The afternoon had been an interminable one, wondering what could be occupying the ladies for hours on end. In the lists despite the rain, James had taken a blade to his arm as reward for his inattention. Unable to put off his curiosity any longer, he returned to the castle and to his sister's room determined to simply ascertain that his prisoner was still just that when he had heard her talking. Peeking around the door, he found Scarlett shod in a pair of red slippers, holding her skirts up to her knees. He was entranced by her performance, by her nimble steps and the sight of her trim ankles and shapely calves. The lines of strain around her mouth and the shadows in her eyes that haunted her expression since he found her at Dunskirk had faded. She was entrancing.

Her farcical story was entertaining as well. Some peculiar tale of witches good and bad – Good witches! As if there was such a thing – but her face lit with animation as she imparted the voice of Dorothy in a soft, tentative manner quite unlike the one she had used with him over the past days. Then she had sung. Her spirited voice high and clear.

"My apologies for the interruption," he felt compelled to say. Sorry for himself as well. Sorry that he was the reason she stopped. "Please carry on."

"I... I..." Scarlett held true to her name and flushed a bright, yet becoming bright red. "I didn't know you were watching."

"Does it matter when ye've an attentive audience already?" he asked curiously. "What is one more pair of eyes upon ye?"

To his surprise, she blushed even more, looking away. "Maybe later."

How intriguing.

"Oh! You mustn't stop now," his sister protested. "I want to know what happened to Dorothy."

Remarkably, so did James. But he also undeniably wanted so much more.

"I can tell you the rest later," Scarlett assured her, kicking off the ruby-encrusted slippers. "It's getting late anyway, isn't it?"

"Aye, the dinner bell has just rung," James told them, sweeping his glance over his sister and sister-in-law as well. "Perhaps ye might be persuaded to share the tale wi' us after supper?" James added to Scarlett. "I for one should like to hear it from the beginning."

Scarlett caught her lip between her teeth and James stifled a moan at the sight. "In front of everyone? Really? I'm sure there is someone better to entertain everyone."

"Oh, no," Aleizia protested, leaping up to catch Scarlett's hand. "You are the best storyteller I've heard in a long while. I've never heard such a tale before and with songs to mark each moment. It's simply wonderful. You must share."

Aileen nodded in agreement still Scarlett hesitated. "I told you I can't remember all the words to the songs."

"No matter, whatever you can do. Right, Laird?"

"Aye, lass," he said softly, his brogue rolling lazily. "I am verra keen to see more of what ye hae to offer."

James ran the pad of his thumb absently across his bottom lip as he watched his bonny captive's expressive face as she told her tale.

Her performance showed James a side of his captive he hadn't seen before. A side that was light-hearted, lively. Also one that was more amicable than a skin of whiskey could make her. Personable and approachable rather than hostile and sardonic. This new facet of her character held him spellbound. Confound it, she was a perplexing woman, prickly one moment, engaging with his sisters the next. Giving him a glimpse into a side of her he hadn't imagined existed.

Igniting a spark within him that had long lain dormant as well. He could hardly keep his mind on the convoluted tale of scarecrows, metal men and talking lions, she was such a vision in the firelight. The rough linen gown of the morning was gone in favor of one far more becoming. Though without lavish adornment, the bright blue of the velvet gown seemed to set her uncovered hair on fire by contrast.

And ah, those slender ankles! At least she'd been shod in a jeweled slipper rather than shite this time.

"As thin and tall as she is, without womanly hair or ample bosom, she should look like a lad," Rhys said quietly at his side.

It wasn't a question rather than a statement of fact. And fact it was, James couldn't deny Rhys' observation. The most desirable ladies of the court were petite and plump, though hidden beneath stylish headdresses, their hair would be long. Their bosoms and arse amply fleshed to warm a man's body and plump thighs to cradle his hips.

Scarlett Thomas had none of those assets. She was extremely tall and painfully thin to the point of emaciation, her collarbones clearly outlined. Her wrists were as thin as a birds. Aye, she should look like a lad.

But she did not.

Nay, she was lovely indeed. Her delicate bone structure only accentuated by the heavy gown she wore. Her flawless skin looked as soft as velvet and as pale as fresh cream as if the sun or the elements had never touched her. So frail he could almost see the veins, blood beneath her skin. Not a callous on her fingers.

Her figure might seem to some boyish or wraith-like, but he saw her as long and elegant. Though it seemed as though she might break in a strong wind, her curves were not masculine and her breasts, he knew well, were ample enough to fill his hand and rouse his loins.

Her head was nearly shorn, her auburn hair far shorter than he wore his own. Yet it somehow it suited her, accentuating that fey look.

But most compelling, despite that aura of delicacy and

purity, there was something about Scarlett Thomas – perhaps the constant upward turn of her lips that suggested knowing amusement, the warmth of her whiskey brown eyes or the way they pierced a man's soul – that made a man wonder at what fire that might be kindled beneath.

It made him long to pin her against the castle wall and taste her honey lips once more. To taste much more of her as well.

As wrong as he knew it was, he couldn't stop imagining it.

Those bewitching eyes were warm with laughter now as she brought yet another rare smile to Aileen's lips. Aye, James knew the sight of her shouldn't have been able to conjure an iota of warmth in a man's loins but James would wager that the mere memory of a night with her would sear a man to the core for the rest of his days.

"Laird?"

"Aye, she should," he agreed at last, keeping the rest of his thoughts to himself.

"She insists that she hasnae been ill," Rhys continued though James was only giving him half an ear. "Still it maun be true. I ken nay other reason why any woman of her years would shear their hair as she has. 'Tis against God's will."

James nodded at that, though his eyes never left the lass in question as she once again began to skip across the hall while her small audience clapped along. "Nay, the only other reason I've e'er known a woman to shave her head was because she took the ve…"

Rhys chuckled aloud at the sour expression on James' face. "Aye, and doesn't that just turn yer stomach given the thoughts going through yer head?"

James turned to his brother with a scowl. "What do ye ken of my thoughts, brother?"

"I ken they're the same as any man here." With some surprise, James looked about to find the gaze of many men following Scarlett with more than amusement in their eyes.

His brother laughed some more but James dismissed the other men and considered Rhys' speculation. Short hair aside, Scarlett was quite clever and seemingly educated. He knew she had been reading the King's proclamation the previous night. Not just scanning it curiously as Lady Ishbel did. She looked at a man as if she were his equal and demanded respect for her opinions. She met his gaze steadily without fuss or flirtation. The lasses in Scotland might be bold but never had one leveled him a look like that. As if she were his equal. She had the will of a queen.

No gentlewoman of his acquaintance, not even his Queen, was all those things. Not even his sisters who, while intelligent, could hardly read, or write beyond their own signature. Scarlett was completely unlike any woman he had ever come across. Few stations in life educated women so well. Few vocations. Bitter bile burned at the back of his throat. "If she is for the church…"

"Then ye maun hae something new to confess at matins tomorrow," Rhys said with a grin as he clucked his tongue lightly. "Lusting after a nun, Laird? There maun be some sort of sin against that."

"She isnae a nun," James felt compelled to say, even knowing that the slightest argument would do little more than confirm his growing attraction to the lass.

"Save it for the confessional, brother."

"Why do ye insist on bedeviling me?"

"I take a great deal of joy from it, actually."

"I thank ye for an entertaining evening, my dear Scarlett," Rhys said, lifting her hand to his lips. "Yer by far the most diverting captive I hae ever taken."

"Have there been so many?" Scarlett teased, quenching her thirst with a large swallow of wine, wishing it were water instead.

"More than ye would imagine, I'd wager."

Her lips twitched. "My, my, Rhys, you didn't strike me as the bondage sort."

His wicked grey eyes narrowed as if he were gauging her meaning and the corner of his mouth tilted up attractively. "Is that an offer?"

Scarlett laughed at that, lifting her cup in silent salute. Before she could summon a witty retort however, a curious warmth glided over her and without looking, she knew Laird was behind her.

"Yer in good humor."

Already flushed with exertion, Scarlett's cheeks warmed even more under the banked desire in his eyes. "I had more fun than I thought I would. Perhaps I should turn my efforts to the stage."

It was true. Though she doubted that the grand design for her time traveling adventure – assuming there was a reason to this madness at all – was to provide endless entertainment in medieval Scotland. If it were, Scarlett wouldn't be the one to throw a monkey wrench into the cosmic design, at least when it came to a performance that was as distracting for her as it was diverting for them.

"I thought ye already had."

"A more intimate venue," she amended, not wanting to get into the different avenues for actors in her time.

"Aye, intimate," Rhys drawled in a suggestive brogue. "I

was just telling Scarlett how interested we are in what more she might offer."

More of what she had to offer?

That roguish question – Laird's, not Rhys' – was back like a wrecking ball, shattering Scarlett's composure to bits. Though not a single smile had graced Laird's lips during her performance, she'd been all too aware that he had watched her intently. Her nerves had been thrumming like the steady rhythm of a Tardis all night, though she was professional enough to disguise her jumpiness.

Was he flirting with her? Was he serious? She wished she knew.

Laird's brow furrowed tightly as he leveled a dark scowl on his brother. "Yer no' as amusing as ye think ye are, brother."

Rhys cast her a wink. "Aye, I am. 'Tis getting late. Can I escort ye to yer rooms, my dear?"

"Than –"

"I will see to her," Laird grumbled and turned away as if he expected her to follow. Scarlett waited until he turned back impatiently.

"If it's a choice between being escorted and seen to, I'd rather have the escort."

Rhys chuckled but Laird only sighed impatiently and offered her his arm. Scarlett slid her hand into the crook of his elbow, immediately second-guessing her testy command. Already shaken by his proximity, touching him made her all the more conscious of his raw masculinity. Through his fine linen shirt, she could feel the heat of his flesh and the bulge of his bicep beneath her fingers. Against the back of her hand, the brush of his torso caressed with every step.

"I'd like to thank ye for being so kind to Aileen," he said

as they climbed the stairs. "She's had little to find joy in of late."

"That's no problem. She's a sweet girl."

"Aye, she is." Laird fell silent once more but Scarlett wasn't surprised. He wasn't much for conversation. It was more of a shock when he spoke again. "The usual entertainment at Crichton is a bard Lady Ishbel retains. She's determined to get her penny's worth from him. Having heard him but once, I dinnae believe that is going to happen."

Scarlett's jaw sagged. Was he making a joke? Stoic, serious Laird trying to be funny? "Glad I could help then. I suppose it's a good thing Lady Ishbel didn't join us for dinner."

"She was abed wi' a sick headache," he told her as they stopped at Scarlett's chamber door. "Remarkably, they come upon her each time I visit."

Another joke, as self-depreciating as it was. She wavered, wondering at the change in him. Perhaps, maybe Laird was just a wee bit likeable after all. "An amazing coincidence."

With just the light of a single sconce in the hall, the stillness felt more intimate than uncomfortable. Still, she couldn't look at him. "Well, goodnight."

"Scarlett." His hand covered hers as she reached for the door latch. "Ye should be wary of Rhys. He has a reputation among the ladies at court."

Scarlett snorted skeptically. "Oh, I doubt that."

She looked up and up again past his powerful chest, noticing again just how huge he was. Just how delicate he made her feel. How feminine. How the flames licking at his steely eyes radiated toward her.

"I don't think that will be a problem." Instead of the sarcasm she had intended, the words emerged breathlessly.

Laird's warning was laughable. It would be more appropriate to warn her of the danger Laird himself posed to her. Rhys was more handsome than any man had the right to be but he couldn't rouse her desires the way Laird could with a single glance. It would be far better for her peace of mind, in fact, if her feelings for Laird were as platonic as those she had for Rhys.

The dim hallway felt as though it were shrinking around them. Scarlett was dangerously aware of his every breath, the rise and fall of his chest beneath his linen shirt. Her breath slowed to match his, the very air compressing against her breasts as she inhaled.

"Laird." Whatever she might have been planning to say was swept away as his lips covered hers. Lightly, like a soft caress then deepening as he drew her into his strong arms. Crushed against that captivating chest, he lifted her, propelling her into her chamber and nudging the door shut before falling with her on the bed.

No man had ever kissed her like this. Other men waited for her permission, or worse, her initiation of a kiss. Laird took what he desired, devoured polite objections. Forced her body into an honest, if shocking, response. She felt wild. Wanton.

Panicked by the loss of control, Scarlett tore her lips from his, panting, "Laird, we can't do this."

Laird tugged her gown off her shoulder. First pressing a kiss there, then nipping at her collarbone. His lips dragged upward, his beard scraping until his tongue curled around her earlobe. He drew it between his lips, biting gently and Scarlett swallowed hard. "It's ridiculous, really." Scarlett gasped as his rough palms enclosed her tender breasts and he bent his head to take her sensitive nipple between his teeth.

A tortured moan formed at the back of her throat. "You're not my type at all."

"Yer type?" he asked against her breast.

"The kind of guy I normally find attractive," she explained haltingly, panting for breath as his tongue lapped over her nipple. "Overly handsome, domineering." Domineering? Oh, would he be? Scarlett felt a little thrill at the thought. No, that really wasn't her type at all! "You're too big."

Laird's hands slid to her hips pulling her roughly closer as he thrust his hips forward, clearly illustrating his immense length. "Too big?"

"Big, as in overpowering," she explained and a smile lifted the corner of his mouth. But that demonstration had sent her blood pressure soaring.

"Och, lass, I'm every woman's type."

Of course he was. He was tall, dark and ridiculously handsome. Even a saint would want him for his sensual brogue alone. Scarlett released a pained laugh. "Ego."

"Experience," he whispered and kissed her again. His tongue plunged deep, sweeping along hers seductively. He tasted of heady whiskey and almost undeniable temptation. Powerful hands roamed over her body, gliding from her waist to her shoulders and back down again before he clasped her bottom in his palms and lifted her against him.

His hips rocked and Scarlett helplessly arched against him. Her heart pounded hard against her ribs. Desire pulsed through her veins. Desire unlike anything she'd ever felt before. Laird hiked up her skirt, one broad finger slid between her damp folds. Her thighs quaked, tensed. Clinging to his shoulders, Scarlett prayed for mercy.

"Yer wet for me already, lass. Open and let me in."

"Oh, God," she cried, warring with herself. Battling

against the naked passion Laird roused it her. It was so incredible. Could it possibly be wrong? "O-kay."

Laird stilled against her.

"Ye hesitated," he said, using her words from that morning.

Only the sound of their heavy breaths broke the silence.

"I did. Oh, God, what am I doing?" This wasn't her. She just didn't do this! Not like this. For all of Hollywood's foibles, she wasn't easy. She didn't sleep around like many actresses might. She was, in fact, highly conscious of what people saw and assumed after having a lifetime of her parent's not-so-fine examples to follow. And because of her visibility, she had been very careful about who she had been with if only because she hadn't wanted her relationships blasted about for everyone to hear. She could count on one hand the number of times she had slept with a man.

Hell, she could count on two fingers! And neither one had been terribly memorable. Neither one had left her shaking like this.

The problem was, she wasn't entirely opposed to giving it a try. His hold slackened and he pulled away, cooling air found its way between them. Scarlett grasped his wrists before he slid entirely away. "Laird, I want to. I do. It's just..."

"Yer a virgin."

"No." Scarlett scrambled to her feet as he lifted himself away. His chest was damp and heaving when she lifted a hand to his heart. Felt his surprise. "No, it's not that. I just not ready for this. Please understand, I'm not that girl who sleeps around. I don't do this on first dates or... or like this, without even one date."

"Dates? What does fruit hae to do wi' it?"

"Ugh! I'm sorry. I know I'm sending all kinds of mixed signals here."

"Mixed signals? Lass, I dinnae understand."

"I know you don't. I'm just so… I don't know what to say. Laird, you're taking me down a road I'm not sure I want to travel." She glanced down at the still raging erection lifting his kilt. Oh! She wanted nothing more than to turn back time just five minutes this time and tell her capricious conscience to take a hike. She wanted him badly. Why not?

Because she was his prisoner, remember?

Bull shit! The devil on her shoulder taunted her. *Take the road. Do it because you want to. Do it because you can finally feel free.*

With a sigh, Scarlett closed her eyes.

"Laird, I'm…"

"I dinnae need yer apologies, lass. I ken the situation well enough."

"Laird…"

"Mind what I said aboot Rhys. I ken ye think he's the bluidy nice one, but mark my words. Beware. Else ye find yerself thoroughly seduced."

The door closed behind him before she could say another word.

Scarlett pressed the heels of her hands against her eyes. She was already finding herself thoroughly seduced.

"Well, if it isn't the bloody nice one," Scarlett said when she answered the knock on her bedroom door the next morning and found waiting Rhys in the hall.

"I had thought to escort ye to dinner, dear Scarlett." A sly grin spread across his lips. "Perchance, were ye expecting someone no' so nice? My brother perhaps? Should I offer my apologies for disappointing ye?"

A hot blush crept up her cheeks. Such humiliation burned through her on how things had ended between her and Laird the previous night. Laird had brought her to the edge of release and she had left them both hanging. How was she to face him after that?

It certainly wasn't what she had planned on and he had every right to be angry with her or worse. Honestly, after the way they parted, who knew what he was thinking?

"You have a dirty mind, Rhys. No, actually I was expecting... or rather hoping for a bath. I asked Graeme a half an hour ago if I could have one." Two days without a bath was two too many. Scarlett felt grimy and was afraid she was starting to smell something awful. The steward had reacted like she was asking for the moon. For such a religious group of people, they didn't take the cleanliness is next to godliness theorem very seriously.

"Did the servants no' bring ye water to bathe?"

"They brought a bucket of water and a cloth. That is not a bath."

"Ye wanted a full bath?" His voice held more than a little surprise. "While some, like Laird and myself, prefer to totally submerge ourselves as well, opportunities to do so in the castle are rare. We will often bathe out of doors in the rivers or streams."

"Why?" Scarlett asked curiously, pushing open the door and inviting him in.

"No' only is it a great deal of work for the servants to prepare frequent baths, but some, like my lady mother, believe that bathing in such a manner opens the pores," Rhys answered as he took a chair near her empty fireplace. "Allowing for evil humours and disease to enter the body."

"Evil humours? What disease?"

"The plague for instance."

"What a load of... You don't actually believe that do you?" Scarlett gaped at Rhys. Dirt was not a protective barrier between a body and the germs. Somehow, she needed to relay that to these people.

"I dinnae, but some are superstitious."

"But that's not how contagions work."

"Are ye so educated that ye ken these things better than the priests?" he asked, slouching back in the seat and propping his feet up on a nearby cushion until Scarlett was treated to a fine view of his muscular legs and a glimpse of his bare butt under the draping of his kilt.

Scarlett chewed her lip, distracted by the thought of what Laird might or might not be wearing beneath his kilt and that long shirt. "I think I know a bit about it."

"Yer educated then? Can ye read, Scarlett?"

Scarlett shifted her gaze up to his. There was a glimmer of keen interest in his eye and she wondered what he was digging for. "Of course. Can't you?"

"I can." Rhys considered her thoughtfully. "No' many ladies of my acquaintance are so skilled however. Can ye do sums and such, as well?"

"If I count on my fingers and toes," she answered dryly, bringing a smile to Rhys' lips. "What's with all the questions, Rhys? You don't still think I'm a spy, do you?"

Rhys chuckled, shaking his head. "Nay, but I do wonder if ye might be of the church. Did ye flee the nunnery, Scarlett? Is that how ye came to be at Dunskirk?"

Laughter bubbled up inside of her and Scarlett wagged a finger at him. "You do ask all the best questions, Rhys."

"That is no' an answer."

No, it wasn't but it was amusing to toy with him when he'd so often done the same with her. "Let me ask you this: why would you think I am?"

Rhys stroked his chin thoughtfully as he studied her. "I dinnae think it myself, only cast the lure to bait another but I began to think upon it and wondered if it might be true enough. Yer a smart lass. Clever. Educated. Ye hae a way of looking upon a man as if he were somehow inferior to yerself. I once knew a Mother Superior at a convent in Edinburgh who looked at me just so. And too, few women other than those in God's service shave their heads. Novices do so to humble themselves before taking their vows."

"So every smart woman with a pixie cut must be a nun?" Scarlett laughed again. Laird might be able to tie in her knots in moments but his siblings were such good company. Rhys, in particular, should have been renowned for his diverting banter.

"Ye hae no' the look of an experienced woman, either, for all yer years and sharp wit," Rhys said, looking her up and down until Scarlett was plucking at the laced sleeves of her linen dress under his scrutiny. "Ye do seem to hae a bit of the devil gleaming in yer eye but even so there is something virtuous about you."

Yes, one that had been a huge part of her Hollywood success story but a nun was the last role she would ever be cast in. "That's quite poetic, Rhys, but I'm not that innocent."

Rhys shrugged as if he didn't quite believe her.

"What do you think says experience? The sultry lady of the night look?" Scarlett shot him a practiced smolder through her lashes that had graced more than one magazine cover and Rhys lifted that brow once more. He was impressed but then she had practiced it often enough. A look that said she knew all men wanted her and knew it well. The photographers had loved that naughtiness juxtaposed against her natural wholesome looks. "Experience doesn't have a look, Rhys. I don't have to be experienced to look it or act it. People fake it all the time."

"Fake it? Bah, I could tell," he said with confidence.

"Could you?" Scarlett chuckled in disbelief, shaking her head. "Could you really?"

"Of course."

"Hmm." Mischief seized her in its wicked grasp. Perhaps it was time to give Rhys a little of his own. Scarlett slouched down in her chair, relaxing against the back. Her knees parted but a tad. Giving him her most seductive look once more, she drew her forefinger slowly across her lower lip and then down her chin and throat. "Mmmm," she sighed and breathed heavily.

Rhys' eyes widened, his mask of deviltry truly slipping for the first time she met him. "What are ye aboot, Scarlett?"

He seemed almost panicked, gripping the arms of his chair as if he meant to stand but Scarlett wasn't about to stop. No, she was going to give him her best *When Harry met Sally* reenactment if only to prove a point and bedevil him just a bit. Closing her eyes, she tilted her head back against the chair, shifting restlessly and moaning with increasing volume until she was tossing her head from side to side, clenching her short hair in one fisted hand as she pounded the arm of her chair with the other. "Yes! Oh God! Oh God! Yes! Yes! Yes!"

When Scarlett opened her eyes, Rhys' eyes were once again dancing with amusement and a newfound appreciation. "So no' a nun then?"

Scarlett bit her lip but joined him when he burst out in laughter.

"Would that be such a horrible thing if I were?"

"No' for me. But for some."

"My, my. How ambiguous. No, Rhys, I am not a nun. There. Happy?"

Rhys nodded. "Ye may no' be a nun but yer a verra fine actor, Scarlett. I might ne'er trust yer words or actions again."

"Then mission accomplished."

Their laughter mingled again until the door was thrown open, crashing against the stone wall and Laird was there, filling the door. His gaze shot first to the bed before finding them sitting far apart near the fireplace. "What the bluidy hell?"

"Calm yerself, brother," Rhys drawled calmly as he levered himself leisurely from his chair and strolled to the door, slapping Laird's shoulder as he passed. "Scarlett was merely treating me to a demonstration of her fine acting talents. Verra enlightening. My thanks again, my lady." He gave her a short bow. "And I will be sure to hae Graeme send ye up a bath straight away."

"Thank you, Rhys."

$$\times \quad \times \quad \times \quad \times \quad \times$$

The door closed behind him leaving Scarlett alone with Laird. Though he hadn't moved any more than she had, she felt his presence as completely as if he were standing right next to her. The tension. The lingering anger. The charged nerves.

No, those were hers.

He unsettled her in every way. She employed more of her acting skills in that moment than she ever had before to radiate a tranquility she didn't feel. "Don't you knock?" she asked lightly. "You never know what you might be walking in on. Or were you thinking to watch?"

Laird made a strangled noise deep in his throat. "What was my brother doing in yer room?" he choked out.

"Obviously not what you thought we were doing. What are you doing here?"

"Oddly enough, I came to offer my apologies."

Glancing up through her lashes, she met his gaze for the first time. There was none of the anger she expected to see considering the way they had last parted. No, his were blazing with a fire she had never seen in a man's eyes.

This was nothing like the soft, simmering desire of the previous night.

She'd seen lust before. On him, it was unnerving. Even slightly terrifying, yet she felt an answering sizzle spark deep in her belly and her pulse raced in anticipation as he took a step toward her. Involuntarily, she backed away, one pace and then another to match each of his until her back was pressed against the wall.

"Your apologies?" she said shakily. "I'm the one who should apologize."

Would he kiss her again? Scarlett spread her palms over the cool stone. Hoping that a similar chill might seep into her? Looking for an escape?

"Nay, lass, the fault was mine."

She bit her lip as he came, step by step, until the radiant heat of his body caressed her. The veins straining in his neck and forearms thrilled her. Lord, she had been around men who were too pretty for too long. Laird was unbearably rugged, too rough. Too devastating to her senses to bear.

She didn't want him so close.

She wanted him closer still.

Well, what are you waiting for? The wicked devil that sat on the opposite shoulder to reason goaded with a wicked chuckle. *He's right there. Yours for the taking.*

Another blush crept up her cheeks. No, she couldn't possibly.

Why not? The devil teased. *He's the best part of this whole nightmare, He's a tempting diversion. Can you think of a better way to pass the time?*

No, she couldn't.

The admission made her more conservative conscience

sigh in disappointment.

But yearning for Laird flared through every inch of her body, setting her afire. Her heart jittered in her chest like a violent water sprinkler, but the flames would not be doused. Primal lust. Lust like she had never felt before even though he hadn't laid a finger upon her yet. Lust she felt compelled to act upon, which in itself was surprising.

"I heard ye from all the way down the hall, lass," he bit out, looming over her until she was cast in his shadow. "I warned ye aboot him, dinnae I? Do ye ken what I thought?"

Yes, she knew what he had thought he had heard and what he had assumed she was doing when he barged into her room. Yet he had barged in anyway, angrier than she had seen him thus far. Or jealous?

Scarlett swallowed back the lump in her throat. Her tongue darted out to moisten her suddenly dry lips. "It was just a joke."

"'Twas no' amusing."

His lips slanted over hers with a low groan, forcing her head back and compelling her lips to part. This wasn't the tender assault he'd employed before. This was an attack on her senses. Her person. His tongue plunged deeply, rasping across hers. Scarlett's head swam dizzily, blacking out her objections. She stretched against him, her arms winding about his neck of their own accord. Drawing him closer. Urging him on.

This fire between them was downright irresistible.

Scarlett tore hers lips away with a gasp. "This is crazy. I don't even like you."

"I dinnae like ye either, lass."

Tugging up her skirt, Laird slid his hand between her thighs. Scarlett's involuntary squeal was muffled against his lips, but instead of withdrawing, she lifted her leg, hooking it around his thigh. Inviting him in. Laird did not hesitate, stroking her wet folds deftly before dipping his fingers into her pulsing heat.

"I mean, look at us," she stammered. "I'm me. And you're so... *you*."

A gasp of rapture robbed her breath and Scarlett threw back her head to find it, but unrelenting, Laird followed, raking his teeth down her neck. "Ye talk too much," he grumbled.

Tension spiraled almost immediately deep within her core as his fingers continued to circle her sleek, sensitive nub. His touch was rough, unfettered but at the same time, gentle. Her body rocked against his hand as if of its own will, seeking, searching. Building to a poignant ache that emanated outward, tensing. Waiting.

He held her there. Hovering between heaven and hell and an agonized moan escaped her between her panting breaths. "Oh, God," she sobbed, burying her face in his sweaty neck as she clung helplessly to him. Pleading. Then with a cry, Scarlett threw back her head once more as her climax burst brilliantly, painfully. A thousand parts of her body exploded.

Laird cupped her bottom, lifting her against him as he rocked her against the wall. His hard, throbbing length beneath his kilt slid against her naked heat, the wool chafing her already overly sensitized flesh. "I want to be inside ye, lass." His brogue was rough, thick. "I want to hear ye scream as ye did before."

"Oh, God," she moaned again, covering her eyes with both hands as she wiped away the tears she didn't even realize were flowing down her cheeks. She was utterly flabbergasted by what had just happened and he just wanted to hear a repeat of what Scarlett now realized was an utterly incorrect imitation of true rapture? Didn't he realize she had experienced so much more than that? Inexplicable. Unfathomable.

Scarlett peeked from beneath her hands and looked at Laird, his features taut with desire that made him even more dazzling.

Did it matter? Yes, it did.

A firm knock sounded at her door and he stilled, saving her the need to make a hasty decision.

The knock sounded again and with a soft oath, he rested his forehead against hers.

"What is it?" Laird barked before she could answer.

"A bath for Mistress Thomas."

"I might hae to do murder." His lips pressed a warm kiss to her forehead before he released her. Scarlett nearly melted against the wall but managed to get her feet beneath her though her heart was still beating madly. Her skirts dropped back down of their own accord as he turned toward the door.

"Laird?"

He stopped with his hand on the latch and looked back.

"I guess, as far as apologies go, that wasn't *too* bad."

Humor lit his eyes; with a wink he was gone as Graeme entered leading a queue of men and buckets into her room.

18

Good timing or bad?

Scarlett couldn't decide though she'd pondered the question thoroughly over the afternoon and into the next day. Laird's tantalizing lovemaking played over and over in her mind. Silly girl, she berated herself finally. Whatever she was here for it probably wasn't so that she might have the liberty to engage in a clandestine affair with a divine, if somewhat ill-tempered, Scotsman.

Such thoughts weren't like her at all, however Scarlett couldn't deny that beyond the seductive freedom of these anonymous days, there was just something about Laird that drew her, enticed her. Lured her to act in a way that she normally wouldn't. *Couldn't*.

Uninhibited. Spontaneous.

Breathless.

But Scarlett wasn't sure if that was what she wanted. She hadn't lied. Laird was turning out to be more than she had bargained for and because of that, key to getting home or not, she'd avoided being alone with him since then. Avoided making a choice. Did she want nothing more than a fling with Laird? That was all it could be, of course, a casual affair to wait out her temporary situation.

Her stomach began to churn at the thought. Surely, this whole kerfuffle was only temporary, right? A moment with the man of every woman's dreams? Or was it to be a life locked in a nightmare? The two conundrums battled for supremacy at the forefront of her mind.

Tucking both dilemmas aside, Scarlett instead spent a large portion of her time with Aleizia and Aileen, finishing off *The Wizard of Oz* and moving on to *The Sound of Music*. On a lark, she had tried to break down the tale of Joss Whedon's *Firefly* but the concept of space travel had been too absurd for them. Surprisingly though, the young women loved chilling tales of the magic and mysticism so Scarlett had begun telling them a convoluted tale about a ring, a Hobbit and an improbable journey with a wizard named Gandalf.

Aileen especially ate it up and Scarlett was happy to spend time with her. Recognizing almost too easily a young girl starved for attention, affection and friendship. Forced to grow up far too quickly.

It was a rare opportunity to enjoy herself, as well. No one at Crichton with the exception of Lady Ishbel treated her as a captive, nor did they treat her as a thing, a paycheck. The publicized product she had become back home. She hadn't had such fun since before *The Puppet War* began filming.

She especially enjoyed the time she spent with Rhys. He never expected to be entertained. No, he just liked to talk, or rather, make her talk. Talking about herself had never come easily but Rhys had a real talent for pulling it out of her. Sometimes Scarlett wasn't sure he would be satisfied until she had bared her soul completely.

His questions – he truly did ask all the good ones – became more probing as he pried tirelessly into her life until she'd provided him an odd concoction of fiction, half-truths and fairy tales.

She was certain he knew that she was holding back but he didn't seem to care. He seemed to simply enjoy her company as Scarlett did his.

But this morning, he'd tried to pull perhaps one secret too many. Looking for answers to questions she didn't want to talk about, things she wouldn't talk about and things she couldn't talk about.

Her life.

Dunskirk.

Laird.

Where she hadn't yet felt the need to escape Laird or Crichton, it was those questions that finally compelled her to run. At least for a while.

$$\times \quad \times \quad \times \quad \times \quad \times$$

"What are you still doing here, bastard?"

Passing beneath an open window of keep as she tried to find her way out of the castle, there was no way Scarlett could miss the disdainful query. She recognized Lady Ishbel's malevolent tone well enough. Her spiteful epithet could have been directed at only a few people. Sure enough, it was Laird who answered. "I am here at yer bidding, my lady. Did ye no' summon me to this room?"

A low feminine hiss followed by, "You know my meaning. I demand you leave Crichton at once. You're not welcome here."

"Upon my father's invitation, I am," Laird said flatly. "And I will await him here to address the coming war and the fate of my captive."

"Captive? Bah! You bring your harlot into my home under such a ridiculous pretense? Do you think I don't know everything that occurs in this castle? I won't have it," Lady Ishbel spat out so viciously that Scarlett cringed even though she wasn't in the line of fire. A harlot was she?

"Ye willnae insult the lass." Laird's voice was as ominous as Scarlett had ever heard it. A thrill shot through her as he came to her defense. "She is a lady born, madam."

"Bah! My error was in assuming the same. She is no lady," Lady Ishbel insisted, maliciously. "Do you think the servants would not comment on your presence in her chamber yester morn?"

"Did they comment upon mine as well, Mother?" Rhys's voice joined the pair. Unexpectedly, given the long silence that followed. He continued, "'Tis naught worth gossiping over this day nor any other. I would chastise yer servants for spreading such rumors and leave Laird be."

"Leave him be?" Lady Ishbel spat out, clearly unwilling to let the matter rest.

"She is a lady true, madam," Laird continued more calmly yet there was resolve in his tone, "and due all the courtesy of her station. She will hae it, am I understood?"

"You dare to command me?"

"I do and upon my honor, ye will regret crossing me in this."

There was a quiet moment. Scarlett could just imagine Lady Ishbel seeing that particular look in Laird's eyes and cowing before it. Even the devil would hesitate before gainsaying him when he had that look.

"I shall be glad to see you gone," Lady Ishbel hissed. "By God's grace, you will find a place in hell and never return."

Scarlett gasped at the woman's viciousness and even Rhys protested. "Mother, enough! Laird has ne'er had more than a respectful word for ye. Would that ye could treat him in kind and let us all be at peace."

"I will never treat this bastard kindly. I want him out of my home!"

"When I hae words wi' mine father and mine uncle, I will depart Crichton and no' before," Laird said tightly.

"Your uncle?" Lady Ishbel snarled. "You dare claim connection to the king? You vile bastard, you... Argh!" The epithets ended in the slam of a door and the lady's screech of frustration, telling Scarlett more clearly than words that Laird and Rhys had left Lady Ishbel to spew her venom in solitude.

Even with the woman's spiteful glances upon their arrival and her insulting assumptions, Scarlett never imagined that Lady Ishbel felt such animosity toward her husband's son. As if Laird were the one to blame.

Turning away, she found her way to the open portcullis and out of the castle, heading toward the small village she had spotted upon her arrival to Crichton.

It was just so wrong. Sympathy for Laird washed over her. Had he had to deal with such open malice his entire life? Still he treated Lady Ishbel with nothing but respect in public. Even in private, he had been civil. Until Lady Ishbel had cast aspersions on Scarlett, that is.

Underneath that stoic, warrior-like exterior was a good man. A patient one. More patient than some deserved. She could do worse in a captor.

You could do worse in a man, her inner devil teased.

With a sigh, Scarlett shook the thought off and focused on

183

the village ahead. It wasn't large, just a few dozen small stone cottages roofed in sod. The short grass growing there undulated hypnotically in the light breeze, soothing her troubled thoughts. The smoke billowing from the chimneys smelled like burning dung. Peat, she supposed, but mingled in with it was the scent of savory food, meat that twisted Scarlett's empty stomach with envy this time reminding her that she'd eaten little at dinner.

She did not feel such a sentiment for the inhabitants of the village. Alas, no one wanted to go to the renaissance fair as a peasant. Men, women and children moved in and out of the buildings, laboring over their work or bearing large bundles on their backs. They were clothed in simple tunics and dresses made with rough fabrics in muted colors. Most wore long caps on their heads.

For the first time, history intrigued her. Probably because it was living and breathing right in front of her. It was a captivating picture. She was seeing something historians from her time might envision and hypothesize about but would never see for themselves. Life how it really was. Castles could be preserved, but all of this was gone forever.

Determined to get a closer look, Scarlett lengthened her stride but a strong hand caught her around the upper arm and yanked her to a halt. Scarlett cried out in surprise. Turning, she found Laird glaring down at her, and as her sharp spike of fear faded, she glared right back at him and slapped his hand away. "Sweet baby Jesus, Laird! You almost gave me a heart attack. You can't just sneak up on people like that."

"I dinnae sneak up on ye. Ye simply dinnae hear me. What are ye aboot, lass?"

"I was just going to the village."

He shook his head. "There is a pox in the village," he

explained quickly, as if he knew she meant to argue.

"A pox? Which pox?"

"Small," he answered and Scarlett shuddered at the thought, looking back on the inhabitants of the village. Though she couldn't see it from a distance, it seemed many of them were sick and perhaps dying from a disease that had been eradicated in her time. Scarlett looked up at Laird to find him still watching her inquisitively.

"Will they die?"

"No' all of them."

Not all of them. As if were just a fact of life. Lord, what kind of world was she living in? Moments ago it had all seemed so innocent and untouched. She hadn't even noticed the scars though they were right on the surface.

Laird steered her away and Scarlett followed without a fight. It would do no good to try to explain to him about inoculations and immunities and not a bit of good to walk where she could bring no aid. However, she didn't necessarily want to go back to the castle where there was nothing to do but think of him. Or people who somehow managed to turn her attention back to him just when she managed to cleave him from her thoughts.

James could feel her grief as if it were his own when her usually bold voice withered to a child-like quiver of compassion. She was more softhearted than he had given her credit for.

He had just returned to the lists when Scarlett hurried by. The impending war itself couldn't have stopped him from following her. When he had realized where she was heading, he'd had to stop her.

To warn her, he reasoned.

To simply see her, he realized.

Just a day had passed since he'd last seen her, yet somehow he missed her. A day passed since he held her in his arms, still he wanted nothing more than to hold her again. He was in no mood to return her to the castle where she might easily avoid him again. Instead, he turned and lead her toward the river that twisted around the castle. "Ye've been avoiding me, lass."

"No, I haven't." He lifted a brow. "Okay, maybe I have."

"Why?"

Questions like that weren't going to make being outside the castle any better than the inside. "I don't want to talk about it."

"Would ye talk aboot it wi' Rhys?"

Startled, Scarlett looked up. There was a tautness to his expression, a flare in his eyes. "What do you mean?"

"Ye talk wi' him for hours at a time." She hadn't seen him all day but he must have been around if he had noticed that.

"I like him. He's easy to talk to."

"And I'm no'?"

An incredulous laugh gurgled low in her throat but Scarlett swallowed it back. He wouldn't like it if he thought she was laughing at him. "No, you're definitely not. I can hardly think around you much less hold a normal conversation," she admitted and realized it was true. For the most part, his presence either flustered or irritated her. Besides being a man of few words, Laird was too intense, too disturbing to allow for normal thought processes or casual dialogue.

Moreover, the little time she spent in his company wasn't being passed verbally.

"Ye think too much."

"I thought you said I talk too much."

He didn't smile but Scarlett could feel his mien lighten as they reached the shady bank of the Tyne River. Laird dropped down on the grassy riverbank and pulled the long length of plaid from over his shoulder, spreading it out on the ground next to him. Then he removed his sword and laid it down next to him as if it were a line of truce between them. A symbol of peace. Scarlett sank down on the woolen cloth, appreciative of his courtesy.

"Why does Lady Ishbel seem to hate you so much?" she asked tentatively, testing the waters of conversation.

Lifting a brow, Laird only contributed a question of his own. "Ye overheard that, did ye?"

Tepid at best. He certainly wasn't helping! Pulling conversation from her stony Scot was like trying to take pie away from Dean Winchester.

"Yes. I'm sorry. I was just walking by and happened to pass beneath the window," she explained. "Thank you for defending me as you did, by the way. Even though she was right. Not the harlot part, of course, but I am not a lady in the sense you intend it."

"Aye, ye are, regardless of yer occupation," Laird covered her hand with his and squeezed before drawing away. "I hae been as guilty as she for no' treating ye as such."

Scarlett didn't know quite what to say to that. She supposed he was referring to their times together but couldn't find it in herself to hold that against him.

Silence fell over them like a shadow. Then he spoke quietly, "Lady Ishbel spews her hatred upon me because she cannae expel it on the one person she believes deserves her wrath the most."

"Your father?"

Laird shook his head. "Nay, my mother."

Doubly a bastard. Vaguely she recalled Rhys saying something more about it but couldn't remember it all now. "Who was she?"

Laird picked up a handful of pebbles, tossing one after another into the creek's swiftly moving waters. "'Tis no secret, really. My mother was the auld King's bastard, Lady Mary Stewart."

Oh, that's right.

"She was born just nine months after the King's marriage to Margaret of Denmark. 'Twas rumored to be quite the scandal when the Queen might hae born the King his first child if he had only kept to their marriage bed."

"How did your father meet her?" Scarlett couldn't resist asking. A part of her wanted to know more.

"Father met Lady Mary long before his marriage to Lady Ishbel. Long before their betrothal even. I've heard from some at court that they were much in love and wished to wed. The King even supported the match but Father's father, the auld Earl of Bothwell, forged a betrothal for him wi' Lady Ishbel. Her dowry from her sire, the Earl of Errol, was quite large, ye see. For all that he loved and spoiled Lady Mary, the auld King wisnae willing to dower her so. So Father wed wi' Lady Ishbel even knowing Lady Mary was already swelling wi' his child."

With him. "How sad for her. Your mother, I mean."

His shoulder lifted in a dismissive shrug. "'Twould no' hae mattered in any case. Lady Mary died no' long after birthing me and the auld King shortly thereafter."

"Still, I feel for your mother, losing the man she loves," she said then added, "I suppose I can sort of understand

Lady Ishbel's position, too, bless her heart. It couldn't have been easy for her knowing her husband only wanted her for her money. That she was your father's second choice."

"That's no' why she hates me, lass," he said, looking down at her, his silvery eyes shimmering beneath his thick brows.

"It's not?"

"Nay, Lady Ishbel hated my mother for giving my father his firstborn son," he explained. "She hates me because I might hae been his heir. Mayhap because she suspects I should be."

Scarlett shook her head confusedly. "What do you mean? I thought illegitimate children couldn't inherit titles."

"They cannae," he said. "But my father once told a tale… Och, he was drunk. This I ken, but there are times when I wonder if it is true and Lady Ishbel knows."

"What?"

"My father claimed to hae wed secretly wi' Lady Mary ere I was born. 'Ere he wed wi' Lady Ishbel," he explained. "If it were true, I would be his heir and all her children would be the bastards."

"Oh." Scarlett's eyes widened at his confession. Yes, she could definitely see why Lady Ishbel might hate him then. Why she would feel the need to constantly remind him of his place, just to assure herself that it was the truth even if it wasn't. What a soap opera. "No wonder she doesn't want you around now."

"No' just now," Laird corrected. "Upon her insistence, Father kept me at court as a bairn. It wasn't until I fostered wi' the Earl of Drummond as a lad that I met Patrick and Rhys. Lady Ishbel dinnae ken that Father fostered us all to him so that we might grow up together."

"You don't resent them? Knowing that all they have might

actually be yours?"

"Nay. 'Struth I dinnae envy them a'tall. They are good men all, my brothers, but subject to Lady Ishbel's wishes where I am no'."

"They care for you very much, you know." Laird's brothers gave him all the respect Lady Ishbel did not. Rhys especially was very protective of him.

Laird shrugged again. "Mayhap. I dinnae see Patrick often as his mother often calls him home and I am rarely here at Crichton. After Drummond, I was squire to the Auld King's second son, the Duke of Ross, until he was made Archbishop of St. Andrews. Rhys went to court to serve as a squire for the King. I did battle in France whilst Rhys cut the King's meat."

All because he wasn't completely welcome at Crichton. What a sad childhood. Compassion for Laird flooded her. It sounded like a rather lonely life. Something Scarlett understood all too well.

"Now ye ken all there is to know about me, lass," he said. "I think the time has come to learn more aboot ye. Ye cannae avoid my questions forever. I hae nae forgotten where I found ye. Who are ye, lass? More importantly, I need to discover how ye came to be in my holding. Why were ye at Dunskirk?"

A pinpoint of cold prickled against her arm and a shudder racked her body as her dread over those first few questions froze in her veins. "Dunskirk?"

"My keep," he said, tossing the last of his pebbles into the water and dusting off his hands. "Ye should kent the place well enough, lass. Since it is where we found ye. Why were ye there?"

Another icy prick. Scarlett shivered as her vision

darkened. Stretching her fingers outward, she slid them over the blade of his Claymore, finding the steel warm to the touch. What was going on here? "You *own* Dunskirk Castle?"

"Castle? 'Tis little more than a pele tower, but aye, 'twas gifted to me by the auld king. I've told ye this before."

He hadn't said it was Dunskirk he owned, had he? Now, his link to her future was stronger than just the sword beneath her fingertips. All the years she had spent there while filming! It had been as much a home to her as it was to him.

Her bare skin tingled again. And again. Scarlett looked up at the dark clouds overhead. Not a metaphorical shadow then, but a real one. She hadn't paid them much attention with the sky to the north so clear.

More drops fell, splashing on her nose and chin.

"Shouldn't we get out of the rain?"

Laird looked up at the sky and shook his head. "No' for a mere sprinkle. Now, dinnae change the subject, lass. Answer me true."

The rain might have taken that as a challenge. Big, fat drops fell. Faster, harder. Within minutes, Scarlett would be drenched and cold if she continued to sit there. "Laird!"

"It will pass quickly, lass. Dinnae fash yerself."

"I'm a sweet, southern belle, Laird," she drawled tightly, fruitlessly covering her head with her arms. "Pure sugar melts easily, you know?"

His shoulders heaved. Was he laughing at her? Probably. But without comment, he scooped her into his arms as she squawked in surprise and carried her to the cover of the beech trees, depositing her beneath their dense branches. She was still getting wet though and as if he knew another complaint was lurking, Laird dropped down beside her and flung the long length of his kilt around her. With a forearm, he tented the wool over her head and held her close.

"Is that better?"

His questions had been put aside for the moment. So there was that to be thankful for but when Scarlett looked up at him looming over her, so close, she was incredibly aware of his powerful body. Warm, wet and masculine, his presence was surrounding her.

No, that was definitely not better.

Exhaling slowly, she tried in vain to forestall her racing pulse. She couldn't even remember what they had been talking about. Or why she'd been avoiding him. All she could recall was the memory of his lips on her, his mouth on her body, his fingers playing her so skillfully. Wide-eyed, she looked up at him only to find him looking down at her.

He had a smolder Flynn Rider would envy.

The temperature rose. Hot. Steaming. Charged. Still goose bumps spread across her flesh. Scarlett bit her lip and his gaze fell.

He was so close. His breaths no more even than hers.

"Laird."

What was she doing? Again?

Laird's fingers tickled the shell of her ear, sending a shiver skittering through her. Scarlett inhaled raggedly. It was so warm beneath the plaid, his body next to hers so powerful, so electrifying. A shiver of anticipation raced through her as his calloused fingertips trailed down her neck.

He tilted her face to his. So much for conversation.

What is it about you that I simply can't resist?

19

He kissed her.

James wouldn't have been able to stifle the urge to do so if his very life had depended on it. Deep down he knew he should leave her be, avoid her as she had been avoiding him. She was a lady at heart and due more respect, just as he had told Ishbel.

But bluidy hell, her kiss was a seductive thing. Headier than the finest whiskey and far more intoxicating. The sweetness of her lips haunted him. Her unleashed passions tormented him since the previous morning. He wanted to be the one to incite her passions, to make her scream. Her fervent whimpers and rapturous moans echoed in his ears until possessing her was all he could think about.

And Scarlett! She had done naught but go about her business. Och, she didn't know the torture she had inflicted upon him. She laughed with his sister when he could do nothing but grimace. Talked endlessly with his brother while he gnashed his teeth in frustration.

All to abide by his father's wishes. Well, enough of that.

Never had he felt a lust so strong. Never had he wanted beyond his own will. All thought, all logic had fled. James knew he could not trust her. He didn't know who she was or what she wanted from them.

But he knew what he wanted of her. What he had to have.

Twisting her about, James lowered her onto her back, never breaking their kiss. She welcomed him, parting her lips. Parrying her tongue playfully with his. Encouraging him with provocative noises wrested from deep in her throat. Her arms wrapped around his neck pulling him closer but he wanted more than the taste of her lips. Tugging down her bodice, James cupped her breast, rolling her nipple between his fingers. Her gasp of delight was like an angel's chorus to his ears. Her skin soft as the finest silk. His lips trailed down her neck, tasting salt, rain and woman until he reached her breast and drew her hardened nipple between his lips, sucking deeply.

Her cry urged him on, her fingers tangling in his hair. Pulling him closer.

James gathered up her skirt. She wore no petticoats, no hose. It was just his flesh against hers. Her thighs fell apart with little hesitance. James dipped his fingers between them and was welcomed by hot moisture. Already she was weeping for him. She clung to his shoulders, biting his neck as his fingers circled the opening. Her cry of delight muffled against him.

Her open, unfettered desire, stoked his all the hotter. No pretense, no coy advance and retreat. She simply wanted him as much as he wanted her.

He trailed a finger up between her nether lips, circling the nub of her desire. She cried out hoarsely again, locking her legs around his hand.

"No," she cried, pushing his hand away and James felt his disappointment like a weight around his heart. His arousal was so painful he wasn't sure how he could walk away from her again but he could not, would not force her. For all his savage ways, he was a courtier still.

Bracing his arms, James lifted away from her but to his amazement, Scarlett followed, pushing him on to his back and rolling on top of him until she was straddling him. She looked down at him. Her brown eyes were dark, hot as coals as she panted heavily, shaking her head even as she stroked his chest invitingly.

Then she kissed him. Hot. Open-mouthed. Taking control, surprising him. Never had he been so challenged by a woman. He was aflame with the need to plunge within her heavenly body. To ravish her with all the primordial hunger burning within him. Her hips undulated, grinding her heated core against his rampant staff. Her hands spread over his chest and moved downward until she reached between them and grasped his erection.

Their moans intermingled. Her pleasure. His.

He flipped her beneath him, showing her just how dominating, how masculine he was as he held himself above her. Then he shifted downward, his hard chest grazing over her breasts and belly until he was cradled between her thighs. His fingers sought her heat once more, curling into her as he moved downward to trail kisses and bite at the tender flesh of her moist, quivering thighs.

Scarlett gasped and tensed. Alternately tugging at his hair to pull him away and grasping him closer as if she alternately welcomed and dreaded what was to come.

In the shadows beneath his plaid, James paused, studying

her while she squirmed in anticipation. "Laird!"

With a groan of surrender, James buried his face between her legs. Scarlett arced off the ground with a cry of ecstasy. His passionate lass coming almost immediately as his lips closed around her. His blood roared in his ears but still he circled her with his tongue, draining every last throb from her until she was begging for him to stop, weeping in her surrender.

Primal satisfaction surged through him when there should be shame. She was his captive, his responsibility. He should never have touched her, never coerced her into this but now that he had her beneath him only the pain of death could have separated him. Scarlett tried to close her thighs and roll away but James forced them apart once more and bent his head to taste her again. For all her teasing words, she was as sweet as fine sugar. She tensed, her hips retreating before arching upward. "No, no," she moaned.

"Aye."

James teased her gently with the tip of his tongue, her still pulsating opening drawing him inward. He thrust his tongue deeply then withdrew, savoring her hoarse, rapturous scream. One finger, then two. He pushed inside her scalding depths as he tormented her with his tongue. Her thighs quivered as he pushed her to the brink, then retreated only to push her higher once more until she begging for release once more.

Never had he known any woman so impassioned, receptive. A woman who might wring him dry before he even possessed her body. His raging body screamed for satisfaction, but still he denied himself for the pure joy of watching his lass soar again to the gates of paradise. He could do this all day.

"Please, please! Laird!"

Ah, never had that sobriquet sounded so good as it did when torn from her lips. James suckled her throbbing nub and finally gave her the release she was begging for. Her muscles contracting strongly around his fingers as she came, hot and liquid.

He imagined her milking his rod just so and nearly spilt himself at the thought. "Lass?" The question was pained. He wasn't sure what he would do if she denied him again.

"Oh God. *Yes.*"

This time there was no hesitation.

$$\times \quad \times \quad \times \quad \times \quad \times$$

A horn blasted through the silent forest, startling them both but Scarlett relaxed almost immediately, lifting her legs high around his hips. "Laird?" She nudged him with her heels as one might spur a horse into action.

Her hot hands found their way beneath his kilt, grasping his arse in her hands. "Aye, lass." James bent his head and took her lips again as she lifted his kilt out of the way. His hard length brushed against her bare thigh and upward, toward her scorching, inviting heat.

The trumpet sounded again. Three times.

Ah, bluidy, fookin' hell!

"What's wrong?" Scarlett whispered, her soft panting against his ear sending a shudder of pure lust raking through him. Every fiber of his being demanded James ignore the call but he could not. Not for long. Not long enough to finish this properly. And he did want to do it properly and without a rush.

"My apologies, *mo chroí*," he murmured, brushing his lips against her ear. "We maun go."

"Now?" Her sweet voice was incredulous with regret. It gladdened him to know that she was no more pleased by the interruption than he.

"'Tis the King's herald, lass."

"And that's more important than *this*?"

"Upon my honor, no one is more saddened by the fact than I."

With one last kiss, he leapt to his feet, throwing the trailing end of his plaid back over his shoulder. Retrieving his sword, he helped Scarlett to her feet and took her hand in his as he gestured to the north.

Scarlett followed his arm. To her surprise, she could make out what did look to be an army bearing down on Crichton. Bannerman at the front of the brigade were visible, even at a distance.

"Come we maun make haste."

Subdued by the sight, Scarlett followed him back to the castle staying close to his side as they entered the keep.

20

"Lift yer arms, please, mistress."

Peigi was one of the three maids on hand to help her, Aileen and Aleizia 'prepare' themselves for supper, dressing for the affair in a fashion Scarlett was quickly realizing was far more ceremonial than the formality she had already witnessed in this time.

To meet the King.

Despite the gravity of the occasion, it was still a tantalizing and thankfully distracting thought. Meeting Queen Elizabeth once a few years back had been one of the most nerve-wracking moments in her life but the occasion hadn't had this sort of pomp.

To think, it had taken a five hundred year leap backwards to experience it.

If they were to ever get there. Dressing, so simple that morning, had become a process proving that she had been wrong before. This wasn't *Braveheart* or a renaissance fair. This was *The Tudors* but with far more layers.

Oddly enough, their stockings and shoes had gone on first, when usually they were the last thing Scarlett donned. Then a fresh chemise of fine linen, petticoats – one, two, three – and then the farthingale. They'd had to tell her what it was called since Scarlett had labeled it a hoop skirt. A half-remembered image was forming her mind and she could begin to imagine where this was all going.

Then the corset, but this wasn't the kind of corset she was familiar with, one that strove toward an hourglass figure. Besides flattening her breasts, this one squared her out from chest to hip. From there down it was all about width and volume. Now, she lifted her arms – again – while Peigi added a thick roll around her hips. "What is this called?"

"A bumroll, mistress."

Why not? "Of course it is."

Next came a ruffled gold lace parlett that would cover her shoulders and bosom modestly beneath the low neckline of her gown, then the underskirt. It was a bronze silk that was pleated into a diamond pattern with a tiny topaz sewn in at each point. Finally came the gown itself. Lush bronze velvet edged with woven gold embroidered trim and strings of pearls and topaz. More of the same draped across the bodice. It laced up the back, allowing for a tight fit, which was a good thing since even twelve-year old Aileen had more going for her up top than Scarlett did. The skirt parted in the front to show the underskirt beneath. The hems on both had been let out but still only reached Scarlett's ankles. The long draping sleeves were lined with the same silk as the underskirt.

Unlike *The Tudors*, there would be no heaving bosoms and bare shoulders in this gown. She was covered and bound securely. Thankfully the day had not been too hot, but she would likely lose ten pounds in water-weight sweating under so many layers.

Finally a matching, jewel-encrusted French hood covered her pixie cut, curving over her head from ear to ear with all the heft of the Crown Jewels.

"You look just lovely, Scarlett," Aleizia enthused as she sat motionless at her vanity. One of the other maids was braiding, looping and weaving her long blond hair into an impossible configuration. It made Scarlett glad that she didn't have the length of hair needed to be tortured so.

"Do you like the dress, Scarlett?" Aileen asked. She was all ready to go, and clearly excited as she danced from foot to foot anxiously.

"I do like it. It's very beautiful. And very heavy." She felt royal and wished there was a full-length mirror so that she could see the whole outfit. It was certainly a weighty feeling, she thought, grinning at her pun.

Scarlett ran her palms down the rich velvet, wondering if Laird would think she looked pretty. Ugh! She was gushing like a schoolgirl. You'd think she'd never orgasmed before.

"Thank you for letting me borrow it. You look beautiful too," she told Aileen. It was true. Aileen looked almost grown up in an even more heavily decorated gown of blue silk covered with pearls and with sleeves trimmed with fur that draped nearly to the floor.

Aleizia was also in blue, though hers was a darker shade that complimented her blue eyes. Done with Scarlett, Peigi placed a matching French hood upon Aleizia's head seemed to frame her hairdo like a piece of art from the back. She could have been a queen. "Your hair is just amazing."

Aleizia patted her hair with a satisfied smile. "Our Lady Mother has a very fine wig, if you'd like to wear it."

Scarlett shook her head with a laugh. "That's okay. I'm

good."

A trumpet sounded and Scarlett's heart leapt with giddy excitement. For the first time since arriving in this time, she was completely devoid of worry and the anxiety of her predicament. Right now, it was all about joy and pleasure, and she meant to embrace it. More openly, Aileen clapped her hands, the long ropes of pearls she wore swung from side to side as she leapt up from her chair as did her long, unbound hair. Even Aleizia could hardly hold still as Peigi hurriedly slipped several long strings of pearls over her head as well.

"Come, Scarlett," she cried, grasping Scarlett's hand and tugging her out of the room.

Laird was waiting for them at the bottom of the stairs. Without his kilt, he looked like a completely different person than the rugged Scot Scarlett had become familiar with. More severe, more stoic but for the molten desire still warming his gaze. His dark blue velvet doublet was subdued, modestly quilted and embroidered with black threads. Beneath it he wore a more tailored kilt of navy and red plaid. He wore thick matching hose beneath it and embroidered leather shoes. A short, matching cape was flung over his shoulders and a heavy-looking sporran was slung low on his hips.

If he hadn't still managed to radiate pure masculine sexuality, Scarlett might have been hard pressed not to laugh at the sight of him with those jeweled garters above his knees.

"You look good," she said with a slow nod, as she looked him up and down. He did. She especially liked how having his shaggy hair clubbed back accentuated his gorgeous face. He'd trimmed his beard close as well, drawing attention to his squared jaw. "You can't be comfortable though."

Laird smiled and inclined his head. "Nae more than ye, I'd wager."

He passed soft greetings and compliments on to Aileen and Aleizia but his eyes strayed in her direction once more.

"Ladies!"

Rhys and Patrick appeared at Laird's side. While Patrick was as soberly dressed as Laird, Rhys was more flamboyantly attired in a jewel-encrusted crimson doublet and matching skirt instead of a kilt. The sleeves of his doublet were slashed to reveal gold silk beneath. His black cape was heavily embroidered and lined with the same gold silk. The colors reflected in his shoes and hose.

"My dear sisters, my dearest Scarlett," he swept an extravagant bow, pulling a matching velvet cap off his head. "Yer all a vision to behold."

Aileen giggled, but bobbed a curtsey, as did Aleizia. Scarlett tried to bite back a laugh but it was hard to keep a straight face with a guy who dressed like that. "I gotta say it, Rhys. You are rocking that doublet like nobody's business."

All four of them looked at her quizzically and Scarlett laughed merrily. "It's a good thing. Trust me."

"Father awaits. Shall we go?" Patrick asked.

Rhys nodded and offered his sister his arm while Patrick towed his young wife away leaving Scarlett alone with Laird in the empty stairwell. Her pulse fluttered under his steady gaze.

"What is it? Do I look okay?"

"Ye've covered yer ears," he murmured, cupping his hand around the back of her neck. His thumb swept upward beneath her hood to tickle her lobe and the air in the stairwell rose by more than a few degrees.

So Laird had an ear fetish, did he? "Should I take it off?" she asked, suppressing a delicious shudder.

"Nay, but mayhap I can take it off ye later?"

So that they could finish what they had already started, was his unspoken implication. "Maybe. If you're nice."

"I can be verra nice. In fact, here." His husky brogue shivered along her spine, sending a reverberation of desire and anticipation through her. A reminder of their truncated interlude. He held out his other hand to reveal a spill of pearls and golden topaz. "I thought ye might like to wear these tonight. I thought they might match yer eyes, but I suppose they will match yer gown as well," he told her, holding it out by the ends to show her the necklace, loops of pearls meeting at a topaz as large as a robin's egg with more pearls and smaller topaz dangling along the way.

"It's stunning. Thank you."

"'Twas a gift to my mother from auld King James. Obviously 'tis just a loan."

"Of course, but it is sweet of you." And surprising. "Do you treat all your captives this way?"

Laird looked disgruntled by her teasing and shrugged. "No' all my captives join the King's table. Nae lady should go into battle wi'out the proper armor."

Obediently she rotated so that he could clasp it around her throat. Her hand lifted reflexively to cover the jewels and felt her heart racing beneath her hand as his warm fingers tickled the back of her neck. "How do I look?" she asked shakily, feeling more confident of the answer than she had been the previous morning. Well-armed, indeed!

"Like heaven," he whispered, his lips grazing a

hairsbreadth below her covered ear.

"You didn't even look," she protested, turning to face him.

"Yer a bonny lass, as ye well know." She quivered as his finger traced a path up the side of her neck, feeling the truth in his words right down to the toes of her borrowed shoes. Never in her life, her career had she been covered in so many layers, concealed from head to toe and yet made to feel so beautiful.

Something had shifted in his attitude in just a matter of hours. What? How? She didn't know but that change sent her heart thrumming. She really wasn't thinking this through.

"Cease yer dallying," Rhys hissed, sticking his head into the stairwell. "King James is nigh approaching!"

21

"*That* is your king?"

Amazing.

"This is nae time to be yerself, Scarlett. Ye dinnae dare offer him insult."

"I'm not insulting him, but I'm just saying." To make him happy and not ruin the good mood between them, Scarlett kept her other thoughts to herself.

James Stewart was an inconspicuous looking guy. He might have been Laird's blood uncle, but there was nothing about him that bespoke a genetic resemblance. No taller than she, lanky though richly dressed, the King didn't have any of the presence she had come to associate with royalty. He had long dark hair cut straight at his shoulders and across his forehead. Scarlett had seen the hairstyle in old portraits but hadn't really thought anyone actually wore their hair like that.

King James made slow progress through the great hall, nodding here, lifting a hand there. Everyone in the crowded room pressed forward to greet him, shake his hand or merely get a glimpse of him. He worked the room with an ease Scarlett envied.

Here was the A-List superstar of the time. Everyone was looking at him. None of them were looking at her. Any curiosity the castle's inhabitants had felt about her in the preceding days was gone and she savored the novelty of having not a single set of eyes upon her. Scarlett didn't begrudge him the attention in the least.

Well, perhaps one but she didn't mind that single admiring gaze today at all.

"Are we going to meet him?" she asked Laird.

"Nay, no' today." His eyes dimmed. "Is it something ye were hoping for?"

Scarlett shrugged. "No, not really. Just excited. There's just something about getting all dressed up, you know? I've always loved that part of it."

"It?" he asked curiously but Scarlett just shook her head.

"Who are all these people?"

"Retainers of the King, his traveling companions and counsel," Laird told her. "My father, Sir William, is at the King's side."

She would have realized it the moment she had seen Sir William even if Laird hadn't said a word. It was like a glimpse of what Laird would look like in the years to come. Unlike Lady Ishbel who was aging poorly, Sir William for all his fifty years was still a vital, striking man.

Perhaps she could see now why he managed to have so many illegitimate children. Women probably had a hard time keeping their hands off of him. Except Ishbel, who managed somehow to give the impression that she was avoiding him even as she stood right by his side. Instead, she was fawning over the King who seemed not to notice as he gave all of his attention to a gorgeous, dark-eyed woman on his other side.

"Is that the Queen?"

"The Queen remains at Linlithgow I heard," Laird told her.

"Then who is that?"

Laird only took her arm and steered her after the throng of people who followed the King's party into the dining hall. More tables had been added as the crowd present for supper far exceeded that at dinner but the King and the other noble visitors paraded immediately to the high table along with the Hepburns. The benches below began to fill.

"Come share a trencher with me, Scarlett," Aileen invited, capturing her hand and tugging her toward seats just below the high table.

Lady Ishbel caught her eye then glanced down at the jewels around Scarlett's neck. Her eyes burned with green flames. Scarlett could almost envision the green fog gathering around Lady Ishbel, all she lacked was a raven on her shoulder to make the picture complete.

"Sorry, Aileen, I think it would be better if I sat down here."

With the little people. Scarlett had heard of seating by rank and would never have thought they took it so seriously but at the moment she was glad they did. The high table was the last place she wanted to be.

"Can I sit with you then?" Aileen asked in a small voice. "I don't want to be a burden."

A glance at the high table told Scarlett that Lady Ishbel was again occupied with the King and unlikely to take a headcount of her children, so Scarlett nodded her agreement as Laird found them a place far along one of the long benches, scooting down to make room for her young friend.

A richly robed man seated near King James made a lengthy, solemn blessing over the food. In Latin, Scarlett thought. When he finished at last, the conversation picked up once more, filling the cavernous room with an overwhelming din.

A young gentleman on Aileen's other side would share a trencher with her, leaving Scarlett to share with Laird.

"Thank you," she said when he poured her a goblet of wine.

"Bread?" he asked, in a low husky voice. "I ken it's yer favorite."

"How did you know that?"

A shrug answered her. He thoughtfully served her salmon and tattie scones along with a thick slice of bread but kept the other meats on the far side of the trencher. While she wasn't a vegetarian, strictly speaking, she tended to avoid most red meats because of their fat content. She was surprised Laird had taken note.

"Who's that next to the King?"

"That's the King's mistress, Janet Kennedy," Aileen told her when Laird again declined to answer. "She's why the Queen isn't here."

"Sweeting, ye shouldnae ken such things," Laird scolded, frowning at her over Scarlett's head.

"I know more than you think I might, Laird!" She poked her tongue out at him surprising Scarlett with her sudden spunk.

Laird only grimaced. "Then ye shouldnae speak of them."

"Is it true?" Scarlett asked him and continued when he nodded shortly, "Then let her be. She not hurting anyone if it's common knowledge."

The two women shared a grin before Aileen continued, lowering her voice. "She is by far his most enduring mistress to date. They've three children together already though it is rumored that the King is not the only one who enjoys her favors."

Laird groaned, shaking his head. "Sweeting," he released a long-suffering sigh.

"Now, that sounds like pure speculation," Scarlett chided gently. "Rumors can hurt if they were spread with malicious intent." *Believe me, I know.* "Tell me about the others up there. Who are they?"

Farther along the table were three handsome boys in their late teens and early twenties who bore the Hepburn stamp clearly.

"Those are my other brothers, Alexander, Arthur and Adam who just returned with Father. That one over there," she poked a finger out quickly, "is our cousin Adam, the Earl of Bothwell, his wife, Lady Agnes. Did you know she is a bastard as well? Her father is the Earl of Buchan. No, it's true! How did you say? Common knowledge. Over there is our uncle, Sir Adam of Craggis; our uncle, George who is the Abbott of Arbath and the King's Lord High Treasurer; our aunt, Margaret and her husband, the Earl of Glencairn and over there is…"

The list went on, impossibly including more Margarets, Patricks and Adams than any one family should have. Aunts, uncles, cousins. The Hepburn family needed a different baby name book. There was no chance of remembering one Margaret from the next.

Scarlett nodded as the list concluded with a rundown of the noble earls of Angus, Huntly and Home that were also present with their wives. "And that other man? The one speaking to Rhys?"

Aileen looked suddenly downcast. "That is Robert

Sutherland. He is my betrothed."

Scarlett nearly choked on her tattie and reached for her wine. Catching Laird's eye, she cast him a quizzical look but he only nodded grimly. The man had to have been thirty years older than Aileen. A paunchy, balding and humorless looking man. "That's your fiancé?"

Aileen nodded miserably. "We are to be married by Michaelmas. He is the Earl of Sutherland. Mother says I should be happy to be a countess. That I will outrank her one day."

"Are you?"

"I shall be his third wife," Aileen explained without answering the question. "He has a son already to carry on his title one day." She looked up again, quickly glancing away with a blush and Scarlett followed her gaze to a nice looking, ginger-haired boy of about twenty sitting across the U from them.

"That's his son?"

"Yes, that's Dickie. I mean, Lord Richard."

Aileen had seemed to have lost her appetite and Scarlett felt bad for unknowingly bringing up what was obviously a sore subject. How horrible to have to marry a man so much older than herself when she was obviously infatuated with the man's son. Clearly, he felt the same. How tragically Oedipal.

Wasn't there something someone could do?

Probably not. It was a pretty messed up family dynamic.

It broke her heart to think of it. Scarlett hated to know that the girl had such a dismal future awaiting her.

"Don't worry, Aileen. I'm sure it will all work out in the end," Scarlett said, patting the girl's hand. "You never know what the future will bring."

"I don't think there is anything that can change this. I

doubt the future will bring me the love I desire."

Scarlett looked up at Laird. He was as solemn as usual but there was that new, incessant heat in his eyes.

"Perhaps a bit of magic might pick you up and drop you into another place and time," she said. "I've heard it can happen."

"Like it did with Dorothy?" Aileen asked, perking up enough for a twinkle to appear in her bright blue eyes and a smile to deepen her dimples.

Like it did with me.

× × × × ×

A small group of minstrels armed with two flutes, a lute, a psaltery and a Scottish hurdy-gurdy played in the great hall after the meal. One song after another. Spritely tunes that set Scarlett's toe tapping. Her cheeks were pink with delight as she smiled up at him. James thought he'd never seen a sight more becoming.

The music soon transitioned to a statelier tune and King James set his wine aside and rose from the monstrous wooden chair that had been set upon a raised dais for him at the end of the room. Holding out his hand to Janet Kennedy, he led her to the center of the room. Other couples joined them and began to weave an intricate pattern across the floor.

For Scarlett, it was enchanting and lovely to watch but to her it didn't look like any sort of dancing she was familiar with. It was more like a promenade of careful steps to the front, side and rear.

"Would ye care to dance, my lady?" Rhys asked.

"Oh I would love to, but…" *I don't know any of your dances.*

It was on the tip of her tongue but Scarlett bit it back. She'd had too fine a day to risk rousing the dragon once again. "Thank you, but no. I'd rather just watch, if that's all right?"

Too bad really, she would have loved to dance. With Laird especially, though he hadn't asked. He was so graceful in every way; surely he would be a joy on the dance floor.

Perhaps in the days to come she could ask Rhys to teach her some dances or offer to teach them some of hers. Scarlett stifled a laugh, struck by the hilarity of showing them all the Dougie, how to do the Wobble, or worse, how to Twerk. If she could keep a straight face, perhaps they'd all join in. How ludicrous. She'd probably be laughed off the dance floor!

"Mayhap we can find some wine to refill our drinks then?" Rhys offered.

"That would be lovely."

"I'll escort her," Laird cut in.

Rhys looked set to argue but Scarlett only shook her head. Thanking him again, she let Laird lead her away.

"Ye ken nothing of our dances, do ye?" he asked quietly as they strolled around the perimeter of the hall.

Scarlett briefly considered a lie but shook her head. "Nothing."

Silence fell heavily. A new dance had begun. Patrick and Aleizia had joined the dancers and Rhys led a beaming Aileen on to the floor as well.

"How is that possible?"

It was the same thing he had said each time she told him something like that. She wished she could tell him as she knew it frustrated him deeply. "I'm not from around here. You must realize that by now."

"The Lindsay raid…"

"I think you know very well that I'm not the Lindsay's daughter, sister or even a distant cousin," she said, quietly. "I can't tell you how I ended up in your castle, Laird. I don't really know myself."

"Who are ye, lass?" he asked quietly. "Ye come here wi' yer nonsensical speech and yer peculiar walk..."

"What's wrong with the way I walk?" she asked, interrupting him.

Laird shrugged. "'Tis like an untutored youth wi' little restraint. Always rushing this way and that. Aye, 'tis clear enough that yer no' from this place but where are ye from then? What are ye hiding? Or hiding from? I hae seen fear in yer eyes. Mayhap I can help ye."

Oh, if only he could.

"I'm sorry, Laird. I can't but I am no threat to you. I promise." Most of it was half-truths but that last, at least, was true enough. They came to a small alcove off the hall just as the music changed its rhythm again. A soft, haunting ballad played sweetly on the flute that seemed to sing to her very soul. It was romantic, stirring.

It also provided her an excuse to change the subject before it progressed farther than she could safely negotiate. Before Laird had time to pelt her with another round of questions, Scarlett took him by the hand and smiled up at him. "Will you dance with me?"

"Ye just admitted ye dinnae ken our dances."

"No, but I could show you one of mine, if you like," she said, tugging him into the alcove and out of sight from the rest of the room. "It's called a waltz." Taking his right arm, she placed his hand at her waist.

"Ye think to distract me?" he grumbled.

"Maybe. Now, put your hand here and give me your other

hand." She held her right hand up for him to hold.

"Ye jest."

"Not at all." She grinned up at him, enjoying his astonishment when she put her hand on his shoulder. "Now hold me closer."

"Perhaps we should retire to yer room for this," he murmured, his breath teasing against her cheek as he tightened his embrace. "'Tis no dance to be sure."

Scarlett laughed. "No, it *is* a dance. Not too tight. There! Now, we move like this." She guided him through the simple one-two-three motion until he got the hang of it. "That's it. You've got it."

Slowly but with growing confidence, Laird moved her around the small room. He pulled her closer and closer until her breasts were pressed against his chest and his growing arousal was pressed against her belly. His pale eyes held hers steadily as they moved together, filled with dark promises for the night to come.

"Like this?"

Her body sighed and her heart fluttered. "Yes, just like that."

Growing desire clouded around them until they were nearly lost without more than touch between them. Laird bent his head to nuzzle the hollow below her ear, inhaling her sensual scent.

× × × × ×

"What is this?"

Scarlett looked up, gulping in a deep breath at that all too familiar face. At her side, Laird stiffened and withdrew to an arm's length.

"May I introduce my father, Sir William Hepburn, Lord High Chamberlain," Laird said, his voice tight. Angry? "Father, this is Mistress Thomas."

Sir William offered a short bow and Scarlett dipped a curtsey as she had seen some of the other ladies do. If nothing else, she was a good enough actress to blend in. "How do you do?"

"Verra well," he said in a chilly voice then speared Laird with his flint-like gaze. "My wife tells me that my sons found ye at Dunskirk during a Lindsay raid yet they welcome the clanswoman of my enemy as a guest in my castle."

"Father…"

Sir William cut him off with a look that whisked away any familiarity he shared with his son. While Laird had shot her looks containing heat of anger and passion, nothing in his eyes had ever been so cold. An Azkaban dementor couldn't have produced such a sudden chill! "I would have words wi' ye, James. In private."

Laird stiffened beside her. She felt more than saw his curt nod. What an awkward moment. Hardly like she would have imagined meeting anyone's parents.

"My apologies, Father," Rhys said quietly, coming up behind Sir William. "The King would hae a word wi' ye before he retires. Ye as well, I'm afraid," he directed this to Laird. So it hadn't been just a rescue attempt then.

Sir William cast around one last sour glance before he turned on his heel and left them. Laird looked down at Scarlett but his gaze, so warm and open all evening, was shuttered and closed. "I maun apologize for my father's rudeness, Scarlett. There are other issues at play ye dinnae understand."

Explain them to me, she wanted to say. Scarlett had

217

wondered at Lady Ishbel's malice but his father's coldness was little better. She wanted to know the reasons behind it but this was not the time.

"You shouldn't keep the King waiting. I hear monarchs hate that."

Just a hint of humor flashed in his eyes before it dulled once more. "Indeed they do."

"Dinnae worry, Laird," Rhys said jauntily. "I shall see Scarlett to her rooms."

"*Safely* to her rooms," Laird corrected but with a nod, departed.

Scarlett's eyes followed him until he was lost in the crowd before she turned back to Rhys. To her surprise, his gaze was troubled.

"What is it?"

"I worry for ye, my dear."

"For me?" she asked. "You should be worried for him. My parents may not have been the best in the world but at least they had some warmth. They cared about me."

"I cannae excuse my mother, but our father favors Laird," Rhys said.

"If that's an example of his favor, I'd hate to see what his disapproval looks like."

Rhys only shook his head. "It might no' show, but I think our father genuinely regrets that Laird isnae his legitimate son, his heir."

Scarlett scoffed at that. If Sir William cared so much for Laird, he would have acknowledged him as his heir if it were true and not just admit as much in a drunken stupor.

"They are actually quite similar beings, ye see."

"I doubt that." Comparing the two men was like equating the icy hell of Hoth to the raging fires of Modor.

"Nay, lass. Look at Laird. He can be as imperfect as he pleases, doing what he likes. He is laird of himself, if nothing else. Yet even wi'out the position in name to do so, he commands everyone he meets. Just like our father. Including our father in many ways," Rhys said with a laugh. "We all love him, myself included."

"Yet you constantly goad him just to rile him up."

Rhys shrugged. "How else am I to show my love?"

22

"I wish I were going with you, Scarlett."

Scarlett caught her wistful expression and hugged Aileen tightly, whispering in her ear. "I wish you were, too. Aleizia will be so busy with Patrick, I will have only Laird and Rhys for company along the way."

As they parted, a smile brightened Aileen's vivid blue eyes. "What a torturous labor for you. Perhaps I shan't envy you at all! Promise you'll write me and let me know how my brothers fare? They are horrible correspondents, all."

"I will but don't worry over them, okay? We will all see you soon."

A shadow passed across the girl's eyes. "I wish that you might be able to promise me that."

"I can," Rhys assured her, leading his mount along behind him as he came to her side. "Ye well ken that I am too arrogant to die. Hae I no' said so before?"

"A hundred times!" Aileen flung herself into her brother's arms and squeezed him. "I shall hold you to it this time."

"Ye hae my promise as well, Sweeting."

Laird appeared behind them and braced himself as his sister turned and hugged him fiercely too.

Over Aileen's head, Laird's silvery eyes met hers. Once again he wore his worn and faded kilt and linen shirt without even a vest or doublet to subdue the impact of his broad chest. She much preferred him like this rather than in the finery of the previous night. His savage magnetism was undeniable.

She hadn't seen him since he'd left her the previous night, but this morning a buxom young woman named Maris had appeared at her door and introduced herself as Scarlett's new maid and companion. Her duty, Maris informed her, was to see that Scarlett was ready to travel and to accompany her for propriety's sake. While picking out a half-dozen dresses for Scarlett to take along with her, Aleizia had explained why Scarlett required a chaperone as a young, unmarried woman traveling among the soldiers.

It was an amusing concept since Scarlett had been kidnapped forcibly and traveled alone with a dozen Hepburn clansmen without any one of them worrying for her reputation. She didn't see much of a point in starting now but Maris was insistent and helpful in carrying along the heavy valise Aleizia had packed for her. Now it and Maris were safely aboard a small wooden cart being pulled by another of Laird's horses. Along with it, Aiden, Laird's squire was loading Laird's clothing, arms, shields and chain mail along with his tent and supplies that would see them through the journey.

The squire was now waiting, holding Laird's horse patiently but Scarlett was sure it would be awhile before Laird would be able to peel himself away from Aileen. The King, who was already mounted and moving among the thousand or more men who had been camped overnight outside Crichton's walls, probably couldn't have rushed him.

Scarlett's heart ached for them all. Even Lady Ishbel, bless her heart. For all her glacial stares and scathing insults, all the men of her household were going off to war. Not that she seemed troubled by her husband's departure, but Lady Ishbel had almost had a tear in her eye when saying her goodbyes to her five sons. Especially Rhys.

Scarlett had never had to send someone off to war before. The uncertainty of the days to come without cell phones, emails and Skype to send frequent assurances would be harrowing for the women left behind.

But not all were being left behind. Aleizia refused to be parted from Patrick. Lady Agnes, the young Countess of Bothwell, was also accompanying her husband, as was the Countess of Glencairn, Laird's aunt. In fact, there were many women of all ranks coming along, children as well. Something Scarlett was having a hard time comprehending. Historically speaking, she'd always had the impression that men marched off to war alone, even during transport to the battlefield itself.

"Dinnae cry, wee lassie." Laird was down on his knees now before Aileen, smoothing back her hair with a tender hand as he spoke to her softly. Words of caring, affection and cocky assurance until he coaxed a smile from her. He grinned then, dropping a kiss on her forehead.

Something deep within Scarlett stirred at the sight.

It occurred to her then that she had never known what a real man was.

Oh, she knew guys who went to the gym to bulk up. She knew geeks, stars, soldiers and gentlemen but never all that combined in one man. Laird was everything – fierce, strong, chivalrous, protective and caring of his women.

His women. Those who belonged to him, even if they weren't directly related.

Like her.

Scarlett knew that there was some feminist part of her that should be offended on behalf of them all. Though it was a more modern ideal, she had been raised to believe that she was as good as any man. That she could do anything a man could. That she could be anything.

In the process, women in her time had lost the femininity of centuries past.

Damn, even decades past.

When women expected to be taken care of because they were the weaker sex. Not that they were weak. She could see that now. Under all the frippery and fawning, she had seen incredible strength in the women who were waving their men off to war that morning. To endure what they did, to face loss of husbands, brothers, sons and daughters to war and disease every day.

Without complaint, they took on what looked to Scarlett might be an often ugly life and tried to see and be the beauty in it.

Her whole job since finishing her movies had been to look fantastic on magazine covers and in person. Even at the grocery store. Heaven help her if she were caught on film without makeup and designer clothes. Sometimes that was hard enough with an assistant and a personal trainer to keep her ready at all times for shoots, sets and days on a plane. Living out of a suitcase for weeks on end.

That was it.

There were no real worries in her life, no horrors to be

faced.

Or course, her life didn't have an ounce of the intrigue and ambition these women had despite her celebrity status. According to Aleizia, the ladies of the upper classes wanted nothing more than to one up each other with the best marriage, best castle. Having friendships – Scarlett used that term loosely – with anyone who could promote their social standing.

From one perspective, the lives of the peasants seemed more enviable. They worked hard, yes, but for the most part just wanted to love, eat and be happy.

One was Hollywood. The other an average American life.

Perhaps their times weren't so different after all.

Laird turned to Scarlett. His eyes were turbulent, yet resolved as he lifted easily up into her saddle. Gathering up the reins, he adjusted her hands around them until she was holding them properly. "She's docile enough for ye, I promise. Just hold on and she'll follow along wi'out a fuss."

"You okay?" she asked softly, clasping his hand.

"Aye." His calloused thumb stroked over her knuckles before he bent his head, pressing a kiss to the back of her hand. "I maun apologize again for last night. My father can be a difficult and autocratic man."

"I noticed."

"Bear wi' me, lass. 'Tis all that I ask."

It was a bizarre statement but before she could ask him about it, Laird strode to his horse, pulling a length of plaid from his saddlebags. Returning, he held it out to her. "'Twill rain soon. Wrap it around yerself. The wool will shed the water."

Scarlett nodded but he turned away again, moving toward his horse, finding the stirrup and mounting smoothly. Lifting his hand, he waved goodbye to his sister one last time before kicking his horse into motion. Shoulders set and stiff, he rode away without sparing her another glance.

What was that all about?

A moment later, Rhys rode up beside her, slapping her horse on the rump. It lurched forward reluctantly. "How are ye faring this morn, dear Scarlett?"

"I'm fine."

"Fine?"

"Well, I am back on a horse." Scarlett gestured to the animal as if Rhys weren't perfectly aware of her position. "Again."

"Och, did ye get more riding in last night then?"

A blush blossomed hotly on her cheeks at his innuendo. "You do have a dirty mind, Rhys."

"Aye, but by yer own word, I ask all the best questions." He flashed her a wink.

They had given her a side-saddle this time and she wasn't sure if it were a good thing. It might have been more practical given the long skirts of her brown linen riding habit but she didn't feel any more stable in the saddle than she had before. On the bright side, she didn't feel any less stable either and maybe her thighs wouldn't ache so badly this time since they wouldn't be spread wide all day to accommodate the huge beast between them.

No, but they might ache pleasantly enough if you let another huge beast between them, her inner devil teased. Ugh, this was getting out of hand.

"Is it a long ride today?" she asked, hoping to change the subject and divert her thoughts. "I've never heard of this Ellenfort."

"Ellemford," he corrected. "Ellemford Haugh. It's the

traditional muster point in the area. 'Tis just over a score of miles southeast of us. We should be there early this afternoon," Rhys said as if about seven hours, by her quick calculation, was little more than a jaunt in the park. With twenty cannons being pulled at the head of their procession, she could see why their progress would be even slower than before. Plus, many in the cavalcade were walking as well, some pulling small carts behind them.

It was going to be another one of those days.

Scarlett wasn't certain that she could handle another full day in the saddle. The last one she'd spent there had been hard enough.

Yes, but Laird must have held you in his arms for a good portion of it, her inner devil reminded.

Because I was his prisoner.

The devil smirked. *You don't seem like much of a prisoner any more.*

"Where are we this time, Rhys?" she asked as they stopped to make camp three days later along the banks of a river called the Blackadder Water. The area seemed familiar to her though Scarlett couldn't pinpoint why.

"Do ye no' recognize the place, my dear?" he asked curiously as he unsaddled his horse while his squire, Willem, emptied a small horse cart of his tent and belongings. Aiden and Maris were taking care of setting up Scarlett's tent, neither one appreciated her interference, leaving her at loose ends. "Ye should, since it is where we found ye just a sennight past."

"We're back at Dunskirk?"

"Merely passing by, dear Scarlett."

Interest pricked. "Do you mind if I go look around a bit?"

"Hoping to see Laird?"

No, she'd given up that hope days ago. Scarlett hadn't seen hide nor hair of Laird since they'd left Crichton. His abrupt abandonment after such a focused seduction was confusing. Whatever he wanted her to bear with, she assumed it had something to do with his continued absence. She hoped that it was something in his private talks with Sir William or the King that prompted him to avoid her company and not just regret over their brief but passionate interludes.

"If ye'll wait, I'll escort ye," he said. "Or ye can take Maris."

Maris paused in her work but Scarlett shrugged off the option. No doubt her maid was again itching to run off with a burly Scotsman or two as she did each afternoon after seeing Scarlett settled in. She wasn't sorry to see Maris go, as the woman wasn't much of a companion by Scarlett's definition of the word.

"That's not necessary."

Maris turned back to her work, no doubt pleased with Scarlett's decision.

"Don't get lost," Rhys warned.

"I won't and I promise I won't run off either."

"I wisnae worried aboot that."

Having conquered the maze of tents, Scarlett strode off in strides as long as the skirts of her blue flax gown would allow. Heading west where Rhys pointed, she enjoyed the burn of her thighs and calves after another long day in the saddle. At least she could walk on her own this time, Scarlett realized. She must be getting used to it.

The skies above were thick with clouds but clear on the horizon. The descending sun swept across the rolling hills far to the west, awakening the shadows between and glowing off the treetops of the woodland park nestled between the encampment and the castle. Through the trees, she could make out just a hint of Dunskirk's easterly elevation silhouetted against the ball of light. Bright beams speared around the tower, casting their rays on the large pond at the center of the woodlands and bouncing off the placid surface like a mirror.

Scarlett shaded her eyes as she plunged into the trees, finding in the lacy shadows beyond her first hint of the familiar since arriving in this time. With a smile, Scarlett stroked the leather soles of her shoes over the mossy stones of a recognizable arched footbridge. Trickling streams below called out to her like an old friend. Moss covered rocks rolled out a welcoming carpet and the hanging branches of the trees waved hello.

Once upon a time, she'd spent days on end within this fairy-tale landscape. It was untouched. Unchanged. Beautiful and savage just as she remembered.

Through the trees, the reflection of the sun off the pond sparkled like diamonds. Long beams of light angled through the canopy of leaves. Meandering slowly, Scarlett skimmed her fingertips along the tree trunks as she circled this way around one, that way around the other. Reaching the shoreline of the pond, she spotted the tiny island where the mini castle tower of her time had once sat. Now it was missing. The realization saddened her but missing Laird made her almost as melancholy.

Much as she tried not to dwell on implications of her continued stay in the sixteenth century, Scarlett tried not to dwell on his continued absence either.

She'd become something of an abandoned lover.

Was he regretting their love play? Or regretting having her come along?

Both?

Part of her wanted to find him and ask, rather than dwelling on the worst-case scenario, but the crowds within the encampments were too vast to even consider such a futile search.

Thousands of men, women and children from the Brough Muir muster, which had marched out of Edinburgh, combined with those gathering from Midlothian at Ellemford. Pages, squires, wives, and children. People to care for them all. To feed them and clean up after them.

The military encampments were a marvel to Scarlett, whose idea of camping was far removed from the ever-expanding spectacle around her.

Ellemford Haugh – the 'haugh' meaning only a meadow near a river, Rhys told her – on the banks of the Whiteadder Water, became a city of tents that first night. Big ones, small ones. Flamboyant and humble. Tents of all colors set in long avenues and cross streets like it was a metropolis unto itself.

Her tent – Rhys had been very clear on that point – was modestly sized with red and white stripes. Laird's squire, Aiden had pulled a large feather mattress from the cart for her to sleep on as well as the small table and chairs for her comfort.

Not far away from hers were two large tents of red and yellow bearing the Hepburn coat of arms. One Rhys was sharing with his father and brothers. The other was for Patrick and Aleizia. Theirs had been fully furnished with all the comforts of home. Scarlett could only imagine how lavish King James' was.

Or Laird's.

Rhys had made no mention of where Laird planned to sleep.

Rhys had taken her on a tour of the Ellemford

encampment the previous night after supping with Patrick and Aleizia. Everywhere the Scottish accents of Highland and Lowland blended as men prepared for battle, sharpening swords and knives. Stringing bows and mending chainmail. All through their walk, her eyes strayed left and right, wondering where Laird might be but she never caught sight of him among the growing throng.

Today, when they had left Ellemford and moved southward, she wouldn't have imagined they were stopping near Dunskirk. Scarlett was glad for it though. The idyllic tranquility of the place was a long lost friend, soaking into her and washing away the moment of melancholy.

Skirting the shore of the pond, Scarlett made her way to the postern gate of Dunskirk and slipped inside. The halls were dark with shadows but she knew her way well enough and the keep was but a fraction of the size she remembered. Working her way through and up the second floor of the pele tower, she took note of what it was. What it could, no, would someday be.

Near the center of the great room, she found the spot she'd been in when she'd traveled through time. She circled the room, playing the moment over and over in her head once more. And the questions came again. How? Why? Would she ever know?

It was also the spot where she'd first encountered Laird. Amongst all the confusion and chaos, he'd brought an element of excitement into her life. Anticipation that had long been lacking in her days. She couldn't find it in herself in that moment to regret the unexpected journey.

Not that she wanted it to last, of course.

So much was waiting for her back home.

Her mind blanked but Scarlett shook the unnerving

moment away. Of course, there would be a thousands moments to look forward to even if she couldn't enumerate them now.

Bracing her palms against the casing of the narrow window, she leaned out inhaling deeply as she looked back over the path she'd taken to the castle and the encampment in the distance.

She loved this place, missed it terribly in the years since the filming for *The Puppet War* wrapped up. There'd never been another place in the world where she'd felt such peace. Of course it was half the castle it used to be, or would be, but the spirit of it was still there. Now it was Laird's. Scarlett wondered if he adored it as much as she did.

She hoped so.

Footsteps shuffled through hall below and Scarlett pushed away from the window, climbing the winding staircase to the top of the tower to avoid discovery. Though she had told Cormac that she was afraid of heights, her phobia was only mildly pathetic rather than neurotic. Besides the parapet walk was wide and the view remarkable. From up here, she could clearly see the layout of the castle within the curtain walls. In her time, there were four towers like the one she was in and two flanking towers breaking up the enclosed walls that connected them. Now there was just the single, mammoth pele tower and a small keep within the open walls surrounding the bailey. Everything else was gone.

Again. How? Why?

She was still pondering the question when a rough, burly brogue spoke close by. "Lovely day to be in Scotland, isn't it, Miss Thomas?"

"I'm sorry, have we met?" she asked, turning to the wizened old man who leaned against the tower wall. His arms were crossed over a rough woven tunic and he wore leggings with leather straps criss-crossed over his calves and down to his leather shoes. Pushing his cap back on his balding head, he gave her a wink. An all too familiar grin creased his cheeks. "Wait... Mr... Donell? Is that you?"

"Aye, lassie, and how are ye on this fine day?"

"What are you...? How did you...?" she stuttered, gawping at him like a strangled fish.

"Just a few days away from the press and already yer no' minding yerself every word in public." He nodded approvingly. "Quite an improvement, I'd say."

Such relief bulleted through her that Scarlett hardly gave his words a moment's thought. She grasped his hand excitedly. "Oh, thank God I'm not the only one caught up in this nightmare! Do you know how we can get out of here and go home?"

"A nightmare, is it now?" Donell tilted his head questioningly. "Is that what ye want, lass? To go home?"

"Of course, I do! How can you even ask such a thing?"

"But this is what ye wanted, wisnae it?" he pressed, his eyes boring into hers and Scarlett's heart thumped heavily in her chest as she realized what he was saying.

"No, no. Why would you think that?" Dropping his hand, she took a step back, pressing two fingers to the sudden ache building at her brow.

"Och, lass," he chided. "Isnae it what ye said? That ye wished ye could just get away from them all?" Donell matched her step, catching her by the elbow just as the back of her thighs brushed the battlements and tugging her toward him. "Och, careful now, lass. 'Twould no' do to fall and ruin all my efforts, now would it?"

"Efforts? Away from them all?" She shook her head,

denying the implication of his words. "You? You did this? Why? What did I ever do to you?"

The mischief fled his gaze and concern took its place. "Ye did nothing, lassie. Yer nothing but kindness. All this… 'tis what I do for ye. And others. Yer no' the only one, lassie."

Her head still swung uncontrollably from side to side in rejection of his words. "Only one what? I don't understand."

"The only one to feel alone, lass." he said with some exasperation. "Ye think yer the only one who feels lacking in control? Who feels they cannae trust anyone?"

"You think *this* helps?" she asked, flinging an arm toward the castle. "You think *they* trust me?"

"Trust given and received needs to be earned, lass." His impatience was evident as he crossed his arms over his barrel-like chest but Scarlett was filled to the brim with irritation of her own.

"I don't need you to teach me a lesson, Donell. Send me home now!" She stomped her foot and jabbed her finger down insistently.

Donell only compressed his lips tightly, sending out a whole new network of wrinkles to show his dissatisfaction. "Bah, 'tis too soon." He waved a hand scornfully. "I dinnae ken what I was thinking. I'm getting impatient in my auld age and yer no' yet ready for more."

"I am so ready," she cried desperately. "Donell… Wait! Get back here!"

But he already turned away toward the tower. "I will see ye again soon enough, lassie. Ta-ra, for now."

"What the hell?" Scarlett blinked in astonishment as he disappeared through the door with a wave. "Oh no, you don't!"

Dashing through the door, she found the upper hall empty but swore she heard his mischievous laughter drifting up the spiral staircase. Snatching her skirts high, she chased after the mysterious man who claimed responsibility for her nightmare as fast as her feet could carry her but she never caught sight of him.

How could such an ancient human being be so fast? He must be an elf to vanish into thin air like that! Down another flight and a wrong door later, she raced into the bailey just as the old man disappeared through the postern gate.

Gasping for breath, she ran after him wondering all the while how he managed to elude her when he appeared to be taking nothing more than a leisurely stroll.

Still his lead grew as he headed toward the woodlands. Scarlett lengthened her stride as she dashed through a stand of trees but when she broke through the other side, he was gone.

Scarlett bent over, panting as she stared in disbelief. Where the hell did he go?

Damn it, she wanted answers.

Holding her side, she continued doggedly onward around the pond, determined to find Donell make some sense out of his rambling.

24

Dusk had fallen by the time she returned to the encampment still she hadn't seen Donell again. It was fully dark by the time she found her way back to her tent an hour later. Rhys was nowhere in sight, nor was Maris or even Aiden.

She didn't worry much about Maris but where was everyone else?

"Scarlett, there you are." Aleizia exclaimed as she came out of the next tent. "Where have you been? We thought you'd gotten lost."

It was shocking that Aleizia could scold so well when she was little more than a child herself, but the point was well made. She'd hardly been able to find her tent and it wasn't even mobile. It had been like trying to find The Pirates of the Caribbean ride at Disneyworld without a map. She wouldn't leave it again without a GPS handy. "I walked to the castle. I told Rhys that."

"You did but we never expected you to stay away so long.

Laird was worried for you. We all were."

"He was?" Scarlett's heart leapt. "Where is he?"

"Right where he's been all this time. At the King's side."

"Oh." As far as excuses went, she supposed it was a pretty reasonable one.

"Come, we'll let the men know you're all right," Aleizia looped her arm through Scarlett's arm tugged her away down the tented lane. "They're all at the King's table this night but I know they'll want to see that you're back safe and sound."

King's tent wasn't far away. The quality of the tents got more elaborate as they neared. Aleizia explained that the clan chieftains, lairds, lords and earls would be closer to their monarch. Scarlett equated it to the Beverly Hills of the encampment.

"...And I welcome my friends from Clan Hay and the other border lords who hae today answered the call of their King and country."

King James voice boomed out as they reached the fringes of a clearing around the most elaborate tent Scarlett had seen yet. Silken luxury meets the big top. Before it, King James sat at the head of a long table with at least fifty men dining with him, though no ladies were present. Clearly they were talking business.

"Yer King thanks ye one and all for yer service. Tomorrow we shall cross the Tweed into England."

Scarlett was hard-pressed to give the King even an ounce of her attention as she scanned the men lining the table and spotted Laird sitting about half way down the opposite side with Patrick, Rhys and Sir William.

His eyes lifted and met hers immediately, as if he had felt her gaze upon him. Whispering something to Rhys, he rose unobtrusively and disappeared between the tents behind him.

She started forward but Aleizia held her back. "No, wait here."

"I ken that there has been some debate o'er my decision to honor the Auld Alliance wi' France, but as Henry threatens to reassert what he calls his God-given rights as feudal overlord of Scotland, I believe we hae nae choices left in this matter."

Some of the men sounded their approval but the sound was drowned out by the roaring of her blood in her ears as Laird's powerful arm slid around her waist. "Laird," she sighed, leaning back against his chest as he bent his head to nuzzle her ear.

"I, uh… I'll just leave you then," Aleizia said with an awkward smile before she turned and fled.

The King's voice ricocheted through the camp again. "I hae sent word to the regent, Catherine, and Henry that we shall meet them on the field of battle."

The men banged their goblets on the table in approval.

"Where hae ye been?" Laird whispered. "We were worried for ye."

"Were you?" she asked. "You didn't come looking."

"Would that I could hae and spared us all the wondering."

Scarlett sank into his warm embrace, pleased by his open concern.

"Wait," she said under her breath as the King's words began to sink in through the clamor of banging cups. "Your king *told* the enemy that he's planning on invading England?"

"Shh, lass," Laird said. "Aye. How else would our enemy know where to meet us for battle if we dinnae arrange a meeting? Scotland is a big country. England larger still."

King James droned on, "On the morrow, we shall cross into England."

"I kind of thought the point of an invasion was that the

enemy doesn't know you're coming," Scarlett persisted, pulling away to look up at him.

Laird shook his head. "Lass, we arenae reivers to sneak aboot like thieves in the dark."

"I thought that's exactly what you were," she reminded him.

"Not in this endeavor," Laird clarified, his fingers tightening over hers when she started to speak again. "Scarlett, now isnae the time."

"But you're giving them plenty of time to raise an army of their own."

"Scarlett, ye cannae question what ye dinnae understand."

"We will take every Sassenach hold along the way!" the King announced and the men at the table shouted their support.

"How can I not question that?" Scarlett asked over the din, drawing the attention of the guards standing nearby. "How can you not? I mean, it just stupid to let the enemy know you're coming."

One man at the end of the table turned in his seat, narrowing a menacing look on her.

"Pax, Angus. She's been ill," Laird explained quickly, pulling her away from the clearing with a firm hand. "I will see her back to her tent."

"I have not been sick," Scarlett hissed. "I wish you would stop saying that."

"Then offer me another explanation for these mad ramblings and questions," he said as he dragged her through the encampment. Holy crap, she didn't know a man's stride could cover so much ground in a single step but she was practically running to keep up with him. "I myself cannae think of another reason that ye would dare to question our practices so insolently if it no' for an addled head."

"You think I'm addled?" Scarlett tripped on her heavy skirts before lifting them high. Laird was in no mood now to see that she didn't fall, not that she wanted his help in that moment. She didn't like being dragged around like a doll any more than she liked being told what to do or say. "I'm not the one who thinks the plans to invade another country should be announced ahead of time. It sounds to be like you're all pretty nuts. You're going to get yourselves killed."

"'Tis becoming easier to believe that yer no' from this country at all if ye hae such questions about our ways. I ken 'tis no' for a female mind to understand a gentleman's code of chivalry but 'tis how it is done."

Scarlett just shook her head. "Chivalry says that? I don't remember reading that anywhere. What else does it say? Stand across the field from each other and hold still like gentleman so that they can get a better shot at you? That's ancient idiocy, that's what that is. In modern warfare…"

"Enough!" Laird roared, opening the flap of her tent and shoving her through with enough force to send her stumbling. He had to be pretty incensed to get so rough but Scarlett was reaching the end of her good sense as well.

"Don't you get all medieval with me, Laird Hepburn." she snapped, jabbing a finger into his chest. "I'm not some wilting flower you can just push around. And don't think you can feed me that crap about female minds either. I'm not feeble or stupid. I have a right to my own opinions, and in my opinion, this whole thing you've got going on here is pure bullshit."

"I've had enough of yer prattle, yer questioning our practices. I demand that ye cease acting as if ye hae no familiarity wi' our ways."

"I don't have any familiarity with your 'ways', Laird," she said, making air quotes around the word. "I don't live with them, I haven't practiced them and frankly, with the little I've seen of them, I am as thankful as all hell that I grew up in a better time."

"Bah! What is that supposed to mean?"

"It means exactly what it sounds like."

"Yer the most maddening woman I hae ever met."

"Yes and what's supposed to happen to this maddening woman when you go off and fight this war?" she asked, her heart pounding sickly. Ah, now she was getting to the crux of the matter wasn't she? He was going to war, for Christ's sake. And by the sound of it, he was going to get himself killed in the process. The image of that dripping, bloody sword emblazoned itself in her mind once more, sending a chill through her heart. "Am I supposed to stand by and watch you get yourself killed?"

"That is no' for ye to decide," Laird replied. "Ye'll remain here at Dunskirk until this is over."

"Stay here? Uh-uh, I'm not going to sit around and wonder what's happening. This is my life, too, and I'm going along."

"I said ye'll stay here where ye belong."

"This is not where I belong!" she shouted at him.

"It is!" Laird grasped her by the shoulders and gave her a little shake. "Yer my responsibility, lass. Mine."

"Yours?" Scarlett shot back mockingly. "You think just because you almost shagged me back at Crichton that I'm yours? I don't *belong* to anyone."

"Shagged?" Some of the heat faded from his eyes, his grip relaxed ever so slightly but Scarlett was still mad. Madder than she had ever been.

"Yes, shagged. As in screwed, did the nasty, got busy, fornicated…" His eyes blazed with comprehension at last. "Fucked," she spat the ugly word. "Admit it, all of this is just because you want to fuck me and haven't managed to get under my skirts yet."

"Ye think all I want to do is fook ye, lass?" he said in a thick, dangerous brogue. "I can fook any lass in Scotland if I wanted to. 'Tis no' that hard to get beneath their skirts."

Braggart. Bastard. Scarlett sneered but bit back the stab of hurt that followed his words. I don't care, she told herself. He could screw all the 'lasses' on the planet if he wanted. All she wanted from him – until she tracked down Donell and knew otherwise – was that damn sword and a way home.

"Go to it then." She swept her hand toward the door. Tears clogged her throat. No, that was it. A way out and nothing more. "There's the door. Have at it."

"Ye want me to find another to warm my bed?"

No! "Sure, knock yourself out."

With a hard look, Laird turned toward the door. Her heart pounded with something akin to panic, and Scarlett was hard put to restrain the bit of herself that wanted to chase Laird out that door and beg him to come back.

But Laird didn't leave. Instead he drew down the flap, casting the tent in near darkness but for the single tallow candle Maris had left burning for her. "I'm afraid I cannae do that, lass."

"And why is that?"

"Because there is only one woman I want."

25

"What do you think you're doing?" she asked apprehensively as James unpinned his kilt from his shoulder and tossed it to the side.

His molten eyes met hers but he didn't answer. Instead he toed off his boots and proceeded to unfasten his sporran. Slipping it off, he advanced slowly. He lifted the hem of the loose shirt he wore and peeled it over his head in a smooth motion.

There were no words on his tongue now; only a memory of the taste of her and James had to have more. Scarlett gasped and backed a step away but there was nowhere she could run from him.

Not anymore.

The muscles in his chest bunched and leapt as he balled the garment up and flung it to the side. His chest was incredible. Massive with thick bands of muscle reminiscent of a certain Shreveport werewolf she and every other red-blooded American woman had admired on TV. But this was real, incredibly lifelike and right in front of her.

"What are you... Geez... You can't just... wow," she exhaled the exclamation with a sigh and shook her head as her eyes drank him in. Just so many muscles. Her fingers itched to touch him.

Laird prowled toward her until he was almost within reach. His chest was wide and magnificently sculpted in the candlelight with just enough dark hair arrowing downward to draw her eye and make her mouth water with anticipation. "I'm still... mmm, those ... I'm still mad at... wow, just *wow*."

His abs rippled like sand dunes under his taut, tanned skin as he unbuckled his belt. He certainly looked hotter than the Sahara. "Don't think you can... Oh my God."

Her Scottish laird flung the kilt aside as he reached her. His arm wound around her waist and lifted her against him, carrying her backward. She slammed against the support post as his lips descended upon hers, muffling her gasp of surprise. A gasp that transformed into a moan readily enough as he forced her lips to part. Desire kindled within her as his tongue plunged deeply and Scarlett raked her teeth across it, biting down gently. A low growl escaped him.

Then the fires began to rage once more and Scarlett surrendered. She was done fighting with him. Done fighting the irresistible hunger he inspired in her. She doubted that this was all in the grand design of her temporal displacement. Surely there was more to it. She could have gotten laid anywhere. Whatever her purpose was, she didn't care. She had never wanted anything so much as she wanted Laird. Never *had* to have anything more.

Drawing on his lower lip, Scarlett nipped there for good

measure before kissing him fully. His short beard pricked at her chin but she held him close, urging him closer as she ran her hands over his naked chest, thrilling at the smoothness of his skin and the rigidity of his fine physique. Kneading upward, she wrapped her arms around his shoulders. Her fingers digging, curling into his long hair.

Lifting her legs, she entwined them tightly around his hips as his pushed up her skirts and his hands cupped her bottom, squeezing hard as he fit them together, thrusting erotically against her. His erection was long and thick, insistent. She welcomed the invasion, already hot and ready from her thoughts of him, from the sight of him. Any reservations she had about where this all might lead were fading fast.

His lips branded a path down her neck, his whiskers rasping, exciting. Scarlett bit his shoulder, his neck. Provoking him, then licking away the sting.

"Ye drive me to madness." His brogue was thick, nearly indecipherable.

"Honey, I'm already there," she whispered in his ear before nipping on his lobe.

A pained groan rumbled up from deep within him, shaking them both.

Turning, he carried her to the bed and fell with her on to the mattress. His eyes met hers, fierce, dark with passion. Hunger. For her. "I'm going to take ye, Scarlett. No' because I want to *shag* ye but because I long to possess ye."

Scarlett trembled at the resolve in his rough brogue. Possess. It sounded so complete. So devastating. "Yes."

With a savage growl, Laird thrust hard, driving deep into her ready, willing body. They cried out in unison, possessor and possessed. He was so big, too big but still she wanted more. Wrapped tightly around him, every part of her became his as Laird pounded a steady rhythm into her depths. His chest against hers, his thighs against her. It was a full body possession.

"Laird," she moaned, urging him on as she held him with her thighs. Stroked him with her hands. "Yes, oh yes!"

Laird buried his face in her shoulder and quickened his tempo, his fingers biting into her hips. Euphoria coiled deep within her and spiraled out. Pulsing, searing, singing through her veins. Incredible. Impossible. She wanted to savor it, as always her passion for him spiraled out of control. Too soon. Too quickly. Lost, helpless against the waves as they began to crash. Drowning beneath the waves of ecstasy as they lapped over her. Consumed her.

Harder. Faster. An agonized keening filled her ears and Scarlett realized it was her. Rapture called to her. A whimper escaped her, and then she cried out.

"Laird." She shattered with a hoarse scream, coming apart at a cellular level as he plunged hard once more and tensed. His own groan muffled against her neck as his heavy weight pressed her deeper into the mattress.

A moment later, he shifted and Scarlett felt him unlacing her gown. He trailed soft kisses down her neck and shoulders as he bared them, tossing her linen parlett aside. Her corset loosened and Scarlett drew in a deep, revitalizing breath. "Stand," he commanded.

Scarlett rocked her cheek negatively against his damp chest. Silent laughter shook them and Laird clapped a hand lightly over her bottom. "Contrary lass."

He lifted her to her feet and Scarlett swayed, clinging to his shoulders as he untied her skirts and petticoats. She wore no corset so her clothing fell to the floor as he swept it all downward, leaving her in nothing but her stockings and shoes. Laird looked up at her for a long moment, his eyes skimming like flames over her body. His calloused palms closed over her breasts and he released a ragged breath.

Lifting her, he laid her back on the mattress. Climbing to his knees, he lifted her leg and grasped one foot to remove her shoe. The muscles in her calf and thigh tensed and jumped as he fingers skimmed upward. Unrolling one stocking slowly, his lips followed it down. Kissing, licking and raking her with his teeth. His eyes, shining like silver plate now, held hers with wicked humor. He bit her ankle, the arch of her foot before lowering her limb and repeating the process on the other leg.

Scarlett watched him, her fingers curling into the counterpane as she twitched and tensed with every touch. Her body was still pulsing with satisfaction from their quick, hard mating but heat was already began to pool between her thighs once more.

Finishing with the other leg, he crawled slowly up and over her bending his head here and there to graze his lips or stubbled cheek along her sensitized flesh. He held himself above, arms bulging as he looked down at her.

Scarlett was trembling, shaken by his size as he loomed over her. He was so big, so broad; Scarlett should have felt suffocated by his overwhelming presence. She didn't. That tightly leashed power was the freakin' sexiest thing she had ever experienced. His arms were like steel beneath her hands as she caressed them, moving over his chest once more, unable to resist touching his deliciously sculpted body. He was a colossus.

"You are so beautiful," she said softly, feeling his body tense even more with surprise.

"Nay, *mo chroí*, 'tis ye who is the beautiful one, for never hae a seen a more bonny sight in my life than ye right where ye are." He stared down at her intently, cupping her breasts.

God's breath, but he had missed looking upon her.

She was a vision in the candlelight, her short auburn hair aflame in the flickering light. Her skin flushed and dewy from her exertions. Her modest bosom heaving distractedly beneath his palms.

How could he have ever thought her scrawny, James wondered? She was dazzling. Perfect.

Enticing. She made his blood heat on a normal day, but like this! Ardor was scorching through his veins. Even having just taken her, he was impatient to have her again. To ravish her fervently, though a part of him wished he could make love to her tenderly. His fey, fragile lass deserved tenderness but such delicacy had no place among the riotous passions that consumed him. Having known the paradise her body could bring, having tasted of her bliss, he was only that much more eager to plunder her again and again.

Perhaps one day.

This was not that day.

He moved between her thighs once more, pleased when she wrapped them tightly around his hips in a welcoming embrace. His muscles tensed and twitched as her palms smoothed over his chest and ribs, around his back and downward to his arse.

Scarlett cast him an enticing glance from beneath her lashes then lifted her head. Her tongue traced an erotic line up his throat. By the time she nipped at his chin, his arms were shaking with lust. He rocked his hips forward, unerringly finding her. She blossomed around him, welcomed him.

Bending his head, James caught her lips and thrust hard as she arched her hips to meet his, tasting her gasp. Her delight. She was a bold one but her passion matched his. Withdrawing slowly, he tried to savor the sensation of her encasing him but the urgency was building undeniably again. He drove into her welcoming depths, again. Deeper. Her wild cries and helpless gasps spurred him on until Scarlett was clinging to him. A sob sounded in the back of her throat, a cry that told him she was reaching heaven's gates once more.

James lifted her bottom, tilting her hips upward and quickened his pace. His lips found her neck, that enticing earlobe. "Come for me, *mo ghrá*," he urged and her heavenly body contracted and pulsed around him as a thready cry passed her lips. He couldn't stop his body from answering in kind.

"Ah, *mo ghrá, mo chroí. Adhrodh métú!*"

His fingers eased, then massaged before James lifted himself away. The mattress dipped as he rolled over on his back next to her.

In the silence, their harsh breathing matched as they caught their breath.

His hand found hers and their fingers entwined.

"Ye are mine." The words were quietly spoken but brooked no denial.

"Then take me with you."

He said nothing but she felt his nod.

Bloody hell but she was getting to him. Had she managed to break through his defenses so easily? He was beginning to care about more than what she might know. What she might want from them. Who she might be.

He cared about what she thought about him, the person. Whether she liked him more than Rhys.

Aye, that was the problem, wasn't it?

He might have her passion but it was Rhys she gave her friendship to. Rhys who she talked with at length. Rhys who provoked the sweet laughter that reached his ears even through the din of a thousand men.

It was his brother's arms that she fell into upon reaching their encampment each night, his company she sought while the servants were erecting her tent among the village of soldiers and followers. Rhys who she dined with outside her tent, whispering into his ear while James was absent.

All of it ignited a fierce, hereto unbeknownst envy within him. He knew not who she was or from whence she came, but for now, in this moment of time she was his. His father be damned.

James pulled Scarlett into his arms, wrapping his arms tightly around her. He had missed her so dearly these past days even an edict from the King himself couldn't have stopped him from having her at his side in the days to come. His threat to leave her there had been spoken in anger. Anger built by the sight of Scarlett laughing again and again with his brother over the past days.

Now that he had tasted joy on her cherry lips, leaving her behind was no option at all. It had been extraordinary, how her desire had infused him as if drawn from her lips to permeate his soul. The experience had been like no other. He'd been so in tune with her body, captivated. He hadn't thought himself capable of such an all-consuming passion. A passion not just of the body.

James shook of the mawkish thought but couldn't refrain from admitting aloud, "I've missed ye these past days, *mo chroí.*"

Scarlett looked up at him, feeling a jolt of surprise and maybe a little annoyance, too. "Missed me? Really? I thought you'd forgotten all about me."

"How could I forget aboot ye, *mo chroí?*" Laird traced his knuckles along her jaw before gently rubbing her ear lobe between his fingers. She savored his touch and the husky burr of his softly spoken words even though she had no clue what they meant. "There's been little else on my mind all these past days."

"Really? I couldn't tell with the way you were ignoring me," she said, biting her lip. Ugh, she berated herself. No man, regardless of the century, appreciated a clingy, controlling woman.

"I wisnae ignoring ye, lass," he sighed, tucking her head into the curve of his shoulder. "I stayed away from ye because I cannae be near ye wi'out wanting ye, lass," he whispered, bending his lips to her ear. A little shudder raced through her and a blush blossomed on her cheeks. "Yer utterly beguiling. My father would ken how I felt the moment he saw me wi' ye. He would ken I'm bewitched."

"Would that be so bad?"

"For yer sake and mine, my father cannae think that there is anything more between us than my returning ye to the Lindsay. He has enough suspicions already. I couldnae appear too close to ye whilst he was nearby. Appearances are everything."

"Appearances, huh? Doesn't he care that Rhys appears

close to me?"

"Rhys disnae care. 'Tis his way of thumbing his nose at Father."

"But you wouldn't dare." It wasn't a question.

"No' whilst my future is in his hands."

"How is it in his hands?" Rhys had told her Laird didn't answer to anyone.

"I will tell ye my secrets when ye reveal yers, lass."

He must have known that would be enough to shut her up.

But he wasn't just avoiding her because he regretted their passionate encounters. If he did, he had shown none of it tonight.

At least there was that.

26

"How do ye fair this morn, Scarlett?" Rhys asked, drawing her horse up alongside Scarlett's the next morning.

"I'm fine."

"Are ye certain? I heard the oddest moaning last night."

"Did you, now?" Scarlett winced, wondering if Laird had given his brother an accounting of their night together.

"Aye," he persisted. "I only mention it because ye seem a bit flushed this morning. A fever perhaps?"

"Oh, dear, I do hope you aren't falling ill," Aleizia said from her other side.

True to her name, Scarlett blushed mightily all the way up to her hairline. "No, I just..." Scarlett pressed her lips tightly together. She had ne intention of sharing the details with Rhys or Aleizia. "I'm fine."

"Hmm, must hae been an auld tom maun hae been caught beneath some of the supplies stacked behind yer tent." He flashed her a wink and smiled knowingly.

"Must have been," Scarlett responded weakly, shifting in

the awkward saddle and it wasn't only because she found it so uncomfortable. She was still tender from the previous night. That second bout might have been just one too many. She wasn't used to it.

Their lovemaking, as hasty as it had been, had been explosive. There was something appealing about being utterly ravished. She had never felt such urgency in her life, had never known that desire could be so intense, all consuming. He had taken her to a plane of rapture she hadn't even known existed.

No, he had propelled her there, ratcheting up her desires to match his as if he would accept nothing less. It was a far cry from her experience with her former partners who had both worried so much about whether or not they were pleasing her that they'd forgotten to actually do it.

One of them had spent so much time asking her over and over 'Do you like that? Do you like that?' that she'd nodded just to hurry him along because it had been so distracting. She'd had to take charge of the progress just to see it through.

And in the end, she had been nothing but a conquest for them. Bragging rights to Scarlett Thomas' bed. It was why she had never taken another lover.

And now she had taken Laird Hepburn. A man who was desperate to have her. Just her. Scarlett. Yet even in that impassioned haste, he had seen to it that she found her own pleasure in the moment before he found his own satisfaction.

Scarlett squirmed in the saddle, memories of magnificent his body against hers renewing the tension between her thighs.

Even a minute on horseback was a burden but she was only making it worse thinking like that.

"Are ye looking for someone?" Rhys continued. "Laird,

perhaps?"

With a blush, Scarlett returned her focus to her traveling companions. No, she hadn't been searching the crowd for Laird, but she had been absently scanning the amassed troops hoping to spot the elusive Donell. What if the peculiar old Scotsman was really the source of her predicament, as he implied?

Of course, he had to be. What else would he be doing here as well? Did that mean that Laird and his sword weren't the key to her way back home after all? That she didn't need to stay close to him?

That she didn't need him at all?

No, some instinct told her that her future – and with it, her return to her own time and place – was linked directly to Laird. While it might be against her best interests to travel with Laird and leave Dunskirk and Donell behind, she somehow knew Donell would be back around when it suited him to be and not a moment before.

"No, I wasn't looking for anyone," she lied. "I was just thinking what a tedious day it's going to be."

"Perhaps we can pass the time with a story," Aleizia suggested.

"Aye, a story would be just the thing," Rhys agreed, though his curious smile told her that he knew she was lying.

"Do you know a good one?" she asked and smiled when he chuckled.

"Mayhap. Mayhap." Rhys looked up thoughtfully. "The *Nun's Priest's Tale* perhaps?"

Chaucer. "Heard it. What else do you have?"

"The *Treatise on the Reformation*?"

Aleizia shook her head vehemently and Scarlett wrinkled her nose playfully. "Sounds a little dry for a road trip and I don't dare doze off on this beast. Nothing else?"

Rhys laughed. "There are some old poems and a bard's tale or two I might relate, but truth I'd rather hear another of your stories. They are unlike any I've ever heard before. I love this... What did you call it? Musical theater?"

"Of course you do," she said with a smile. "But I'm not about to sing out here with all these people around."

"Such a great misfortune," Aleizia said sadly.

"For me as well," Rhys teased, laying a hand over his heart. "Have you no other tales?"

"How about the tales of Robin Hood and his band of Merry Men who robbed from the rich to give to the poor when Prince John ruled England when Richard the Lionheart departed on the Crusades?"

Rhys' eyes widened. "I believe I might hae heard tell of such a tale before. That might verra well be the first time ye've spoken of anything I might find familiar."

"Well, we can't have that, can we?" Scarlett joked, then an idea came to her and she pulled out her purse and dug inside for her paperback copy of *Pride and Prejudice*. She had brought it along to read on the plane but had almost forgotten about it. "How about this?"

"What is that?" he asked, taking the dog-eared old thing from her and studying it curiously.

"It's a book," Scarlett said, resisting the urge to add a 'Duh'. "You do have books, don't you?"

"Aye, we hae books. Large, heavy tomes for the most part." Rhys smoothed a palm over the cover before running the pad of his thumb down the even, laser-cut edge as Aleizia looked on curiously. "It's so... tiny. The color on the cover... the pages are..." Rhys shook his head as he trailed off.

"Let me see it."

Scarlett looked up in surprise to see that Laird had fallen in between her and Aleizia. Rhys leaned across her and handed him the novel. Like Rhys, he examined it with some awe before opening it reverently and running a finger over the typeface print. "I've ne'er seen such uniform script. 'Tis so small, yet there is so much space left blank at the sides."

"It's the margin."

"'Tis a waste of fine paper," he said, rubbing a single page between two fingers. "'Tis verra fine, true. I've ne'er seen the like. Where did ye get it?"

The bookstore. How Laird would glaze over with awe and wonder if she told him the tale of huge bookstores, mapped in a maze of shelves with thousands of books full of wasteful margins? And pictures! Good thing there were no illustrations to explain. "Uh, my director bought it for me."

"No' yer father?"

No, the only book her father had ever bought her was about how to make it big in Hollywood. "No."

"Yer director maun be verra wealthy to gi' away such treasure."

What would he say if she told him that she owned hundreds of books? Keel over in shock? Die laughing? That was more like it. "Yes, books are a treasure. Would you like to read it?"

"Nay. To my shame, I cannae do so easily."

Laird handed the book back to his now curious brother who opened the book and scanned a page with a frown. "Some of the words are most oddly spelled. Others unfamiliar."

Having seen the difference between the old English spellings and sentence structure as compared to relatively modern writing, she wasn't surprised.

"Will ye read from it, Scarlett?" Aleizia asked. "Twould be a most pleasant way to pass the journey."

"I can, though I'm not sure the men will like it," she told her as she flipped through the pages. "It's just a silly story about love and marriage. Things that matter to a woman."

"Ye think it matters naught to a man?" Laird asked. "Ye think we dinnae wish to find comfort in the arms of our wives if we can?"

"Given what I've heard," Scarlett pointedly cast a sidelong glance at Rhys, "I guess I hadn't gotten the impression that many of the men around here particularly cared whose bed they found comfort in. You seem to do as you please regardless of your marriage vows given the number of illegitimate offspring running around Scotland. No offense."

"None taken." Laird stroked his chin thoughtfully, scratching his short beard along his jaw. "Many more men would be faithful to their wives, I think, given the choice and the chance."

"Infidelity is always a choice," she pointed out.

"I was referring to the wife," he said. "Given the choice of a wife. A marriage bed can be a cold, unwelcome place for a man to rest his head, much less warm his body. A man fortunate enough to love where he lies is a happy man, and me thinks, more often a faithful one."

"Would you be such a man?"

His eyes were bright as polished silver when they met hers. "I could be given a chance."

"A chance to do what?"

"Och, enough already," Rhys groaned, rolling his eyes. "Get on wi' it!"

"Hey!" Scarlett pinned him with a fierce frown. "We're

talking here." Lord knew it was a rare enough occurrence. She wanted to savor the moment.

"My apologies for my discourtesy."

"Thank you." She started to turn back to Laird but Rhys wasn't to be denied.

"Och, lass, would ye no' just read the bluidy book already?"

Scarlett shook her head, but Laird only grinned. His eyes promising to continue the conversation later.

"Well, since you asked so nicely," she said wryly and opened the book to the first page. "'It is a truth universally acknowledged, that a single man in possession of a good fortune, must be in want of a wife. However –'"

Rhys burst out in laughter but more to her surprise, Laird did as well. "What is it?"

"Nothing, lass. There is much truth in those words indeed, though I cannae recall that has yet been universally acknowledged." Rhys chuckled again. "'Tis an amusing thought."

"Read on," Laird nodded with a wink. "I begin to like this tale already."

Scarlett's lips twitched but she looked down and continued, "'However, little known of the feelings or views of such a man may be on his first entering a neighbourhood, this truth is so well fixed in the minds of the surrounding families, that he is considered the rightful property of someone or other of their daughters.'"

Laird's shoulders shook again and with a smile, Scarlett did indeed read on.

"I have to say, as far as invasions go, I'm pretty underwhelmed," Scarlett told Rhys that night when he joined her at the dinner table Aiden had set before the small campfire outside her tent.

Laird estimated that between seventy and a hundred thousand men, women and children now comprised the supply train that had funneled over a narrow bridge crossing the River Tweed into England that afternoon. Even if they hadn't announced they were mounting an invasion, the English would have to have been idiots not to see it coming, assuming they had any sort of spy network at all. Scarlett was fairly certain they did.

"*Under*whelmed?" he asked, pouring her another glass of wine. "What do ye mean?"

Scarlett shrugged. "I guess I just thought it would seem more invasive somehow."

Rhys chuckled. "The time will come, my dear. On the morrow, we will take Wark Castle. While that willnae provide the action ye feel lacking, from there we will move on in a fashion that will hopefully meet wi' yer expectations."

"No, if this is all the violence you're expecting, I'm fine with that. I like an invasion where no one gets hurt." Scarlett twirled her wine around the bowl of her goblet. "I worry for you all."

"I've said before, I'm too arrogant to die."

His conceit was incredible, she thought, pursing her lips. "No one is."

"Speaking of worries," he segued as she set her cup aside and absentmindedly began picking her way through a piece of bread. "Tell me, dear Scar, hae ye nae family who might be worrying over yer absence?"

"None nearby." Ha, what an understatement!

"We've undeniably established that yer nae nun but hae ye nae husband?"

"No."

"Yet ye maun be nearly a score of years in age?" Rhys asked, pushing a plate of food her way. Scarlett absently picked up a piece of some sort of poultry and nibbled at it.

"I'm twenty-four," she corrected and was rewarded with a look of surprise.

"Truly?" he said, diverted from his interrogation. "I would hae thought ye much younger. I ne'er would hae guessed we were of an age."

Astonishment of her own coursed through Scarlett. Of an age? Rhys was only twenty-four? She would have thought him closer to thirty, easily. That meant Laird was probably not much older than that when she would have thought him in his early thirties with that bit of gray in his beard. What did that make Lady Ishbel? If she had married at about thirteen or fourteen like Aleizia, that would make her around forty rather than the sixty Scarlett had guessed. That was a revelation.

"Hae ye been widowed then?" Rhys' squire, Willem, approached offering to refill their wine glasses and Scarlett shook her head before turning back to Rhys.

"No-o-o." Scarlett drew out her answer. "I doubt I'll ever marry."

"Why is that?"

"Well, partially because of my parents." He truly did ask all the interesting, if occasionally tough questions. "They were a constant scandal. It was almost embarrassing. Each time they divorced and married and divorced and married again…" Scarlett rolled her wrist to indicate the progression as she trailed off.

"Divorce? That is scandalous. How many times?"

"My dad has been married three times… I don't know why I tell you all of this."

"I'm easy to talk to. All the ladies say so."

A grin tugged at the corner of her lips. "I'm sure they do."

"Please continue." Rhys waved his fingers encouragingly.

"Okay. Anyway Mom was planning on marrying her fifth future ex-husband when I… saw her last," Scarlett finished jerkily, just realizing that she might never see her mother again. She stared down into her wine as if it might hold some undiscovered wisdom before lifting it to her lips. As odd as she was, she missed her parents. Did they miss her though? That was the question.

"Astonishing. I've known a widow or two who married four times but always because their spouse died and they needed another protector," he told her. "And yet ye hae none? Do ye no' long for a home? Bairns?"

"No. Maybe." Scarlett scowled at the bone in her hand and tossed it away. "It doesn't matter what I want. That's the thing about being in a public position. I've never been able to get past the fact that men probably wanted something more from me, than just me. My cache. My fame. I am a product to them. Not a person. I doubt that makes much sense to you."

"Ah, but it does," Rhys drawled. "I might be the mere second son of a second son but I hae discovered well enough that there are many things beyond my person that motivate some ladies to pursuit me."

"Your charm and good looks aren't reason enough?"

"No' for many. 'Tis my purse that attracts them. My family, my position. Rarely my person."

"It appears we have more in common than I thought."

"'Twould seem so. Yer lucky I suppose no' to hae anyone forcing ye to wed."

"Forcing you to wed?" Scarlett repeated in disbelief. "I guess I'm not surprised that your mom mapped out your life from the cradle but is she really that big of a control freak?"

Rhys smiled at her curious choice of words. "'Tis the way it works at our station in life but ye mistake the matter. It is by my father's behest, no' my mother's that I will soon wed."

Understanding and sympathy washed over her. "And how do you feel about being a husband one day? Having a wife?"

"We all do what we must, don't we?" Rhys offered the surprisingly maudlin thought as he twirled his whiskey around his glass. "I ken something of playing a role, lass. I might make a fine thespian myself."

"Is there no other option for you?"

He looked up at her softly spoken words. Surprise lighting his eyes. "Yer a perceptive lass, Scarlett Thomas. 'Struth, I had desired to dedicate my life to the church."

"You? A priest?" Scarlett couldn't help but laugh at the thought. He did have the face of an angel, but a priest? "I'm sorry but you don't strike me as a man of the cloth."

He would be fabulous in the confessional though, if he could pull revelations from his parishioners as easily as he did from her.

Rhys flicked a dismissive wrist. "Och, it isnae all piety and celibacy, my dear."

"Isn't it?"

"An appointment in the church would no' necessarily require either," he said. "My cousin, John, is the Bishop of Brechin. He manages two mistresses and a half dozen bastards in his time away from the nave."

Scarlett inwardly cringed, reaching out to cover his hand. "How terrible. And that's the life you want for yourself?"

"It matters naught what I want. 'Tis my father's will that matters." Rhys turned his hand beneath hers and laid his other hand atop hers, sandwiching it between them. "Alas, I am no' alone in ha'ing to obey an undesirable command. Take Laird for example."

Just his name had her heart leaping into her throat. Rhys must have felt her tense because his fingers closed around hers. "The mighty Laird of Achenmeade? Who would dare tell him what to do?"

"Och, lass. Ye ken nothing of how our world works, do ye?" There was something in his voice. Sympathy, maybe? Dread washed over her and Scarlett unconsciously braced herself before he even spoke. "Even ha'ing a title and living of his own cannae save Laird from a fate similar to my own."

"A fate...?" Scarlett gaped as she grasped his meaning and drew her hand away.

He was engaged? Her contrary heart sprinted and Scarlett scolded herself internally. What did it matter? Just because he kissed her and more? In her time – and not just in Hollywood – sex didn't seem to mean that much at all anymore. Whether one was married, engaged or not.

"Forgi' me for speaking plainly, dearest Scar, but I hae to say something," Rhys said, reclaiming her hand and squeezing it gently. "I should hae sent ye away when I had the chance but I kept ye close to taunt Laird. I dinnae expect ye to engage so deeply."

"What are you talking about?"

"I ken what ye were aboot last night and I hadnae thought much of it, but something has changed between ye two today and as I said before, I worry for ye. I had hoped ye were safely wed and just looking for a dalliance but I can see I was a fool to think so. I dinnae want to see yer heart broken, knowing he's gotten to ye."

Scarlett pushed away from the table in astonishment.

"Ahh, dinnae shake yer head at me, dear lass. I'm nae blind."

"I'm not in *love* with him." Scarlett protested hotly. No, if there was one thing fame had taught her, it was not to get too attached to a men. In truth, she learned not to care too deeply for anyone at all because she never knew if anyone truly cared for her as a person. She had major issues with trusting someone's word on the matter. She'd seen her parents get sucked in by pretty words and torrid affairs too many times. "I hardly know him."

Rhys shrugged and retrieved his goblet. "I've known him all my life but doubt I will ever truly know him. Time matters naught in these matters nor does familiarity."

"I'm his prisoner, for crying out loud!"

"Are ye truly? And how is it exactly that he holds ye? I see nae bindings, nae cage that keeps ye here."

Scarlett turned away, walking in long strides down the lane between the tented rows. She was appalled by Rhys' erroneous assumption. Heaven forbid Laird thought the same thing!

She wouldn't have any man thinking she was mooning for him. Why if the press were to latch on to such a notion, it would be the scandal with Grayson all over again. She wouldn't have it.

Not that she seemed to have much control over it. Scarlett's pace slowed as the spurt of incredulity Rhys' erroneous assumption roused trickled away. There was something deeper and far more unsettling about the gap Laird's absence left in her life these past few days. She missed his presence – which was absurd enough given their short acquaintance – but combined with the depth of her attraction to Laird and the intensity of her physical response to him, the trifecta of symptomatic caring was disconcerting. Even that shallow psychoanalysis had deterred her from trenching any deeper.

Sometimes life was easier without having all the facts.

✕ ✕ ✕ ✕ ✕

Strong arms caught her around the shoulders. With a start, she looked up into Laird's smiling eyes. "There ye are. I was just coming to find ye. The King is well done wi' my services for the night and my time is yers. What shall we do?"

Scarlett drew herself together, focusing only on the pleasure seeing him brought her and not at all on the reasons why.

"I don't know. There are so many choices here at camp," she teased. "What would you like to do?" Flames lit his eyes and a flutter answered in her chest. "Besides that."

"A walk perhaps around the camp to stretch yer legs? I ken how ye like to get some exercise."

"Yes, that would be wonderful."

With her hand tucked into the crook of his arm, Laird led her down the lane of tents. It was dark but small campfires dotted the path at intervals to guide them as they walked along.

"You're verra quiet tonight," he said after a long stretch of silence.

"Quiet?" she chuckled. "My voice is nearly raw from reading to you all day long. You wouldn't let me quit."

Laird shrugged. "And yet, we're still no' finished wi' the story, but that is no' what I meant. There is something amiss and I dinnae think that another day on horseback is solely to blame."

"It's nothing. How was your night?"

He shrugged, covering her hand with his. "Just taking possession of the armaments France sent through Dunbar and making final plans for the morrow."

"Rhys said you were going to take Wark Castle tomorrow. I've never heard of it. Will it be dangerous?"

"Do ye worry for me, lass?"

More than she cared to admit. "Yes."

"Ye need no' fear, lass. Wark has changed hands so many times 'tis unlikely we'll need to do more than knock at the gate. I shall return by supper."

"Without a scratch?"

"Ye hae my word."

"Good." They walked in companionable silence for a

while before Scarlett thought to ask, "Laird, do you know Donell?"

"I ken many a man named Donell, lass. Can ye be more specific?"

"An older man, looks like he's a hundred but about as spry as a ten-year-old? He lives at Dunskirk maybe?"

"Ye mean auld Donell?" he asked, lifting his brows in surprise. "Wee fellow aboot so tall with tufts of hair o'er his ears and face of a troll?"

Her eyes flared. "I would have gone with elf, but yes. Do you know him? Where I can find him?" she asked anxiously.

"Nay, lass. He's no' often at Dunskirk but only passes by occasionally. I dinnae ken that he had joined the muster as he is too auld to fight," he said but curiosity would not let him leave it at that. "What do ye want wi' him?"

"Nothing. I just want to ask him a few questions. Can you help me find him?"

Scarlett could see the curiosity raging in his eyes at her evasive answer. The questions. What could she want with Donell? How did she even know him? Hopefully, he wouldn't press her for more information than she could offer.

"I couldnae find anything in this camp even if I kent where to look but mayhap, I can ask aboot." Laird scratched at his bearded cheek, and noting her impatience, added, "Later. Gi' o'er, lass, what do ye want wi' the auld man?"

A sigh escaped her. Scarlett wished she could explain it all to him, but she couldn't. Laird hardly trusted her at all. There was no chance he'd believe her if she told him exactly why she wanted to talk to Donell. "It was nothing. Never mind."

She would just have to keep a watchful eye for the old

man. When she found him next, there was no chance he'd escape her again.

×　×　×　×　×

Bagpipes played a lively tune not far away. Attracted by the music, James let the subject drop and turned to lead Scarlett that way. They stopped to watch as one of the kilted Highlanders laid his swords down on the ground and began to dance over them. Scarlett's red skirts swung from side to side like seductive flames as her hips swayed enticingly. She smiled up at him. Her amber eyes alight with joy.

"Yer smiles are so verra bonny," he said softly. "Ye gi' them so freely."

"And you hoard yours," she said teasingly. "I'm surprised as you are, though. Would you believe that not so very long ago every smile I had was forced?"

"Nay."

"Yes, it was exhausting."

Another curious statement from his ever-enigmatic captive.

Or was it he who was now the one held in thrall?

Scarlett applauded the dancer when the tune was finished and the piper launched into mournful ballad. A crusty old Scotsman seated by one of the tents joined his voice to the melody, slightly off-key but sweet all the same even though she couldn't make out the words.

"How lovely," she said softly, leaning into Laird as he slid an arm around her waist. "What language is that?"

His brows rose. "'Tis Gaelic, lass. Do ye no' even recognize our ancient language? True our own King hardly knows a smattering himself but 'tis the language of our people."

Scarlett grimaced, biting back the urge to retort that she wasn't one of his people. Though their argument the previous night had been spurred by another example of her not any 'familiarity' with their ways and had resulted in an extremely satisfying night of rapture, she wasn't eager to rouse his anger now. Lord knew she had at least enough acting ability to fit in if only to maintain the status quo.

"You speak it, I take it?" she asked instead, recalling the foreign words he had spoken. What did *mo chroí* mean, she wondered? *Mo ghrá?* It would be too embarrassing to ask.

"Aye."

"Then maybe you can teach me one day."

His eyes were full of questions and doubt again but he only said, "Mayhap."

"And I can teach you how to play the lute," she offered.

Astonishment and pleasure – probably because there was finally something she knew that was familiar to him – leapt into his eyes. "Ye play?"

"Yes." Sort of. She played the guitar, but six strings were six strings, right? How hard could it be? "My mother's second husband was a musician." – A guitar player in a Seattle grunge band in the nineties, but close enough – "He lasted the longest of them all and was actually inclined to give fatherhood a chance," – at least for a little while – "He taught me when I was little."

"Ye shall hae to play for me. Music is a pleasant way to pass an evening."

"Oh, I think we could manage to pass an evening pretty well, don't you?"

"Yer a saucy lass."

"And you're a roguish laird," she shot back. Laird relaxed and laughed, keeping his arm around her as they turned back toward her tent. The music faded behind them as they wound their way through the encampment. Here and there, men greeted Laird. As Rhys had long said, he was well liked.

Rhys had said a lot of things.

"Rhys told me that your father wants you to get married."

Laird was silence for a moment but then admitted, "Aye, he does."

"Is that what you didn't want to tell me about? How your father holds your future in his hands?" she asked. "It's a pretty big piece of information to withhold."

"Aye."

It was a fairly unhelpful response but it was enough for Scarlett to understand that Laird was no happier with his father's arrangements than Rhys was.

"Who does he want you to marry? Some old, withered hag?"

A smile quirked the corner of his mouth and Laird must have been feeling chatty for a change. "Nay, my cousin, Jean Scot of Buccleuch. Young, comely and well-dowered wi' lands attaching my own."

Something irksomely bitter lumped in her throat but she swallowed it back. Jealousy? No, that would be ridiculous. "Your cousin? How close of a cousin? There are laws against that sort of thing, you know?"

That half-smile broadened to a full-on grin as he looked down at her. It might have been the first time he had ever smiled at her so and the sight of those long dimples creasing his cheeks, of his humor-filled eyes shining like chrome with humor sent Scarlett's heartbeat galloping yet again. God but he was dazzling.

"No' close enough to offend the church," he said, his smile slipped away. "But nigh close enough for me to feel nae more than sisterly affection."

"Then why do it?"

"Hae ye much triumph in yer life of keeping yer father from interfering in yer life, lass? If true, tell me the key to yer success so I might use it to unlock my own freedoms."

Scarlett cringed inwardly at his challenge. No, she had never had much success in telling her father 'no'. If she had, no one in the world would know her name. She'd be just another southern girl in a southern town. "What would happen if you didn't marry her? I mean, if he loves you, surely he wouldn't force you into something you didn't want to do?"

"Ah, *mo chroí*, do ye truly understand so little of our ways?" he asked, echoing Rhys' sentiment from earlier. "My father cares far more for position and connection than affection. Were I to deny him in this, he would withhold his aid in refurbishing my keep. I am no pauper, but the task requires ready funds. I need his investment."

"Why? You could get a job, couldn't you?"

"A job?" Laird repeated and shook his head. "By God, lass, but ye've a strange manner of speech. Where did ye learn such words that I can no' e'en ken yer meaning?"

"Employment," she clarified, not daring to explain. "A trade."

"A trade? My father would be appalled. Lady Ishbel e'en more so." A look of mischief passed across his face. "The idea has merit. But, nay. I hae no tenants, no fields. The ground of Achenmeade has lain fallow for many years."

Achenmeade! Scarlett knew she had heard the name before. Now she remembered why. Why the Achenmeade label was one of the oldest brands of Scotch in the world. Almost, well, five hundred years old. Wasn't that a coincidence? "Scotch," she blurted out. "You could make scotch. The best the world has ever known."

"Scotch."

"Whiskey," she hurried on excitedly, turning to catch his hand between hers. "All you need is to go dig up that friar of yours and start bottling the stuff. You could sell it and get rich."

"I cannae fathom." Laird shook his head, but he was thinking about it. Scarlett could see the wheels turning in his mind. "Mayhap I could keep Dunskirk wi'out Father's aid."

"Wouldn't you rather have a trade than be at his beck and call?"

"The idea does hold some appeal."

"You could be free to do what you want."

"Could I?" Tilting her chin up, he brushed his lips across hers and she felt the ever present spark between them ignite once more. "How aboot right now? 'Tis been a long day wi'out ye, *mo chroí*."

"Has it?" she teased breathlessly, parting her lips to deepen the delicious kiss.

Wrapping his arms around her waist and lifted her against him as he backed her into the tent without breaking their kiss. She lips softened, parting beneath his with a sigh. "*Mhianliom tú, mo chroí. I maun hae ye.*"

"What about propriety?"

"Fook propriety."

"Okay."

28

Gasping for air, Scarlett pushed away from Laird and pulled off her headdress. She flung it to the side and began untying the laces on the sides of her gown as she watched him strip away his kilt, hose and shirt. Already the delirium of her desire was setting in. Her heart was fluttering madly, her head woozy. Her body feverish and aching.

She'd had illnesses that were more mildly symptomatic.

His eyes darkened with hunger as she peeled the dress off her shoulders, leaving her in only her chemise. Laird eagerly aided her in seeing to its dismissal, sweeping it over her head and throwing it aside. Her nipples hardened, aching as his calloused palms curled around her breasts.

"I don't know how you do this to me," she moaned as his lips scathed down her neck to the hollow of her throat.

"Ye enflame me much the same," he murmured softly.

"I'm not sure if I like it." Contrary to her words, Scarlett wrapped her arms around his head, pulling him closer.

His warm chuckle puffed against her sensitive skin sending

a wave of sensual chills down her spine. "Neither am I."

Scarlett gasped as Laird cupped her bottom and pulled her flush against his long, hard body. "You might be more than I can handle."

Even knowing that, she couldn't resist him.

"Let's find out."

Laird lifted her and carried her to the mattress, falling with her onto the feathered depths and turning her beneath him. Scarlett pushed against his sweaty chest, harder still until he rolled onto his back, chest heaving, and a quizzical look on his face.

"What are ye aboot, lass?"

With a smile, she crawled over him until she straddled his hips. The rough hair of his thighs abraded her tender skin but the feel of him hard and naked below her only roused her more.

Clasping his face between her hands, she ran her fingernails over the scruff of his beard before dipping her head and kissing him passionately. She ran her tongue over his lips, nipping gently before she trailed kisses to his ear.

"Possession," she whispered, breathing hard. "You had your chance before. This time it's my turn." She shifted from side to side, inching upward until he was nestled tightly against her groin. Her body was trembling, shaken be the force of her desire and by the frantic pounding of her heart. "I am going to take you, Laird. And not only because I want to shag you."

Laird tensed beneath her with a swift intake of breath, Scarlett could feel his surprise in every line of his body. Grinning wickedly, she lifted her hips and positioned herself over him. Her breath seized, her body quivered as she descended slowly. Spreading for him, moisture gathering.

His throbbing erection was poised for entry and Scarlett was aching for him. Laird sat up, wrapping his arm around her waist, lifting her. "Let me."

"No," she released a ragged breath. His intent, she knew, was to flip her beneath him and take control. She wanted this. Wanted to see him. Scarlett pushed him back once more, bracing her hands against his chest. Closing her eyes, she threw back her head and slowly took him in.

God, he was huge! Inch by inch she took him, a long moan torn from deep within escaped her as he filled her. She clenched around him, adjusting to him until she was seated completely. Savoring the moment, she ran her palms over his shoulders and chest, marveling at the feel of him, velvet over steel. Across the swell of his pecs, over the rise and fall of his abs.

"Lass. Scarlett," his voice was harsh. "Look at me."

Opening her eyes, Scarlett met Laird's gaze, churning beneath hooded lids. Molten. His hands ran up her legs, roughly kneading her thighs until his fingers dug into her hips. He flexed his hips, his manhood jerking inside her.

"Are ye done wi' this game of yers yet?"

Biting her lip, Scarlett shook her head. "Oh, it isn't a game." Rising up, she slid down his silky length but was up again quickly, then descending faster, harder. Her gasp was drown out by his agonized groan but again she was up. This time Laird was ready for her. His grip tightened on her hips and he pulled her down roughly, arching beneath her. Sensation shot through her, stealing her breath. Her heart stuttered. "Oh God," she moaned. Lifting her, he urged her on, each time driving upward, more fervently. Meeting her frenetic pace.

Her climax was on her almost immediately, splintering

through her like explosive charges and she cried out her release.

Laird bowed beneath her with a harsh yell. *"Mo ghrá!"* Sitting up, he held her tightly against him. Cupping the back of her head, he drew her lips to his. He kissed her deeply, swallowing her moans.

Scarlett collapsed against his sweaty, heaving chest. His heart was pounding hard; jumping against her cheek while Laird nuzzled her ear, his soft brogue nearly incoherent with murmurings of praise and nonsensical words.

He ran his tongue along the edge of her earlobe. "I've never had a woman mount me before."

"Did you like it?" she asked, smiling against his chest as his arms tightened around her.

"Aye. There is some merit in being at someone's mercy."

Scarlett drew back to look up at him curiously. "Mercy?" she whispered, her voice surprisingly throaty.

His nod sent a tantalizing ripple through the muscles of his shoulder and chest. "Aye, let me show ye."

A shudder of longing rippled over her at the promise in his voice. "Okay."

Rotating her beneath him, Laird's lips moved downward, nipping at her collarbone and the top of her breast before closing over her nipple. His tongue was hot, rough against the sensitive peak. Lacing her fingers through his hair, she held him against her but then he drew on her nipple more deeply. With a gasp, she tried to tug him away. Laird chuckled and suckled harder, sending bolts of pleasure/pain rocketing straight to her groin and Scarlett cried out, bowing off the mattress.

Grasping her wrists in one hand, he pinned them above her head and turned his attention to her other breast, giving it the same treatment. Scarlett sucked in strangled breath. "Laird!"

Laird lifted his head and grinned down at her. "'Tis part of being taken, lass. I only seek to ignite in ye the desperation ye rouse in me. If ye dinnae like it, tell me to stop and I will."

He lifted a brow and waited while Scarlett panted indecisively beneath him. Not because she wanted him to stop but because of the way he said that. Taken. It sounded so primitive, so controlling to a modern woman like her. Did she want to be *taken* like that by this man?

The answer came quickly. Oh, hell yes.

Scarlett looked down the length of his body poised over her. Every muscle was defined, flexed and bulging. He was magnificent. "Well, what were you waiting for?" She had intended the words to come out as a bold dare but instead they were breathless with anticipation.

With a groan, his lips descended on hers. His tongue swept over hers before he tore mouth away. It was back, hot and wet, on her breast. Picking up where he had left off.

Her breast, a small but perfect mound, rising and falling beneath his lips. James suckled hard once more, savoring her cries of delight. The musky scent of her filled his senses. Releasing her hands, he cupped her other breast in his palm, rolling the nipple between his fingers until Scarlett was again fisting her hands in his hair, now urging him on.

She was glorious in her passion. Her ivory skin flushed pink in her excitement, her flesh warm, damp with perspiration. Tasting of salt, heat and Scarlett. Dipping his head to her belly, he turned his head from side to side, knowing his lass loved the chafing of his beard against her delicate skin. She stiffened and moaned, nearly tearing his hair from his scalp.

With a dark chuckle, he flipped her over onto her stomach, licking, biting, sucking as if he might devour her. His long fingers bit into her bottom, kneading. The hair on his chest, prickling her as his body caressed hers. Then his mouth followed behind. Down each leg and up again until he tasted every inch of her.

Her blood was surging through her veins like fire. Her panting breaths became shallow and frantic. Her head was swimming but she refused to faint. She didn't want to miss a second of this.

She was on her back again; his hands and mouth working their way back up her legs. Laird was not gentle with her. In fact, he seemed utterly abandoned as if he couldn't help himself. Couldn't control himself. Couldn't get enough of her. The thought thrilled her even more. Desperation, he had said. If he was feeling anything of the feverish yearning he provoked in her, she could well understand his lack of restraint.

His hot breath blowing against her was her only warning before his mouth closed over the throbbing nub at the juncture of her thighs. A hoarse cry escaped her as his tongue circled her, then he bit down lightly. The orgasm came so quickly, Scarlett arched off the bed in shock as pleasure swept her like a whirlwind. Frenzied charges sparked and flared. With his tongue, Laird soothed her with soft strokes but the moment she relaxed, he was at it again.

He let the storm build more slowly this time, the tension escalated, knotting almost painfully until Scarlett was panting desperately, begging. Her release when it came was as blinding as a flash of lightning sending electricity cursing through her.

Then again. This time when she came Laird lifted himself over her, hooking her leg over his shoulder until her thighs were spread wide to welcome him. His eyes were hot, holding some emotion Scarlett couldn't identify. He ran his fingers through her short hair and kissed her gently, then again more deeply as he plunged within her. He hissed as he sucked in a sharp breath.

His brogue was sensual, throaty. "Yer so hot. Ah, lass!"

Laird's lips took hers as he began to move, slowly at first as if he were trying to draw it out. His chest rocked against hers, hearts pounding as one. Dragging over her tender nipples. He cupped her bottom in one big hand, urging her to match his rhythm. The languor was only fleeting, however. Desperation had its own demands. Their tempo hastened. Laird lifted himself over her, changing the angle of his thrusts. With a gasp, Scarlett wrapped her free leg around his hips, dragging her nails up them until she could grasp his hard buttocks as he flexed with every thrust.

Faster. He slammed into her. Deeper and deeper still until she was caught in rapacious agony, caught in the tempest once more.

Words of passion, words she couldn't understand were on his lips. "*Tog den. Bhful don.*" She could hear no more as she reached the eye of the storm. Her blood was raging in her ears, the torment too much to bear. A sob was torn from deep within.

Scarlett." His voice was commanding and she looked up at him. So beautiful, so intense. "Let me see ye, *mo cridhe. Guilleadh don.*"

"Yes," she whispered hoarsely, taken by the torment in his eyes. It didn't matter what he said. "Oh, Laird… yes!"

"*Comhlanaigh dom, mo ghrá.*"

With one last blinding thrust, he pushed her over the edge once more. Scarlett cried out as it ripped her apart body and soul. Laird joined her rapture with a harsh groan, stiffening before he slumped over her. Continuing to pump languidly within her as she pulsed around him. Drawing out her climax until tears were rolling down her cheeks.

He cleared them away with the back of his knuckles, brushing tender kisses down her cheek and along her jaw.

She had never imagined there might exist such a lover as he. The sensations he had evoked in her were really almost too much to bear.

No, she really hadn't thought this through, had she? The road he had taken her down was becoming treacherous indeed.

29

"More rabbit?" Rhys asked, holding out a piece of juicy meat as he rejoined her at the table.

"Thank you."

"More wine?" he asked, sprawling back in his chair. He had shed his doublet, his shirt open at the collar and hanging over his kilt.

"Yes, please." Scarlett was almost as informally dressed, having shed her parlett and untied the sleeves of her finely woven flax gown, which were normally laced tightly from elbow to wrist, and pushing them up her arms. Her jaunty Italian bonnet – favored by Laird over the ear-covering French hood – was hanging on the back of her chair.

"Another bottle, Willem." Rhys nodded to his squire, a young man of about twenty who brought a bottle of wine to the table and poured for them both.

"Did we finish one already?" Scarlett asked, staring down into her cup in surprise.

"Two, my lady," Willem said with a smile.

"Oh, that's a lot." She tipped up her goblet again.

"Yer no' verra talkative this night, dear Scarlett," Rhys said softly. "Hae ye no' forgiven me my hasty words? I beg ye, dinnae bear me a grudge. I apologize truly."

Scarlett sighed. Whatever Rhys' misconceptions, he was only trying to be a friend. "I'm not angry with you."

"Then what vexes ye so?"

Not what. *Who.*

Hence the alcohol.

"There is something troubling ye." It wasn't a question this time. "What is it?"

Scarlett looked around warily. The night was dark, moonless. There was little to see beyond the glow of their small fire except similar spots of flickering light in the darkness.

"Laird won't be back for hours," Rhys told her, reclaiming her attention. "Fear no', he has returned from Wark unharmed. The castle taken smoothly and now under Scottish garrison. 'Tis the King who demands his attendance again this night."

Or perhaps it was their father who demanded it, determined to keep Laird from her side. Either way, it didn't matter. His absence wasn't the problem. In fact, for the first time, Scarlett was glad Laird was nowhere in sight, however Rhys didn't need to know that.

"Yes, he told me. Why aren't you there?" she asked evasively.

"I, thankfully, am not my father's favorite son," he said with a smirk, tipping up his goblet. "Therefore I get to spend the night as I please. With you. Now, come. Talk to me. I assume the problem is wi' Laird?"

"Yes," she admitted. Damn, Rhys and his insight! "And

that is why I cannot talk to you. Besides, I've drunk too much. If I open up now, I might not be able to get the flood gates shut again."

"That might be most amusing."

"Or humiliating," she countered. "Depending on which side of the conversation you're on."

"True. True," Rhys nodded, swirling his wine around his goblet before lifting it and downing the contents in one swallow. He held his cup up once again for his squire to refill.

Thankfully, Rhys seemed content to let the matter lie. Something Scarlett was grateful for. She couldn't talk about what was troubling her.

She thought she'd known what she was getting herself into by giving into her desire for Laird. She thought that once they'd slept together, the edge would come off the intensity that had so shaken her that first time. That she could just lust after him like a normal person.

She had been a fool to think she would feel so deeply just the one time, not every time. The road Laird had taken her down was too intense to be taken casually. It rocked her to the core and terrified her more than a little.

For the first time since arriving in this time, Scarlett truly felt the urge to run.

To do *something* before she became too attached to him.

"Did the King command him to go?" she asked but rushed to add, "Not that I care about whether he was forced to go, I'm just wondering if they are close. King James is Laird's uncle, right?"

Rhys shook his head but took the bait. "To my knowledge, the King has never acknowledged the connection. I dinnae think he means to shun Laird in so much as he knows verra well that he wisnae his father's favorite child any more than I am my father's. It has never bothered me much but the King wisnae so forgiving."

"That seems odd. I would think any monarch's heir would automatically be his favorite child – if he were to have one, of course. Who was his favorite then?" she asked simply to perpetuate the conversation. "Laird's mother?"

"His favorite daughter perhaps but nay, 'tis well known that the auld King favored his second son above all his children. Perhaps that is why Laird served as his squire, at the King's bidding," Rhys shrugged and swallowed more wine, tipping up his cup to get the last drop before holding it out to be refilled once more.

"Thank ye, Willem."

The young man beamed, his eyes filled with adoration for his master.

"Top me off, too, Willem." Scarlett pressed her fingers to her lips as a hiccup escaped her. "I heard about him. The Duke of something?"

"Ross."

"Yes, that's it."

"Perhaps it was the duke who taught Laird to be the way he is. He inspires such love from his people yet he cares naught for any of us."

Scarlett thought Rhys was wrong about that. Laird did care, thought he hid it well. Perhaps he even cared about her as well.

Ha, she must be tipsier than she thought.

"He might have made a fine King," he went on. "He is the only child of the auld King's oldest child. In another world, in another time, he might have been King."

"Naw," she scoffed, waving off the notion with a flick of

her fingers. Laird might have been legitimate but his mother was not. Scarlett bit her tongue from blurting out Laird's secret and said instead, "That would never happen. The laws of primogeniture will never change that much. A daughter, sure, but not an illegitimate child."

"And how can ye ken such a thing, my dear?" he asked, slurring his words a little. "Are ye a mystic seer?"

"Nope," Scarlett brought her goblet down on the table with a punctuated thunk. "I'm from the future."

Rhys blinked at her in a moment of silence and then burst out laughing, slapping his knee and almost spilling his wine. "The future! Ha! Ha!"

"No, it's true," she insisted, ignoring the little voice in the back of her mind that was telling her to shut her mouth. "I can prove it. Go ahead. Ask me anything."

He laughed some more but interest flared in his eyes as he leveled her a serious look. Or as serious a look as he was capable of producing in his inebriated state. "Verra well. Tell me, Scarlett my dear lass, who will be the next King of Scotland?"

Scarlett rolled her eyes. "That depends, which number on you on now? I never thought to ask."

"James is the fourth of his name."

"Oh, well, then that's easy. The next one will be James the Fifth."

They shared a look and then they both fell into a bout of laughter. Even Willem was grinning from ear to ear.

"Well played, Scarlett. Well played!" Rhys leaned across the table and lifted his cup. Scarlett tapped hers against it before they both drank deeply again.

"No, really," she said, twitching her fingers in invitation. "Give me another one."

"I dinnae know. If I ask ye who will follow King Henry, ye will probably only say Henry the Ninth." Rhys waved a finger at her.

"Henry the Eighth?" she said, her jaw sagging in amazement. Tucking one leg beneath her, she hooked her other heel on the seat of the chair and rested her chin on her knee as she stared at him with fascination. "The King of England right now is Henry the Eighth? Holy shit. Imagine that. Meeting Henry the Eighth."

"He is in France right now," he pointed out. "Ye cannae meet him."

"That's too bad," Scarlett said with honest disappointment. "Which wife is he on right now?"

"Which wife?" He raised a brow in bewilderment. "You mean Catherine?"

"Catherine? Which one?"

"What do ye mean?"

"Aragon, Howard or Parr?"

"Aragon." Rhys drank deeply once more, eyeing her over the rim of his cup.

"Ha! There you are, then. I can prove it to y'all." Scarlett waved her goblet at him triumphantly, the wine sloshing over the sides. "Henry the Eighth will have six wives. Catherine of Aragon, Anne Boleyn, Jane Seymour, Ann of Cleves, Catherine Howard and Catherine Parr."

"Six?" He jeered dismissively. "Nae man is widowed six times."

"No, he was never widowed at all." Scarlett counted them off on her fingers. "It goes divorced, beheaded, died, divorced, beheaded, survived."

Rhys spat out his wine and howled with uncontrollable laughter, rocking back in his chair until he almost tipped over before Willem caught him. Still he didn't stop, laughing so uproariously that he couldn't catch his breath and was holding his sides as Laird walked into their circle of light.

"What's all this?"

Scarlett offered up a lopsided grin. "I think I broke him."

"Yer blootered again, are ye?" James looked between them, at the empty bottles on the table and at Willem, who hastily shoved the third bottle behind his back. Rhys hollered hysterically once more.

"Hey, don't judge me." Scarlett waved a finger at him.

James snorted. "To bed wi' ye, lass."

Rhys looked set to argue but Scarlett only shook her head, leaning across the table to kiss his cheek and wish him good night before James led her off.

"Willem, be sure Rhys reaches his tent. We've an early day before us."

"Aye, my lord."

Willem took Rhys away, wrapping an arm around his waist as he stumbled away.

"Spoil sport," Scarlett mumbled as James propelled her into the tent.

"Ye've become a veritable maltworm, lass," he said, clarifying when she frowned, "A drunkard."

"Yeah? Well, I didn't grow up drinking with every meal like you did. You're going to make a drunk out me before I make it home. Then I'll have to go into rehab. The press would get a cheap thrill out of that."

Ignoring Scarlett's drunken rambling, James ignored her and looked around the tent. "Where is Maris? I hired the bluidy wench to see to yer needs no' her own."

"She's been gone since we got here. Again." Scarlett sniffed dismissively but turned to face him. "Hey, this is my tent. Mine. Remember? Propriety and all?"

"I kent whose tent it is verra well, lass," he ground out.

"You're not supposed to be in here. You should go."

"Would ye rather Rhys shared this tent wi' ye?" he asked bitterly, feeling the jealousy rising up to bite him once again. Scarlett had ignored him in favor of his brother's company again this day. After their powerful lovemaking the previous night, James was hard put to find an explanation for her suddenly aloof demeanor. Nor had she offered one.

"Rhys schmees," she mumbled. "He wouldn't share this tent with me for a million bucks. Whoa, I think I need to sit down."

Dropping on to the end of the mattress, Scarlett cradled her spinning head in her hands as the striped tent swirled like a carousel around her. "I swear I'm never drinking again."

"Yet ye will nae doubt hae another cup in yer hand on the morrow."

"Only if it's water. Is it really bad as I've heard to drink it?" she asked as James undressed her like a child.

"Where would ye hear that?" he asked.

"I think that's what they teach, isn't it? Somehow it's an embedded certainty that they didn't drink water in the past."

Such nonsense was falling from her lips, James didn't

know how to address it. "There's nothing wrong wi' water from a spring, lass, though some claim any water can chill the stomach and hinder digestion. 'Tis only standing water that ye should avoid." But she should know that. Any person would know it. It brought to mind once again all the mysteries about Scarlett and reminded him of the answers he still didn't have.

With the nonsense she was talking, there was no chance he would have them now.

"To bed wi' ye, lass," he said, pulling down the coverlet and lifting her between the sheets.

"Are you going to leave?"

"Aye, we depart in the morn to take Norham," he told her.

"No, are you going to leave me now?"

"Do ye want me to?"

"No, you should stay."

Relief swept through him. "Then I shall stay."

✕ ✕ ✕ ✕ ✕

"Awake wi' ye, lass."

Scarlett rocked from side to side as she was shaken roughly. With a groan, she rolled on to her stomach and buried her head under the pillow. She was never go to drink again. How did these people do it every day? "Go away."

"How do ye manage to live a life where ye can sleep the day away?"

Pulling her head out from under the pillow, she glared at Laird who was kneeling next to her bed. Nothing more than a silhouette in the gloom but he still managed to look appealing. And appallingly awake. "Sleep the day away?" she grumbled. "It's still dark. Go back to bed."

"Mayhap if ye were there to share it wi' me," he teased then clapped a hard hand down on her bottom, the sting searing through her thin chemise. "Make haste, lass, we maun away."

Stretching, Scarlett sat, not noticing how his gaze fell to her breasts as they pushed against the taut linen. "You are too freakin' happy. I hate morning people."

"Lass." His light caress tickled down her arm.

Running her hands over her face and through her hair, she kicked off her coverlet and rolled off the mattress. "'Kay. I'm up. I'm up."

Standing, she tugged down her chemise and jumped when his hot palms ran up her thighs, pushing it up once more. Cupping her bottom in his hands, he pulled her closer and pressed an open-mouth kiss to her belly. His beard rasped teasingly as his lips drifted southward. Scarlett clenched her thighs together as heat pooled between her legs.

This was the problem. This incessant need for him was getting out of hand. Even when she tried to dominate him, he was in charge. He left her feeling helpless and overwhelmed.

Cherished, her conscience reminded gently.

Perhaps, but he reached deeper, demanded more from her than she had ever freely given. She'd spent too long having her will overridden. She didn't like the way her body quivered at the slightest touch, her heart ached at the merest glance.

Liar, her inner devil retorted. *His protective nature tugs at your very soul and well you know it.*

Scarlett shook her head. No, she wasn't used to the concern for her well-being any more than she was used to this tempestuous desire.

True, she was in way over her head. What was she going to do about him?

Somehow she needed to put some distance between them. Find some objectivity as best she could. This wasn't her future. *He* wasn't her future.

But what if he was?

Scarlett stiffened at the thought and pushed him away before his tormenting lips might find themselves in a place that would dissolve her determination.

"I thought you said you were in a hurry?" she asked when he looked up at her quizzically.

"What troubles ye, lass?"

No more willing to talk about with him than she had been with Rhys, Scarlett only provided the same answer. "Nothing. Let's do this."

$$\times \quad \times \quad \times \quad \times \quad \times$$

Dressed in a bronze linen dress and wrapped in Laird's plaid against the morning chill, Scarlett crossed her arms protectively around her waist as she watched Aiden load Laird's possessions into his cart. Laird was clad in a thin metal armor that covered his chest beneath his kilt and sleeves of chainmail covered his massive arms. He wore no helmet, nothing at all on his legs. For a man considering doing battle, he looked alarmingly unprotected.

Surely he meant to wear something else? Scarlett couldn't help but put the question to him.

"We go to lay siege," he told her. "Norham willnae fall as easily as Wark. 'Twill take time and many cannons to defeat them. What I wear now will be unneeded."

"Really?" she asked doubtfully. "You'll be careful?"

"I always am."

"Now you're sounding as arrogant as Rhys," she mumbled not noticing the frown that furrowed his brow and darkened his eyes.

"Yer up early, Scarlett."

Scarlett turned to find Rhys strolling toward her, not from his adjacent tent but from the opposite direction. He wore the same clothes he had the previous evening and his dark auburn locks were untethered, skewed every which way. Obviously, he had just awoken.

"I wanted to say goodbye. You're going, aren't you?"

"Aye, I'm ready to be off. See?"

She turned to see Willem leading a pair of heavily laden horses over to the tent.

"If we're to Norham this day, we need to make haste, if ye dinnae mind, Rhys."

Rhys glanced curiously at Laird, taken aback by his snappish tone and hurried to Scarlett's side. Looping his arm around her waist, he turned her away and whispered, "Is something amiss?"

Scarlett shook her head. "I don't know. He was perky enough this morning but something's eating him now."

"I'll try to pry the truth from him," he assured her. "I shall write ye of that and our progress assuming I dinnae lose a hand or other more valuable limb along the way."

Scarlett bit her lip. "That's not funny."

The two of them shared a long look and tears stung at the back of her eyes as the implications of the battles awaiting them truly hit her. If the worse were to happen, she might never see Rhys again. Or Laird. The thought was staggering. "Rhys."

"Come, Rhys, we maun go," Laird barked harshly.

Casting a look over her shoulder, Scarlett turned back to the man who had started out as nothing more than a mordant scoundrel spewing nothing but mischief but had rapidly become her unlikely ally, a friend and confidante.

"Rhys." She reached up to rest her palm against his unshaven cheek. "Damn it. Don't get dead, okay?"

Humor twinkled in his eyes. His big hand covered hers before he pressed a kiss to her palm. "I wouldnae dare disappointment ye, my dear. How would I ever face ye again?"

"You're not as funny as you think you are," she chided him but couldn't help the soft smile that curved her lips. "Just be careful. Promise me."

"I shall see to it wi' all the care I am capable of mustering," he said. "Ye hae my word."

Scarlett pursed her lips. "I guess I cannot expect any greater effort than that."

"And ye, as well?" Rhys's eyes clouded over briefly. "I ken there is something bothering ye. Whatever it is, hae a care for yerself and patience for my brother. He is just as conflicted, me thinks."

Laird was glaring at them now, she noticed as she shot him a sidelong glance. "We'll figure it out." Lifting herself onto her toes, she kissed him softly on the lips then smiled as they parted. "You're a good man, Rhys."

"Yer the only one who thinks so," Rhys laughed and led her on his arm to his horse, kissing her one last time before he leapt into the saddle. "Fare thee well, my dearest Scarlett."

Scarlett nodded and turned to Laird, wringing her hands worriedly. For all that she was uncertain of how she planned to proceed with him, or if she wanted to at all, the last thing she wanted was for a hair on his gorgeous head to be harmed.

"Laird." She reached out to him, running her hand over his forearm as he checked the cinch on his saddle, but he ignored her. "Laird? What's wrong?"

"Are ye done wi' yer goodbyes?"

Blinking at his harsh tone, her hand slid away. His cheerful friskiness of the predawn hours long gone. Now his shoulders were stiff, his spine rigid. "No, not even a little. Laird, look at me, please. You're angry."

"I'm no'. Now I maun go."

"Without a goodbye?" she asked, reaching up to rake her nails along his bearded jaw. Framing his face in her hands, she forced him to look at her. "Be safe. Promise me you'll come back in one piece."

Laird scoffed and tried to look away but Scarlett held him firmly. Lifting herself up on to her toes, Scarlett pressed a kiss to his chin. It was all that was within her reach. He held himself stiff, unbending and Scarlett knew she should just leave it at that. She should let him go, let him walk away and be happy that he was putting the distance between them that she could not force herself to create, but she couldn't let him leave like that. If this were the last time she would ever see his face, she wanted the memory of a smile to carry with her always.

Or at least not a frown.

"Laird, please." She pressed her body against his and nipped lightly at his jaw. Then at the tendons at the side of his neck. At his collarbone. He resisted at first, then a shudder ran down his body and he was kissing her back. Bending her over his arm, he plundered her mouth as if that kiss would save his soul.

"James," a sharp voice barked out.

Laird's lips eased away, but not in haste. With one last lingering kiss, he drew back with a frown. Not for her but for his father.

"Let us go."

Sir William kicked his horse into motion and trotted by with Patrick, Alexander, Adam and Arthur following close behind. All of them but Sir William looking down at her with bemusement written clearly on their faces.

Chucking her chin lightly, Laird brushed one last kiss across her lips and turned away. Just a moment later he was mounted. With a wave but no smile, he was gone.

Soft hands took hers and Scarlett clasped Aleizia's tightly as they watched their men ride away.

$$\times \quad \times \quad \times \quad \times \quad \times$$

"Brother."

James stiffened as Rhys rode up beside him but ignored him, spurring his horse to a greater pace.

"Laird," he said more insistently. "I maun talk to ye aboot Scarlett. She said the strangest thing last night."

"Last night when she was bladdered wi' wine?" Laird asked caustically. "Away wi' ye, Rhys, I hae better things to do than to listen to ye this morn."

"Nay, Laird, I maun tell ye. 'Twas nonsensical to be sure but she dinnae seem deceitful. I cannae fathom, but–" Rhys put a hand on his arm but Laird shrugged him off, refusing to listen. "Bugger it, Laird, I'm worried for her."

"Enough! She isnae yer concern, Rhys." Laird kicked his horse into a gallop and left his brother behind.

31

August 26

We lay siege to Norham with our score of large caliber cannon under King James' order but not the Mons Meg, which I believe would be more effective. It's taken nearly a week already to break down the castle defenses. We have taken the outer ward and hope to have surrender from the castle garrison soon.

Worry not, mo chroí; *I am in no danger of dying from anything more than the want of you.*

James

August 27

My messenger returned without a letter from you in hand. Will ye write, lass? A note from you would bring me great pleasure and a relief from the tedium of long nights without you.

James

August 27

Would that you were here, dear Scarlett. I've naught but Laird to bear me company and his mood is stale, though I can easily guess the reason. Our supply train remains camped at Wark whilst we move on to lay siege to Norham Castle and ye wi' it. Best we take it quickly before we expire from rations of cheese and bread.

Word has reached us that Surrey (an Sassenach Earl, in case you are not aware) has taken up residence for the summer nearby at Pontefract Castle. By now he has heard of our movement and will muster the Sassenach forces to meet us.

By God's will, this will all be over soon.

Rhys

August 30

Our forces are now garrisoned at Norham Castle securing the eastern end of our supply route across the Tweed. We move on to Etal Castle on the morrow. When it, too, falls we will have gained control of the bridge over the River Till located just west of there, securing our flank against the Sassenach attack.

Will you not write me, lass?

~~Iam~~ Laird

September 1

The Lindsay joined our muster at Etal, my dearest Scarlett. In my ennui during these dull days, I find some humor in the fact that Laird will not approach him though no one else takes note as the Lindsay clan has long been a Hepburn rival. While I know he doesn't believe you to be the Lindsay's kinswoman any longer, I believe he avoids the Lindsay simply forestall any news to the contrary. He will not allow any circumstance to part you.

Perhaps he cares for you more than I had imagined. This

possibility causes me to worry for you both all the more.
Rhys

× × × × ×

The days at the Wark encampment were interminable. Letters came from both Laird and Rhys as promised though Scarlett had to enlist Aleizia to read their odd handwriting for her. For a girl used to the instant gratification of email and texts, the notes seemed unbearably infrequent and uninformative. It ate at her, not being able to Google what was happening. To have access to an instant newsfeed. There were no online videos or newscasts to keep her up to date; leaving her with long stretches between those few hastily written lines and a vivid imagination to fill in the rest.

It would have been better for her if he had left while they were still at odds with one another. When she had anger or even indifference to buffer her troubled thoughts. As if was he had left his masculine scent upon her sheets and the imprint of his last kiss in her memory.

She missed him.

The fact didn't sit well with her.

Independence played a key role in her life, self-reliance compensated for the lack of supportive relationships. Not that her parents didn't love her (she was moderately certain they did) but parenting wasn't their priority. *She* had never been their priority and she'd learned to live without deeper intimacy. If she were honest with herself, Scarlett didn't really know what to do with it now.

Being too close to Laird made her as twitchy as a golden snitch on Quidditch day. Then again having him be too far from her and in dangerous circumstances didn't leave her feeling any more serene.

That winding path Laird had somehow convinced her to

travel with him was become more and more perilous as the days passed.

She simply couldn't write him back. With no news of her own to report, Scarlett feared what else she might reveal in writing.

Unfortunately the encampment provided little in the way of distraction. Scarlett sat with Aleizia on most days, but without sewing or embroidery, or the skills to take up the task, there was little to occupy her hands or thoughts. Fortunately for her, her young friend did have that distraction because it turned out that sunny, optimistic Aleizia was a serial worrier. If she didn't have a needle in her hands, she paced restlessly, too nervous to even listen to a story.

That constant apprehension transferred itself to Scarlett so horribly that she had taken to escaping the tent for long walks or finding ways to make some modern improvements in the encampment. It had become a horrible, stinking place with slop and sewage running between the tents as people emptied their waste along the tented avenues. So, she whipped Aleizia's servants and Maris into shape, making sure they kept their area of the camp clear and clean, boiling water for washing and drinking since she hadn't discovered any clear springs during her walks. Wine was no longer an option.

When that didn't work, she found some peace in the solitude of her tent with yoga. Child's pose, dolphin pose, anything to quiet her mind and reduce her growing anxiety. To fill her days.

The long nights alone were worse.

As her stay in the sixteenth century extended with no end in sight, it should have been easy to dwell on her fears for the future more and more, mentally beating her problems to death. Even thoughts of Donell, where he might be and if he were looking for her could not overcome her worry for Laird and the battle being fought. She fretted over his safety and Rhys' until it was almost too much to bear. Even her own plight could not plague her so.

There were injuries at Norham, she knew. Some men had been brought back, injured and bleeding though none severely. It made her wonder what Laird and Rhys might not be telling her. Then another letter came. This one delivered with the instructions that she should read it personally and written in square, precise lettering that made the request possible.

September 2

Etal has been taken and our encampment has moved once more to a neutral site but a few miles away now. I cannot leave by King's command but I beg you to come to me, Scarlett. This war is a dismal thing. Only the thought of you brightens my days. Only the sight of you can cast away the darkness completely.

Also, Patrick has suffered an injury to his leg. I do not believe his life will be threatened but Patrick asks that you gently forewarn our Plumpy so as to spare us her hysteria by the time you reach us.

Yours, Laird

Though his poetic words made Scarlett's heart leap, she could only shake her head at that last. War and bloodshed they would take without a second thought but when it came to the truly difficult jobs, they left it to a woman.

× × × × ×

They obviously knew Aleizia far better than she did.

Despite a gentle breaking of the news, assurances that everything would be all right, and a shoulder to lean on, Aleizia had been a nervous wreck from the time Scarlett told her of Patrick's injury until they were well on their way to the new encampment with the supply train the next morning.

She had been in such a state that Scarlett had finally dragged Aleizia from her horse and insisted that they walk the short distance – to Scarlett, that's all a few miles was – rather than wait on the slow progression of the cavalcade. Luckily, her quick pace had calmed Aleizia's nerves or at least wore her out enough that, by the time they found Patrick lounging in a chair before his tent, Aleizia only flung herself against him with a quiet sob.

Patrick stroked his wife's blond hair with a gentle hand as she lay her head in his lap and smiled up at Scarlett. "Whatever magic ye worked, lady, ye hae my thanks. She is far more calm that I imagined."

Scarlett wanted to point out that Aleizia was only sixteen years old. An adolescent with too much energy and no outlet for it but only nodded. "You're welcome. Is Laird around?"

"No' presently, he should be back soon though."

Scarlett tapped her fingertips against her thighs impatiently. "How's the leg?"

"It pains me some," he admitted, gently patting the side of his thigh.

Beneath the hem of his kilt, she could see a bloodied and horrifically dirty bandage. She was no doctor. She hadn't even played one on TV but that was just wrong. "Do you, er, do you mind if I take a look?"

"Hae ye experience in nursing?"

Scarlett shrugged. Her medical knowledge might be

limited to what she'd garnered from medical dramas but she couldn't do worse, could she?

No, she definitely couldn't, she realized as she peeled the bindings away. The wound was dirty and already inflamed. Still gaping despite the crust of scabbing. Thankful to have a purpose, Scarlett set everyone to work finding clean cloths, needles and thread to stitch the wound, making sure everything was boiled first.

She flushed the wound again and again with their strong whiskey then had Aleizia's maid, Peigi, do the stitching since Aleizia was again working herself into a panic. Scarlett covered it with a clean linen bandage made from one of Aleizia's petticoats wishing she had some antibiotic cream. All she had were a couple acetaminophens she found in her purse, but hopefully combined with her strict instructions for his care, it would be enough to stop the infection.

"Did ye learn all that in the nunnery?"

Scarlett leapt up at the teasing brogue with a wide smile and threw herself into Rhys' welcoming embrace. "Are we back to that again?" she teased. "You're unharmed?"

"Aye, my dear, I live a charmed life."

"I know you do." Scarlett pulled back with a smile and looked around. "Where is Laird?"

"He'll be along soon. He's just ha'ing a final word wi' the King's council. Och, dear lass, yer a sight for these weary eyes." Rhys drew her close again, bending to kiss her cheek.

From the corner of her eye, Scarlett saw a flash of red and immediately forgot about her friend as she spotted Laird not far away.

Her eyes ate him up hungrily as she took a step in his direction. He was dirty and bloodied but in one piece. Looking oh, so alive and dynamic. Relief swept through her.

He was safe.

Was she a fool to feel such a thrill?

Casting aside her restraint, Scarlett ran to him, throwing her arms around his shoulders and pressing kisses to his cheek. He was solid and powerful against her. Not until that moment did she realize how much she truly missed his presence. Often so quiet but still so overwhelming. Wrapping one leg around his thigh, she pressed herself flush against him, seeking his lips but Laird was stiff. Not returning her kiss just as he had not before he'd left Wark.

"What's wrong?"

His eyes were as frigid as a steel plate when he finally looked at her. Scarlett was taken aback by the anger reflected there.

"Wow, are you mad?"

A shutter fell over his gaze. "I'm nae more mad than ye."

"Not crazy. Angry," she clarified. "Are you angry with me?"

"Nay."

"Are you sure? You seem angry."

"I'm no'…"

"What is this?"

With a sinking feeling, James turned and faced King James and the half-dozen retainers who followed him, including his father, as they appeared behind him.

"Your Grace." He stepped away from Scarlett and bowed low, aware that Sir William was watching them with a frown.

"Aren't ye to wed wi' my goddaughter soon, Hepburn?" King James asked, raking his eyes down Scarlett with a lingering look at her nearly exposed bosom, since she had once again forsook her parlett. "Who is this?"

"This is Mistress Thomas, Your Grace."

The King held out his hand to her and Scarlett took it uncertainly, dropping into a deep, unsteady curtsey. "Your Majesty."

"Majesty, eh?" King James chuckled, grinning around at his men. "I like that. I should have all my loyal subjects address me so, shall I?"

Agreement was murmured among the men but the King

only turned back to Scarlett, lifting her chin with one finger and turning her face this way and that as he studied her thoroughly. Too thoroughly for James's liking. "Why have I not seen you at court before, Mistress Thomas?"

"She is nae one of importance to ye, Your Grace," James said before she could speak, squeezing her hand to keep her from contradicting him. Lord only knew what might come out of her mouth. She was the unpredictable sort.

Sir William stepped to the King's side. "Your Grace, my son claims to hae found the woman upon countering a Lindsay raid of his keep at Dunskirk."

"A Lindsay raid?" King James tsked sternly. "Hmmm. Is she one of yours, Lindsay?"

John Lindsay, Earl of Crawford stepped forward. James held his breath but the Lindsay only shook his head. "Nay, Your Grace. I dinnae ken the lass."

The King nodded speculatively, looking Scarlett over once more as if she were a prime mare at auction. She stiffened at James' side, clearly uncomfortable with his perusal but to his relief, she retained enough good sense not to rebuke the King. "Mayhap, I should take her under my wing, as it were. See her safely back to her clansmen myself. It is my duty to see to my subjects welfare after all."

Aye, James knew how the King was thinking of protecting her. It seemed Janet Kennedy might finally have some competition for the royal affections after a decade in his bed. He bristled at the thought and Scarlett's hand tightened in his. "Nay, Your Grace."

He felt more than heard her exhale in relief but James was well aware that the matter was far from settled.

The King speared him with a sharp look. "Nay? Are ye daring to deny my will, James Hepburn?"

The retainers behind him all stilled and Scarlett was once again radiating tension, though he dared not look at her, even to cast assurances. Sir William was also glaring at James with a dark warning written in his eyes but James couldn't bear the thought of Scarlett becoming a royal plaything. He wouldn't allow it, King or not. "That is no' my intention, Your Grace. I only meant to say that Mistress Thomas is in no need of any protection beyond my own."

"I believe that would be for me to decide," the monarch said. It was a command without words. If King James wanted Scarlett even if it was only for a night, it would not be James' word that gainsaid him. Scarlett's might but James couldn't take the chance that her wishes on the matter would be taken into consideration. To his knowledge, no woman had ever denied the King but his lass was a contrary thing.

"Nay, Your Grace," he repeated more firmly, a decision made even as the words passed his lips. "She is mine by handfast. I will gi' her all the protection she needs."

Sir William stepped forward, his eyes dark with anger but James only leveled him a look of the same. "'Tis done, Father."

"'Twill be undone."

"Nay, it willnae," he said decisively. "I am hers and she is mine."

The two men stood, meeting eye to eye. The tension was palpable.

"Ye've no' asked my permission," King James said.

"Nay, but I ask yer blessing, Your Grace."

The King stared at him long and hard and James tensed, waiting.

"Verra well," he relented and the tension eased.

"Thank ye, Uncle," James said quietly as he bowed low

before the King. "I am in yer debt."

"Then I shall expect repayment."

James nodded as the King and his retainers turned away, continuing their tour through the encampment. Sir William lingered behind, clearly angry as his gaze shifted between his son and Scarlett, who was now clinging to James' arm. "Leave the lass and come along, son. Now. We need to discuss this."

"I will join ye at my leisure, Father," James replied evenly, shaking his head. "But there will be no' discussion. I'm nae bairn but a man and a laird in my own right. I will do as I please."

"Ye would dare disregard yer father's demands?"

Pressure seized him, banding about his chest, but James couldn't, *wouldn't* relent now. "Aye, as I just countermanded a King, I believe I can do the same for my sire. As I said, I will join ye shortly."

Leaving his father speechless and fuming, James grasped Scarlett by the elbow and guided her into his tent. Thankfully, Sir William did not follow.

I am hers and she is mine.

Scarlett couldn't deny the thrill those words brought her. The promise, the commitment in them.

Nor could she deny the panic.

"Handfast?"

"'Tis like marriage wi'out a priest. A promise to wed," he explained. "'Tis as good as a vow in Scotland."

But they weren't in Scotland and no promises had really been made. Scarlett took a deep, calming breath. "You just lied to your king. And your father."

"I would hae lied to the Saint Peter himself to keep ye out of my uncle's lecherous hands," Laird said, his hands fisting at his sides. "Sparing ye would be worth any sacrifice."

"Why?" she asked, trying to ignore how her pulse raced at his words.

He frowned down at her. "Would ye rather hae been his next mistress? Are ye like all the others longing for a higher position in life?"

"I never asked for the position I'm in right now."

He lifted a brow at her pert response. "Blast it, Scarlett, this is nae laughing matter. Did ye no' see how he was looking at ye?"

"Rather like you look at me, I think," Scarlett said tartly though inside she was awash with awe at the truth of what he had done. Laird had stood up to a reigning monarch for her! In a time like this, something like that might have been enough to get him thrown into the dungeon and put on the rack. Kings did hate to be contradicted.

"Ye need a hand taken to yer backside, lass."

"Ha, I wouldn't even try it. And while I appreciate you going to so much trouble to save me from your King, you didn't need to go to such lengths. Do you think he could have forced me to do something I didn't want to do? I can take care of myself, remember?" she reminded boldly.

"Ye wouldnae dare to strike the King," Laird said in surprise, his hand flexing at the memory of how able she was. "'Twould be treason." Suicide, really.

"How can it be treason? He's not my king."

Curiosity flared in his eyes, but he only shook his head ruefully. "Och, lass, it dinnae matter. He has all the power."

"Not over me," she insisted staunchly.

"'Ye need to clear these delusions of grandeur from yer mind." Laird kissed her forehead and turned her toward the mattress with a swat on her behind to hasten her along. "As much as I would like to stay, I maun go."

"To your father?"

There were questions in her eyes. Doubts. Laird sought to reassure her. "Dinnae fash yerself, lass. I swear I will let nae harm come to ye. On my honor and life."

"You sound like you care."

"I would take on King James' entire army for ye," he confessed tersely.

Good answer.

"Then why were you so angry with me before?"

"Are we back to that? I told ye I wisnae angry," he growled. The anger, which had faded with the King's departure, once again flamed in his eyes at the reminder. She should have left well enough alone but a part of her needed an explanation.

"Okay, let's choose another word then. How about enraged? Furious?"

"I take it back, I maun be mad indeed to tolerate yer vexing natter. Cease, lass."

Scarlett shook her head. "I will when you tell me what's bugging you. I haven't seen you in more than a week. What did I do?" Nothing. "Is it because I didn't write you?" Still nothing. "Geez, you're not still mad because I got drunk with Rhys, are you?"

His back stiffened even more. She was getting closer. Not that this guessing game was how she wanted to pass the time after being parted from him for more than a week.

"You weren't around, you know?" she said defensively. "I could have just sat alone in my tent without a bit of company.

If Rhys hadn't come by…" Her eyes widened. "It's Rhys, isn't it?"

"Let it be, lass."

"Like you are?" she taunted. "You cannot be mad that your brother…"

A choked snort died in his throat, interrupting her.

"Oh, my God!" Her eyes widened as the truth hit her. "Are you jealous?"

A low growl this time but it was answer enough. Scarlett shook her head, biting back a grin. "Laird, you cannot seriously be jealous of Rhys, can you?"

"Ye spend all yer time wi' him," he grumbled under his breath, scowling even more. He was none too pleased by his confession.

"I think you're making a mountain out of a molehill, Laird. I told you before, I like him but that's it. Besides, I spend a lot time with your sister, too. Are you jealous of her?"

Another short snort but the glower was back in his eyes. No, it was just Rhys. Why?

"I warned ye aboot him, did I no'?"

Scarlett rolled her eyes. "Sure, but I can't think you really meant it."

"Why would I no'? He might verra well take advantage."

Scarlett lifted a brow at that. "Seriously? I mean, come on."

"I cannae fathom how ye would so easily dismiss me."

"Oh, my God! Laird, he's *gay*!"

Laird scowled again with a shrug before turning his back. "Aye, he is at that. I cannae deny it. Clearly, that must be why ye prefer his company to my own."

Scarlett shook her head, rejecting what she saw only as Laird being obtuse. "That's not what I meant. Rhys is homo…"

Scarlett bit off the word with a frown, thinking about what she was about to say and the implications it might have for her newfound friend. This wasn't the twenty-first century where a growing percentage of the population didn't give a fig whether someone was gay or straight. Before that acceptance and acknowledgement, there had been widespread prejudice. Before that… Scarlett gnawed at her lip. Before that it had been not just a moral issue but a criminal one as well.

"Rhys is what?" he asked, looking back over his shoulder.

Unsure of where the matter stood during this time in history, she was hesitant to say anything that might cause problems for Rhys. Or worse, cost him his freedom or even his life. She doubted the LGBT had any presence in medieval Scotland. Scarlett shook her head again. "Nothing. Never mind."

"'Tis always 'nothing' wi' ye," he muttered, turning away once more and Scarlett knew that on some level she had wounded him once again by denying him the truth.

Would it really hurt in this case? Laird was Rhys' brother and friend. Surely he would understand. Surely he *knew*?

"Laird, I like Rhys very much but he… uh, *prefers* the company of men."

"Aye, but ye prefer his company. Ye gi' him yer smiles, yer laughter. Yer kiss."

How could he not know? Scarlett had known by that first morning after her abduction but either Laird was being thickheaded or Rhys had proven himself to be a finer actor than she could ever dream of being. "Laird, look at me," she said, laying a hand on his steely arm and waiting until he turned to her at last. "My passion, my desire is all for you.

There is no need for you to worry over my friendship with Rhys. I promise you, he is only just that. I spend time with him because he seeks my company."

He didn't look at all mollified by her assurance.

Aye, it was jealousy plain and simple that ate at him, James admitted, if only to himself. Those smiles Scarlett cast upon his brother, that laughter and warmth. Her constant natter streaming into his ears.

Scarlett was right.

It was ridiculous to be jealous of his brother, but even so James was. He might have her passion but Rhys had her friendship.

Strange he had never desired such a thing from a woman, but now...

Aye, he begrudged them all. He wanted the hours with her by his side. Wanted her supple body straining against him once more. Their passion was incredible but there was much more to his captive beyond her appetites, beyond the questions. And there were many.

There was so much more.

What a conundrum she was. Caring of his sisters, of people she'd never met. Full of love to give yet she was afraid of it. As if she didn't trust in it being returned. By him or anyone.

"And his company alone loosens yer tongue? He kens everything aboot ye."

To his chagrin, Scarlett nodded. "It's amazing really, talking to him is like being at the therapist's office." The word was unfamiliar and she must have realized it, trying a different comparison. "It's like being in a confessional, Laird. He just drags it all out of me."

Aye, he understood that one all too well even if he didn't appreciate the honesty of her admission. "And how does he do that?"

"He asks." James was surprised by her simple answer and Scarlett flushed with embarrassment. "It's stupid, I know. For so long people have just assumed so much about me. Rhys asks. It opens a floodgate. You could ask, too, if you wanted to."

"I hae asked ye questions," he reminded. "Questions ye've refrained from answering."

"Well, we don't seem to have a whole lot of luck with long conversation, do we?" The words were as provocative as they were bitter. She didn't sound like she appreciated the fact any more than he did.

Still, a slow smile lifted the corner of his mouth. "Nay, we don't."

"And whose fault is that?"

"Yers, naturally." Amusement lightened his spirits at her mock outrage but when he spoke, his brogue was heavy with the feelings weighing upon him. "'Tis indeed yer fault, lass, as I cannae be near ye wi' out wanting ye, wanting to touch ye. 'Tis unbearable."

"Is that why you eavesdrop on my conversations with Rhys? I know you do."

James only shrugged. He had said more than he intended, but still she pressed him further. "Or is it because you're still trying to figure out whether I'm a spy or not? To find out if I lied to you?"

"Aye," he said unapologetically, clearly surprising her with his direct answer. Especially since it wasn't the one she was expecting and dreading. James lifted her chin, forcing her golden eyes to meet his gaze. "But also to learn more aboot ye. Scarlett Thomas. I want to ken everything aboot ye."

Only mildly appeased, Scarlett shrugged aloofly. "You want to talk? Fine. Let's talk then. Tell me, do you read much, Laird?"

"When I am fortunate enough to borrow a book. I recently read *Le Morte d'Arthur* by the Sassenach, Thomas Malory."

Scarlett nodded. It was the go-to source on Arthurian legend for almost all the years between his and hers. "Yes, I've read it. I thought it was…"

James dragged her into his arms. His lips covered hers cutting off her words.

"I dinnae want to talk, lass. No' now."

"Good, neither do I."

Laird made love to her more tenderly than he had before. The urgency was still there to overwhelm her and Scarlett was still wary of the power he wielded over her, but something had shifted between them.

Scarlett cuddled against his broad chest with his powerful arms wrapped snuggly around her. Occasionally he would nuzzle the back of her neck or inhale her scent but while his hands might roam every now and then, they were finally talking.

"I don't think I've had a real friend since I was in grade school."

"I dinnae think I've e'er had one a'tall."

"Yes, you have," she said. "You do. For all his teasing, Rhys cares for you deeply as does Patrick. I think you know that and you're lucky to have them."

Laird grunted noncommittally. "Be ye feel ye had none?"

"No, as a child, they'd frown down at me for my parent's scandals or want what they might gain by a slim connection them. It was even worse when I became famous myself. I couldn't trust anyone's motives. Rhys has none beyond rousing your jealousy, I think. He truly cares for me. He gets me."

"Gets ye?"

"He understands me but he doesn't at all assume he knows me." Well, except for that one very flawed assumption. "I hope you won't feel the need to take that away from me."

The tent was quiet for a long moment before Laird released a deep sigh. "I willnae part ye, but I think I ken ye as well."

In the biblical sense, maybe, Scarlett thought. Or as friends with benefits.

"Why did ye no' like being an actress?" he asked after a long moment of silence.

Scarlett tilted her head to look at him. "How do you know I didn't?"

"I told ye. Rhys isnae the only one who understands ye," he said softly. "Come, tell me more about yer life on the stage. Why did ye no' enjoy it?"

"It wasn't the acting itself I didn't like. It was the fame. I never wanted it," Scarlett admitted, catching her bottom lip between her teeth. "Not like some people do. I was actually an introvert growing up. Do you know that word?"

After a pause, she felt him shake his head. "Latin root? Intro would be inward...?"

"Shy, awkward around people. Happy with my own company," she explained. "Plus, I was not very pretty growing up. Thin and gangly."

"I find that hard to believe."

Scarlett smiled. "Aren't you the one who called me a bag

of bones?"

Laird's lips brushed the top of her head. "I ne'er meant it. I wanted ye from the verra start."

The dichotomy of her feelings when he said things like that was annoyingly contradictory. Triumph. Trepidation. It was easiest just to push it all aside. "Anyway, I was extremely awkward, especially with other people. On top of that, I was a huge geek."

"A geek?" Laird tested the word with a frown. "Such an unsavory word."

Scarlett grinned at that. "Ahh, but better than being a nerd. It's an important distinction. I was just a blissful fangirl."

"Fan girl? I thought ye were an actor?"

"Someday I'll explain all that to you. The point is I was happy as I could be far away from all the hoopla surrounding my parents. It was magnificent to hide from the world, fly beneath the public radar, you know?" she asked, then promptly shook her head. "No, of course, you don't."

"Then why did ye do it?"

"My parents," she hesitated, not wanting to confuse him further with talk of a future he couldn't understand, but the truth of it was yearning to get out. To voice what she had never dared to say aloud before lest she find it printed in some gossip blog the next day. "Roles, good paying ones, were getting harder for them to find." Scarlett laughed inwardly at that. What a delicate way of interpreting the past. Truth was her mother hadn't wanted to admit that she just wasn't the screen siren she once was. She refused to play anyone's mother. "Times were getting tough when my dad landed a bit part in this new movie franch... uh, production," she continued. "It was being developed from a young adult paranormal book series about a group of teenagers in a post-apocalyptic world who escape the destruction of London and gather at an old castle to fight the invaders taking over the world."

"I dinnae understand any of that."

"Don't worry. It's not important. What ended up happening is that my father told the director that he knew just the right person to play the role of the geeky, shy but brilliantly techno-savvy Finley Adams. Me."

"Nepotism." He shrugged, his chest shifting against her back with the motion. "No' an unusual way to win a place in the world. The Hepburns hae relied upon it for generations to advance the clan."

"Some called it nepotism, others said it was just in my genes. Either way, the part was mine. I spent most of my teen years making those fil... uh, playing that one part," she modified.

"Tell me more aboot the plot of this tale. Post-apocalyptic? Was it a religious work?"

"No," she paused, considering how to answer in a way he might understand. "How can I explain this so that you'll understand? It just refers to a time when the human race as managed to nearly destroy itself without God's help. Does that make any sense?"

"Aye, we are well on our way, me thinks."

Scarlett smiled. "Oh, I think the world's safe for a while yet, but in this story it wasn't. Imagine a time far in the future, all right? Society was nearly destroyed but had begun to build itself up once more, and had come to realize that humans were not the only intelligent beings in the universe."

"What a sacrilegious notion," he said, his arms tightening around her as he stiffened in shock. "I cannae fathom that the playwright wisnae immediately imprisoned for propagating such blasphemy."

"Are you going to let me finish?" Laird paused but then nodded against the top of her head. "All right, so the humans have been interacting with the alien beings for some time..." His chest heaved against her back as he scoffed. "Really? Now listen. One of the races of aliens, called the Umbrut, brought with them another species that they kept as pets. Harmless, innocuous dragon-like creatures called Harquinians. Little," she held her hands out to indicate something the size of a basketball, "and as cute as pie."

"Pie isnae cute."

Scarlett just pursed her lips in exasperation and continued. "Well, it turns out that the Umbrut were the ones who were the pets, so to speak. The Harquinians had been controlling their minds for generations, feeding on them. They came to Earth with the same intention for the human race. Before long, most of the world's population was reduced to a zombie-like state, uh, puppets in the hands of their masters before the threat could be countered, in part, by a group of young people who took refuge in an ancient castle. In the last segment, *Broken Strings*, they manage to vanquish the alien enemy and save the human race from eradication."

"I've ne'er heard such lunacy in my life," he said with a dry laugh. "I cannae imagine a person succumbing to such control."

Turning in his arms, Scarlett looked up at him curiously. "Can't you? Aren't the people here controlled to some extent by religion and superstition? By fear of hellfire and warnings of eternal damnation?" Her question was met by a dark scowl.

"Ye speak dangerously close to heresy, lass. Now I ken

why Rhys sought yer company as he is oft an irreverent fool. No' doubt he enjoyed such stories greatly."

"In fact, he did. Millions of people did. It was wildly popular."

Laird laughed, assuming her number an exaggeration, no doubt. In truth, it was rather conservative. "And ye say ye played this same role for years?"

"Yes. The role wasn't much of a stretch for me and to some extent I enjoyed it, but it was never my dream." It had been her parents dream. Her co-stars as well, who one and all desired nothing more than fame. Scarlett hadn't wanted it. She hadn't lied to Grayson about that. Growing up as she had and seeing the impact 'fame' had on her parents, she wanted nothing to do with it. Regardless of her wishes, she had been a reluctant star, but was just finally getting a grip on her life.

"What was yer dream?"

It was Scarlett's turn to shrug. "I'm not sure. I never had much of a chance to really think about it. I did go to college when I was done with the role. University," she clarified. "I studied English Literature. I'm not sure what I thought to do with it. Teach, maybe? Write? Other than becoming a professional student, the options for a popular movie actor are surprisingly limited."

"I kent that ye were well educated."

"Did you go to school?"

"I was trained for a knighthood but since I do hae mine own property, I was well-tutored on how to manage it." Thoughtful silence fell as he stroked his thumb idly over her knuckles. "Were yer parents supportive of such a change?"

"Not really." All through those years at school, her parents and Tyrone had been there, trying to guilt-trip her into living her life for them, making them more money. The modeling. The appearances. It had been all been her parents and Tyrone. Pressing her. Pushing her. Each time she had given in until she couldn't any longer. "But I was done with it before I ended up here," she said to Laird. "I had finally put my foot down. No more cameras. No more celebrity. No more having people tell me where to go, how to dress or what to eat. I wasn't going to bow to their expectations anymore."

"Did it work?"

"I don't know."

She had been whisked away from her time before she had a chance to find out. On the other hand, there was no chance of continuing that life here, so in a way she had succeeded. Scarlett almost laughed at the irony. She should have been careful what she wished for. She'd wanted freedom and she'd gotten this. Somewhere the fates were mocking her. "Maybe I'll never know. What about you? You're going to be in trouble with your father, no doubt."

Laird's lips pressed into a thin line. "Mayhap. My wishes align wi' his no more than yers did wi' yer parents. Like ye, I dinnae live the life I ha' wanted."

He paused, as if surprised by the confession and the truth behind it. It seemed he didn't like the life he led any more than she did. "I've always done my duty but I've spent years at loose ends. Father wills me to be a soldier, a courtier but this disnae please me."

Scarlett cocked her head. "What would please you?"

Their dark tent was cloaked in silence as James contemplated the question he'd never been asked. "To see my holdings grow." Again it was a surprise but James felt the truth in those words. "I've held my own land since birth yet

I've no' known the satisfaction of toiling wi' my own hands, of making it my own."

"How would you do that?"

"Expand Dunskirk. Add to the existing pele tower and bailey until it is a force to be reckoned wi' in the borderlands." His burr was soft but full of conviction. "It could be a grand, bonny castle."

"I can imagine just how it should look."

James raised a brow. "Can ye now?"

An impish smile tilted the corner of her mouth as if she were privy to something he was not. "Yes, I could draw you a picture of exactly how it should be."

"I may hae ye do that and we shall see if yer vision matches my own."

"I bet it will," she said smugly.

Some of her words and terminology had been nothing but gibberish, though that was nothing new when speaking with Scarlett, but not for the first time, James got the impression that Scarlett was hiding something from him. Something far more important than the state of his keep.

Everything about her was a mystery but he could get no answers from her – at least on matters of more import to their relationship than her life on stage. Despite hours of conversation, he knew little more about her than he had before. Oh, he had learned more about the person she was beneath the surface but not the hard facts that would help him make some sense of her and her presence in his life.

It was all nothing, but it meant something.

What a complicated lass she was, he thought, looking down into her golden eyes. They were as direct as always, charged with vitality and fortitude.

Who was she really? From whence had she come? How

could she know so much about some things, yet so little about others?

He couldn't fathom how such a determined lass so assured of her own opinion and cleverness might ever be compelled by another to do something beyond her own will.

She was not an innocent when it came to matters of the flesh. Was she married? Widowed? Was the Tyrone she had called to for aid at Dunskirk her husband? A lover?

He might never know the answers when she refused to respond to his queries on the matter, but if he were honest with himself, James knew he was less and less interested in knowing.

The raw beauty of the area was as stunning to Scarlett as when she first arrived in this time. Endless hills of green with a touch of burnt umber and bronze that hinted at the coming fall. One after another they rolled as far as the eye could see with little to break the picturesque landscape. A small village in the distance. A church spire or two.

There was nothing around her that Scarlett recognized, nothing at all that reminded her of modern day England. No landmarks, no roads.

Nothing.

From the fringes of the latest encampment, she'd been able to watch the cannon fire at measured intervals upon a castle about a mile or two to the east. It was just four towers connected by curtain walls. It had taken less than an hour before the portcullis was raised and the Scottish troops entered the keep.

It was not at all like she imagined when first hearing about the 'invasion' of England. But for Norham and that excruciating five day siege, the castles of northern England were giving in to the Scottish forces without much of a fuss and it left Scarlett wondering whether the English were planning on fighting back at all or if, as Laird said, the border holds and castles were so used to being fought over that they merely cleaved to and hoped for the best.

"How goes the war?" she asked when Laird returned to their tent a few hours later. One advantage of Laird's lie to his father and the King was that they were able to share a tent.

"'Struth I never wanted to be a soldier any more than ye enjoyed life as a thespian. I believe the life of a courtier to be even worse each day I'm am commanded to be at the King's side." Shedding his weaponry, Laird poured himself a glass of wine and dropped into a chair with a sigh.

"That distillery must be looking better and better."

"Far more promising even in theory than my father was in keeping his word in truth. Father strings me along wi' promises to aid me but has ne'er acted on them. Nor hae I spoken of my impatience. 'Twas always much easier to let him have his way than it was to argue wi' him."

"I so get that. Isn't it interesting that both of us dream basically of living our own lives unfettered by the will of others?" she asked softly.

Yes, they were more alike than Scarlett had realized.

"No' terribly grand, is it?"

"I think they are. Our dreams are our own. As great in importance as the kid who dreams of ruling the world," she said and Laird chuckled.

"I see yer point."

Scarlett nodded, massaging his shoulders and bending to kiss his neck. Laird turned his head to capture her lips.

Beneath his, her lips parted welcoming his languid exploration as he pulled her into his lap.

"Lass?"

"Hmm?" she murmured against his mouth.

"Why would a goat long to rule the world?"

Scarlett's laughter joined his as she turned, hiking up her skirts to straddle his lap. Wrapping her arms around his head, tangling her fingers in his shaggy locks, she spread kisses along his jaw and down his neck. Shifting, she undulated slowly until his thickening length was snug and throbbing against her. Already she felt heat coiling at her core but she was in no rush. There was urgency but also contentment just being within the circle of his embrace. In feeling those strong arms wrapped tightly about her, holding her securely as if she had become a part of him.

"Ah, *mo chroí*, there is nothing sweeter than the feel of ye in my arms," he murmured thickly in his husky brogue, burying his face into the curve of her neck.

She never knew what to think when he said things like that. Never knew how to deal with the incompatible emotions of pleasure and alarm they inspired. It was as if he wanted to be with her always though he never said anything about the future. Scarlett didn't either but for entirely different reasons. "So you've conquered another castle today?"

"Conquer is a strong word. Ford Castle belongs to Sir William Heron who is currently held prisoner by King James at Holyrood. 'Tis his wife, Lady Elizabeth Heron who surrendered the castle to us wi' the promise to secure the release of two Scotsmen being held by the Sassenach in exchange for us sparing her castle," he told her.

"And what if she doesn't?"

He shrugged. "Then we will destroy it anyway."

Sure, Scarlett thought, why not? No biggie. "So, what's next?"

"I dinnae ken. Seems King James has found the company of Lady Heron to be most congenial. He remains at Ford Castle this night."

"Poor Janet Kennedy. She might be in danger of losing her prized position."

Laird chuckled softly. "I dinnae care, as long as she disnae lose it to ye."

"How could she?" Scarlett teased. "I'm 'married' to you now, aren't I?"

"Och, ye've no ken how to behave like a proper wife."

"Submissive?"

"Aye."

"Oh, I could be submissive," she raked her teeth along his whiskered jaw, enjoying his sharp intake of breath at the promise in her words.

"Aye, for aboot an hour's time then yer back to yer usual sass."

"You like it."

"Aye, *mo chroí*, I do," he admitted, his arms banding even more tightly around her. "Och, my sweet lass, would that ye might be my bride in truth."

Scarlett laughed nervously. Was that a proposal? He was joking, wasn't he?

"But I'm not," she said lightly. "It doesn't matter, I suppose. I'm terrible at relationships." True enough. She wasn't really looking to be anyone's girlfriend much less wife. She'd never gotten serious with anyone before simply because all the men she met already had a preconception of who she was and their expectations of how things with her would be.

"I would only disappoint you."

"Ne'er, lass," he whispered in her ear, brushing his lips across her lobe. "Ye delight me in every way."

"Until I don't anymore," she said firmly. He deserved fair warning. She knew well enough how these things went. "Nothing good ever lasts forever. We won't either."

His arms tightened around her. His disappointment at her words was palpable. "Hae ye somewhere else to be?"

Scarlett shrugged noncommittally. "Not just now, but I may not have a choice in the matter. Any more than you do."

$$\times \quad \times \quad \times \quad \times \quad \times$$

He'd never met a woman like Scarlett Thomas. She was an enigma in so many ways, but especially in this. To be so caring in one moment but to deny the reasons for it in the next. He'd never known a woman so guarded with her affections, so hesitant to give her heart. But then, James had never known himself to be so willing to give his own.

If the truth were known, he already had. He'd told Scarlett things about himself he'd never shared with another. He'd lied for her, to have her for his own. To his family. To his sovereign. Yet James knew he would go further still to keep her safe. To keep her at his side.

She would realize soon enough that some good things could – and would – last forever.

$$\times \quad \times \quad \times \quad \times \quad \times$$

It was some minutes later before what Laird had said finally sank in.

Her eyes popped open, searching his face as her heart

began to flutter a rhythmically, sickly. "Wait. Did you say Ford Castle? Laird!" she shook him urgently as she scrambled to her feet. "Ford Castle. Is that what you said?"

"Aye, lass. What of it?"

"I thought you said King James planned on invading England through Newcastle? Isn't that what you said? I'd never been there. Hell, I probably wouldn't have recognized it now if I had. But we're nowhere near there, are we?"

"Nay, Surrey's forces were gathering to the east at Dunbar so James decided to cross at Coldstream. What is it, lass? Ye look faint."

That's because she was. She hadn't recognized any of the castles the Scots army had defeated in the past week. Wark she had never even heard of. Oh, the other names, Norham and Etal, might have rung a distant bell but many of the dozens of castles on the Scottish Borders and Northumberland were nothing but ruins in her time. Hardly anything for a tourist to see.

She hadn't recognized this last one either. Not because it was a ruin in the future but because, like Dunskirk, the castle itself looked nothing like the one she knew from the twenty-first century.

But she recognized the name. Ford Castle didn't just ring a bell; it set off a peal of church bells.

Scarlett's mind thundered as her pulse rate skyrocketed. Shutting her eyes tightly, she pressed her fingers to her throbbing temples. No! She had to be wrong! "What day is it?"

"Lass, what is it?" he asked, concern clouding his eyes as he caught her hand and tugged gently.

Her eyes flew open, filled with anguish. "The date. What is the date?"

Laird rose to his feet as her agitation extended to him. "'Tis the fifth day of September."

"The year," she demanded urgently.

"'Tis the year of our Lord fifteen hundred and thirteen," he said slowly and ironically echoed Rhys's concern from weeks past. "I hope that dinnae come as a surprise for ye, lass."

1513! Oh, what a fool she was! Why hadn't she listened before? Why hadn't she paid more attention? How could she have been so stupid? Half-truths and misconceptions. A world that looked nothing like the one she knew. She hadn't been able to recognize the path they were taking.

Well, she recognized it well enough now.

"Lass? Scarlett?" Laird's fingers trailed across her jaw as if his touch might calm the anxiety building in her, but Scarlett was very afraid there would be nothing that could. Not now. "What is it?"

Scarlett struggled to find the right words in the sudden vacuum of her mind. Words to make him understand. To make him believe.

Pushing away from him, she paced anxiously to the open tent flap and back again. Too much of her life had gotten out of control because she hadn't spoken up. She couldn't let that happen now.

But panic was gurgling up inside of her. She couldn't make a rational argument in such a state. Ugh, could she make one at all? Was there one he could possibly believe?

"Scarlett, what's amiss?" His strong hands closed over her shoulders, turning her to face him.

"Everything. You cannot fight this war, Laird," she said carefully, tilting her head back to look at him. He was so precious to her. She couldn't let this happen. She had to find a way. "You must find a way to stop it. Talk to King James. Tell him he must draw back."

Laird frowned warily. "Yer talking nonsense, lass. Why would the King want to withdraw?"

She squeezed his hand, trying to convey some of her urgency and none of her panic. Becoming hysterical wouldn't garner a bit of faith. "Because you are going to lose this war, Laird. You are going to be utterly defeated," she told him, remembering that detailed oil painting from the exhibit at Dunskirk of the Battle of Flodden. So much red. "You need to tell the King and make him withdraw."

"Och, lass, tell him what? That ye've had a flight of fancy? A premonition?" There was concern in his eyes but it wasn't for the war ahead. It was for her. "Och, lass, how can I do that? He'll no' believe it."

Because Laird didn't believe it. Scarlett took a breath. How could she make him understand? His knuckles traced a path along her jaw before he tweaked her chin and tilted her head back.

"Ye worry for naught, lass," he said soothingly. "We hae far more men than anticipated, lass. More than thirty thousand men already and even more still arriving each day. Henry fights in France wi' his regular army. Our spies tell us, Surrey has no' more than twenty thousand. I admit to ha'ing my own doubts aboot this. But there is nae way we can lose with those odds. We will outnumber our enemy."

Scarlett drew in a deep breath. "It won't matter, Laird. It won't be enough. Now I want you to listen to me carefully. Because I'm about to tell you what will really happen."

"Lass…"

"No, hear me out. Please," she begged, pushing him back into the chair and dropping to her knees before him. Relief swept through her when Laird settled back in the chair. He was doubtful but at least he was listening.

"There's going to be another battle. A big one on the ninth of the month."

"Ye dinnae ken what yer saying, lass."

Scarlett sighed in exasperation. "I *ken* that just a couple of miles away is a field where you plan on fighting the English army. And I *ken* you are going to lose. Talk to King James. Tell him he must draw back."

"Lass…"

"No, hear me out." Scarlett gripping his knees, rotating her thumbs. The words were slow in coming; she kept hoping some inspiration would hit her. That some vague fact from a quickly thumbed through brochure would pop into her mind.

The brochure!

Running to her trunk, she dug through the depths until she found her purse. Burrowing through the contents, she withdrew the pamphlets Donell had given her and shuffled through them until she found it. *Flodden: 500 Years.* "The battle will be fought at Flodden Field, not far from here." His eyes narrowed and a heavy sigh lifted her shoulders. "No, I'm not a spy."

"Then how do ye ken such a thing? Did Rhys reveal such a detail?" he asked.

"No. I know it because I read it in this." Scarlett flipped through the pages, scanning them quickly. "Four days from now. Thousands of men will die."

"Scarlett, lass." He leaned forward, propping his elbows on his knees and took her hands in his. "'Tis war, lass. Aye, men will die."

Frustrated, Scarlett shook her head again. "Look at this,

Laird." She waved the brochure at him again. "Your countrymen are going to die for nothing. Even the king. You have to stop it."

"'Tis treason to threaten the life of the king, lass."

"Let's not go there again, okay? I'm not threatening him," she enunciated clearly. "I'm telling you flat out that he will *die* if this battle is fought." She pressed the brochure into his hand. "Look at it. This is your Kobashi Maru, Laird."

"My what?" he asked, running his fingers hesitantly over the glossy cover.

"It's a no-win situation," she desperately explained. "I mean, maybe Captain Kirk beat it because he cheated but you don't have that option. You cannot win. You *will not*. Read it, Laird. Don't believe me if you want but believe that. Read what it says. Read the names of your family and friends who will die on that field. Nearly ten thousand of them." Names that had once sounded familiar and now she knew why. "Your uncles, your cousin. All of them will die. And if that sword of yours is any indication..."

Scarlett's words broke off with the crack of her voice. How had she not seen it all before? Why hadn't she realized the truth? "You will die, too." The words emerged dully as she rocked backwards and she sank numbly down on the ground.

"'Tis nothing but nonsense, lass," he scoffed.

"It's true." Her voice was barely a hoarse whisper. "It's all true. I saw it. Your sword. In the museum."

Scottish claymore, found on the battlefield of Flodden.

Even when she had first seen it, she had realized why it had been in the exhibit. Because the Scotsman bearing it had fallen in battle. Because he had died.

Because *Laird* had died.

"It was found on Flodden Field after the battle. So either you left it there or…"

Emotion tightened at the back of her throat painfully, making it almost impossible to breathe. Tears stung at her eyelids as she sat there in stunned silence. Her heart pounded in hard, slow thumps, knocking against her ribs. Her stomach twisted sickly. She could hardly breathe, suffocating under the numbing weight of the truth.

He was going to die.

"'Tis madness ye speak of, lass. Ye cannae ken such a thing." He flipped through the brightly colored brochure. "'Tis words on a page, nothing more."

"No, it's history."

And for the first time in her life, the subject evoked real emotion in her.

"Lass," Laird sighed, shaking his head as he left the chair and dropped down on his haunches in front of her, taking her hands in his once more. "Scarlett. Look at me, *mo chroí*."

Scarlett lifted wide, dazed eyes to his, seeing the cynicism, the disbelief written there. "If you say one word about female nerves or hysteria, I will hurt you bad," she warned. "I know what you're thinking, Laird. I'm not mad or hysterical. It is far simpler," – and way more unbelievable – "than that."

"What is it then?"

"When I told you I wasn't from around here, Laird, I wasn't joking," she told him. "I'm from a place far from here, not in distance but in time. This isn't my time. I came here from five hundred years in the future. I came here, I think, to warn you. To stop this war because everything I've told you is true. I know what will happen because to me, it's history."

After a long moment of silence, his eyes searching hers

347

intently, Laird stood and crossed his arms over his massive chest. He stared moodily at her for a long while. "Now I ken ye maun be overwrought to be speaking such nonsense."

"It isn't nonsense, Laird." Resisting the urge to roll her eyes, Scarlett hastened to his side and laid a pleading hand on his arm. "I think somewhere deep down you know it. You're thinking that it actually makes sense. You've never met anyone like me. Anyone who talks like me, acts like me, right? It makes sense now why I wouldn't know how to ride a horse or eat with a knife or dance your dances."

"Nay, lass. None of this makes any sense a'tall." Brushing her hand away, Laird strode toward the open flap. Fighting back a flight of panic, Scarlett knew she had to stop him. She had to make him listen and believe. Not for her sake but for his and for everyone he knew.

Turning back to the bed, she upended her purse spilling the contents out on to the mattress. Her phone, wallet, passport, mints, pens... her gun. "Look at this, Laird! See the proof for yourself. Any of it will show you that I'm telling the truth."

But he wasn't listening. Instead he was walking away.

She couldn't let that happen!

An earsplitting explosion echoed off the tent walls and through his head, dragging his feet to a halt. James spun around to find Scarlett standing at the foot of his bed with one arm raised and pointing at the ceiling. Above her, a ragged hole pierced the roof of the tent, spearing a thin shaft of sunlight down upon her. "What the bluidy hell was that?" he yelled above the ringing in his ears.

"That is a hole in your ceiling," Scarlett said calmly. "This is a called a Smith &Wesson Bodyguard .380 or in this case, it is more commonly referred to as 'irrefutable proof'. I am not mad, Laird, and here is undeniable evidence of that fact. It is a handgun, a weapon made to fire small projectiles called bullets at a very high rate of speed for the purpose of harming or killing an attacker or enemy... or in this case, a ceiling. Come here and look at it. Hold it. Believe it and then maybe you can believe me. Just don't walk out that door."

She said it all so matter-of-factly, James was almost inclined to believe her right then and there but curiosity consumed him. He paced slowly back toward Scarlett, never taking his eyes from the small black object in her hand. "Let me see it."

Knowing that she finally had his complete attention, Scarlett ejected the clip and pulled back the barrel to release the bullet from the chamber. Turning the pistol, she offered Laird the butt end. It was an extreme length to go to; to secure his faith but she hadn't seen any other options. She needed to stop him before he got on his horse and left the truth behind. It had been either the ceiling or him.

Hopefully she wouldn't regret her choice.

"What is it?" he asked, rolling the handgun in his hands. It looked so small in his palm. Harmless.

"I told you what it is," she said. "The best I could relate it to for you is a hand cannon I saw at the exhibit."

"This disnae look like any hand cannon I hae e'er seen," Laird said, still examining the weapon. "'Tis too small and frail looking to do much harm."

Scarlett held up a small shard of metal and he took it rolling it between his fingers. It was smoothly tooled and oblong. "That's a bullet. Like a cannonball, it is propelled from the barrel at a high rate of speed. Fast enough to do more than enough damage, especially at close range. Now tell me, have you ever seen anything like it before?"

He hadn't. That fact unnerved him but he wasn't keen on accepting her far-fetched explanation for it just yet. "I've heard of places far to the east that have developed advanced weaponry." It was an inadequate option and his lass knew it as well given the soft, sympathetic smile that was curving her bonny lips.

"It's overwhelming, I know. Believe me, I had my fair share of shocks when I arrived in this time. But I accepted it, sooner rather than later, and you need to, as well, Laird."

So simple a request, yet so difficult despite the evidence in his hand. Nay, James did not believe it had come from the farthest countries to the east but it was no simple thing to believe her explanation either. It was an unholy option. More heretical than anything that had yet fallen from her lips. The logical part of his mind revolted, the other part exulted for he hadn't wanted to accept that Scarlett was naught but a madwoman. "It *is* beyond belief."

"Yes, there's no questioning that," she agreed. "So now that we've got that settled, will you tell the King that he must withdraw before they reach Flodden?"

"Nay, lass, I cannae do it."

"Why not?"

"I am in the King's service but I hae no' his ear," he said evasively. "Even if I did, I doubt he would believe me. *I* dinnae truly believe it yet and I hae nae desire to be thought mad."

"Mad as me, right?" Scarlett shook her head, frustrated with the lack of progress she was making with him. "What else can I tell you, Laird? You cannot let this happen. I cannot let it happen. I think I must have come back here to save you. But I'll need you to believe in me if I'm going to make that happen."

"Ah, lass," he said, tweaking her earlobe. "I always kent ye've been hiding something from me. But I cannae simply accept this reason as truth."

"Even with the evidence in your hand?"

James looked down at the wee hand cannon once more and tossed it on the bed. Aye, he was curious and a large part of him wanted to believe her incredible tale. To believe that the woman who had come to mean so much to him in such a short amount of time wasn't fit for Bedlam. But it was just too bizarre, too ungodly a fable for him to just set aside everything he knew about the world in blind faith.

He needed time to think.

36

"We've languished here for days whist ye dally wi' Lady Heron as if we've nothing better to pass the time!" Lord Lindsay slammed his fist down on the thick wooden table with a solid thud. "Our men sit idle, some are beginning to drift away and still we've nae progress forward. Surrey hae nae such hesitation. His son brings ships filled with supplies and arms. The Sassenach forces hae left Alnwick and arrived at Woller Haugh this day."

"Beware how ye speak to yer king, Lindsay," King James uttered darkly. He must have tired of Lady Heron's bed, at least for the time being, to take some interest in the strategies for the days ahead. "We will carry on as planned."

James lounged back in his chair placed far away from the crowded council table, brushing the pad of his thumb thoughtfully across his lower lip as he listened to the Lindsay rant against the King. Enemy of the Hepburns the Lindsay might be but his arguments made far greater sense than they should. Given the words he had read over and over again these past two days, he was beginning to agree with the Lindsay's assessment.

Slipping his hand into his sporran, he ran his fingers over the pamphlet he kept there. Ten pages of thick, glossy paper emblazoned with colorful artwork such as he had never seen. Paintings so finely detailed he could see nary a brushstroke. He'd marveled over them for hours. It had taken even longer for him to work out the words printed so tightly on the pages.

The first were clear enough. *Flodden: 500 Years.* The field of Flodden sat no more than two miles to the west of Ford Castle. A wide-open space with a ridge excellent for the strategic placement of their troops. Troops that were already gathering there.

Below the broadly written heading was a statement of an exhibition honoring the five hundredth anniversary of the battle. Five hundred years. If Scarlett spoke true, she had come to him from a time far beyond his imagination. That more than anything made it difficult to grasp the veracity of her claim. Ironically enough, James had gotten to a place in his mind where he might have accepted a hundred years, perhaps even two but five hundred was mind-boggling.

Perhaps in another day or two he might wrap his mind around such a great number but...

According to prophecy contained in the pamphlet, they didn't have that long.

"Surrey has troops pouring in from all over the northwest and northeast corners of England," Lindsay pointed out. "He's sent a bluidy challenge to remain in this area so that we might meet him in battle on the ninth day of September. That's bluidy well two days from now!"

James had seen the letter and the one that had followed it

from Surrey's son, Thomas Howard, the Lord Admiral. That more insulting missive had concluded in the brash statement that he would 'expect no quarter and will give none, other than to your majesty, should you be delivered into my hands.'

According to the words in Scarlett's brochure, Howard would not have that chance. King James IV would die on the field of battle. The last reigning monarch to do so.

Ironic given his cocky response to Surrey's letter. 'To meet the English in battle is so much my wish, that had your message found me in Edinburgh, I should have relinquished all other business to meet you in the field.'

And meet them they would.

"Surrey expected us to stay near Ford Castle. He willnae like it that we hae crossed the River Till and positioned our forces on the high ridge of Flodden Field," Sir William explained. "'Twill gi' us an excellent advantage in meeting Surrey, leaving him to face an uphill assault when he comes to us. Already our defenses are prepared for battle."

Surrey's intelligence had taken note of their fortifications. Strong on the eastern and western flanks. Another letter had arrived from, complaining about the advantageous location and challenging King James to come down off his hill to do battle.

Aware of its contents, the King had refused to receive it.

According to their own spies, Surrey was leaving Woller Haugh to take up a better position and a new challenge had been received that day urging King James to come forth and meet him there, hoping, no doubt, that James would leave his more strategic position. The King had responded to the challenge by saying 'it beseems not an earl to handle a King after this fashion.'

King James would not be told what to do. There was

some relief in that, at least. But it wouldn't be enough. None of their efforts would if the words in the brochure were made true.

Ten thousand men. The number echoed through James' mind. Friends, family. His father. His cousin. Uncles. Mayhap brothers and as Scarlett pointed out, himself. He was no coward but neither was he a fool.

If it were truth, indeed.

"Your Grace, we've gone o'er and o'er the intelligence that we hae at this point," the Lindsay told him. "Many of our troops hae deserted, taking the booty thus far won and running back home. We are short of provisions as well. It is my advice and counsel, Your Grace, that we withdraw from this meeting and reassess our chances for victory."

"Nay, I willnae hae it," Sir William shot back, while others on the King's council nodded their agreement. "Henry has forced our hand and we cannae back down."

King James inclined his head. "I find I maun agree wi' my council on this, Lindsay. We cannae let Henry's insults stand. We hae the manpower and the position. We'll ne'er hae another chance like this."

"'Tis yer fault," the elderly Earl of Angus, known as 'Bell the Cat' said, glowering at La Motte, the French emissary, who along with his cohorts had been training the Scottish troops in the use of the long pike over the last month. "Ye encouraged him in this folly to gain our fleet for yer own use."

"I've done no such thing, *monsieur*," La Motte replied tiredly. "The choices of your monarch are his own."

King James sighed, waving his hand dismissively. "Angus, if yer afraid, go home."

Angus bristled up like a cock and stood. "And so I shall.

Yer an arrogant fool, Jamie Stewart." Then he was gone, the door slamming behind him.

"Anyone else?" the King asked, glancing about the room with narrowed eyes.

"Your Grace," James began hesitantly but continued more assertively as he levered himself from his chair. "Perhaps it might be to our best advantage to listen to the Lindsay's opinion on the matter."

Everyone in the room stopped and stared at him, including Sir William and the Lindsay himself. Even the King himself was nonplussed by the verbal support of a Lindsay by a Hepburn. "Ye agree wi' the Lindsay, Hepburn?"

"James," Sir William hissed under his breath. "Enough."

But now that he'd begun, Laird couldn't back down. Scarlett's dire warnings rang in his ears. What if she were right? Shaking his head in his father's general direction, he took a step toward his sovereign. "Aye, Your Grace. I believe the Lindsay's arguments are valid. We may hae underestimated our foe and waited too long to press forward."

"Is that so?"

James nodded.

"Then yer as much a fool as Lindsay if ye think I'll gi' up an inch of ground now," King James said. "I've come this far. Ye think I'll turn tail like a whipped pup? Nay, we press forward as planned and regardless of yer arguments we will win this battle for Scotland."

× × × × ×

"What was that all aboot?" Rhys asked, pouring them each a cup of the King's finest whiskey after the council had vacated the room and Sir William had taken his fill of soundly berating his oldest son for 'such foolish nonsense'. His lecture included a long rant over James' attachment to 'a worthless lass' who brought him neither position nor plate, and an extended lecture on how he had failed the Hepburn name. "'Tis no' like ye to support the Lindsay much less speak of surrendering before a fight."

James shrugged, tilting up his goblet. In that moment more than any other, the burn of the whiskey down his throat was welcome. "I hae a bad feeling aboot this, that's all. It cannae end well."

"And Scarlett has nothing to do wi' it?"

"What's that supposed to mean?" he asked warily, wondering if she had made such claims to Rhys during one of their many long conversations.

"Ye feel for her," Rhys said quietly. "Deeply, if I'm no' mistaken. I cannae blame ye for she is an intriguing lass. If I were interested, I daresay nothing would stop me from assuring a long future at her side."

"I'm nae milk-livered coward, Rhys," he ground out. "I will fight wi' all I hae for my country."

"Och, I dinnae imply any such thing but what is it then?"

James sighed heavily. "Scarlett claims to hae foreknowledge of the battle ahead. She says we will lose most egregiously."

"And what makes her say such a thing?" Rhys shook his head. "Is there more to it than maidenly worry?"

Swirling his whiskey around his cup, James tipped it up and downed it all in one swallow needing fortification to say it aloud. "She claims to ken that we are destined to be sorely defeated by the Sassenach. No' because she is a seer or because she's had a premonition of failure but because she is from the future and to her, it is naught but history."

"Hmm," his brother murmured into his cup.

"Ye dinnae seem surprised."

"I'm no' really." Rhys tossed back the remainder of his whiskey and poured himself another, larger portion. "If ye had listened to me before leaving the encampment at Wark, I would hae told ye that she made the same claim to me. That night we over imbibed on the wine. I thought her drunk, naturally, I was as well. But it makes sense, does it no'?"

"Sense? Och, surely ye cannae take stock in such absurdities?"

Rhys lifted a shoulder. "Why no'? It makes more sense than her no' knowing anything aboot how we live every day."

"I told her ye were a blasphemer," James grumbled.

Laughter spilled from his brother. "If ye dinnae believe it, why do ye even speak of it a'tall? I'll tell ye why. Because ye do believe her. Because it makes sense of so much. How is it that she can ken so much yet ken so little at the same time? Her manner of dress? Her speech? The way she fought ye? That book? Have ye e'er seen the like? I'm sure she offered something in the way of proof?"

James pinched the bridge of his nose between his thumb and forefinger. "She has a weapon. A handgun, she called it. It expels a shot similar to a hand cannon but it is only the size of the palm of my hand. It dinnae look dangerous a'tall but I saw first-hand the damage it can do."

"And ye still dinnae believe her?"

"I dinnae want to," James sighed, dropping down onto a low, cushioned seat. "If I believe her, it means that everything else she said might be true as well. If she spoke true, we are on the verge of losing most everyone we know. She says it will be a crushing defeat."

"How crushing?"

James dug into his sporran and retrieved Scarlett's brochure. Unfolding it, he handed it to his brother. "Read this."

Curiously, Rhys took the page and pondered the tiny print. "I cannae. I assume ye managed a way through it?"

"I've taken two days to do so." Two days where he'd denied, aye, denied the truth. Two long days since he'd seen Scarlett, uncertain what to say. What to admit. What to accept. "It says that the casualities among the Scots fighting in this battle numbered more than ten thousand, including at least one family member from every noble house in Scotland. Including King James. Here." He flipped to one of the pages. "I'd wager ye can make this out well enough."

"Other notable casualties include…" Rhys trailed off as he skimmed the list, taking note of the names of men he knew. And family, too many. "Adam Hepburn, 2nd Earl of Bothwell, Lord High Admiral of Scotland, Adam Hepburn of Craggis, George Hepburn, Bishop of Isles, Sir William Hepburn, Lord High…" His voice trailed off and he swallowed deeply. "Father."

James retrieved the pages, refolding them carefully. "And Angus and Glencairn as well. My old master, Ross, and even the Lindsay for all his gainsaying of the King's plan. All dead, if this is true. If Scarlett is right. And who can ken those no' listed?"

"What do ye propose we do then?" Rhys asked.

"What can I do? Ye heard the King, he is set on this madness. Aye, I suppose I can admit as much now. 'Tis madness." He scratched his whiskered jaw, hoping some heretofore-unseen option might raise its head.

"Show these pages to Jamie then," Rhys suggested. "Let

Scarlett speak wi' him. Convince him of the truth herself. A woman can change the world if her head is on the right pillow."

James' fist clenched around the paper. "I'm going to forget ye said that."

"Och, Laird, would ye no' gi' up a woman's virtue to save yer King, yer father? Me as well, perhaps?"

"I cannae ask her to do that."

"I can," Rhys said. "And I will if ye dinnae."

"Ye speak a word of this, I will kill ye myself." James swallowed the last of his drink and slammed the goblet down on the table. "Ye cannae change history."

"Ye can try."

Thus far yoga, which had done much to calm her nerves in the past, wasn't working. As she did each morning now, Scarlett stood before the open window flap in the tent bathed in a bright ray of light as the dawn arrived, poised in the Tree position. A slow inhale did nothing to relax her mind, nor did the exhale. Her clothing might be to blame. Without proper workout wear, she'd had to make do with her own cotton panties and a thin, short camisole of sorts that didn't offer much in the way of elasticity.

But she didn't have her own gear here, did she? Whose fault was that?

Donell's? How had he done it? Why? What had he thought to accomplish in bringing her here?

The questions tumbled over themselves.

The encampment was practically deserted that morning. All of the troops had moved into position on the ridge above Flodden Field to await the English who were on their way for the battle.

Tomorrow.

Would she even see Laird before then? He hadn't been back to their tent since he stormed out after her revelation more than two days before. She'd seen Rhys, talked over the upcoming predicament and Rhys' idea that she speak directly with the king, to sacrifice herself on the altar of his bed, if necessary, to gain his ear. With little hope of getting through to Laird, she had done as Rhys asked and walked to Ford Castle hoping to speak to King James directly, but despite hours of waiting, hadn't been able to get past the first tier of his security.

Upon her return to camp, a pale-faced Rhys had been almost glad for her failure, apologizing for coercing her into such a dissolute situation. Scarlett was inwardly relieved as well but frustrated nevertheless by her failure to gain the king's ear.

And by Laird's continued absence.

What if she didn't get to see him again? What if he went off to battle and died before she could hold him once more? Panic bubbled within her at the thought.

Stop it, focus on the distance.

Relax.

Even from a distance, the mass of men assembled on that ridge with their cannon, waiting for death to come to them was surreal. More a step back in time than anything she had experienced so far. Witnessing first-hand those medieval concepts of how a war should be fought.

Where was Laird? She hadn't had a single message from him. What did that mean? Did it mean anything at all?

No, don't go there.

Scarlett closed her eyes and inhaled through her nose, focusing her energies on her body. She eased into Warrior II, feeling the stretch of her muscles. Both feet on the floor, one knee bent in a sideward lunge, she reached her arms out to the sides, holding on to her control, in this at least. Where she had some. Exhale. Good.

Inhale. Better.

Opening her eyes, she stretched slowly into a modified side angle, stretching one arm over her head as she leaned to the side.

Yes, much better.

Straightening her legs and arms once more, she slowly transitioned into the Triangle, bending to the side and touching her fingertips to her toe. Exhale. Much, much better.

Downward Facing Dog. Scarlett felt her blood rushing to her head, drowning out the last of her chaotic thoughts. Tranquility. Finally.

Laird.

Unfortunately, her peace of mind – so ruthlessly focused on to achieve – was short-lived as his named popped into her mind again. Had the truth gotten her anywhere at all? Had she changed anything? What madness had consumed her that she thought she had the power to change history? To fix one thing when she screwed up so much? History was too big for one person to affect.

In exchange she had only lost precious days with Laird.

One leg lifted skyward. Half Downward Dog.

Her mind galloped once more. But she wanted to change history. At least that one thing.

She didn't want him to die.

A shudder ran through her but Scarlett pushed the thought away and lowered her leg until she was again in Downward Facing Dog position.

Laird.

What would happen to her when he was gone, as he surely would be? Would staying in the sixteenth century alone and homeless be her punishment for thinking that she had the power to make change? That just once she deserved something good – truly good for *her* – to happen in her life?

And what she had found in this time was good. She had found friendship. In Rhys and even Laird. Sisterhood that she'd always lacked in Aleizia and Aileen. People to care about. People to live for.

Laird.

She had always wanted to be desired for something more than her fame, even if it was only for her body.

Would that ye might be my wife in truth.

Was that what he wanted? Did he truly care? Would she ever know?

Ugh, even if there was something more to it, did *she* want it? If sex was all Laird wanted from her, she might be content with that and not wish for more if only she could manage to save his life. It wouldn't do either of them any good to hope for more when she finally made her way back home.

When? It was starting to seem more like an 'if' to her.

With a groan, she straightened her body as she sank to the floor in a smooth motion and swooped forward into the Cobra position.

"What in hell are ye aboot, lass?"

It was as if he had known she was thinking about him and just magically appeared. Scarlett didn't even bother to look at the door but only hung her head between her arms. Whatever peace she might have briefly found fled as her heart rate accelerated. At just the sound of his voice. Already she felt more alive, wired with anticipation.

Every fiber in her being begged her to race across the room and fling herself into his arms.

She might have if she knew where they stood.

"Don't you ever knock?"

✕ ✕ ✕ ✕ ✕

He'd never seen such a sight in all his days.

Contrary to her impudent accusation, he had called for admission before entering, uncertain of his welcome but wanting to see her. To make peace. When she hadn't answered, he'd only meant to peek in quickly to see if she was still abed.

The sight of her posed like a statue awash in the morning sun had caught his attention and stolen his tongue. What a body she had! She was thin, aye, but her long limbs were sleekly muscled and firm. Her hips weren't broad but her waist dipped in alluringly. Her breasts strained against the thin fabric of her shift. And the way she bent...! Such a graceful, lissome creature. He had been caught in silent admiration.

Until she had bent over, her bottom presented to him with no more to cover it than a babe's swaddling. Less even. The thin fabric clung to her arse, stretching with her until he could see her flesh through it and all the secrets in the dark shadow of the valley between her thighs as well. Then she arched her body against the floor and all his good sense had fled him.

He'd hardly recognized his own voice or recalled the words that escaped him.

Now she was watching him as she stood. She did not bless him with the greeting he had been hoping for, in fact,

367

she did not greet him at all. Nor did she attempt to cover her near nudity as she drank deeply from a clear canteen of sorts. But her eyes never left his as she swallowed again and again, her throat flexing with the effort. At last she lowered the drink, wiping her mouth on the back of her hand. "Are you back for your armor?"

He should have waited for her to come to him. He should have turned away. Hell, he should have at least bathed first after working all night to fortify their defenses on the western flank but James did none of those things. Instead, his feet propelled him by their own will across the room.

He came at her without hesitation, his eyes – hot and hungry – locked with hers. Once he was within reach, his hands followed his eyes roamed hotly over her, from shoulder to hip and back up again. Scarlett trembled at his touch, relief and yearning battling for control. Laird framed her face in his hands, tilting her head back until she met his eyes. "Is that all ye hae to say, lass?"

"Well, it would be rude of me to point out how badly you stink, wouldn't it?" Her voice was husky, breathless. Quivering with emotion that he would have to be a fool not to notice.

His thumb brushed over her bottom lip and she parted them involuntarily. "Did ye miss me, lass?"

Scarlett inhaled shakily. "Hey, who left wh–" She gasped as his lips covered hers, swallowing the rest of her words. His tongue plunged deeply, their tongues dueling and drawing a long, rumbling moan from deep within his chest. Then his body was wrapped around hers, pressing her against the center tent post. The heat of his broad chest radiated through her thin chemise. Another groan shook him, the vibration chafing against her tender breasts through the gauzy linen. They might well have been naked already.

Laird caught the front of the flimsy garment and ripped it away. The tightly leashed violence of his passion was exhilarating, sparking the same urgency within her. However much the intensity of their passion might scare her, it thrilled her just the same. Feelings she had been denying all week, flooded her. She arched against him with a silent cry as his lips closed over her nipple, suckling hard. She tugged on his hair but he only sucked harder, holding her tighter and tighter still. Her heart beat hard against her chest, clamoring to get out just as her breath was encaged within as well. Her head swam, her vision blurred.

As if he knew just how far he had pushed her, Laird's mouth trailed upward once more and her breath finally left her in a rush as she clung to him.

His fingers were on the move also, finding the way inside her panties and thrusting deeply into her. Scarlett cried out, clinging helplessly to his shoulders as ecstasy ripped through her. She couldn't have cared less that he hadn't bathed.

"Did ye miss me, lass?"

Lost in sensation, she could only shake her head against his sweaty throat. His low growl rumbled against her. Winding his fingers around the side of her panties, he tore them away. Her only pair of real underwear but Scarlett couldn't mourn the loss. They were gone for a good cause, she knew, when he brushed his kilt out of the way and lifted her legs around his hips. His forceful entry should have torn her apart but Scarlett was more than ready for him, so ready she was nearly swept away by the possession.

"Did ye, lass?"

Laird pinned her against the post and flexed his hips, pumping deeper into her. Her breath caught but she didn't answer.

"Lass?"

He drove into her hard. Again and again until Scarlett's thighs were quivering around him. His fingers bit into her bottom, holding her just so to receive him more deeply. Pleasure arced through her, her back bowed to draw him even deeper.

"Lass! Scarlett!"

He was insistent, as if knowing that he held her on the precipice of rapture's waiting abyss. He wouldn't let her leap, wouldn't allow her to fall. Pleasure became torment, aching poignantly through her every extremity. "Och! But ye'll be the death of me." Increasing his pace, Laird carried her over the edge. His hoarse cry outweighed her soul-wrenching sob as they succumbed together, soaring instead of plummeting.

Transcending instead of crashing.

Laird carried her to the bed and curled around her, spooning her bottom against his groin and hugging her tightly against him. Scarlett wiggled even closer, finding the contentment that had been missing all week, the peace of mind that even yoga had denied her.

"Did ye no' miss me, *mo chroí?* Even a wee bit?"

Miss him? How inadequate, really. She hadn't missed him. She'd agonized over his absence, worried for his safety, pined for his company. Longed for his body. Even his absence hadn't managed to dull the emotion he roused in her. The power he had over her was unnerving. Stunning. How could she ever give this up?

Scarlett shrugged, biting back the urge to tell him just that.

"You knew where I was this whole time."

His chest trembled behind her. "How can ye torment me so? Tell me true, lass, did ye miss me a'tall?"

"Did you miss me?" she countered softly.

"I've ne'er felt so bereft in all my days than those when parted from ye." His brogue was thick, heavy with feeling.

Rhys might ask all the good questions, but Laird had all the right answers.

"I may have missed you, just a little," she conceded and was rewarded with a light swat on her bare behind for her efforts. She turned in his arms so that she could face him, reaching up to caress his cheek. Taking note of the few additional gray hairs that joined his shaggy beard. The sight of him brought such joy to her heart. She'd never be able to adequately describe it much less confess it. She only knew she didn't want him to leave her alone again.

Relaxing in his encompassing embrace, she absently stroked his hands and arms as he held her tightly. Content with the steady beat of his heart thumping comfortingly against her cheek. Having not slept well in days, she snuggled closer and drifted into the hazy netherworld feeling at peace at last.

Finally it occurred to her that Laird might have been right. She was right where she belonged. In that moment, everything was perfect and Scarlett was content.

"Are you still angry with me?"

His silvery eyes danced over her face. He must have been consoled by whatever he saw there because a tender smile lifted the corner of his lips before he brushed a lingering kiss across hers.

"Nay, lass. I was ne'er angry. Only in denial, doubting what I prayed couldnae be true. But I couldnae go another day wi'out seeing yer bonny face."

Scarlett nodded, biting her lip worriedly. "Do you still doubt me?"

"Ah, *mo chroí*, I only wish I could." He held her in silence for a long while. "Lord Lindsay has advised the King to withdraw. I, too, extended my opinion that we should do so."

"Supporting the enemy of the Hepburn clan?"

"Supporting the man in the right," he corrected.

"Then it's over?" She pounced on that tidbit.

"Nay, lass." Laird tweaked her earlobe. "He wouldnae listen."

"But did you tell him all of it?" she persisted.

"I tried. I swear," he said. "The King wouldnae see reason perhaps because there was none to be had. He thought me mad as I thought ye. And before ye say it, all yer proof would mean nothing to him. He wants this war. Naught will change his mind on that."

Taking his hand in hers, Scarlett looked up at him beseechingly. "Then let's leave this place. Let's get your brothers, even your father and go back to Dunskirk or even Crichton."

Laird shook his head. "Nay, lass. I willnae turn tail."

No, of course he wouldn't. Even knowing certain death awaited him, Laird would still want to be first over the wall, so to speak. She was going to lose him either way.

"So you'll just leave me here?"

He bent his cheek to hers. "Nay, lass, I'll no' leave ye again. I cannae. The Hepburn motto is *Keep Trust, Keep Faith*. Have the same in me. I will make it through this is one piece."

"And if you don't?"

"Then I'll still ne'er leave ye. No' really."

"*Omnipotens Deus: ut in nobis et imperio istis beneficiis inceptum. Fac eos uictoria et pace.*"

"Amen," Laird murmured beside her, his head bowed reverantly as the priest blessed them. Or at least, Scarlett hoped that's what the elaborately robed man was doing. Lord knew, they needed every bit of help they could get.

"Amen," she echoed.

Scarlett wasn't the religious sort at all but when King James called his nobles to attend mass with him that night at the chapel of Ford Castle, she knelt beside Laird with her hands wrapped around his. Praying harder than she had ever imagined herself capable. Praying for his safety and for his family's.

Praying for something, anything to change what was about to happen.

The priest lifted his arms heavenward. "*Hoc petimus in nomine Domini Dei nostri, et Pater noster, qui vivit et regnat in unitáte Spíritus Sancti.*" He signed a large cross in the air before him.

"Benedicat vos omnipotens Deus, in nomine Patris, et Filii, et Spiritus Sancti."

"Amen," they all said again and stood, waiting as King James left the pew at the front of the chapel and exited down the aisle. Scarlett wrestled with the urge to latch on to him as he passed.

Laird's hand holding tightly on to hers might have been all that was between her and the moment where she prostrated herself before the monarch and begged him not to be such a huge idiot. Pride had no place in a situation like this.

Other lords and nobles filed out behind him. Some faces Scarlett recognized and then finally the Hepburns, all of them. Names on a long list. Sir Adam of Craggis, the Abbott of Arbath, the Earl of Glencairn, the young Earl of Bothwell who would leave behind his wife and new son, and the Bishop of Brechin who would leave behind those two mistresses and a dozen fatherless children.

Scotland would be filled with orphans and widows by this time tomorrow and there was nothing she could do to change it now. No matter how much she wanted to. No matter how hard she prayed. It was futile.

Unlike the others, Laird knew exactly what he was getting himself into. She had read the brochure to him in its entirety since he'd labored through the unfamiliar print. She, too, knew more than she had before. More than she wanted or needed to know.

Still, he would fight.

Rhys caught her eye as he passed. Scarlett hoped it wouldn't be the last time she saw that roguish wink. Then all the younger Hepburn sons. Patrick limping by with Aleizia on his arm.

Scarlett followed them out at Laird's gentle prodding.

"I hope yer happy wi' yerself," a deep voice hissed in her ear and she looked up into Sir William's glowering face. She had been so wrong. He looked nothing like Laird who might scowl for all he was worth but never conveyed a quarter of the malice this man managed so easily. "Ye've bewitched my son and ruined his life. He will hae nothing now."

"Didn't you do that yourself when you denied him his birthright?" she asked and his eyes widened in surprise. But not confusion. "Wow, it's true, isn't it? How could you do that to him?"

"Sometimes connection and power are more important than what the heart wants," Sir William said through clenched teeth. "My son has forgotten that for the moment but he will remember soon enough."

Scarlett shook her head. No, if history had its way, he wouldn't. But even if he survived, Laird wasn't like his father.

"Scarlett, come," Laird said softly, not bothering to meet his father's eyes. "I disnae matter any longer."

No, it probably didn't. Not anymore.

Making her heartfelt goodbyes to Rhys and Patrick, and promising to see Aleizia the next morning, Scarlett fell in at Laird's side for the long walk back to the tent.

Stars stood out like beacons against the dark night sky. Scarlett had never seen so many, so clearly. She felt like she and Laird were utterly alone together in the cosmos. Wrapped in the length of plaid he had given her weeks before. It was like being wrapped up in him.

It was a flawless moment there with his arm around her shoulders as they walked through the night, his hard body so solid and alive next to hers, his lips grazing her temple.

She would never forget it.

"Will ye go back, do ye think?" he asked quietly. "When it's over?"

"I don't know," she whispered. "Maybe." If she could find Donell and figure out if this whole trip was meant for anything more than the destruction of her heart.

"I would miss ye if ye were to go."

Would he even be around to miss her? Perhaps. Knowing what he knew now, conceivably he would be more careful and find his way to safety.

"I would miss you, too." A tight ache built in her chest. Oh, God, she'd miss him for the rest of her life either way.

"Mayhap ye could stay."

"I'm not sure I have a choice either way."

"Ye could stay. Be my wife," he whispered, his lips close to her ear.

Scarlett bit her lip, feeling tears burning at her eyes and thickening in her throat. "My greatest fear is that you would always regret it."

"My greatest hope is that you would no'."

The tears fell then, splashing on her cheeks. Scarlett dashed them away quickly with the back of her hand, wishing she could banish the ache in her heart as easily. Drawing in a deep breath, she tossed her head. "I told you I'm no good at relationships," she said briskly. "I couldn't give you what you're looking for."

It was true, she told herself insistently. What he would demand from her was too consuming. She would lose herself too easily.

The thought frightened her.

Almost as much as losing him.

"I would ne'er ask ye to be anything other than what ye are. And my darling lass, yer exactly what I'm looking for."

Laird pulled her to a halt in front of their tent, tilting back her head so that she would be forced to look into his eyes but she closed hers, not wanting him to see the tears still shining there. His thumb brushed at the corner of her eye, catching a tear. "Ah, *mo chroí*, I've ne'er met a lass so stubborn as ye. Ye'll admit to nothing, will ye? What hurt ye so that ye must guard yer every feeling?" His soft lips kissed at the corner of her eye and then the other, tasting her tears. "Look at me, Scarlett lass. I've kent all along that ye were hiding something from me. But dinnae hide from this. Do ye no' ken what *mo chroí* means?"

"I told you I don't speak Gaelic," she said, sniffing softly.

"It means 'my heart'. Ye hold it in yer hands already." His brogue was deep, thick with emotion. "*Is breá liom tú, mo Scarlett. Bhfuil tú m'aman. Is mise, agus beidh go lá.* I love ye, my Scarlett. Ye possess my soul. 'Tis yers and fore'er will be."

He possessed her lips in a tender kiss, his massive arms binding her around the waist and lifting her against his chest. He didn't give her time for words but Scarlett wasn't sure what she would have said in any case. She was too overwhelmed by his confession and those heart touching words.

Pushing her into the tent, Laird worked the laces on her blue dress until he freed her from her clothing and lifted her in his arms. Laying her back on the mattress, he undressed quickly and stretched out next to her. Scarlett savored the feeling of his solid mass pressed against her, memorizing every muscle, every plane. The sensation of his skin against hers. His hair teasing her sensitive flesh, his calloused palm stroking her hip. Longing washed over her, not just for the passion he could wring from her body but for the yearning he could squeeze from her heart.

She didn't want this to end. Ever.

He kissed her again with painstaking tenderness, his lips grazing across her cheek, jaw, nose and forehead as if he were trying to memorize her every feature. His fingers followed, glided lightly behind. Then leading the way, down her neck, shoulders and belly. Then his lips, so gentle, as he worshiped every inch of her. Desire fluttered deliciously in her belly but that wasn't all the feeling he roused in her.

Finally he rose above her, his elbows propped on either side of her head so that he might look down at her. Laird held her gaze firmly as he slowly entered her until they were fully joined. Her body absorbed him, memorizing the sensation of his possession, the hard thighs between hers, the rippled abdomen pressed against hers. His shoulders, massive and wide beneath her hands. His bristled jaw, shaggy hair. His eyes, molten pewter, churning with feeling. "*Chomhlánú tú dom, mo ghrá. A dhéanamh tú go hiomlán mé. Beidh mé grá duit that am féin. I gcónaí.* Ye complete me, my love. Ye make me whole. I will love ye across time itself. Always."

Again he didn't give her a chance to speak, but took her lips as he began to move inside of her. Deliberately, as if the pace itself could stop time in its track. Aching, devastating emotions such as Scarlett had never known, gripped her chest like a vise. Even as pleasure cascaded over her, it scored her soul. Sobs built up inside of her and she buried her face in his neck as the tears began to stream down her cheeks but his lips were there once more, taking the tears away. Murmuring again words that branded her heart. "*Tá tú mianach, mo chroí.* Always mine."

Yes, she was. Losing him would be even more heartbreaking because of it.

Her body bowed beneath him as her release came with

bitter sweetness. She cried out in exaltation. In anguish. For what she had found and what she was to lose. Laird's chest rumbled as he moaned throatily against her lips. He collapsed on top of her, nearly crushing her beneath his massive body but Scarlett didn't care, wrapping all of her limbs around him and holding him tightly.

Yes, she was his.

But he would always be hers as well.

"Don't go," she whispered into the darkness just before dawn, compelled to try one last time to keep him safe. Scarlett had lain awake all night holding Laird in her arms even as he held her. Savoring, memorizing and cherishing every moment with him, knowing... fearing that they might be her last.

"Ye should sleep," he said, buckling on his armor and chainmail. He wore thick leather padding beneath them today but Scarlett knew deep inside it wouldn't be enough.

"I can't. Stay, Laird. Please. For me," she begged, scrambling to her knees to wrap her arms around his shoulders as he sat on the edge of the bed to pull on his boots.

"We've been through this. I hae nae choice, *mo chroí*. I maun fight."

"But you know what's going to happen. You can't do this, Laird. It's suicide."

Laird only shook his head. "I'm uninterested in hearing

more of yer protests on the matter, lass."

"And I'm uninterested in a life without you," Scarlett retorted and realized in the space of a heartbeat that it was true. "I don't want to stay here without you if you die. *When* you die. I don't want to go back to a hateful world filled with hateful people either. To go back to where there is no real life for me."

"Hae ye nae one... there?" He added that last word hesitantly as if he could not give it any other name.

"Other than my parents, I have one older brother who wants nothing to do with any of us. A slew of stepfathers and stepmothers, if you can call a woman not much older than you that," she said. "I don't want to go back to that. I don't want to be alone anymore."

"Then stay here wi' me."

"Will I be with you, though?" she asked. "If you die..."

"Och, enough now, lass. I cannae be a coward and hide myself away. I maun fight wi' my clansmen and watch over my brothers."

Of course, he would. He was a brave man. A caring one.

Scarlett lifted a hand and raked her fingernails lightly through his whiskers and then curled her fingers into the shaggy, mahogany locks at the nape of his neck. Pressing her body flush against him, she tugged his head down until she could reach his lips. She brushed her lips across his, running her tongue over his luscious lower lip before drawing on it and gnawing gently. He threaded his fingers through the short hair at her nape and pulled her head back to kiss her more fully.

The kiss was full of promise and passion but over too soon. Laird pulled away and looked down at her, his fingers toying with her earlobe and the hair behind her ear. "Ye'll hae curly hair when it's longer, me thinks."

"Yes, it is."

"I should like to see that."

I would like you to see it, too. Scarlett swallowed back a tortured sob. "Laird, I…"

"What is it?"

Her blood roared in her ears, buzzing in protest. "Nothing."

"I ken that particular 'nothing'. What's amiss?"

Scarlett stared up into those remarkable eyes that would haunt her forever. "I'm just so terrified by the thought of losing you."

It was true. All true. Her heart pounded like a drum in her chest as if she hovered on the brink of a precipice but Scarlett pulled back from the edge, a skitter of nerves chasing down her spine.

A man who wanted nothing more from her than her heart and the love she could give him. Everyone else had wanted something more from her, from her parents or from their fame. A piece of the Scarlett Thomas pie, carved out of her soul.

But what Laird wanted from her could not be taken or forced. It had to be given.

Scarlett realized then that it had been. All her attempts to keep an emotional distance from him had been pathetic. She'd fought against him in vain. All her denial just a bunch of natter to fill her head and drown out the truth.

She loved him.

This Scottish warrior. This domineering, stubborn, irascible, caring, honorable Laird who was *so* not her type. She loved him. Loved him all the more because of each of those things.

Amazing that a single moment in time could change her perception of reality. But reality didn't care if she loved him. Laird was about to die. Why would Donell bring her here then? To make sure Scarlett knew what love truly felt like before stripping it cruelly away from her?

"Laird."

The words would not come. The feeling was too new, too difficult to assimilate.

"Farewell, *mo chroí.*"

With one last kiss, Laird gathered up his sword and left the tent. Scarlett stared after him, her blood pounding in her ears. Throbbing in her chest. No, she couldn't...

NO!

"Laird!" she cried, running after him and throwing herself into his arms when he turned to look back. Wrapping her arms tightly around his neck, she buried her face in his shoulder, dampening his skin with her tears as they fell freely. "I love you," she choked out, her voice strained to break through the lump in her throat. "I love you so much. Please, come back to m-"

His mouth covered hers, swallowing the last of her plea and devouring her heart and soul as he held her so tightly against him that Scarlett could hardly breathe. It didn't matter; she'd give her last breath to make sure he knew how dearly she loved him.

Just in case.

Laird set her back on her feet just as the sun broke the horizon, spilling its rays upon his face. His eyes glittered like polished silver as he framed her face in his hands and looked down at her. The slash of dimples appeared above the shaggy line of his short beard as a smile of pleasure such as she had never seen on him graced his handsome face. "I will be back to hear ye say that again, if for nae other reason." He kissed her lightly and drew back, still smiling. "I love ye as well, my bonny lass. 'Twas the grandest day of my life, finding ye at Dunskirk."

"Mine, too. Be careful."

"I will."

Boom!

The first blast echoed over the camp in the late afternoon. The hideous reverberation was followed in waves by another and then another. Scarlett had seen enough historical battle scenes on film to recognize the firing of the cannon. That would be the opening volley King James had promised would set the English on their heels but Scarlett knew better. Scotland's heavy artillery wasn't going to scare anyone off.

Even from the distance, the shots sounded ponderous, as if the cannon was too fatigued already to spit out the cannonball without effort. As if the cannon knew its efforts were in vain.

Soon enough a more rapid fire responded. The English counter attack with its light artillery, aimed at taking out – not the Scottish forces waiting to fight – but the Scottish cannon that would impede their immediate advance.

Scarlett circled the clearing outside Aleizia's tent restlessly, pleating the fabric of her skirts with nervous fingers. "How can you all just sit here like this?" The question was torn from her as she whirled back to the group of women gathered there, stitching away as if nothing were amiss. "Your men are out there dying! Your husbands. Your sons! How can you just sit here without doing something?"

"What is there for us to do?" Lady Glencairn asked. "Should we take up arms with them? Have them die even faster from the distraction of worrying over us rather than themselves?"

Scarlett gnashed her teeth in frustration. It was the same point some soldiers made even in her time about having women on the battlefield. Even a bigger point in a time when chivalry was still very much alive. She turned to Aleizia. "I thought you were a panicker."

"I am," Aleizia whispered, staring down at her sampler. "I want my husband safe. I want my babe to have a father."

She pressed a hand to her abdomen and Scarlett felt her own stomach drop. Aleizia was pregnant? Oh, God, she was a just a girl! Too young to be a widow and a single mother. But still, even if the worst were to happen, she would always have that piece of Patrick and Scarlett had to envy her that.

The thought sent a shudder down Scarlett's spine. Bearing a child in medieval times? No, thank you.

But what if it was Laird's baby? Another sort of shudder ran through her. One of longing and yearning. It would be worth the risk. "Forgive me, Aleizia," she said. "I know you're worried."

God, they were a brave bunch. It was easy enough to love a man who sat at home by the hearth each night and another thing entirely to love a man who might never return. It gave Scarlett a whole new respect for military wives in any time.

"It's quite all right. We all are." Aleizia's words were calm. Sensible. Scarlett felt anything but.

"I just wish there was something we could do."

Pacing away from the group, Scarlett started in surprise when a strong hand caught her around the arm and pulled her behind the tent. Donell! His wrinkled face was folded into a severe frown.

She didn't feel much like smiling either.

"Och, lassie, what are ye still doing here?"

"Still doing here?" she screeched through clenched teeth. "You tell me."

"I thought ye were clever enough to figure it out on yer own."

"I thought I had. I tried to stop it," Scarlett protested. "They wouldn't listen."

"Och, lass," Donell spat in disgust. "Did ye think ye could change the minds of a thousand bull-headed Scotsmen? Ye daft lass, why did I choose ye? Only a knotty-pated beldame would think she could singlehandedly stop a war." He clucked his tongue lightly.

Scarlett ignored his insults, determined to get to the heart of the matter. "Why then? What am I here for?"

"To save him, lass. Not the whole bluidy country. *Him.*" Donell shook his head in disgust. "I'm all for second chances, lassie, but ye've got to take them when they come along."

"Why the hell didn't you just say that right from the beginning?" she snapped, gathering up her skirts and turning to run to Laird. To the battle.

"How do you expect me to find him?" She spun back to ask the meddling old man. "There are tens of thousands of men out there. Arrows. Cannonballs. I'll never find him now."

"You'll find him, lassie. Just follow your heart."

"Follow my heart? What kind of fairy tale bullshit is that?" she asked but Donell was already turning away. Scarlett didn't try to chase after him, knowing that it would be a useless endeavor and besides, she had something far more important to do right now.

Running back through the circle of women, Scarlett raced on to her own tent.

"Scarlett, what are you doing?" Aleizia asked, scurrying after her.

"Something very, very stupid," she said, snatching up her purse and slipping it over her head. She had to save Laird. She'd known it all along. Laird was going to be as mad as an enormous, green rage monster when he saw her on the battlefield. He'd likely hulk out completely, but at least he would be alive to do it.

"I'll go with you," Aleizia said. "It would be better than waiting here for news."

Scarlett shook her head as she pulled out her pistol and checked the magazine. "No, you're not. You stay here and take care of that baby." She hugged the girl hard. "And pray. God, pray for us all."

The sound of the battle was her compass as she lifted her skirts and began to run. The smoky haze gathering overhead, the pall hanging like buzzards over the bloodshed.

Reaching the top of a hill, she paused, watching the battle. A battle that no film could depict the essence of. No director – not Coppola, not Scorsese – could capture.

The reality of war was not something anyone would truly want to watch, especially for entertainment. Cannonballs flew flinging earth, blood and body parts into the air. Arrows zinged by, taking down the unshielded, unarmored Highlanders. Pikes lurched upward, piercing man and bone. And the noise! Beyond the explosive of the artillery, the clash of metal and screams of man where horrifying.

The Scots warriors were fighting like demons but it wouldn't be enough. It would never be enough.

Then Scarlett saw Laird as if she were looking into a crystal ball. Through the swirling smoke, there he was.

And he was fighting for his life.

The English army left its baggage train at Barmoor and set out in two parts. The vanguard under the command of Howard, the Lord Admiral, crossed the River Till at the Twizel Bridge. The Rearguard led by Surrey had crossed at a little known ford point at New Heaton and the two regrouped on the northern edge of the battlefield.

Learning that they were being outflanked, King James ordered a rapid redeployment northwards from Flodden Hill to the top of nearby Branxton Hill. It was an equally commanding position, but without any of the defenses already prepared on Flodden, it was an ill-considered move.

They'd had another chance to gain advantage whilst the English army was crossing the Till. Borthwick begged the King to let him release cannon fire upon the unwitting soldiers but King James denied the request, insisting that his enemy meet the open plain before they met battle. They were waiting until their enemy was in position before the two sides began bombardment by cannon fire simultaneously.

The English compounded the attack with a rain of arrows from their longbow men, their archers far outnumbering the Scots. Screams were drown out by the artillery, masked by smoke and fire.

Five battalions of Scotsmen waited on the ridge for their enemy to advance. They had the advantage on the hill, so James was struck by horror when the King was provoked so quickly by the English cannon and sounded the attack, forcing them to give up their strategic position once again.

But give it up they did. The far left flank under Lords Home and Huntly charged diagonally, picking up troops from the middle as they marched forward. Under pressure, the English right flank was forced to divide. Riding with them, James approached the foe through the fog of battle.

The English scattered under the force of the wild and willful force of Home's Border Scots and Huntly's Highlanders. They fought as they always had, in close combat with sword, bill or bludgeon. They took Howard's standard. The battle was flowing in their favor but it wouldn't last.

Their center vanguard under the earls of Errol, Crawford and Montrose and another battalion under Bothwell and the Frenchman, d'Aussi, walked straight into a bog, heretofore unseen until they were ankle deep in the mire. King James left his command position at the top of Branxton Hill to take charge and urge his soldiers on, bringing his division into the fray with him, a division populated by the bulk of the Scottish nobility.

James watched it, helpless to change the tide of history. Surrey was massacring the Scots in the center, Scots exhausted from their charge through the swamp. A barrage from the English longbows was let loose on their right flank,

Argyll and Lennox, their Highland warriors not wearing a stitch of armor were easily shot down as they too slogged through the mire.

Determined to meet his foe on equal footing or perhaps to inspire his troops, King James dismounted from his horse and ordered his nobles to do the same. Clad in full armor, they were nearly immobilized by the mud and James' heart seized in anguish as he saw his young cousin Bothwell fall. Then his uncle, George.

Leaving behind his successful flank, the soldiers of which were now looting the dead and injured English soldiers as much as fighting them, James forged a path atop his powerful steed in aid of his sovereign. He hadn't been called to the King's side for battle but he couldn't stand aside and watch Fate take its course without lifting hand to stop it.

For hours they fought. The pikes they'd trained on with the French were useless in these tight quarters. So many of his countrymen were nearly defenseless with the unwieldy spears in hand. Again James lashed out, sparing one man from certain death, uncertain if it would save him in the end.

"Your Grace," he shouted as he neared his monarch, cutting down the enemy around him. "The battle is lost. We maun see ye to safety."

"I cannae withdraw," the King protested, then looked at James. "See that Home secures Coldstream for our retreat. Go! See that it is done."

"I willnae leave ye here to die, Your Grace," James said tightly, dismounting and hoping to urge his monarch up on his horse.

"It is not my day to die."

Brave words but James knew better. Everything Scarlett had warned him of had come to pass. Everything was happening just as Scarlett's pamphlet had said. Everything. His King was worn out and on the verge of death. In all likelihood, James would die today as well, though his death had not been imprinted on the paper.

"We are blood, James," King James said under his breath. "I hae ne'er admitted it aloud, perhaps no' even now is it loud enough for another to hear. Ye are the only Stewart ne'er to envy my place, to conspire against me. Ye ne'er did."

"No," was all James said.

"Watch over my son. Guide him. Protect him."

James wanted to protest. To beg his King once more to retreat but only nodded. He knew stubbornness well enough. He was a Stewart in part, at least. King James would not give in. If he himself could make it out of the day alive, he would do as King James commanded, not because he was James' sovereign but because he was family. "I swear it."

"Go then."

James fell back, hacking his way through the English who had them nearly surrounded. Stepping on the bodies of his clansmen, his countrymen as he fought. Some dead, some yet alive but not for long as they drown in the muck and blood of their fallen comrades. His shoulder screamed in protest as he lifted his heavy sword again and again. Slashing, stabbing his way through the mob. Fighting to survive.

For her. For Scarlett.

He had been alone for most of his life. From his grandfather, he'd gotten a name. From his father, a family of sorts. But they couldn't give him a home. They could not bring him the sense of belonging he'd always longed for.

He'd never known a mother's love. Never known a woman's love. Never known that a woman's soft arms could cradle him, surround him with something more than a physical release.

He knew those things now. Knew them because of the appearance of a single extraordinary lass who had nearly brought him to his knees. James didn't want to lose that now. He didn't fear death in battle as much as losing the love of a will o' a wisp of a woman. Now, as he never had before, he wanted to live life to the fullest.

With her. With Scarlett.

Swinging up into his saddle, James saw Home join Huntly as they made good their escape toward Coldstream. James could see the same salvation waiting for him. It seemed wrong that he should survive when so many others would not and was tempted to return to battle but the King's command weighed on him. The prince, the new King was just a bairn. He would have no one on his side.

A Sassenach pike caught James in the side and lifted him off his horse. Staggering to his feet, James fought for breath against the all-encompassing pain and swung his sword once more. Clash of steel against steel vibrating through his aching shoulders. Slash to his enemy's side and the man fell with a hoarse cry.

Clutching his side, James lowered his sword just as an angry cry sounded behind him and he turned to see yet another Englishman's sword swinging for his head and no time to raise his sword in defense.

James closed his eyes waiting for the deathblow to fall, knowing that his end was at hand. A high-pitched pop rose above the low din and opening his eyes, James saw the surprise on the Sassenach's face as a small badge of red blossomed on his chest and unfurled. He lifted his hand to the wound in surprise, his eyes shifting beyond James. Another pop and the man staggered back and fell to his knees as a tiny red dot appeared on his forehead.

In astonishment, James spun about to find Scarlett thirty yards behind him, wrapped in his red Hepburn plaid. Her arm raised and pointing at the man with the small firearm she had shown him in her hand. A delicate wisp of smoke wove skyward from the barrel. She was more pale than ever, her eyes dark with horror as she stared down at the body at James' feet.

"Scarlett!" The word was choked with surprise as he lurched toward her. "What the fook, lass! What are ye doin' here? This is nae place for a woman."

Scarlett brows rose at that, color infusing her cheeks. "Don't you take that tone with me, Laird Hepburn. I just saved your life!"

Another battle cry behind them, and James turned to fight once more but another pop sounded and the Englishman stumbled with a scream of pain as the bits of his knee fell apart. Scarlett again. Reaching her side, James grasped her arm, hauling her away from the fighting. "Are you hurt?" she yelled over the clash of metal and the screams of dying men.

James shook his head. He would survive it if they made their way through this mêlée. Battling, pushing his way through the swamp of combat and death. Ahead, he saw Rhys fall to his knees and rushed forward, feeling a jolt through his shoulders as his sword sank deep into the neck of the man who would dare try to kill his brother.

"Are ye alright?" he yelled above the din and Rhys nodded, wiping blood from his brow as he pushed himself to his feet. His eyes widened as he saw Scarlett behind him but there was no time for comment. Savage cries, echoed around them and the two men put Scarlett between them, facing the English soldiers pressing in.

✕ ✕ ✕ ✕ ✕

Once long ago – or far in the future, depending how one looked at it – Mark Twain was quoted as saying that 'The two most important days in your life are the day you are born and the day you find out why.'

Now Scarlett knew why. She had done it! She had saved Laird, who in turn had saved Rhys. Firing her pistol again and again, she was determined to keep it that way.

The crowd thinned, only requiring a slash here or there to make a path for them. Scarlett fired once more and then they were to safety, running toward the River Till to the east. All around them, the Scots were retreating knowing that defeat was upon them.

The battle was over, but not finished. They had to run as the Englishmen would follow, looking to strike down any stragglers.

Tripping along after Laird's long strides with his plaid trailing out behind her, Scarlett's legs were burning against the exertion. Then numbing. She stumbled as weakness washed over her. "Laird," she cried out, tripping over her skirts and landing on her knees. Something was wrong, terribly wrong. "Laird," she whispered weakly.

Laird turned and frowned down at her taking in her pale face, nearly translucent skin. "What is it? Are ye injured?"

No, that wasn't it at all. Weeks ago, she had taken Laird's sword in her hand and begged for someone to save her. She had come to him and now saved him in return. The circle was complete. She knew it with a sickening certainty. "Laird, oh no! Oh, God, not now. Not yet!"

Her eyes met his beloved gaze, seeing the confusion there. He didn't yet understand what was happening, but he would all too soon.

His gaze narrowed and then his jaw set with familiar stubbornness. "Nay, yer no' goin' anywhere, lass. Fight it."

"I can't," she gasped. Laird dropped his sword and fell to his knees, locking his arms tightly around her. Scarlett held on to his shoulders, hoping beyond hope that she might hold him tightly enough to carry him with her. "Oh Laird. I want... Take care of Aleizia and Aileen. Don't make her marry the earl. And, Rhys." His eyes flared as she cast her eyes north. Realizing they weren't following, Rhys had stopped and turned back. "Don't let anyone make him marry at all. He and Willem..."

Laird's eyes widened in understanding. "I won't but ye hae to fight it, *mo chroí.*"

"I can't." Weakly she lifted a hand to stroke his cheek, but already she was fading. "Be the heir you were meant to be. Maybe not in position, but at heart. Take care of them all. I love you, Laird. I will always..."

"Scarlett! Na-a-ay!"

✕ ✕ ✕ ✕ ✕

James beat his fist down on the ground where Scarlett had just sat but there was nothing there. She was gone.

How? Why?

His fingers found the warm blade of his sword and curled around it, so tightly that it cut into his fingers. His palm. Blood oozed from between his clenched fingers. The pain was nothing compared to that impaling his heart and spiking through his chest as if death itself had seized him in its grip. So much he had gained.

"Nay, *mo chroí.* Stay wi' me," he whispered. "Please,

please, dinnae go."

"Laird," Rhys shouted running back to his side. "We maun go. Now, Laird!"

"Nay, I cannae."

"Aye, ye can, ye spleeny bastard! She dinnae come all this way to hae ye die on yer knees," he yelled, fisting his hand in James' shirt and dragging him to his feet. "Now, come on!"

As dark descended around them, the battle was all but over. His misery was just beginning with her loss.

41

The battle was still raging. Scarlett stared dumbly at the sight as the numbness faded. Hope speared through her but faded quickly. Where it had been blood, guts and ugliness before, the spectacle before her was too small, too clean... too kind.

Staged.

Only a few hundred men were on the field. A field dotted not with the bodies of the dead and injured but with rounded hay bales. Atop a low hill not far away a stark granite cross rose in memorial against the blue sky.

A plane flew overhead and Scarlett's head whipped from the left to the right taking in the evidence of a modern day Flodden. Cars, cameras. Spectators.

It was a reenactment, she realized. It wasn't real at all. Laird was truly gone. Dead now by about five hundred years.

"No, no, no," she whispered, denying the truth. Digging in her purse, she found her phone and turned it on.

But there it was. September ninth, twenty-thirteen. Five fifty-seven p.m. Just as when she'd left, she'd come back through time exactly five hundred years almost to the minute. And almost a month had passed since she travelled back in time.

A month where her life had changed completely.

And now Laird was gone. Torn away from her forever by time and space. Scarlett felt her shoulders heave in a bone-jarring but silent sob, then another that ripped through her chest like an alien trying to force its way out, but even that pain couldn't have matched this torture. She couldn't take a breath; her throat was clenched too tightly. The burning in her breast spread, radiating outward as hot tears rolled down her cheeks.

No.

The cry of her soul echoed by Laird a half a millennia before as her fingers curled into the moist earth of Flodden.

"Oi, there! You alright, miss?" a deep, brusque voice said nearby as a strong hand wrapped around her elbow and tried to help her to her feet. "Are you hurt? Can you stand?"

Could she? Scarlett had no idea. She didn't even want to try. She just wanted to curl up in Laird's plaid cry until she hadn't a tear left to shed.

"Hey, don't I know you? Aren't you that actress who went missing some time ago?" he asked. "Wot are you doing all dressed up like that? Filming a new movie?"

"Something like that," she mumbled noncommittally.

The phone in her hand sounded a series of pings, then again and again. Forty-six voicemails. One hundred and twelve texts. Almost all were from Tyrone, though a few were from her parents.

Flipping through her contacts, Scarlett dialed for help.

"Where the hell have you been?"

Yes, well, welcome home.

Scarlett hung up on Tyrone. Ignoring the buzzing of her phone when he called her back straightaway. She would answer his messages later but not now. Not when she too devastated by what had happened to her to even draw a steady breath.

There were things she needed to do and she would do them on her own.

Right now, there was somewhere else she desperately needed to be.

"Sir, can you help me, please? I need to get to Dunskirk Castle. Can you take me? I know it's a long way…"

"Ain't but a fifteen minute drive or some such, miss," the man said gruffly. "Are ye sure that's where ye want to go? Do ye need the police?"

Scarlett looked up into his concerned brown eyes. "No, thank you, everything I need is at Dunskirk."

Laird. Donell! That old curmudgeon better be there.

A month later

"Good morning, Miss Thomas. We're pleased to have you back again." The clerk at the Dunskirk admissions desk welcomed her back just as she had every morning the new museum was open for the past month. "Nothing yet, I'm sorry to say."

Nothing yet, meaning there was no sign of Donell. Again.

Just as there hadn't been since the day she returned to her time. She had looked everywhere for him but to no avail. Just as she had in the past, Scarlett felt an undeniable conviction that she wouldn't see him again until he pleased him to make an appearance.

Unlike last time, she wasn't certain if that were ever going to happen.

He had gotten what he wanted from her.

Scarlett sighed. "Can I just go back then?"

The clerk nodded. Scarlett gave her points for being so professional. No doubt she was harboring a raging curiosity for the reasons behind Scarlett's daily visits. What could a world famous celebrity want with an ancient Scotsman? Why would she come to Dunskirk each day to wait for him, wrapped in a ragged old tartan?

Still, the clerk had never uttered a word. Never asked. Just remained serene and unquestioning as if she knew Scarlett's sanity was depending on it.

Perhaps it was.

"Just let me stamp your pass."

With a nod, Scarlett drew her monthly pass from her purse and the girl found a blank spot on the oft-stamped card to make another mark. Winding her way through the exhibits, Scarlett found the spot where Laird's sword had once been displayed. His bejeweled Claymore no longer stood there. She had that much to be thankful for, staring at the short bill that sat in place of the claymore. The bladed weapon was about two feet in length but Scarlett had no idea whose it was.

Nor did she have much information about what had become of Laird. He hadn't died at Flodden, that much she did know. He hadn't left his sword on the field to be found.

There wasn't much else she could discover about him beyond that, though she'd spent much of her time lately researching Dunskirk and its former owner. Information on the early owners of the property was spotty at best. She knew he'd continued to serve at court sporadically until James V had been old enough to hold his own. He'd been made Earl of Achenmeade for his service but there'd never been another earl by that time. According to all sources, it had died with him. Whether it was because he never married or not, Scarlett didn't know.

She only hoped he'd returned to Dunskirk and began to live his dream, building on his tower to begin the expansion that would lead to this one day.

She hoped he was happy. Oh, so happy with his life.

If only she knew! If Laird were happy, that would be enough for her.

She could let it go.

But without knowing...

Movement stirred behind her and out of the corner of her eye, she saw an elderly but spry figure slip out of the tower door. Her heart began to pound and she followed but couldn't catch sight of him again. Down the stairs she went and through the halls, past a cordoned-off area and around another corner.

A pair of heavily carved doors with stained glass panels stood ajar and Scarlett went through them. She knew well enough from her time filming there that they led to the chapel. Donell wasn't within but a single candle sat burning at the altar. Another flickered in one of the alcoves off to the side, the light dancing off an amorphous object she was decidedly unfamiliar with. Intrigued, she decided to take a look. Her boots scuffed along the stone floor, breaking the reverent silence.

Her gasp when she saw the carved marble tomb there was like a shout, bouncing off the stone walls. In all her years at Dunskirk, it had never been there before but she recognized the sculpted figure laying on top all too well.

It was Laird.

Scarlett fell to her knees beside it, tracing her fingers over his attractively hewn features, his nose and clean-shaven jaw. Then over the words carved into the side of the tomb:

James Stewart Patrick Hepburn, 1ˢᵗ Earl of Achenmeade.
Laird of Achenmeade.
Born May 2nd in the year of Our Lord 1486
Died October 10 in the year of Our Lord 1552
He awaits Ye still

A tear splashed on the marble, setting the gray marbling out in stark contrast to the white. *Laird, oh Laird,* her heart cried. *I'm here. I'm still waiting, too!*

"'Boot time, lassie. What kept ye?"

Scarlett's head whipped around and she stared incredulously at Donell, who was leaning against a granite pillar not far away.

"What kept me?" she asked incredulously. "What kept you? I've been here almost every day for a month."

She had. Tyrone and her parents had wanted to make a media circus of her 'kidnapping and disappearance' as well as her miraculous return but Scarlett had told them that the paycheck was all dried up. She refused to work for them and be the oh-so-marketable Scarlett Thomas product any longer.

Thankfully, Grayson would have nothing to do with her. He'd finally gotten all the publicity he ever desired, though not in the best light. It seemed he'd been a person of interest in drawn out investigation surrounding her disappearance. CNN instead of Entertainment Tonight. No one had believed his outrageous claims that she'd simply disappeared into thin air.

Even the press had given up on getting a word out of her on the matter but Scarlett had never given up on finding Donell, hiring private investigators to track him down and waiting him out herself at Dunskirk.

"Ye ken what I find surprising?" he continued, as if she hadn't even spoken. "Ye had no' a tear in yer eye when ye left this place and found yerself in the past. No' a tear for what ye'd lost and yet here ye are in tears now. Why is that?"

"I suspect you know why," Scarlett said tartly, wiping her eyes. "Stop playing with me, Donell. Are you here to send me back or not?"

"Tsk, tsk, lassie. Ye've nae patience a'tall."

"No, I don't," she agreed. "Why couldn't you just send him back here with me in the first place? He was supposed to die on that field after all. What harm would there have been in letting him come with me?"

Donell shook his head. "That's no' the way it works, lass. There was more for him to do. A purpose. 'Tis the reason he was spared."

"And what was the reason for sending me there?" she asked. "To break my heart?"

"Is it broken?" he asked curiously. "Or are yer tears because no one has ever cared so much for ye?"

"My tears aren't because he cared for me, Donell. My tears are because I have never been given the chance to care so much for someone else. I would give anything for him. For Rhys and the girls."

"E'en if it meant staying here and being wi'out him forever?"

The thought was like a knife in the heart but Scarlett nodded without hesitation. "If it meant keeping them safe. Yes. I would stay here. Is that why you didn't let me stay with him?"

Donell ambled toward the effigy, tracing his fingers across the marble. "He was just sixty-six years when he died. It wouldn't have a been a verra long life ye had wi' him in any case."

Another tear splashed on her cheek as she looked down at the carefully hewn sculpture of Laird's beloved face. "A year would have been enough. A week. A day. It wouldn't have mattered. I just wanted to live a life with him, no matter how long it ended up being. He never knew that. I never got the chance to tell him that I would have loved to have been his wife in truth." Her voice broke with emotion over those last words.

"Good answer, lass."

Silence fell once again in the chapel as Scarlett gathered Laird's plaid tightly around her shoulders and stared down at the tomb. "So that's it then? I'm here and he's safe?" She sniffed and nodded decisively though her voice lacked the resolve, emerging in a choked whisper, "Okay, that's okay then."

Her chin trembled as her tears began falling in earnest as the agony of loss and heartbreak expanded in her heart with renewed energy. "It's okay, Laird. You're okay," she whispered painfully as she spread her hand out over his, curling her fingers around the stone. Imagining she could feel the warmth of his touch. His hand in hers one last time.

One final touch.

"That's all that really matters. You're good. We're good."

"Och, lass. Enough," Donell said sharply, though a single tear glinted in the corner of his eye. "Ye've nae hesitation do ye? Is there nothing here at all that ye would miss?"

"Toilet paper."

"Be serious."

"The next season of Sherlock? What do you want me to say, Donell?" she asked, shaking her head. "None of it really matters in comparison."

"What aboot this?" he asked, kicking a large box next to his foot. A box she recognized all too well.

"Where did you get that?"

"Answer the question."

Scarlett shrugged. "It was for them. It was all for them. I just... I thought they might like it."

"Ye cannae change their fate, lass."

"No, I've mostly decided that fate isn't so bad. It gave me Laird. Even for a little while," she said, her eyes drawn irresistibly back to the tomb.

"Yet ye still came here hoping to change fate and find a way back."

A sad smile quirked her lips. "I did say 'mostly'."

"Ye'd fight for him."

"I would. Every girl should be so lucky as to be taken by a Laird."

Donell nodded with open satisfaction. "Then go fight for him, lass."

✕ ✕ ✕ ✕ ✕

Darkness swirled around the corners of her vision then the world went black. By bits and pieces, light began to pierce the gloom once again. Here. There. Little haloed flames. Candles.

Set along the wall of the chapel were thousands of little candles, brightening the space and reflecting off golden grill work along the perimeter of the room, gold paint on the details of the murals covering the ceiling and the gold of the plate and goblet laid out on the altar.

It also shone of the dark hair of the man kneeling there, his head bent in prayer. Tears began to roll down her cheeks again, this time in thanks, as she looked heavenward. She was back!

Though she hadn't made a sound, Laird's shoulders stiffened and squared. He lifted his head and cocked it to the side. His hands tightened on the railing before him as he pushed himself to his feet and then finally he turned. His silvery eyes piercing her with wonder and joy. Shining with the glint of tears reflecting off of them.

Her own vision blurred and a tear splashed against her cheek. Scarlett dashed it away as he rushed to her, dropping to his knees before her.

"I felt ye. I couldnae hope... Ahh, *mo chroi!*" Laird wrapped his shaking arms around her hips as he rested his cheek against her belly. Scarlett combed her fingers through his hair, too overcome to speak.

"Ne'er leave me again. Ne'er," he whispered, pressing his lips to her belly. Scarlett fell into his arms, burying her face in his neck as the their tears of joy streamed together.

"I won't. I won't! Never again."

The promise was sealed in a kiss.

EPILOGUE

December 1518
Dunskirk, Scotland

"Are ye certain ye should be reading that to our bairn?" Laird asked, brushing his lips across his wife's forehead as she cradled their toddler daughter in her lap. A lap that wasn't given too much space as her belly was already well-rounded with their next child.

"Absolutely," Scarlett said firmly, her amber gaze warm with love and contentment as she smiled up at him. "We love it, don't we, Hermione?" She dropped a kiss on their daughter's auburn curls and the two shared a satisfied nod.

He was outnumbered.

With a grin, Laird tucked his Hepburn plaid more tightly around his two ladies and moved to throw another log on the fire. The winter was a cold one this year. The wind was whistling through the stone walls of Dunskirk.

Five years had passed since the Battle at Flodden. Since

their bloody defeat at the hands of the English. As Scarlett's brochure had said, King James had died on the field along with most of the nobles of the land, including his father, two of his young brothers and several uncles. Even more cousins. Dozens of titles in the Highlands and Borders transferred to young boys, bairns or in several cases laid dormant until the next heir could be born.

He'd been very lucky to survive, to have been able to save Rhys' life, who had in turn saved Patrick's during the retreat. All because one young woman had been sent to save him.

The years since then had changed his Scarlett. She'd put on weight though she was still slender and willowy. Her auburn hair had grown past her shoulders in long, winding curls though she preferred to leave it down or wear it in a 'ponytail' rather than sporting the popular fashions of the times.

She was a fish out of water, Scarlett would often say. She would never truly be able to blend in completely. It wasn't her way. These were not her times. Laird wouldn't have wanted her to. It was her unique character that captured his heart from the beginning.

Laird felt the rigid scarring that scored his palm and the fingers of his right hand. A reminder of the loss he'd felt when she'd disappeared. He would never forget that or the torture he endured in those long weeks when he thought he'd lost her forever. He'd worked at Dunskirk from before dawn until long after the sun had set just so he might find sleep from exhaustion. Laird would never take her presence in his life for granted.

It continually humbled him utterly that Scarlett would give up the advantages of her time to be with him. That she would choose to live outside of her element simply to share the remainder of her life by his side. Still, it was his hope that she would never find regret in staying with him that had prevailed rather than her fear that he might regret her doing so.

He would never regret a moment of his life spent with her.

"Leave her be, Laird." Aleizia protested, rocking her own babe near the fireplace. Her third thus far in just five years. "I want to hear the rest of the tale."

Patrick nodded his agreement. "I maun agree wi' my wife, Laird. Dinnae spoil it for us all."

"Here, here," Rhys said, emptying his cup of whiskey and pouring another cup for Willem for a change, who was seated by his side.

"You should all just have her teach you to read the words," Aileen laughed, sitting close to her young husband, Dickie Sutherland, in a cozy, upholstered loveseat of Scarlett's design. "Then you'd be able to read them for yourself as I already have a dozen times over."

"You only have time to read them, Aileen, because you haven't a child of your own yet to occupy your time," Aleizia protested.

No, she didn't, but only because Laird and Patrick – who welcomed Laird's counsel, given by the promise he had made Scarlett – had delayed her wedding day until she was of a more mature age to wed. Scarlett had lobbied for eighteen but they'd settled on sixteen. The couple had been wed only a year. "Soon, my sister, soon!" Aileen grinned and blushed as her husband heartily kissed her in front of them all.

Five years had brought laughter and love to Dunskirk and even to Crichton during the visits Laird and Scarlett made there on their way to court each winter. Though not this one, not with the birth of his next child looming. The summers they spent at Dunskirk, building on the castle from the hundreds of sketches Scarlett made, adding the mini castle on the island out in the pond and a vegetable garden behind the castle. Raising a family together.

It had been five years so far of peace and bliss with Scarlett at his side. Laird had never seen hide nor hair of auld Donell again in all that time. If he had he would have felt compelled to shake his hand. Bluidy hell. He'd probably kiss the auld bastard for delivering his Scarlett back to him.

His sisters would probably thank him for sending along Scarlett's small library as well. The box that had arrived at Dunskirk with her had contained books. The complete works of Jane Austen, James Joyce, William Shakespeare, Oscar Wilde, the Scotsman Robert Louis Stevenson, and J.K. Rowling among others.

Scarlett was reading aloud from one of Ms. Rowling's works, *The Half-Blood Prince,* to them that night. Laird had heard the story a dozen times before but never tired of it, neither did Scarlett. He supposed he was a bit of a 'fanboy' and a 'geek' as well. It was one of the many things they had in common.

She'd brought some other small items back with her as well including medicines such as aspirin and antibiotic cream but as Scarlett said, she was *mostly* willing to let Fate take its course. As it was Fate and auld Donell that had brought them together, they figured that it knew what was best for them.

"Laird, how aboot some more whiskey over here to warm us on this cold night?" Rhys called.

"Get it yerself," he said and with a laugh, his brother pushed out his chair and ambled over to the sideboard, uncorking another bottle of Laird's Achenmeade whiskey.

"Hae ye noticed that ye ne'er seen to mind anyone calling ye Laird anymore, brother?" Rhys asked under his breath.

Laird looked around the room. There was love everywhere around him. His family. His child. His wife. How could he mind the name she spoke with such love? "Nay, I dinnae."

"I'll hae to think of something else to call ye then," Rhys said with a smile.

"Best of luck to you, my brother."

✕ ✕ ✕ ✕ ✕

"Och, no, no, no." Donell shook his head worriedly, looking in on the comfortable scene from the hallway as he passed by. "No, this is wrong. All wrong! I dinnae bring her here for this."

After all he had made them suffer, he couldn't let it end the way he saw the future unfolding. They didn't deserve it. But what to do? What to do?

He needed help. Help from someone who would understand. Someone who wouldn't rail and panic, wasting time when none was available.

A grin creased the old man deeply wrinkled face as the idea struck. Aha! That was just the ticket.

Time and space slipped. A different castle surrounded him, one lit by soft gaslights far beyond the innovation of the sixteenth century.

"What are you doing here?" Emmy MacLean neé MacKenzie, the Countess of Stratheclyde, cried out as she rounded the corner of Duart Castle and ran right into the small but energetic form of man she would have been happy enough never to lay eyes on again. "Don't you dare take me away again. I warned you before, Donell, I will take you out."

Beside her, her husband tensed. His massive form bunching with coiled tension as his hands fisted at his sides. Ready to fight for her as always.

"Och, dinnae get yer panties in a twist, lassie. I need yer help," Donell said quickly, breathing a sigh of relief when the lass caught her man's arm. Sparing him from certain harm.

"Hold on, Connor," Emmy said softly. "Let's hear him out."

AUTHOR'S NOTE

I hope you enjoyed *Taken* and all the quirky, fangirl references I put into it. It's my own streak of geek coming out. And the tiny reference at the end to my time travel romance *A Laird for All Time*. Perhaps there might be more to tell from Donell, Scarlett, Laird, Emmy and Connor one day.

If you're interested in seeing the bits and pieces of fashion and history that inspired this tale, you can find it all on my Pinterest board dedicated to this book at http://www.pinterest.com/angelinefortin1/taken-a-laird-for-all-time-novel/.

Recently I was working on my family tree and found a strong connection to the Borders of Scotland. My ancestor was listed again and again as Laird Densmore of Achenmeade. Achenmeade no longer exists, though family lore places it in the borderlands area near Peebles. The name Laird confused me though being used as a first name and I discovered that it was sometimes used as a first name even back then, given to a family of importance or status. Then I discovered it wasn't a given name in my case but an actual title. I have a Laird in my family tree! I knew it, but I still loved it as a first name and used it in that fashion in this book.

My Dunskirk castle is the one fictional setting of this

book. I wanted a location closer to the border than reality and history could provide, but it is based quite closely on the very real, medieval Duns Castle not far north of there. Today, Duns is a hotel that I would dearly love to visit one day. Most of the other castles I reference are nothing but ruins today. Crichton, Etal and Norham, though they are open to visitors. Ford Castle still stands but as I mention, looks nothing today as it once did. Wark doesn't exist any longer though archeologists are currently digging at the site.

Probably my biggest fabrication is the fact that the Hepburns and the Lindsay clans were enemies when in fact, the opposite is true. They were allied clans but I did want to have that connection – not only because the name of Lindsay might be mistaken for a woman's name as it had in the beginning – but because, Lord Lindsay did advise James IV to withdraw before Flodden. I like that touch of reality.

Also unbelievably true, the Earl of Angus, Bell the Cat, did blame La Motte, the French emissary, for leading King James into war. The King responded with the quote, 'Angus, if yer afraid, go home.'

He did.

What is not real is the stories of *The Puppet War*, though I hope they might be one day soon should I turn my attention to Young Adult Fiction. The names of the books, *Ventriloquist, Marionette* and *Broken Strings*, their author, the characters, the Puppeteers fandom and the plot are all born from the imagination of my daughter, Carley, who may someday be a fine author herself. She certainly has the imagination for it.

As for the Battle of Flodden:

James IV did write to Henry VIII and Catherine of Aragon informing them of his intent to invade the country.

As odd as it sounds, it is the truth. I also followed the progress of the Scottish army closely those absolute details are still left to theory and conjecture. Though he traveled directly there without a brief layover at Crichton Castle, King James IV did lead his troops out of Ellemford Haugh with twenty cannon, and rumor had it, a ring given to him by Anne of Brittany on his finger. The nuns at the Coldstream Priory noted their crossing over the River Tweed at Coldstream on August 22, 1513. The details I have given regarding the taking of Norham in a five day siege is accurate to the historical documents I researched as is the taking of Ford Castle. The King's brief affair with Lady Heron was also speculated on and offered as a viable theory for the Scots delay in the area.

By the time sunset on Flodden Field on September 9, 1513, around 10,000 Scottish soldiers (and as I mentioned, at least one member of every noble family in Scotland) lay dead on Flodden Field along with about 2000 to 3000 Englishmen. The English forces also attacked the remains of the Scottish camp and burnt it, killing as many men, women and children there as they did on the battlefield.

The Scottish forces retreated but it was the bloodiest defeat the country had ever seen. The last war they would fight for more than thirty years and the last time any reigning monarch would die on the field of battle.

I could write a book about the Battle of Flodden alone but there are already many, some which I have used to resources in making the details of the Scottish progress into England and the timeline of their activities as accurate as possible. But like any work of fiction, I have strayed from the truth a time or two to suit my storyline. I hope all is forgiven there.

If you are interested in reading more about the battle, you

can   get   a   nice   overview   at
http://www.flodden1513.com/index.php/site/single_panel/
the_battle_of_flodden.

And in case you caught it and wondered, the term 'your majesty' was not used at the time. Though the usage cannot be precisely pinned down, there is one theory that Charles V of Spain was the first to use it following his election as Holy Roman Emperor in 1519. Francis I and Henry VII would adopt it afterward.

I would love to hear your thoughts any time. You can email me at fortin.angeline@gmail.com or visit my website https//www.angelinefortin.com. You can also follow me on Twitter, Facebook, Google+, Tumblr, LinkdIn or my Pinterest page.

Thanks for reading!

ABOUT THE AUTHOR

Angeline Fortin is the author of historical and time-travel romance offering her readers a fun, sexy and often touching tales of romance.

Her first release in May of 2011, the Highland time travel novel *A Laird for All Time*, has steadily ranked in Amazon's Top 100 in Time Travel for the past three years with more than 80 five-star reviews so far.

A Question of Trust, the first of her Victorian historical romance series *Questions for a Highlander*, was released later that year and quickly followed by series additions *A Question of Trust* and *A Question of Lust*. The series primarily follows the siblings of the MacKintosh clan. Ten brothers and their lone sister who end up looking for love in all the right places.

While the series continues on with familiar characters well known to those who have read the entire series, each single title is also a stand-alone tale of highland romance.

With a degree in US History from UNLV and having previously worked as a historical interpreter at Colonial Williamsburg, Angeline brings her love of history and Great Britain to the forefront in settings such as Victorian London and Edinburgh.

As a former military wife, Angeline has lived from the west coast to the east, from the north and to the south and uses those experiences along with her favorite places to tie into her time travel novels as well.

Angeline is a native Minnesotan who recently relocated back to the land of her birth and braved the worst winter recorded since before she initially moved away. She lives in Apple Valley outside the Twin Cities with her husband, two children and three dogs.

She is a wine enthusiast, DIY addict (much to her husband's chagrin) and sports fanatic who roots for the Twins and Vikings faithfully through their highs and lows.

Most of all she loves what she does everyday - writing. She does it for you the reader, to bring a smile or a tear and loves to hear from her fans.

ALSO BY ANGELINE FORTIN

Time Travel Romances:
A Laird for All Time
Nothing But Time
My Heart's in the Highlands
A Time & Place for Every Laird

The Questions for a Highlander series:
A Question of Love
A Question of Trust
A Question of Lust
The Perfect Question
A Question for Harry

Made in the USA
Charleston, SC
13 October 2015